THE COFFIN MAKER'S APPRENTICE

EAST TIMOR CRIME SERIES Nº3

Chris McGillion

coffeetownpress
Kenmore, WA

coffeetownpress

Coffeetown Press books published by Epicenter Press

Epicenter Press
6524 NE 181st St. Suite 2
Kenmore, WA 98028.
www.Epicenterpress.com
www.Coffeetownpress.com
www.Camelpress.com

For more information go to: www.Epicenterpress.com

This is a work of fiction. All characters and events tied to the specific plot are products of the author's imagination.

The Coffin Maker's Apprentice
Copyright © 2024 by Chris McGillion

ISBN: 9781684921553 (trade paper)
ISBN: 9781684921560 (ebook)

LOC: 2023945709

Dedication

For Scruffy

Acknowledgments

Thanks as always to Raymond Harding and Bill Blaikie for their splendid editorial advice. To the alumni fraternity: Elaine Thompson, Philip Porter, Michael Ryland, Joe Divjak, Damian Grace, Michael Johnson, Brad Norington and, of course, their much better halves. And to Epicenter's Jennifer McCord who saw some good and made it much better.

Prologue

Thirty years earlier: 1984

Three men zigzagged down the steep ravine, alert to any sound or movement that seemed out of place. They hadn't eaten in days except for what they could forage in the forest and that wasn't much. They were hungry and losing strength. They had left the security of their cave in this mountainous part of Viqueque on the eastern fringe of the island after a message that a village, ten miles from where they were hiding, had a little surplus food they could take—if they could sneak in between the military patrols. They had decided to take the risk before starvation finished them off.

The men were members of the Falintil—the guerrilla force fighting for East Timor's independence from Indonesia after it invaded in 1975. The men's clothes were rags, hair long and unkempt, beards straggly. The two in front wore boots held together with twine; the one at the rear, a recent recruit, wore flip-flops that were coming apart. The two seasoned guerrillas carried old Kropatschek bolt-action rifles which had been used in Timor by Portuguese colonial troops and then displayed in a museum in the capital, Dili. Between them they had seven bullets. The newer member of the group was armed only with a machete.

As they came to the stream, they stopped to refill their canteens. The village was a mile further on, where the countryside flattened out enough to allow the cultivation of small subsistence gardens of sweet potato, maize and beans. One of the men, squinting through the glare of the sun, thought he could see smoke from the cooking fires of the village drifting over the trees atop the ridge ahead. His companions smiled when he told them, though they saw no sign of smoke themselves, and the three resumed their trek imagining something more enticing than berries and wild bitter beans to eat.

The first shots cut down the leader as bullets tore into his chest, neck and arm. He collapsed in a bloody mess on top of his rifle in the undergrowth by the stream. As the man in the flip-flops crouched to tug the rifle free, his remaining companion fumbled his own weapon only to be cut down in the second wave of bullets. The surviving guerilla ran but his soles gave out, he stumbled and was hit twice in the leg and fell screaming into the water. Camouflaged Indonesian troops emerged from the foliage on both sides of the stream. They encircled him, checking there were no more guerrillas on the top of the ravine. A lieutenant elbowed his men aside and stood over the wounded guerrilla gripping a semi-automatic pistol. The injured man held one hand up in surrender while the other hand gripped his leg. The lieutenant grinned, stood erect, raised the pistol and fired into the wounded man's face. He then ordered one of his men to take photographs of him standing over those they had killed. They left the three dead Falintil to rot where they fell.

A day later, one of the villagers who had overheard the Indonesian soldiers boasting about their exploit, came in search of the dead men. By then the patrol had moved on and so, when the villager found what he was looking for, he alerted others and they retrieved the bodies. The villagers buried the dead in a common grave in nearby woodland. If the Indonesians found out, there would likely be more killings as a warning against supporting the guerrillas. A boy only nine years of age sat to one side as the adults dug the hole and disguised the grave. The boy shaded his eyes from the glare of the sun which made worse the inflammation in his right pupil. He asked no questions and made no comment. Death from Indonesian military operations, from hunger, or from illness was a regular occurrence. Besides, the boy had been taught that, when things were set right, the dead would rise again.

Chapter 1

"He said he was dead and wanted to go back home," the old man was saying. "Back to his village."

The man looked to be in his seventies, perhaps eighties. He had a parched cocoa-coloured face fringed with a white, wispy beard, and whiskers growing out of his nose. His jacket was a curious addition in the tropical heat, shabby and faded, but it looked like one worn habitually despite the climate. Sitting atop a shock of grey hair was a blue cap with a red and yellow Superman shield on the bill. The cap was so out of place on this elderly Timorese man in this island country squeezed between Indonesia and Australia that it made it hard to take him seriously, even if he was talking about a ghost. That, nonetheless, was his subject and he chose his words carefully as though, at his age, he had to ration them. "You know, for a proper burial," he added.

Vincintino Cordero of the Timorese Scientific Police for Criminal Investigations unit was trying to look interested but finding it hard to disguise his impatience. It was Sunday. He was bored with the everyday police work he'd been assigned while most regular police officers were in Metinaro, fifteen miles along the coast from East Timor's capital, Dili. The following Sunday they'd been assigned to control huge crowds expected for a ceremony to rebury a group of former *Falintil* guerilla fighters killed in the struggle against the Indonesian occupation. They were to be interred in a special cemetery established by the East Timorese government.

Cordero was hungry. He should have been enjoying a long lunch at a nice seafront restaurant with the American FBI Agent

Sara Carter. They'd first met three months earlier. She—very reluctantly—had arrived in East Timor to work with INTERPOL. He—rather indifferently—was given the job as her initial police liaison because he grew up in Australia and spoke fluent English. Since then, they'd become friends and were now seeing each other fairly regularly—less for work than because she knew few Timorese well and he was not married and had time on his hands. Today though, his impatience, boredom and hunger conspired to produce a nagging feeling of annoyance towards Carter—as she preferred to be called. Was it because her assignment with INTERPOL was almost up and she'd be heading home to Arizona in less than two weeks and he'd miss her? Well that had always been on the cards since the day they'd met so why be annoyed by it now? Was it because she had come to East Timor in the first place and upset the comfortable assumptions he'd held about his future? Maybe but—

The old man coughed slightly, regaining Cordero's attention.

"*Tiu,*" Cordero started to say, referring to the old man as 'uncle'. Titles are as much a part of everyday etiquette in Timor as saying 'please' and 'thank you' is in the English-speaking world. Whatever Cordero intended to say was interrupted by a young female police woman suddenly appearing by his side and sliding a green manila folder out from a pile she was juggling in her arms. She deposited the folder on the desk behind which Cordero had been told to sit for the day and deal with whatever problems, complaints and enquiries came his way. The young officer blew a loose strand of hair from her face and hurried away. "Ah, here we are," he said turning his focus to the folder and removing a two-page file.

The old man sat quietly, motionless save for a slow blinking of the eyes. Cordero scanned the file. "Here's the report from your visit on Friday. Same thing: the ghost came to you in your sleep on Thursday night, said he'd been killed and wanted to be taken home and reburied. That right?" The old man nodded. Cordero turned to the second page. "But it says here an officer was sent to look around your neighbourhood on the afternoon you came in but he found nothing suspicious."

Cordero looked up.

"Maybe he didn't look hard enough," the old man suggested.

Cordero let out a sigh. "And now you're saying the ghost came back again last night and told you the same thing," he said with a hint of accusation in his tone. "'I'm dead. Find me. Rebury me.'" The old man agreed. Cordero slid the pages back into the folder and closed it with a little too much force.

"Why would a ghost ask you for help, *tiu*, and not the police or the local authorities?"

The old man shrugged. "People call out for help in different ways," he said. "And I have come to the police. Maybe he chose me because he knew I would."

Cordero cleared his throat at that suggestion. "Has a ghost ever visited you in the night before?" he asked.

"Yes," the old man answered. Cordero smiled, thinking this was all attention seeking. "Last Thursday," the old man said. "Like I told you."

Cordero pursed his lips and rubbed his hands on his legs. "Look *tiu*," he said, trying to sound reasonable. "Maybe it's just a bad dream—"

"I wasn't asleep when the ghost spoke," the old man cut across him. "His voice woke me. He spoke to me and left when the dogs started growling."

"The dogs," Cordero repeated without further comment. He swiveled in his chair, rose, placed his hands on the window sill and peered out. Dili lay before him on the narrow strip of lowland between the mountains to the south and the sea to the north. Cordero had lived in other cities: Darwin, in northern Australia, to which his family had fled in 1982, seven years after Indonesia invaded East Timor, Melbourne, where he had gone to university, and Lisbon, where he'd spent six months studying investigative procedures and forensic science before joining the elite unit of the Timorese police. Every place had a personality of its own, but Dili was in a different league entirely.

In the short space of twelve years since independence in 2002 a minor building boom had transformed a backwater outpost into a small city with multi-storey office blocks, fashionable hotels, a bright new shopping mall, and a bustling university. But the city's population of 240,000 people swelled and shrank with the seasons: Timor's one million rural residents largely survived through subsistence farming and many of those who came to the city went back to the districts to help sow and harvest and participate in rituals that tied them to the land, their village, and their kinship networks. Regular movements back and forth meant that, beneath the outward signs of modernity, Dili was home to tens of thousands of people among whom ghosts and demons and witches and land spirits were all too real and all too able to influence much about life—and about death.

The old man coughed softly. Cordero turned back, slumped into the chair, and stared at the weary expression on the face of the visitor beneath the Superman cap. He said he'd walked to police headquarters from the foothills of Balide on the outskirts of Dili. He said he'd return home the same way. That amounted to two, maybe three, miles, in this heat, in that hot, heavy jacket, on those ancient, tired legs. Cordero knew he owed the old man a little more attention.

"Was anyone else woken up by the ghost?" he asked.

"I live alone," the old man said.

"No family?" Cordero asked.

"The ones who didn't die in the time of the *bapa*," the old man said, using a common Timorese term for Indonesians, "live in Baucau now."

It was a town three hours' drive from Dili on the north coast.

Cordero nodded, his sympathy rising just a little more. "Did the ghost tell you his name?" The man shook his head. "Can you describe him?"

"He spoke to me. I didn't see him. He didn't tell me his name."

Cordero picked up his pen as if to write or doodle but put it back gently on the desk.

"Well all I can—"

"He mentioned water," the old man interrupted. "The need to go through the water."

Cordero looked confused. "I thought you said you'd walked from Balide. That's a long way from the sea. Even from the river."

"The ghost didn't say anything about the sea or the river," the old man said. "Just he needed to go through water."

None of this helped Cordero. In fact, it just complicated an already fanciful story. "So the ghost told you—"

"The ghost told me what I told you," the man said. He was not impatient, just insistent. "Maybe he's in a water trough. Not mine. I looked. Maybe another water trough. Did that other police officer look in the water troughs when he came to my house?"

Most houses in Dili had large outdoor water troughs rather than indoor plumbing. The water would be used for cooking, washing, cleaning clothes, and, if the house had one, flushing a squat toilet. All that water meant the troughs were usually big enough to hold a human body.

Cordero re-opened the folder and ran a finger down the edge of both pages. "It doesn't mention anything about water troughs," he said.

"Then that could be where he is."

The old man had a point, Cordero had to acknowledge, but only if a ghost really had visited him in the night and only if the ghost's story about being dead and left in a watery grave was true. And how likely was any of that?

Cordero checked the name of the officer who'd made the report. He then turned to the computer on the desk and pulled up the roster of the few officers on duty in Dili today. He checked the names. "The officer who wrote this report is not working today. I'll contact him tomorrow morning and ask if he checked the water troughs."

"Maybe the storm water drains too," the old man suggested. "They often fill with water and get blocked. I saw a dead dog in one once."

"Yes, the storm water drains too," Cordero conceded.

"What will you do if the officer says he didn't check the troughs and the drains?" the old man asked.

Cordero rubbed the back of his neck and puffed. The age of the man played on his conscience as did his raggedy jacket and the thought of him shuffling along in the heat.

"In that case I'll look into it myself."

The old man stared at his hands nodding his head then back up at Cordero.

"I can't sleep when the ghost comes like this. I'm old and need my sleep. Do you promise me you will look into it? Often the police don't do what they say they'll do."

"I promise you, *tiu*," Cordero reassured him. He looked at the file again, more carefully this time. "There is no address here. It just says *Senyor* Pinto Baptisto from Balide. Off *Estrada de Balide* near the Chinese bakery."

"It's a lane. It has no name. People use it as a short cut. To avoid traffic, I guess."

"No name," repeated Cordero. "I guess no number either."

"No."

"How did the officer find your house on Friday?"

"I never saw him at my house. After I left here I walked to the market, saw a friend there and sat talking. Whether the police officer came to my house or not, I don't know. Doesn't it say on that paper you have how he found my house?"

Cordero guessed that the whole report of the inspection might have been fabricated because the ghost story was ludicrous. Nevertheless he shuffled through the papers again and shook his head.

"There are no details about an address—" he began.

"The Chinese bakery is on the corner," the old man said. "You turn into the lane there but my house is a long way down the lane. It's yellow. Or was. It's behind a gate I made from scraps of iron. I put a buffalo's skull on the top."

Cordero closed the file and stood. He offered his hand. "All right *tiu*," he said. "Thank you for coming in. I'll let you know what I find."

The old man looked uncertain. "I don't have a talking machine," he said not taking Cordero's hand.

"You mean a cell phone?"

"If that's what they call it."

"Then I will come to your house when I get a chance," Cordero said. Again he offered his hand. The old man took it in his calloused fingers and held it softly.

"Good day *senyor*," the old man said. He stood and turned to leave as the young female police officer returned this time with a sour-looking middle aged woman in tow.

"*Senyor*," the officer said to Cordero. "This is *Senyora* Amivi Carla. Someone stole her pig and she is very upset."

"I know how she feels," replied Cordero, resigning himself to a long and tedious afternoon. "Take a seat *senyora*." He slumped in his own chair, picked up the pen and slid a clean sheet of paper in front of him. "Can you describe the pig to me please, *senyora*?"

• • •

Estefana dos Carvalho and her fiancé Josinto Centavo Veddo were strolling along Dili's seafront in the Lecidere district on this pleasant Sunday afternoon. The dry season was coming to an end and soon days like this would be replaced by ones punctuated by brief and violent thunderstorms. The monsoon would follow with days and days of drenching rain and all the moisture of the wet season driving the humidity to barely sufferable levels. But time to worry about that another day: today was a day to enjoy.

Estefana was a pretty girl with bright brown eyes and a smile that made her hard to ignore. She wore her long frizzy hair in a ponytail under a wide-brimmed hat and was dressed in a bright red and blue cotton summer dress that betrayed the outlines of a slim figure when the light was behind her. Around her neck a silver crucifix glittered in the sun against the flawless hazel colour of her skin. Josinto's skin was darker and his body taut from hard physical work. But he had a soft, youthful face, an almost comical thread of goatee on his chin, and dark curly hair tied up in a bun. He wore blue jeans and a clean T-shirt and he and Estefana held hands as they ambled on to nowhere in particular.

"I can't believe my transfer will be finalised next week," Estefana was saying.

"Me neither," agreed Josinto. "I thought it'd take another year or more."

The two had met in their home town of Suai, on the southern coast of Timor, but Josinto had left six months earlier to learn carpentry from *Senyor* Pereira, the only coffin maker in the Dili district of Bidau.

"Well we can thank *Mana* Carter," Estefana said. She had been reassigned, on the American's insistence and after the two had worked a case together on the south coast, to Dili in a temporary capacity to act as an interpreter during Carter's time with INTERPOL. Estefana had been taught by Filipina nuns and her English was excellent. As the reassignment drew to a close, Estefana was able to request a permanent transfer to the Dili police district, had been accepted, and only needed to complete the paperwork to start this phase in her career.

"And now we can get serious about setting up our home together," Estefana added. The transfer represented a new and, for Estefana, much more significant stage in her personal life. East Timor's marriage laws placed a strong emphasis on preserving the family unit and the parties were obliged to live together rather than apart to secure permission to wed. They had provided the authorities with assurances about their intention to cohabit and been given the relevant approval. The transfer removed problems they might have encountered in follow up checks had they been found to be living apart.

"*Doben*," Josinto said, meaning 'beloved' in Tetun. He smiled. "Let's not set our hopes too high. Rents are expensive in Dili now. I'm still waiting for the boss to give me that raise but he's been busy finishing all those coffins for the guerillas they're reburying."

"At Metinaro?" Estefana asked, picking a frangipani flower up off the ground and twirling it in her free hand.

"Yeah," Josinto replied. "And the price of wood shot up after he'd agreed a price. He's not too happy. But I'll ask him about the raise again next week."

"Well my mother's not asking for *barlake*," she said referring to the traditional bride price paid to the wife's family. "That means we should be able to afford something nice."

She slid the frangipani under the hair atop her ear.

"Maybe," said Josinto.

"She does want you to make her that easy chair, remember? So she can play with her grandchildren."

"Not a problem," insisted Josinto. "I've already put aside the wood." He stopped swinging his hand and stood still.

On their left was the *Avenida de Portugal*, on their right what Timorese called *Tasi Feto*—the female sea, so named because of its generally calm and gentle waters. A group of musicians were jamming on a paved area fronting the beach. They were playing 'La Bele Tanis'—the Tetun version of Bob Marley's 'No Woman, No Cry'—and a group of children and six older adults were dancing. Josinto began to sing along and sway to the music. Estefana looked up at him, squeezed his hand and began humming to the melody. It was a perfect day for young lovers, old lovers and soon-to-be lovers.

"Is that police investigator coming to the wedding?" Josinto asked after the tune stopped and the applause died down.

"I hope so," said Estefana. "It's because of him I met *Mana* Carter and we all worked those cases together. He said he can make it."

"He seems nice," said Josinto. "And important too like *Mana* Carter. Every now and then I wish I worked with important people like you do."

"You do important work, Josinto," Estefana insisted. "And I'm proud of you." Most coffins in Dili were made by Indonesians who had settled there over the years. *Senyor* Pereira was unique as a Timorese coffin maker and Josinto represented a new generation of Timorese who would follow him into this and other skilled trades now the country was independent and opportunities for locals were opening up.

"The work never stops now the boss is busy. I even have a job to do tonight," he said. He sensed her disappointment. "Sorry *doben*. It won't take long."

They made their way further along the foreshore. Several groups of children kicked soccer balls on the sand, old couples exchanged small talk under shade trees, and street hawkers tried to interest anyone they could in the pineapples and coconuts they had for sale.

"You've made me so happy, Josinto," Estefana said snuggling up to him.

He pulled a dollar bill from his pocket—East Timor having adopted US currency as its own on independence.

"Haven't even started yet," he replied. "How about an ice-cream?"

• • •

FBI Agent Sara Carter was disappointed when Cordero rang to say he couldn't make lunch. But she went anyway to a small Portuguese restaurant on the seafront toward the center of Dili. He'd promised her that the seafood there was fresh and flavoursome. He'd been right and that had compensated a little for her having to eat alone. She was just returning to her apartment in the old leafy Portuguese district of Motael when her cell buzzed. It was the US Ambassador.

"Agent Carter," he began in a tone that always reminded Carter of something vile oozing off a spoon. "Hudson Taylor here. Sorry to disturb you on a Sunday but I've just returned from official business in Baucau and wanted to speak to you as a top priority."

"Yes sir, how can I help?" Carter answered.

"Your report to the Embassy on your time with INTERPOL is sitting on my desk. I'll read it first thing in the morning. You can bet on that. You've done a really fine job and you're a credit to all of us."

There was a pause.

"Well thank you, sir," said Carter to fill the silence. She ran her fingers through her shoulder-length hair and against her better judgment added: "If there's anything more I can do—"

"Well that's why I'm calling really," the Ambassador broke in and feigned a chuckle. "You see Jacobsen, your INTERPOL Director, apparently wants you to stay on for a while longer. I'm not sure—"

It was Carter's turn to butt in now. "With all due respect sir, I've completed my assignment. I'm due to go back to the States."

"Well yes, of course—"

"And as much as I've enjoyed my time in East Timor I want to go back and take up the investigations I left off when I was"—she wanted to say 'pressed-ganged into coming here' but under the circumstances settled on—"given this opportunity to work with INTERPOL."

"I completely understand," began the Ambassador before demonstrating that he didn't. "One of our Embassy people got in touch with your Resident Agent in Arizona and he says that as much as he values your contribution to the Flagstaff office he's willing to let you extend your time here."

Of course the bastard would, thought Carter. She'd used excessive force in arresting a man who'd raped a twelve year-old Navajo girl back in Flagstaff. That incident had come on top of whispers about her, as an early-career cop in Missouri, shooting another pedophile in the leg in return for the abuse he'd caused. She was thirty years old now and more cool-headed—most of the time. But her Resident Agent had forced her to take the East Timor posting before she caused more serious trouble on his watch.

"I not asking to have my time here extended," she said, her voice rising.

"I appreciate your selflessness Sara and that's why I'm simply asking you to reconsider. You see your involvement here is terrific PR for the Embassy, for your country in fact, and if you were to stay on another, say, three months or—"

Carter was angry but she held herself in check. "Is this a directive because you know I'm entitled to appeal it to the Bureau?" she said.

"No, no, no. Nothing like that," cooed Taylor. "It's a suggestion, that's all. Well, a request really that you think it over. I understand you're staying on in Dili for a little while longer. Vacation I believe. Very sensible. And well deserved, I might add. Perhaps we could talk about it over lunch next week."

"I'm rather busy," Carter said. "I have reports to finish for INTERPOL and then I'm *on leave*," she added emphasizing the last two words.

"Yes, yes, of course. And I don't want to interrupt your vacation," assured Taylor. "But let's get together and talk again soon, eh?"

The Ambassador abruptly ended the call. "Shit, shit, shit!" Carter cursed. "No way you bastard!" she yelled into her now-dead cell before hurling it onto the couch.

Chapter 2

Cordero blocked a solid rip to the ribs with his left elbow, and countered with a right hook that only brushed across its target and shot off into thin air. He was caught with an uppercut and another rip that this time shuddered through his rib cage. He grimaced. The boy was good, he knew that, but he also knew a thing or two the boy didn't know and he was relying on that knowledge to step out of the ring in the same condition he'd stepped in.

Cordero had boxed at university in Australia and fought as a welterweight in amateur competitions. He'd mostly won. But that was a while ago--a long while. He'd put on a few pounds. He'd also aged almost twenty years and what he'd lost in speed he hadn't quite made up for in strength. But he could bob and weave and flick out a lightning jab to keep the boy at bay and he knew how to clinch and maul if everything else failed. Like now, when a straight jab rifled passed his ear and he tried to slip a viscious hook but missed and took it flush on his left eye.

Four heavy bags hung like giant plums from a shelter of sorts off to one side of the grassed courtyard where the ring had been erected in Dili's outdoor boxing gym. It was Monday morning and two boys were tapping rhythmically on bags while another lifted free weights on the lawn. Across the road in East Timor's national university, students attended classes where they were fed information from lecturers and books. In this, the university of hard knocks, you learned by getting knocked down, getting up and fighting on.

That kind of education suited a wiry seventeen year-old by the name of Fidelis Tau. Fidelis was a tall boy composed of muscle, bone and grit. He had spent three years living under a tarpaulin in an internally displaced people's camp in Dili after the new nation's stability collapsed in 2006. That was the year when sections of the Timorese army and police went to war with each other and numerous gangs in Dili took opposing sides and clashed violently. Dozens of people were killed and the widespread destruction of property left tens of thousands homeless. In the camp Fidelis stole to help feed his family. When he ran away from the camp, he stole because he'd become good at it. Soon he'd joined a notorious criminal gang and risen through the ranks to become an enforcer. His ego inflated with the role and one day a few months back, to show off in front of other gang members, he'd pranced into the gym and boasted he could beat to a pulp anyone who dared take him on.

Police personnel had been asked to volunteer as sports trainers to young Timorese men to counter the appeal of the gangs and Cordero chose to sign up as an auxiliary boxing coach. He'd only been at the gym a few weeks when Fidelis strutted in and he answered the challenge. With just two punches Cordero laid Fidelis flat on his ass. That produced an instant respect for Cordero in Fidelis' eyes and a love of boxing in place of the boy's enthusiasm for gang life. But you don't just walk out of a gang. You fade out or you leave in a box. Fidelis chose to fade out, doing less and less and getting paid less for it. Eventually he was largely free of his past—if penniless once more.

Cordero knew all that. He also knew Fidelis was a decent kid at heart and, given the chance, could be a good boxer and might even make some money as a professional. Cordero had been working closely with him, had become something of a father figure, and was preparing the boy for his first bout.

Fidelis clipped Cordero with two quick jabs and a right cross that sprayed sweat from the older man's head. Cordero managed to backpedal, bounce off the ropes, and crouch inside Fidelis' reach to deliver solid body punches. Fidelis pushed away and re-set his attack. As he came forward Cordero landed a stinging jab on Fidelis' nose as a feint and followed up with a powerful right to the solar plexus that knocked the wind out of him. The boy clinched, caught his breath, shoved the bigger man away, and came in again. Cordero admired his opponent's guts but had reached his limit for this kind of punishing workout. He clocked Fidelis with a sharp left hook, throwing all his weight behind the punch. The boy stumbled backwards against the ropes and raised his gloves in surrender. "*Lae tan*," the boy spluttered—'No more'.

"That's what Roberto Duran said to Sugar Ray Leonard in their second fight," Cordero said, sucking in air. "*No mas* in Spanish."

Fidelis was bent over, gasping. "They Timorese too, *maun*?" he managed to ask, using the casual title of 'brother'.

Cordero didn't reply. Boxing had only recently been introduced to East Timor and few Timorese knew anything about the pantheon of boxing greats.

"You did well, *maun*," Cordero said. "Real well." He took in a lungful of air.

"You too," Fidelis said. He was slumped over catching his breath. "For an old guy," he added and grinned cheekily up at Cordero.

"You want me to hit you again you just keep talking like that," Cordero joked.

Fidelis waved 'no' with his gloved left hand.

"You've got to protect your jaw more and keep those elbows in tight against your sides. You doing roadwork like I told you?"

Fidelis nodded, testing his jaw. "Yeah. Along the beach," he said.

"Good. Build up stamina. Do that and you'll be fine in this fight coming up."

Fidelis stood erect. Again he smiled. "Thanks, *maun*."

Cordero tapped him on the back, stepped through the ropes, and headed for the showers—cold showers but the morning was already heating up and he was a lather of sweat from the sparring. It was close to 9 am by the time he'd dressed into a plain blue shirt and jeans and was entering his office. His head was clear, his body energized even if he could feel a sting over his left eye. He was looking forward to an afternoon off and the rescheduled lunch date with Carter they'd organised when he'd finished work the night before and called her on his cell. She'd said that Estefana had to translate her reports into Tetun before she could sign them and so she was giving herself Monday off as well. Lunch at the beach was set for just after noon.

But first Cordero had time to honour his promise to Pinto Baptisto and follow up with the police officer who filed the report into the ghost investigation in Balide. The officer's name was Dodi Ramos and his file, which Cordero was reading on his office computer, showed he'd graduated from the police academy as an agent—the first rung in police rankings—less than a month earlier. That didn't inspire a lot of confidence. Cordero noticed that Agent Ramos had been assigned traffic duties today. He punched in the number for his cell and listened to it ring

"*Hai. You've reached Dodi Ramos. I'm busy now but I'll call you back,*" a sing-song voice said and recited instructions for leaving a message. Cordero followed them. As he placed the cell on his desk, two investigators who shared the office came through the door. One was Lucas Rama Savoy; the other Manuel Fonseca. Each carried coffee and broke into smiles at the sight of Cordero's face.

"Hey *maun,*" said Lucas, the joker of the two. "What happened to your eye? I heard you were a real police officer yesterday," he said without waiting for an answer. Cordero straightened in his chair ready for the put-down. "Let's see. It was Sunday. I bet you had to break up a fight between two old women over a few coins on the church plate. Or did a kid kick a deflated soccer ball into your face?"

Manuel joined in the taunting. "Maybe there was an argument over a two-car traffic jam at the airport when the plane that comes in on Sundays touched down," he suggested.

Cordero rose, came around the desk and took Manuel's coffee from him. "Actually, I spent the day at the beach. A group of pretty girls from Portugal ran out of sun-screen and requested a real police officer go down and rub it on their backs," Cordero replied. "They hit me by accident when they were fighting over which one would take me home."

They knew he'd won—again. "What are you two doing in here anyway?" Cordero asked. "Pretending to work?"

"You know how things are piling up," said Lucas. "Manuel and I didn't get to finish our report on the fraud case last week. Boss wants it first thing this afternoon and —"

Cordero's cell buzzed. It was Agent Dodi Ramos returning his call.

"Wait a second," Cordero said and held a hand up to Lucas. He turned toward the window and asked Dodi about his visit to the home of *Senyor* Pinto Baptisto the previous Friday.

Dodi took a moment to recall the details. He said he'd followed the directions from the Chinese bakery to the fading yellow house with the buffalo skull on the gate. It wasn't hard to find, he told Cordero, but he didn't see anything suspicious. He insisted he'd checked the outhouse in Pinto's yard but nothing further down the lane.

"It's a long lane," he said as though that was sufficient justification for his decision. He'd found nothing in the water trough and that's why, he said, he hadn't bothered to put it in his report.

"Did you check the storm water drains?" Cordero asked.

"Well one, yeah," Dodi said. "It was near the old guy's house. It was clear."

That seemed reasonable and fairly conclusive. Cordero thanked him and ended the call.

He took a sip of Manuel's coffee, collected his jacket and said he was off for the rest of the day unless anything urgent came up.

• • •

"Jacobsen had no right going behind my back to the Embassy, Tino," Carter insisted.

Cordero liked it when she called him by his abbreviated name—even if in a minor rage—because it suggested an easy familiarity. She tended to use 'Cordero' when she was dismissive, insistent, or angry. "It's how the Dutch operate," he replied for want of anything better to say.

They were sitting on the warm sands of Areia Branca—one of the few beaches in Timor where it was rare to see a crocodile and therefore relatively safe to swim. It was a good day for the beach because it was never crowded on a Monday. Behind them were the few bars and restaurants that serviced those bathing or strolling by. Further back were the foothills, parched after the long dry season and in need of soaking rain: in front, the calm, crystal blue waters of *Tasi Feto*. On a ridge top far off to their right stretching out into the sea stood *Cristo Rei*—the 90-foot statue of Jesus Christ, erected by the Indonesians to suggest they respected Timor's culture while they did their best to eliminate its people.

Carter sat on a yellow beach towel in dark sunglasses, a white T-shirt covering her swimsuit, her arms wrapped around legs pulled up to her chest. She had a lean face that was softly finished, sharp, intelligent eyes, and lips that could suggest promise or threat, depending on her mood. Her legs showed a tanning in the Arizona sun that had taken on a slightly deeper tone under a tropical one. Her hair was the same: the brown bleached to an alluring chestnut colour.

Cordero, who had arrived ten minutes late, couldn't help but admire her beauty when she wasn't looking. He sat in a plastic chair, his shoes and socks parked next to him and his toes digging into the warm sand. The sun was high in a sky leached of colour, the heat tempered by a cool breeze off the water.

"This is going to be damned hard to shake," she was complaining. "Ambassadors aren't easy to ignore and that one wants something to boast about back home." She looked up at him and lifted her sunglasses. "That's me, Tino. For want of anything better he can claim credit for. Me!"

"Well—" he began but she cut him off.

"Then there's that prick back in Flagstaff—my resident agent, Slaton. He'll do anything to keep me as far away as he can for as long as he can. That means he's making it easy for the Embassy to put in a strong case that I stay longer." She scooped up a handful of sand and tossed it dismissively in front of the towel. "Jacobsen had no right to do what she did."

"She's short of staff and she values you highly—"

"Well she's got a funny way of showing it!"

She went quiet and he took a sip from his beer. "Are you going to say anything to her?" he asked.

"Not sure yet," she said. "Right now I don't know what's likely to come out of my mouth if I ran into her." She picked up her own beer and finished it.

Waves were lapping gently against the sand and a group of curlews flew low across the water. A woman dipped her very young daughter in the water, lifted her high above her head, and dipped her again, the child squealing with delight.

"What do you think of the beach?" he asked to change the subject.

She cast her eyes across the view from Cristo Rei to the few yachts moored off the eastern side of the city in the distance near the port. "It's beautiful," she said. "Water's so clear. I don't get much chance to swim in Arizona, let me tell you."

He laughed at that and she smiled. "I'll order lunch across the road and they'll bring it here. Grilled fish, fries and a fresh green salad?" he offered.

"You bet. Along with those tomatoes that actually taste like tomatoes, please." She turned to him wriggling the empty bottle in her hand. "And another cold beer?"

"That sounds like a great idea and will help me forget what I'm supposed to be doing." He drained the last of his own beer.

"What's that?" she asked tossing her empty beer bottle into the air and catching it again.

"Chasing a ghost," he said and reached for his shoes so his feet wouldn't be scorched on the hot bitumen as he crossed the road. "Long story."

She shot him a quizzical look then jumped up and threw off her T-shirt revealing a brief black bikini over a sleek and toned body. "You can tell me after a swim," she said. "And lunch and another beer." With that she strode down to the water, Cordero's eyes following her across the sand.

That's when his cell came to life. Something urgent had come up after all and it needed his attention right away. A body had been found off a laneway near the Chinese bakery in Balide.

It was lying in a water trough.

Chapter 3

It had just gone two o'clock on Monday afternoon when Cordero met up with Sergeant Mateo Belo of the regular Timorese police outside the Chinese bakery in Balide. The body had been found in the outhouse of a residence eighty yards down the laneway where Pinto Baptisto lived. Cordero insisted on walking to the outhouse to check if the laneway revealed anything of importance about the body and to familiarise himself with the neighbourhood.

The area was tired-looking but not dilapidated or over-crowded by the standards of residential areas further to the west of the city center. The laneway itself was lined with high fences of corrugated tin or split bamboo across which the bougainvillea vines were dropping the last purple and red flowers of their summer blooming. A few coconut palms grew here and there and a goat grazed on an assortment of weeds growing along the side of the storm water drain Pinto had mentioned.

Halfway down the lane a scrawny boy of eight or nine, grubby-faced and barefoot, popped out from behind a rusting 44-gallon drum. He made a gun of his right hand and aimed it at the uniformed police officer trudging by. "Pew, pew, pew," he fired off and took cover back behind the drum.

Mateo Belo turned toward the boy and raised his hand as if to strike him. "*Semo-lakon!*" he said, meaning 'scram' in Tetun. The boy scampered down the lane, his bare feet kicking dust up as he went. "They get this shit from pirated American movies," he complained catching up to Cordero who hadn't broken his stride.

"What shit?" Cordero asked without much interest.

"You know, *maun*," Mateo said. He took a stick of gum from his pocket, shoved it in his mouth and threw the wrapper into the storm-water drain on the edge of the lane. Cordero disapproved of littering but in this part of Dili, with plastic bottles, used food containers, cigarette butts and pieces of coconut shell already scattered everywhere, it hardly seemed to matter. "Guns and shit," Mateo added but Cordero had already lost interest in the question.

At an open gateway a junior police officer stood giggling at what he was watching on his cell phone. As the two senior officers approached he pocketed his cell, stood to attention and saluted.

"*Bondia Senyor*," the officer said to Cordero by way of greeting. "*Senyor*," he said again and nodded to Mateo Belo.

"Body in here?" asked Cordero ignoring the man's exaggerated deference.

"*Sin Senyor*," the officer agreed, pointing into a yard off through the gateway. "In the water trough."

"How long has this area been secured?" asked Cordero.

"Secured?" repeated the officer with a doubtful look on his face.

"Forget it," said Cordero and stepped through the gateway.

A woman rode by on a motorcycle, taking her time in order not to raise dust over her clothes. She paid the officers no mind, as if trouble was common in this part of Dili. Cordero squatted inside the yard. A heavily pregnant dog, its ribs exposed, lumbered by, sniffing the ground ignoring him. Mateo Belo edged up pondering Cordero's curiosity.

"What is it?" he asked.

Cordero took a kerchief from his pocket and wiped the back of his neck. "Notice the blood splatter?" he said pointing to the hard ground just inside the gate. "The dog's done a good job of spreading it all over the place but you can just make out a pattern from this angle." He paused. "And you can just make out drag marks across the yard to the outhouse where the trough is."

Mateo scratched his head and stopped chewing. "So you're saying—"

"I'm not saying anything," Cordero cut him off and stood. He put the kerchief back in his pocket. "I'm just thinking out loud.

Take photos of this area and these drag marks in relation to the water trough and the gate."

Cordero walked over to the outhouse and stepped inside to where the body lay, just below the surface of the water. He was young, not more than twenty Cordero guessed. He was dressed in faded jeans, a white T-shirt ripped and grubby, and what appeared to be a new pair of sneakers. His hair was cut in the kind of textured crop that suggested a barber's hand and his face was clean-shaven. He'd been a handsome boy but now his face was contorted in agony and, beneath his chin, was an ugly gash that had tinted the water pink.

"Another one," said Mateo, scratching his head under his cap as he joined Cordero. "I sometimes think dying young is a national sport in this country." Cordero made no comment. "What do you think—late teens, early twenties?"

"No more," said Cordero. He examined the body without touching anything.

He stood back while Mateo took photos from different angles and a series of close-ups of the body and the face. When he was finished, he stared at Cordero. "You want me to do it?" Mateo asked.

"No." Cordero moved back to the body, pushed his shirtsleeve up his arm, reached in below the water line and opened the boy's mouth. He searched with his fingers and from under the tongue retrieved a small green package. It was a betel quid consisting of an areca nut wrapped in betel leaf traditionally chewed as a mild stimulant. He held it up to enable Mateo to see it clearly.

"You think it's the same killer?" asked the sergeant. A week earlier another body had been found under a pile of trash in a back street in the district of Bemori, further east of the city center. It was a boy of a similar age, as yet unidentified, his throat had been slashed, and a betel quid found in his mouth.

"Throat cut, betel under the tongue. What do you think?" answered Cordero. He took a plastic bag from his pocket, deposited the betel quid in it, and wiped his hands and forearm on his trouser legs.

"The morgue's sending someone to collect the body," Mateo said. "Should be here soon."

"I want this whole yard and the lane searched for a knife or blade, a cell phone, and any personal items that might identify the boy," said Cordero. "You know the procedure." He headed back into the yard, squinting in the glare. "The owner of this house found him?"

"Apparently, yeah," said Mateo, reaching for his notebook. "Cisco Mola," he read after flipping through pages. "Old. Lives alone."

Half a dozen children who'd returned from school by midafternoon were shoving each other for prime position at the gate and sniggering in amusement at the sight of police officers. "Tell that officer at the gate to keep those kids well back," added Cordero. "I'll go talk to Cisco and catch up with you in a minute."

Cordero left Mateo Belo and walked to the back door of the cement block house. It consisted of two small rooms and an outdoor kitchen all under a sagging roof. Cordero noticed the blue paint peeling off the walls and the trash piled up beside the door. He knocked...no answer. He waited, knocked again and called "*Senyor* Mola!" Again no answer. He tried the door, it was unlocked. He stepped inside.

"Cisco!" Cordero crept slowly through to the front room where an old man sat huddled, eyes closed, wheezing in a chair. "*Senyor* Mola?"

"What?" Cisco said waking with a start. "Who are you?"

"My name is Vincintino Cordero. I am a police investigator."

"What do you want?"

"I understand you found the body out back," Cordero said.

"What? Speak up."

"The body in the water trough?" repeated Cordero raising his voice.

"Yes? What of it?"

"You found it."

"Of course I did. Why do you think I had my neighbour call the police?"

The man cleared his throat of phlegm and shut his eyes again.

"I am the police, *Senyor*," said Cordero. "I need to ask you a few questions."

"Questions? Well speak up," Cisco demanded.

"What time did you find the body?"

"What's that you say? What time?" The man leaned forward and thought for a moment. "Just after lunch. Went out to the toilet," he said and slumped back into the chair.

"And what time did you have lunch?" asked Cordero.

The man took a rag from his pants pocket and coughed into it, his face reddening. "Same time as always." He coughed violently into the rag again and took a moment to settle himself. "When the bells rang." He waved a hand vaguely. "In the church. Midday bells they ring for prayers."

"Did you see anybody else about at that time?" asked Cordero.

"What?"

"I asked," said Cordero raising his voice again, "if you saw anybody else near your yard at that time. When the bells rang."

The man wheezed noisily, brought the rag back toward his mouth but then relaxed. "I didn't go out there when the bells rang. That's when I had my lunch. I went out after I ate. To *tee!*" he said emphasizing the crude Tetun word for defecate.

"Sorry," said Cordero trying to sound reasonable. "My mistake. When you went out, did you see anyone in your yard?"

"No damn it. No one."

"Did you hear—"

"What? Speak up."

"I guess not," Cordero said to himself. "Do you know the boy, *Senyor*?"

"Who?"

"The dead boy?"

"No, how would I?"

"Have you ever seen him before?"

This time the man waved the hand with the rag as if to be done with the questioning and shoo this annoying policeman away. "No, why should I?"

"You have any idea why his body is in your water trough?"

"Of course I don't. Don't be silly. Have you taken him out yet? I don't want him left there."

"We're getting the body out now, *Senyor*." Cordero was getting nowhere and turned to leave. "One last question."

"What?"

"Do you know Pinto Baptisto?"

"Who?"

"Pinto Baptisto," Cordero said, again in a loud voice. "He lives a little further down the lane."

"Old guy?" Cisco asked, although he appeared to be even older than Pinto.

"Yes."

"Know him. But not well. Don't go out much."

Cordero thanked Cisco Mola and walked back into the yard. Two men dressed in scrubs had taken the body out of the trough, wrapped it in a blanket, and were carrying it to a van pulled up outside the gate. The children at the gate clambered over each other to get a better look at the body, their eyes wide with excitement.

"Get those kids away!" Cordero yelled to the officer at the gate. He saluted and threw his arms out to herd the children away from the van.

"Anything?" asked Mateo Belo who was standing nearby.

"No. Deaf as a boot and doesn't know a thing," replied Cordero. "What about the area search?"

"I've a couple of officers coming," said Mateo, spitting his gum onto the ground off to the side of the yard. "Plus the one at the gate. We'll get started once the body's been taken away."

Cordero nodded, took his kerchief out and wiped his neck a second time. "You notice all the motorcycle tracks in the lane? One slid to a stop about twenty yards from the gate. Three or four motorcycles also came to a sudden stop just outside the gate."

"Yeah," said Mateo, who hadn't paid any attention to the tracks. "Maybe the riders were trying to avoid a dog or something."

"Or maybe another motorcycle suddenly blocked the exit to the lane and one rider was caught by others on his tail," suggested

Cordero. "But there's no spare bike around. Or helmet. Tell your officers to look for both. And ask around the neighbourhood. See if anyone knows where the boy's motorcycle is, if they saw anything, heard anything, know the boy. You have his photo on your cell but don't show anything likely to scare people. Know what I mean?"

Mateo puffed out his chest. "I've done this before, you know," he said.

Cordero glanced at him. "Sorry. I'm just annoyed to be called away when I was supposed to have the afternoon off. Worked all day yesterday."

"Tell me about it," Mateo complained. "Damn short-staffed with everyone going to or coming back from Metinaro. I'm supposed to do the deployments for Sunday. Twenty officers—for the whole of Dili! They'll be stretched thin."

Cordero slapped him on the back. "There's someone I need to talk to down the lane. See you later."

Cordero walked to the house with the peeling yellow paint and an iron gate adorned with a weathered buffalo skull. The padlock was unlocked and he made for the front door.

"*Senyor* Baptisto," he called.

He heard shuffling from inside and the door opened far enough to reveal the old man who heard ghosts.

"Remember me? Investigator Cordero. We spoke—"

"Of course I remember you," the old man said. "Have you found the dead man who spoke to me?"

"Do you mind if I come in?"

The old man opened the door wider and stood back to allow Cordero into the house. It was dim and cool and the same size and condition as Cisco Mola's house. Off the area that served as living room, dining room and kitchen was another smaller room. Through the open door Cordero noticed a bed, neatly made, under a window fronting the fence and beyond it the lane. He stopped in the middle of the first room and turned toward Pinto.

"We found the body of a young man, yes," said Cordero without giving any details. "It was in a water trough at the back of a house further up the lane. The house belongs to Cisco Mola. I've just come from there."

"Cisco, you say?" the old man rubbed a hand through his beard. "I know where Cisco lives. So the other officer didn't search the water troughs on Friday but you just did, is that right?"

"Not quite," said Cordero. "The other officer says he did check your water trough on Friday and after questioning I believe him. But he didn't look into yards that far up the lane and I don't blame him for that. It's a long way from here."

"Ghosts can travel, you know," said the old man, casting a knowing look at Cordero.

"Maybe," said Cordero. "But that's not what has me confused. You said the ghost first spoke to you on Thursday night. The body we found couldn't have been dead that long."

"All I know is what I told you," the old man said. "I'm not an expert on ghosts."

Cordero pushed his hands into his pockets. "The body's been taken to the morgue. It will be examined to determine how the young man died. And when. You may be asked to come and look at the body to see if you know the man. To see if he's the ghost who spoke to you."

"I told you yesterday I never saw the ghost. I heard his voice, that's all."

Cordero nodded. "Well all the same—" he said and made to leave. "At least you should be able to get some sleep now. Good afternoon, *Senyor*."

• • •

Carter called him from the hospital around six o'clock that night.

"Shit!" he exclaimed. "Are you alright? What happened?"

"I'm fine. Long story," she said. "But I need you to drive me home. Estefana's not answering her cell."

"I'll be there in ten minutes," he said but he made it in five.

Cordero found Carter sitting in the waiting room, a blanket wrapped around her shoulders even though it was a warm evening. A beach bag rested on the seat next to her, the edges of a towel and a wrap sticking out the end. An old woman was sitting across from Carter, her eyes closed and a young boy asleep across her lap. A faint scent of disinfectant filled the room. Cordero went straight to Carter and put a hand on her shoulder as he took the bag off the chair next to her and sat.

"Are you alright?" he asked.

"I've already answered that question," she said. She looked directly at him and smiled weakly. "Thanks for coming."

"Here's a question you haven't answer: what happened?"

She rubbed a hand roughly under her nose and puffed. "I stayed on the beach after you left," she began. "This guy came and settled himself on the sand about twenty yards away from where I was sitting. Big guy. Not sure if he was Timorese or not. Anyhow he was drinking heavily. Whiskey, vodka, I don't know, something strong. He'd drained almost the entire bottle by mid-afternoon and was getting badly burnt from the sun." She winced as she moved to get more comfortable. "He ordered a late lunch— you know, from that restaurant you were going to. While he was waiting he kept drinking and shouting into his cell." The blanket had slipped from her shoulders and she drew it up again. Cordero could see that she was wearing only her swimsuit beneath the blanket. "Anyhow, eventually a woman comes out of the restaurant carrying a tray with his lunch on it," she continued. "Burger and fries." She looked at him. "I notice the small details."

Cordero nodded. "It'd taken a while," she continued, "I guess because he'd ordered it late, maybe the kitchen had closed for lunch. The woman was followed by a little girl in pigtails, only seven or eight years old." Again she rubbed under her nose. "The woman put the tray on a table near this guy, he grunted and took another swig from the bottle. But before the little girl goes she pinches a French fry and giggles." Carter stopped and coughed.

"I'll get you a glass of water," Cordero said and looked around the waiting room.

"No…it's okay." She raised a hand to emphasize the point and looked away. "Anyhow this guy gets up and whacks the little girl across the face. She went flying and didn't move. Unconscious, you know? Like I said, this guy was big. The woman rushed to the girl and started wailing. The guy stumbles because he's drunk, thinks he'd better shut all the noise down before it draws attention, and staggers over to the woman. He goes to slap her across the face but I got in the way. I went to knee him in the cojones." She stopped.

"That means—"

"I know what it means," he said.

"But I slipped in the sand. He hit me with the bottle. I went down—dazed. By the time I was up and cleared my head a few locals had subdued the guy and called the cops. He stormed off before they arrived. The little girl was still out cold and I must've looked bad because they brought us both here." She sniffed. "Doctor says mild concussion. Wanted me to stay overnight. I said I had things to do. He refused to let me go unless someone came to get me." She threw him a trace of a smile. "That's you."

"How's the girl?" he asked to hide his embarrassment.

"Eloisa. That's her name. I saw her a few minutes ago. She's okay. Good enough to remember her English lessons from school. She thanked me for helping her mom." She rubbed her eyes. "Doctor also insisted someone stay with me tonight." Another smile crossed her face. "That would've been Estefana but I can't raise her. So...."

"We can try Estefana again a little later. If we can't raise her, I'll sleep on your couch," he said. "I can see a nasty welt has formed on your forehead," he added before she could object.

"Don't be judgmental. Your left eye is hard to miss as well," she countered.

"Lucky punch," he said without elaborating.

"No doubt but who delivered it?" she asked.

"Always the cop, aren't you?" he said.

"You think so? Then tell me what you found when you were called away," she said.

"Young man with his throat cut. Don't know who he is or anything more about it at this stage. But that can wait. Let's get you home. Can you walk?"

"I'm fine, really." She stood and reached unsteadily for the bag Cordero had placed down below his chair. He held it open for her. She took out the wrap and exchanged it for the blanket. She took the blanket, walked unsteadily over to the woman opposite and placed the blanket over the boy asleep on the woman's lap. The woman opened her eyes, smiled her appreciation, and closed them again.

"You have to stop intervening in things like this," Cordero admonished her. He knew her half-sister had been abducted as a child and never found and he knew too how much she detested harm of any kind directed toward children.

"I couldn't let the son-of-a-bitch hit the girl and get away with it," she insisted. "Then go after her mother as well. Besides, we're police officers. That's what we do."

"You're finished with INTERPOL, remember," he said.

"Almost but not quite," she corrected him. "Yet to sign my report."

They walked out through the doors of the hospital, his right arm lightly around her waist and his left carrying her bag. He helped her into his vehicle, closed the door behind her, and hurried around to the driver's seat as though she might run away if he wasn't quick.

When they reached her apartment he helped her up the stairs. Once inside he found a bottle of mineral water. He unscrewed the top and handed it to her before calling Estefana once more. She still wasn't answering her cell. He closed his and surveyed the couch.

"Hope she's okay," Carter said to get his attention. "Estefana."

"I'm sure she is," he said placing his cell on the table then picking it up again. "Do you need a hand—with anything?" he asked. He was feeling awkward. His hands didn't seem to know what to do with themselves.

"I'll be fine," Carter said. "I've extra sheets and a spare pillow in my room. I'll get them."

"Good. Yeah," was all he could manage.

She went into the bedroom carrying the water bottle. He heard her rummaging around and she re-appeared at the doorway and tossed the linen out. "I'll just slip out of this swimming costume, take a shower, and fall straight into bed. If I need anything I'll call."

The bedroom door closed. He placed his cell back on the table, arranged the sheets, sat on the couch that was to be his bed for the night, slipped off his shoes, and waited. After five minutes the sound of running water stopped and moments later the bedroom door opened again.

"The doctor gave me a sleeping pill or sedative or something," she said. She'd slipped into a clean white T-shirt that rose to the top of her bare thighs as she toweled her damp hair. "I might sleep in. In the morning could you check I'm alive, please? But try not to wake me if I am." The door closed but quickly opened again. "Thanks again," she added. "Good night. Sleep tight."

"Good—" he said but the bedroom door was already closed shut.

Chapter 4

After a fitful night on the couch, Cordero had just fallen into a deep sleep when his cell woke him. He fumbled for his jeans in the unfamiliar surroundings of Carter's apartment, found them on the floor beside the couch, then remembered he'd put his cell on the table. He stood, grabbed the cell to stop its buzzing from waking Carter, and answered the call. It was Dr Howard Brooks, the English pathologist who had washed up in East Timor after a failed marriage or two, and was temporarily filling in at the Dili morgue.

"Wait a minute Howard," Cordero whispered into the cell. "I just have to step outside." He opened the door quietly and tiptoed onto the landing. "Okay," he said as his eyes adjusted to the glare of the morning sun.

"I hope I didn't interrupt a fruity morning, dear boy," Brooks said to tease him.

"No. Nothing like that. What's up?" Cordero checked his wristwatch: it had just gone eight o'clock.

"I'm about to examine the body that came in yesterday," said Brooks. "Thought you'd like to know. If you want to swing by in an hour or two I should have preliminary results for you."

Two roosters were competing for attention in a house next door and the sun was already a fireball in the sky. Cordero rubbed his eyes.

"Okay thanks. I'll see you soon." Cordero ended the call, realised people passing on their way to work or the market were staring at this stranger in boxer shorts on the American woman's landing, and quickly ducked back inside the apartment. He threw on his jeans, shirt and shoes and quietly peeked through the bedroom door. Carter was curled on her side, breathing softly and evenly, sound asleep. He scribbled a note to say he hoped she was feeling okay and would call to check on her later, and headed back to the house he rented for a quick shower and change of clothes. On the way to his office, he stopped for coffee. By the time he arrived at work the day was scorching and he was glad to get into his air-conditioned sanctuary.

Except the air-conditioning wasn't working. He removed his jacket, slumped into his chair and loosened his shirt. His colleagues Lucas Rama Savoy and Manuel Fonseca sauntered into the room looking more alert than Cordero was feeling.

"Don't tell me the air con's gone again," complained Manuel as he picked up Cordero's coffee from his desk and took a sip. "What is it about air-conditioning and Timor?"

"Heard you found a body yesterday," Lucas said, talking across Manuel. "That the ghost we've been hearing about?"

"Ghosts don't have bodies," Cordero said. "But now that you mention it...."

He called Mateo Belo—the officer he'd left to manage the follow up work where the body had been found in Balide.

"Hey *maun*," Cordero said when Mateo answered. "Just checking. You find anything that would identify our body yesterday?"

"Not a thing, Tino," Mateo said. "Searched the whole area. No wallet, no cell, no motorcycle. Nothing. Looks like a mugging gone wrong."

Cordero could hear Manuel slurping his coffee.

"Talked to the neighbours," Mateo continued. "No one saw or heard anything helpful. If he'd been dragged inside Cisco Mola's yard that's no wonder. As you said, he's pretty deaf. His gate fronts a wall on the other side of the lane but beyond that it's vacant land. Mola's fence is made of tin sheeting six feet high that would shield an assault from view in the lane and block the sound." He paused. "Oh, and no one knew the boy."

"Okay, thanks Mateo," said Cordero. "I'm heading over to get the results of the autopsy soon. I'll let you know if anything turns up." He retrieved his coffee from Manuel. "You get that report finished yesterday?" he asked.

"Sure *maun*," replied Manuel.

"What have you got on today?" Cordero asked as he finished what coffee was left in the cup, stood and collected his jacket.

"Manuel's looking into a plot to blow up the parliament building," Lucas said, staring absently into his computer. "And I'm teaching the female police cadets the ins and outs of penetrating interrogation procedures."

"That's great," said Cordero whose mind hadn't been on the rejoinders he'd come to expect from Lucas. He considered calling Carter to see how she was feeling but figured it was too early still. "I'll be with Brooks if you need me," he said heading out the door.

• • •

Carter had woken at 8.30, feeling fine except for a bruise atop her left eye and a dull throbbing in her head. She showered to come more fully awake and, with a towel wrapped around her, sat down to a simple breakfast of yoghurt and fruit plus coffee she'd brewed. She'd noticed the sheets neatly folded on the couch and the pillow on top and had read Cordero's note— twice. She had rung Estefana earlier and was told she and Josinto had been attending a counseling session with a local priest before their marriage the following week. That's why her cell was turned off last night. Carter had asked if Estefana had finished translating the final reports she'd written for INTERPOL and was told they'd be ready for her to sign by midday. Estefana offered to bring them to Carter's apartment but Carter asked if Jacobsen would be in the office, was told no, and said she had to go to the US Embassy and would drop by herself later. After all, she added, she was officially working for INTERPOL until she'd signed those reports.

Carter thought it best not to mention the assault or her visit to the hospital. She then called to arrange a consultation with the Embassy doctor—a precautionary requirement of her insurance policy—folded the note Cordero had written and slid it into a book on the table. She walked to her bedroom and chose an appropriately dour business skirt and top. The Embassy wasn't her favourite place to visit at the moment so she figured there was no reason to look cheerful about being there.

• • •

"Tino!" exclaimed Brooks stepping away from a sink and wiping his hands on his tattered surgical apron. The Englishman was in his late sixties. Uncombed grey hair hung down atop eyeglasses over a face grown coarse from the sun. He turned the volume down on an ancient cassette player from which Pavarotti was warbling. "How's the day treating you, dear boy?"

"Hello Howard," said Cordero. "Fine, thanks. But I'm surprised you're still here. In Dili I mean. Just how long are they keeping you here?"

Dr Howard Brooks normally worked as the chief medical officer (and pathologist as required) on the south coast. Given the shortage of qualified pathologists in East Timor, he had agreed to stand in for Dili's medical examiner while the man undertook a training program in New Zealand.

"Well now there's a story, dear boy, and another case of the classic brain drain from an underdeveloped country. I've heard that pretender I'm standing in for applied for residency in New Zealand. Goes completely against the terms of the grant he received to study advanced forensic techniques *there* for use *here*, in Timor," Brooks said with appropriate emphasis. "But who gives a rat's ass about such small details? And what with his application to be assessed, then rejected, then appealed, then rejected again and no doubt reviews of the appeal after that, he may not be back for months, Tino! Years even! Can you believe it?"

Brooks was red-faced but he composed himself and projected an index finger skyward to mark a change of subject. "But I digress."

He picked up a clipboard from a side bench and waved Cordero over to the stainless steel examining table in the center of the room. On the table lay the body of the young man retrieved from the water trough the day before. It was covered by a white sheet under the harsh glare of two fluorescent lamps that hung low from the ceiling. Cordero took up a position on one side of the table. Brooks stood at the top end. He put the clipboard under his arm and rolled back the sheet to reveal the youth's head and shoulders.

"As is obvious," Brooks began, "he was killed by a knife run through his throat. I would suggest, a right-handed attacker holding the victim around the head and striking from behind. If you look closely," he said and pointed, "there are faint suggestions of a tight handgrip on the forehead." He leaned across the body. "The point of the knife has been thrust into the side of the neck below the ear and in front of the spinal column. The cut begins near the hilt with the point rotated forward so that carotid arteries and jugular veins on both sides of the neck are cut along with the trachea. You may know that to cut in the other direction requires cutting the trachea first which slows the whole execution down and, in rare cases, can lead to a failed attempt." Brooks stood erect. "All in all, a very professional job."

"Same as the other one?" Cordero asked.

"The body from Bemori? Pretty much. Yes."

"Pretty much?"

"No two can ever be exactly identical but I have little doubt," said Brooks.

"And the weapon used?"

"That, I would say with even more confidence, was identical," said Brooks.

"Any idea of the type of blade?" asked Cordero bending to examine the wound.

"A double edged blade because a single edged would leave a blunter cut. Combat knife or hunting knife would be my guess. And sharp. Very sharp. Just like the other one. I can't say more than that."

"How old and how long dead?" asked Cordero. He stood and circled the body on the table.

"Age?" Brooks repeated. "I'd say late teens to early twenties. Can't be more specific. Time of death? That's somewhat complicated by the fact that the body was fully immersed in water. But there are no signs of decomposition of the internal organs and no significant buildup of bacteria in the mouth." He took the clipboard from under his arm and consulted the second page. "He was found around 2pm Sunday." He let the pages on the clipboard fall back into place. "My guess is he was killed between twelve and twenty fours hours earlier."

Cordero stopped circling, stared at the body and considered what Brooks had said. Brooks put the clipboard back on the bench behind him and waited.

"I don't suppose there was anything in his clothes or on the body to indicate who he was," Cordero said.

"No."

"Anything else?" Cordero asked after a few moments.

"Of course, dear boy," replied Brooks. "I am thorough, you know. Did you notice the hands?"

"Well they were under the water. I did notice bruising on the knuckles," said Cordero. "Like he might have been in a scuffle."

"Quite right. But not just any kind of scuffle. Did you take a close look at the fingers and thumbs?"

Cordero shook his head.

Brooks lifted the sheet over the man's left hand. "Both thumbs have been broken. Bent back and broken. Same with the left *digitus medicinalis*," he said, enjoying his command of technical language. "More commonly known as the ring finger. So too has the right *digitus medius manus*, or middle finger if you will." A smug expression crossed Brooks' face. "I'd say he was roughed up pretty badly. Tortured even."

"Tortured?"

"Yes, dear boy, tortured or tormented. Take your pick. Held down, thumbs and fingers broken. As though someone wanted information from him and he was reluctant to give it up. Then killed." Brooks sniffed. "There's also this."

He wound the sheet down to the waist and pointed to a tattoo across the youth's left breast. It was of a large, intricate, red scorpion.

Cordero examined it. "Look at the design and finish. It's a work of art, dear boy," said Brooks. "Not like the rough gang tattoo on the previous boy."

Cordero straightened. "It shouldn't be too hard to track down a tattooist of this quality. And that could lead us to the identity of the victim."

He put his hands in his pockets but stayed focused on the body. "Anything else?"

"What you already know," said Brooks. "Tattered jeans and T-shirts are de rigueur among the young of Timor of all classes. But the haircut and the sneakers suggest he had more money than most."

"Anything about the betel quid strike you?" Cordero asked.

Brooks clasped his apron straps and looked back down at the body. "Only what you've guessed already I would have thought. Placed under the tongue after death—like the one found in the other young man's mouth. It hasn't been chewed, sucked or interfered with in any way. Looks like a fairly standard quid to me just like the other but I haven't examined either of them closely. I have them in safe storage if you need them." He eyed Cordero over his spectacles. "What do you think? The killer's calling card?"

Cordero rubbed his chin. "I don't know what to make of the quids," he confessed. "Not yet."

Cordero took photos on his cell of the dead boy's face, neck, hands and tattoo. He checked his watch. Brooks placed the sheet back over the body, went to the door and switched off the lights. "Well I guess we've learnt all we can for the moment, Howard," Cordero said. "If anything else pops up you know how to find me."

"You must drop by my place for a drink, Tino. I just happen to have a bottle of excellent English dry gin," Brooks said. "A friend managed to bring one back from Singapore."

"You have friends?" quipped Cordero.

"Careful dear boy or I'll soon have one fewer," replied Brooks. He looked back over his shoulder. "Tonight's good. That is unless you're getting back to whatever I interrupted when I called this morning."

"No, not getting back to anything, Howard," Cordero said as he headed out the door. "But I'll let you know."

• • •

The US Embassy compound occupied an expansive tract of prime real estate across the *Avenida de Portugal* from the waters of *Tasi Feto*. Behind a high security fence and at the end of a long drive was the main building. It was a sprawling white structure graced by a Greek balustrade set back from a lush green forecourt of freshly cut lawn. To the left at the rear was a swimming pool: off to the right a tennis court and smaller, functional buildings were scattered along the back perimeter. The complex would not have been out of place in the antebellum South but this was Timor and it looked like pure American kitsch.

Carter headed to a building where she knew the medical examiner worked, although they had never met.

Dr Andy Morrow was in his late thirties, freckled complexion, a permanent grin affixed to his face. He took her pulse, blood pressure and checked her reflexes before examining the wound on her forehead. "You say the bottle he hit you with was nearly empty?" he asked.

"Yeah," answered Carter. "He'd drunk most of it."

"Well I'd say that's what saved you a lot of grief," Morrow said. "The near empty bottle I mean. A full bottle packs far more punch than an empty bottle." He removed his gloves and threw them into a bin beneath a sink on the side wall. "It's a nasty bruise but you'll live. We could have X-rays taken if you want but I don't think there's a fracture." He walked back and stood in front of her. "I'll give you analgesics to take. You've been prescribed antileukotrienes. Ever heard of them?"

Carter shook her head.

"They're an anti-inflammatory but not a pain-killer as such. They're mainly used to treat lung inflammation and you don't have that." He chuckled to himself. "It's probably all they had in the hospital. They often do that—give you what they have on hand rather than what you need—but they're not taking your pain away and that's why your head is throbbing. Go home and rest. You should be completely back to normal in another day or two."

Carter thanked him and hopped off the examination table.

"You're normally based in Arizona?" Morrow continued as he slipped off his gown. "I took my kids there on our last leave home. What a place! The kids loved that meteor crater. Could've hung out there all day. And me? I love that desert high country."

"So do I," said Carter. "*So do I.*"

"You miss it?" he asked.

"Hoping to be back there in a couple of weeks," said Carter. "I've been here three months, with INTERPOL. Mostly documenting war crimes. Cold case stuff. Even if you identify the culprits, they'll never be brought to justice. Back home I usually work on child abduction cases on the reservations. You know, hot cases. Red hot. That better suits my temperament."

She finished adjusting her clothing and looked at him. "They're trying to keep me here for another three months but I want to go home."

Morrow ignored what sounded like a complaint. "I love Timor-Leste," he said, using the formal name for the country. "The people, the climate. I'm from New Jersey originally but I've been doing this kind of work for the past eight years. Ethiopia, Solomon Islands. Been here nine months. I'm employed by a healthcare service that contracts to US diplomatic missions."

"Don't your kids miss home?" asked Carter. "Don't you?"

"Me? No, not at all. The kids? At first they did," he shook his head but retained the smile. "But now they're old enough to love all the experiences they know they'd never get back home. Think about all the friends they've made for starters." He picked up a folder to check his next appointment. "And they're old enough now to know that home will be there when they get back."

There was a knock on the door and Morrow said "Enter". A heavy-set, middle-aged woman dressed for a colder climate in dark stockings and a grey cardigan entered the room. A string of white pearls, more suited to a stuffy dinner party in Washington than the informal nature of social life in Timor, hung from around her neck. Carter recognized her as the Ambassador's secretary.

"Doctor," the woman said, tight lipped as though her mouth held something a smile might risk spilling out. "And Miss Carter. How are you feeling?"

"Fine thanks," replied Carter.

The woman seemed uninterested in further details. "That's good. The Ambassador has asked me to extend his invitation to you for dinner this evening"—she looked over to Morrow—"provided that doesn't contravene doctor's advice." Morrow merely shrugged his shoulders.

"Could you thank the Ambassador but really—" Carter began.

"Shall we say seven o'clock for dinner at seven-thirty? An Embassy car will pick you up at a quarter to seven." She turned abruptly. "Good day Doctor and I hope you get some rest this afternoon Miss Carter."

With that the woman left. Carter glared at Morrow. "You could have said bed rest was essential for the next few days," she grumbled and grabbed her things.

Morrow opened the door for her. "I know people who'd give their right arm to have dinner with the American Ambassador," he replied.

"I'd rather use mine to punch him on the nose," Carter said and stomped out through the door.

Chapter 5

Carter arrived at the INTERPOL office just after lunch. She walked down the now-familiar corridor to the room where she and Estefana worked. Estefana's broad smile turned into a look approaching horror when she saw the bruise on her friend's forehead.

"*Mana*! What happened?" Estefana asked, skipping a greeting and rising from her desk.

"It's nothing, Estefana. I slipped and bumped my head, that's all," Carter lied. With Estefana's job re-assignment, wedding, vacation, and house-hunting to contend with, Carter wasn't going to burden her further with tales of her own misadventures.

Officer Furaha Oodanta—the African member of the INTERPOL team in East Timor—sat upright at her desk, eyes glued to her computer terminal as she tapped slowly and deliberately, two-fingered, onto the keyboard. Officer Oodanta never appeared to move from that position or do anything other than tap on her keyboard and she never engaged with her colleagues much beyond 'Hellos' and "Goodbyes".

"*Botarde*, Furaha," Carter said, offering an afternoon greeting.

"*Botarde, mana*," came the tepid response.

Estefana continued frowning as Carter motioned her to sit back down.

"Those reports finished?" Carter asked. Once they were signed she was finished with INTERPOL for good, on vacation, and then due to head back home. She'd taken the vacation leave primarily to attend Estefana's wedding the following week.

"Yes, *mana*," replied Estefana. "Would you like me to read them to you?"

"No, I'm sure they're fine," said Carter. "Just hand them over and I'll sign them. That's it for you here at INTERPOL too, I guess." "The Director said she won't be back in the office today. I'll have to give the reports to her tomorrow morning. Then I have to go to police headquarters and sign papers for my permanent transfer. Once that's done, I'm on vacation like you. For two weeks, *mana!*" The frown had transformed into a smile but momentarily returned. "There is still much to do to organise the wedding."

"Well speaking of the wedding," Carter began as she signed the reports. "If you've no work this afternoon how about we go shopping for a wedding present?"

"A wedding present, *mana?*"

"Yes, a wedding present. You don't think I'm coming to your wedding without giving you and Josinto a present do you?"

"But *mana—*"

Carter held up a hand. "No buts, Estefana. I have to sit through a boring dinner tonight with the US Ambassador. At least I can have fun with you this afternoon and the day won't be a total waste." She handed the signed reports to Estefana and stood to forestall a protest. "Anything we can get for you, Furaha?"

"No thank you, *mana.*"

"Good. I'll wait outside. I have to call Cordero and tell him I'm tied up tonight. Get your things and let's go, Estefana."

• • •

Cordero drove to the main police headquarters building to catch some of the younger officers returning from their lunch break. He wanted to ask those who sported tattoos they didn't try to hide if they had any idea what the scorpion tattoo on the dead boy's body signified and who might have done the tattooing. The first question drew a blank but the consensus seemed to be that the tattoo was the work of Octavio Cristarao, one of the best tattoo artists in Dili. Cordero could find no current address for Octavio but he was told that he made most of his money in the bars and restaurants along the seafront, especially as tourists wandered back from their day's activities and started to unwind with beer and cocktails. The more they drank, the more money Octavio stood to make.

Cordero found him around four o'clock in the third place he visited—*Tasi-Boot* or the Big Ocean bar—tattooing the shoulder of a plump Spanish woman who was trying to look much younger and more attractive than she was. The two were laughing as Octavio coloured in the outline of a crocodile—revered in Timor as the mythical creature that turned itself into the island. The woman's companion, an overweight man in shorts and a sweat-soaked singlet, sat to the side, guzzling beer while he watched a re-run of a European soccer game on a television affixed to the wall. At the rear of the bar was a young couple playing pool. By the way they constantly joked with each other Cordero guessed them to be Australian tourists. He ignored them and approached the tattooist.

"Octavio Cristarao?" Cordero asked holding out his badge. The woman turned, angered by the intrusion, noticed the badge and gawked over her shoulder at the man with the needle in her back suddenly terrified at the possibilities. "We need to talk— when you're finished," Cordero said. "But don't take too long." He walked over to the bar and ordered a mineral water.

Octavio was tall for a Timorese and thinly built. He wore his hair in a bun, sported a thin moustache and a light growth along his jaw, and displayed tattoos of brightly-coloured snakes and birds down both arms below a sleeveless light blue T-shirt. When the Spanish woman and her companion had retreated to a back table near the pool players, Cordero came over with his mineral water and sat opposite the tattooist. Octavio was slowly collecting needles and inks into a metal tin he'd taken from a small backpack, a hand-rolled cigarette hanging off his bottom lip.

"How's business?" Cordero asked.

"Was looking good 'til you came," said Octavio. "You want a tattoo?"

Cordero ignored the question and placed his cell with the photo of the dead boy showing on the table in front of Octavio.

"You know this boy?" he asked

Octavio took the cigarette from his mouth, picked up the cell and examined the photo. "No," he said.

Cordero took back the cell and pulled up the photo of the scorpion tattoo on the dead boy's body. "This your work?"

Octavio admired the photo, smiled and nodded. "Yeah. You want one like that?"

"The tattoo was on the boy's left breast," he said. "He's dead."

Octavio showed no emotion. He nodded again and stubbed out his cigarette. "I remember now. Came up to me at the *Surfista* a couple of months ago," he said referring to another tourist hang-out along the seafront that foreigners knew as the Surfer Bar. "Know it? Had this scorpion he'd roughed out on a sheet of paper. Said he wanted it tattooed to his chest." Octavio finished packing away his tattooing gear, taking his time. He clasped his hands together and placed them on the table. Cordero noticed the fingers were covered in ink stains. "I drew a proper scorpion on the paper. He wasn't an artist, I can tell you that. I gave him a price and did the job."

"Nice job, too," said Cordero. "What was the price?"

Octavio looked over the balcony out toward the sea.

"There's different rates I charge, you know *maun*? If the customer is a good looking woman, I charge less. If they're drunk, I charge more."

"But he wasn't a woman and I'm guessing he wasn't a drunken tourist," Cordero said.

"True, but he was keen. Know what I mean? And that ups the price too."

"What was the price?" Cordero asked as he pocketed his cell.

Octavio turned to face Cordero and spread his hands. "I tried fifty dollars on him, expecting him to bargain it down to maybe twenty-five, thirty."

"And?"

"He pulled the money out of his pocket and slapped it on the table," said Octavio.

"Lot of money for a young boy like that," said Cordero.

"Like I said, he was keen."

"That the first time you saw him?"

"First and last."

"Did he tell you his name?"

Octavio shook his head. He ran a finger around the lid of the metal tin in which he kept his tattooing gear and looked up at Cordero. "His girlfriend simply called him *maun*."

"Girlfriend?"

"Yeah." Octavio smiled and fingered for the makings of another cigarette to roll. "She wanted a scorpion tattoo, too. Smaller one, sure. Didn't want it to distract from her nice tit, you know?"

"Another fifty dollars?" Cordero asked.

"She was pretty." Octavio's smile had now become a smirk. "I did it for thirty. He paid."

"You know her?"

He shook his head, ran his tongue along the length of cigarette paper in his hands, and rolled and lit the result. He shook his head.

"She have a name?"

Octavio drew smoke into his lungs and it came out with his answer. "He called her *doben*." It was a common moniker among Timorese and told Cordero nothing. She could have been a live-in partner, longtime girlfriend, or just a girl the boy had met on the night.

"Just *doben*?"

"Yeah. Just *doben*."

"The two seem close?"

Octavio shrugged.

"You said this boy wasn't an artist. Any idea what he did for a living? What he did to get eighty dollars he could waste so easily?"

"Waste?" Octavio snapped. "I'm an artist, *maun*. You know how much these needles cost? Only professionals use them. They're hard to get, *maun*!"

"Sorry," Cordero said. "I didn't mean it like that. But the money? Where'd he get it?"

Octavio slowly lifted his shoulders. "Never told me and I didn't ask."

"Anything unusual about the way he spoke, you know, that would indicate where he was from or maybe what kind of work he did?"

"Not that I noticed." Octavio took another drag and blew out a stream of smoke that drifted toward the ceiling fan and was gone. "He didn't say much."

"What about the girl?"

"Same."

"How old was she?"

Octavio made a gesture with his hands as if the answer was anyone's guess. "Hard to say with girls these days, *maun*," he said. "Maybe eighteen, nineteen, twenty. No more."

"How did they get to the bar?"

"What do you mean?" Octavio asked.

"I mean, how did they get there? Did they walk, take a taxi, come with friends—what?"

"How should I know, *maun*," Octavio said growing bored with the questioning. "I'm not the doorkeeper. I don't keep an eye on the street. They came by motorcycle like everyone else I guess."

"And you say this was a couple of months ago. Can you be more specific?"

"No. Don't have no diary. I do this every day, every week. Dates are a blur, you know?"

Cordero picked up his bottle of mineral water and sat back in his chair. "Where were you last Sunday night?"

Octavio extinguished his cigarette, leaned across the table, and worked the index finger of his right hand through the condensation left by Cordero's bottle. He traced a fish with the moisture on the wooden table top.

"Working the bars, *maun*, like I said. I work every day, every night. But especially on weekends. Tourists like to drink more than usual on Saturday and Sunday nights and that's good for my business." He placed his hands on his thighs under the table and began to jiggle his feet. "Went home about midnight."

"Anyone vouch for that?"

He shrugged again. "Ask around. Someone will have seen me."

"You can be sure I will," said Cordero. "Where's home?"

"Caicoli," the tattooist said, indicating a district in the center of Dili.

"You live alone?"

"Yeah. Just me. I like my own company."

Cordero took a pen and notebook from his pocket. "Write down your address. I may want to talk to you again."

• • •

After he heard from Carter that she'd been summoned to the Embassy for dinner, Cordero called Brooks to take up his invitation for drinks. He felt disappointed, a little flat. Another missed meeting with Carter? Or a day that brought him no closer to establishing who the dead boy was, why he was killed, or by whom?

In the end all that mattered was he felt like a drink and that was something the Englishman could always be sure to provide.

Brooks had been given use of a small two bedroom bungalow on a hillside overlooking the beach at Areia Branca. The timber veranda at the front had a perfect view of the sea which was now shimmering in the breeze as the sun went down. Waves of wispy clouds were turning from subtle pink to a sharp magenta.

The Englishman filled two large glasses with gin and tonic and brought them out as Cordero was settling into a comfortable wicker recliner. Cordero took a sip, uttered a satisfied sigh, and stretched his legs out to relax. Brooks took his chair, raised his glass in a mock toast, and took a long draught.

Cordero stared out across the water. In the near distance two fishermen were casting nets from their outrigger canoes. Closer, but further down the hillside, a man was walking a track through windswept grasses and spindly trees to his house, a thin bundle of firewood perched on his head. A small boy was waving a stick as he followed close behind and a pale moon had begun its ascent above the eastern horizon.

"I chased down the scorpion tattooist," Cordero said. "Seems our victim had plenty of cash to throw around. Paid eighty dollars for his tattoo plus a similar one for his girlfriend."

"Surely not—"

"Smaller. Atop her left breast." Cordero turned to face Brooks, knowing where his imagination was taking him. "Remember your age Howard."

"Oh must I, dear boy?" There was a pause. "Even so, that's a lot of money for a young Timorese," Brooks added.

"You're telling me. Even I don't have that much ready cash," said Cordero.

"Well remember the haircut and the sneakers," said Brooks. "He wasn't your typical out-of-work, young squatter."

"I can only think of one place where a kid like that could get that much money."

"Let me guess," said Brooks. "He robbed a bank."

"Have you been to a bank in Dili recently, Howard? You'd get more robbing the new Burger King outlet." He raised an eyebrow. "It's just possible he could make that kind of money in a criminal gang."

Brooks nodded to himself, raised his glass and finished his gin in one gulp.

"Two young men murdered in the same way within a week of each other," he said. "One with obvious gang markings and one with a possible gang association. Do you think we are looking at a turf war?

Cordero rubbed his chin. "All I know is that you don't kill a person that way under any usual circumstances I can think of," he said. "And you don't leave a betel quid in the victims' mouths. Someone's trying to make a statement that's for sure but what and to whom is anyone's guess." He too finished his gin. "But I think I need to investigate the gang angle." He looked across at Brooks. "The first victim? Those crude scars formed the sign of the 4:4 gang. I'll start there. Last thing we want is another gang flare-up."

Brooks checked Cordero's drink, stood and went inside the house. A minute later he came back with a large tumbler of gin and tonic, topped up Cordero's glass, and filled his own. He slumped back down in his chair.

"There's only one problem with that idea, Tino," Brooks said.

"What idea? Pursuing the gang angle?"

"Yes, the gang angle. The violent, criminal kind of gang angle," said Brooks.

"Okay. What's the problem?"

Brooks sniffed.

"I've never known anyone in Timor brave enough to open up on a criminal gang's activities. It's not just the wrath of their fellow gang members they have to worry about but the higher ups, Tino." He glared across. "And that can include police officers, politicians, influential bisnessmen. You name it."

Cordero picked up his glass. "You've got a point, Howard. I know. But I've nothing else to go on. And if this is a gang-on-gang thing it could lead to 2006 all over again."

They sat in silence.

"Rather beautiful looking out over the sea, isn't it?" said Brooks to change the subject. "Smooth, soft, calm."

"Hmm," offered Cordero.

"Talking of things smooth and soft at least, how's your American friend?" Cordero took more gin. "Come now, dear boy. Tell Uncle Howard."

Cordero topped up his glass. "She was called to a dinner at the US Embassy tonight. I think they're trying to pressure her to stay on with INTERPOL. Jacobsen wants her to stay on because she needs all the help she can get, and the Ambassador because it makes him look good back in Washington."

Brooks whistled faintly. "And she doesn't want to stay, I'm guessing."

"No. She never wanted to be here in the first place and now she's wants to go home." Cordero gestured with his glass toward the sea. "Tide's running out," he said. "Just like her time here."

"Very lyrical of you, dear boy," said Brooks.

"Well she doesn't belong here," Cordero said as if trying to convince himself. "She should go home."

"What is she going home to?" asked Brooks.

Cordero turned to Brooks, a puzzled look on his face. "What do you mean?"

"Well, is there a man?"

Cordero shifted slightly in his chair and drew his legs in tight. "It appears not."

"Appears?"

"Well she's never mentioned a man in her life, except her father who she talks about a lot. He was killed years ago."

"A family—you know invalid mother, sisters, brothers, that kind of thing?" Brooks persisted, swatting a mosquito on his arm.

"Her mother walked out on her when she was a child. Her half-sister was abducted when just a little girl. Her father was shot dead trying to prevent it. Apparently she never got on with her step-mother and hasn't seen her in years." Cordero took a sip of gin. "So no, no family."

"Okay then, bosom buddies? Friends she can't bear to be without?"

Cordero thought for a moment. "Work colleagues seem to be as far as it goes," he said. "But she never talks about them. I think she's closer to Estefana than she is to anyone back in the US."

"Estefana? That cute young police officer from Suai?"

"There you go again Howard," Cordero corrected him. Brooks feigned a chastened expression. "Yeah. That one," Cordero said.

Neither spoke for a moment.

"Then what's drawing her back?" Brooks asked.

Cordero rubbed a hand across his face. "I think she's still looking for her half-sister. I think that's the reason she became a police officer."

"Oh dear," groaned Brooks and he shook his head. "Grief, remorse, regret. The lives ruined by such things!"

"Don't you have regrets?" Cordero asked. "I mean your marriages for a start."

"My marriages?" Brooks scoffed and took a drink. "My first wife was a nurse, of course. Penelope was her name. Dear Penny. We enjoyed a good six years together."

"And then?" asked Cordero.

"You might say I strayed, dear boy." Brooks took another drink. "Eventually, after the divorce, I moved to Portugal for a change of scenery. Met Yara. It means 'lady of the water.'" He leaned over slightly and grinned. "She wasn't a nurse. She was an actress. Big difference. Oh we had a torrid time of it. So torrid I went with her to Brazil. Lived in Sao Paulo for several years. Marvellous time. Marvellous." Cordero waited. "Then you might say *she* strayed," Brooks added and giggled. "Another divorce. Love grows cold."

"I think you're talking about passion not love, Howard," Cordero said.

"Is there a difference, dear boy?"

"Love is deeper, more complex." Cordero raised the glass to his lips but didn't drink. "I'm guessing you didn't see it in your parents as I did."

Brooks laughed at that.

"Hardly," he admitted. "Have I ever told you about my father? He was a mid-level civil servant in England. Spent his life shuffling papers from an 'in' tray to an 'out' tray across his desk. One day his 'in' tray was overflowing with things to check and sign. He was in a bad mood so he took a pile off the bottom, went upstairs to the men's washroom, tore up the papers and flushed them down the toilet. But here's the thing: what ate him away was that nothing ever came of it. Nothing! No questions, no complaints, no requests to find what had gone missing. He realised then how useless his entire life had become and started drinking. He never stopped."

Brooks fell silent for a moment.

"Your American friend?" he began again. "Perhaps she needs saving from the direction her life is taking, dear boy."

• • •

She was shown into an anteroom off the Embassy dining room by a Timorese staffer wearing a light jacket and tie despite the warmth of the night. To her surprise INTERPOL's Director Danique Jacobsen was sitting across from the Ambassador and they both rose to greet her.

"Ah Sara," Taylor beamed while Jacobsen merely smiled and nodded. "I'm so glad that you could make it. Can I get you a pre-dinner drink?"

"A cold beer would be nice," Carter said to the staffer. "Thank you."

"Do sit down, please," said Taylor gesturing toward a chair next to Jacobsen. "Dinner will be in fifteen minutes or so."

Carter hesitated a moment, offered the slightest hint of a smile to Jacobsen, and took her seat. She didn't quite relax into it.

"That's a nasty bruise you have," said Jacobsen.

Carter went to touch her forehead but held herself in check.

"It's not as bad as it looks," she said.

"But you saw our doctor today," interjected Taylor, a grave look on his face. "He said you were involved in an altercation on the beach."

The Timorese staffer returned and handed Carter a glass of beer on a tray. She took it, nodding her gratitude to avoid commenting on the incident.

"Tell us what happened," said Jacobsen.

Carter sipped her beer. "It was nothing really," she said. "The man was drunk. It was a minor incident."

Taylor was now staring at the wall above Carter as though trying to recall something.

"Violence is such a part of this troubled country," he intoned. "Do you know, they say at least forty thousand Timorese died during the Japanese occupation of the island in the Second World War. About a third of the entire population is said to have perished during Indonesian times. Then there's the history of inter-tribal conflict." He looked directly at Carter. "Did you know some tribes actually engaged in head-hunting?" He shook as if to rid himself of the thought and turned his gaze back to the wall. "And the incidence of domestic violence—oh my goodness. On some estimates more than half of all married women in this country experience it at some stage in their relationships."

He's reciting briefing notes, thought Carter. *This is going to be a long and painful night.*

• • •

Cordero drove slowly home across town, the streets deserted at this time of night, many of the shop fronts locked behind security grilles and shutters. The moon was now bright and high in the sky. He'd had too much to drink, he knew that, and, as he entered his own district on the western side of Dili, the street lights appeared to be out which made him even more careful with his driving.

He was careful, except that his mind was wandering onto the notions of love and passion. He had certainly seen the first in his parents, as he'd told Brooks. Cordero's father had been a journalist with the weekly *A Voz de Timor* until the newspaper was closed down over its criticism of the Portuguese colonial administration early in 1975. He had then found work driving a microlet by day and stringering by night for a number of European newspapers eager for news about East Timor following Indonesia's invasion later that year. It was this work that brought him to the attention of the occupation forces and made him and his family flee to Australia.

In Australia, Cordero's father became a laborer working on the hot, dry roads around Darwin in the country's north. Cordero's mother took a job as a cleaner in a cheap motel. Each morning his father would bring coffee to his mother in bed before he left for work. Each evening she would hand him a cold beer as he came through the door covered in dust. After dinner they would take the time to talk, laugh and walk together. As far as Cordero knew, they still did.

Of passion, though, he was less certain. There had been a girl at university he'd been keen on—Diana—but she was Australian and well-off and, at that time, he was a young, impoverished member of the tiny Timorese exile community. Their friendship never became more than that. After he'd returned to East Timor there were several women but none he'd let get too close. Eventually he'd been honest enough to admit they'd been his attempt to grab something of a lost youth in his native Timor.

Then there was Carter. Her initial aloofness had gone and she was now friendly, and, occasionally, even quite warm toward him.

He, in turn, liked her. In fact, the more he saw of her the more he liked. Could 'like' be the beginning of either love or passion? *Silly question*, he told himself. They were worlds apart in culture, personality and ambition. But what did 'like' mean in terms of saving her from her life's direction, as Brooks had put it?

He hit the brakes suddenly to avoid running over a dog that had dashed across the road. "Shit!" he swore but the shot of adrenaline brought him to his senses. He shook his head, rubbed his eyes and accelerated slowly. He would do everything he could to help her get back home. That's what 'like' required of him—and no more.

But as he drove into his street he began to wonder what would happen if Danique Jacobsen and the Ambassador had their way and managed to force her to stay. She'd be angry. No, she'd be mad as hell, flaying out in all directions, and impossible to get on with.

Compared to that, Cordero thought venturing into the territory of violent criminal gangs would be child's play.

Chapter 6

Early Wednesday morning Cordero rose, took a cold shower and dressed in slacks and a white shirt he left untucked. By then he was feeling much better than he had when he first woke after a night of drinking too much gin. He was beginning to contemplate breakfast when his cell rang. It was Carter and she suggested they catch up at the *Tasi Vista* or Sea View café near her apartment. He agreed without hesitation and drove straight over.

He was the first to arrive and commandeered a table and two seats in the open air outside. A fig tree offered a little shelter from the sun although a breeze off the water brought the morning's warmth with it. Carter soon appeared, wearing a blue cotton frock, her hair brushed in a way that covered as much as she could of the bruise darkening on her forehead, a bag slung rakishly over her shoulder.

"Morning, Tino," she said standing at the table and smiling.

She cut such a stunning figure silhouetted against the sun that Cordero dropped his cell while standing to greet her and say hello. He bent down to pick it up, knocked his head on the underside of the table when he did, and upended a chair as he resurfaced. "Sorry," was all he could manage to say.

"You ordered?" she asked, accustomed to the affect she could have on men.

"Ah—" he said.

"What do you feel like?"

He looked from her to the table. "Um, not sure."

"The black eye of yours is darker today. You had it seen to?"

He put a hand to his face without thinking but she didn't wait for an answer. "The muesli's good here. Made on the premises, not store bought. Comes with yoghurt, wild honey and fresh fruit. That's what I usually have at home—or here when I run out. I'm having it with a coffee."

"I'll have the same," said Cordero, cursing his awkwardness when she'd gone to the counter to place the order.

By the time she'd come back and sat down he'd pulled himself together. "How's the head today?" he asked.

"Much better, thanks," she said. She placed her bag on the back of the chair and sat. "I went to see the doctor at the Embassy. He put me on the right pain killers and said to take it easy for a while. That's what I intend to do." She made herself more comfortable in the chair. "I signed off on my reports for Jacobsen yesterday. Now I'm more or less on vacation." She waved an arm out over the sea. "There's nothing to do at the office so let's say 'more'. No, let's say 'on'. Maybe I'll head back to the beach later."

"Well promise me you won't take on any more drunks," he said only half-jokingly.

She smiled. "After I'd finished with INTERPOL yesterday, I took Estefana shopping for a wedding present," she said.

"Did you find anything?"

"She didn't want anything, of course, but I pressed her and we settled on a breadmaker," she said as their coffees arrived.

"A breadmaker?"

"Yeah, you know—"

"I know what a breadmaker is," he said. "Just seems a strange wedding present."

"Well we are in a strange country, remember, and she said she'd always wanted to make her own bread," Carter raised her shoulders. "Go figure."

"Timor's not that strange," he complained.

She threw him a look.

"Timorese think they're origin ancestor is a crocodile. The country's in Southeast Asia but Caribbean reggae is all I hear from my apartment. The President strolls unaccompanied across the road from his residence to an Italian restaurant, sings some karaoke to those dining in, and walks back with a take-out pizza. I've seen him do it. You don't think any of that's strange?"

Cordero glanced down at the table. She took her coffee cup in both hands and sipped.

"Did you hear Josinto's workplace was broken into overnight?" she asked.

"The coffin maker's workshop?" he asked, looking up.

"Yeah. Estefana told me when she called this morning to say she was taking the INTERPOL reports in for Jacobsen."

"Funny place to burgle," he said, reaching for the sugar. "What'd they take, tools?"

"Well there's the thing," said Carter. She replaced her coffee cup on its saucer. "They didn't take anything. Apparently all the coffins had been opened, the cabinets and drawers were rifled but nothing was taken. It's like they were looking for something."

"What could they be looking for in a coffin workshop?" he asked.

"Who knows," she replied.

"How'd they get in?"

"Ripped off a grille and smashed the back window."

"When?" he asked, stirring a spoonful of sugar into his coffee.

"Like I said. Overnight," she repeated. "Late last night, early this morning."

"Probably just kids," Cordero suggested and found the coffee now to his taste.

"You went to see Brooks?" Carter asked. "How is he?"

He drank more coffee. "Very English," he said.

She took another sip as well. "You do that a lot, you know."

"Do what?"

"Typecast people on the basis of their nationality. Jacobsen's very Dutch, Brooks is very English." She tilted her head and gazed at him. "Am I very American?"

"Only when you're headstrong," he said and drained his cup.

She nodded. "And am I often headstrong?"

He considered his answer more carefully this time, unable to predict her reaction. "Occasionally," he said. "How was your dinner at the Embassy?" he asked to change the subject.

Her expression darkened. "The bastard invited Jacobsen," she said. "Didn't give me any warning. Caught me in a nice pincer movement." She lifted her cup but didn't drink. "Started off telling me what a great job I'd done. First her, then him. Wonderful work, blah, blah. Couldn't have done it without me, blah, blah. I just sat there and held my tongue." She glanced up at him in case he found that hard to believe.

"Well you *have* done good work here," he offered but she wasn't looking for compliments.

"Then it was poor INTERPOL, poor Timor, so much crime, so much to do, so little aid coming from other countries, blah, blah."

She stopped and put her cup back down. He waited. She said nothing.

"And?" he asked delicately.

She swept a stray hair back from her face. "As I said, I held my tongue. When they took a breath I said I'd completed the last of my duties for INTERPOL that very day and I was looking forward to heading home." She sniffed. "Bastard nearly choked on his tuna salad." Her eyes were afire with indignation. "But I wasn't going to give them anything to work on, Tino. 'Keep it simple' I told myself. 'I'm done here and I'm going home,' I said again."

"What did they say?" Cordero asked, leaning forward.

"Well they looked at each other as though trying to telepath a response. Then Taylor gets all ambassadorial. 'I want you to stay on, Agent Carter,' he says deepening his voice in a pathetic attempt to sound convincing. 'I'll take it up with your superiors if you force me to'. I said 'So will I. If you force me to.'"

Cordero whistled.

Carter lifted her coffee cup again and this time drained it. "Well that was the end of their idea of a pleasant dinner, let me tell you. I passed on desert and coffee and stood to leave. Said I had packing to do just to drive the message home that I was out of here. And this is where it gets interesting, Tino."

She bent across the table toward him and lowered her voice. He lent in.

"Jacobsen says 'I'll give you a lift, Sara'. I say 'No, I'll be fine, thank you.' She says 'But I have a car outside and I insist.' In the car I keep shtum." She looked at him a moment. "That means I didn't say anything. 'I wish you'd reconsider,' she says. 'There's a lot of work coming our way at the moment and I could really use your expertise.' Expertise my ass! So I say again 'My assignment has been completed and I really need to go home.' And you know what she says?" She looked at him, more pain than anger in her eyes now. "She says 'Then I guess Estefana will have to go back to Suai as well.' I say 'What? She's getting married. She's been approved for a permanent transfer to the police in Dili. It's their call not yours.' She didn't reply. But the threat couldn't have been clearer. The bitch! If she doesn't sign off on Estefana's work with INTERPOL she could cause problems. I jumped out and slammed the door of her fucking car."

Cordero blinked as though a car door had just been slammed in his own face. "Sorry," she said. "About the language."

He sat back, thoughtful. "Jacobsen doesn't have any say over police appointments," he said.

"Get real, Tino! She meets with senior government officials every other week," Carter said. "Don't tell me she doesn't have strings she can pull."

"I'm not sure that—"

"She's all business, that one," Carter cut him off. "I doubt anything else figures in her life."

Cordero thought it best not to argue. "So what now?" he asked.

"Not sure—yet," Carter said as their bowls of muesli arrived. "Taylor's a political appointee, nothing more. Sold farm equipment or some shit back in the States and was a big political donor. He's out of his depth here. Thinks diplomacy's just another form of closing the deal. Well I've got news for him—you can bet on that." She lifted a spoon to start on her breakfast. "Anyway, I spent too much time going over it last night to worry about it this morning. Enough!" She took a scoop of yoghurt and wiped her lips with a finger. "Tell me the full story about that shiner on your eye."

He started on his muesli. "I help train a couple of boys at the boxing gym on Monday mornings most weeks."

"You never mentioned that," she said. "I'm impressed."

He shrugged his shoulders. "Police community engagement thing. Anyway a lightweight there—you know what that is?"

She nodded. "My dad was a big boxing fan," she said. "Always getting into arguments about who was the best pound-for-pound fighter."

"Sugar Ray Robinson," he said without hesitation.

"Well I *am* impressed," she replied. "That's who my dad always said."

"Right. Well this kid's name is Fidelis Tau. He's coming on well, real well. I was sparring with him the other day and he slipped one past me, I'm ashamed to say. Maybe I'm getting beyond it."

She sat back in her chair and was quiet for a moment, staring at him while he ate the muesli. "Think so, eh?" she grinned. "By the way, thanks again for the other night. I'll have to make it up to you."

"Don't mention it," he said.

She took her eyes off him as a sea eagle glided past on the breeze and she stood to watch it go over the trees. When the bird was lost in the glare of the sun, she sat back down. Her mood had brightened considerably. "I love eagles," she said. "Remind me of home." She rested her elbows on the table. "So," she began. "What've you been working on?"

He quickly finished his muesli, put the spoon in the bowl, and wiped his lips with a paper napkin. "Body turned up on Monday when we were at the beach? Young guy. Nineteen or twenty. Fingers broken like his killer was trying to get something out of him. Then his throat was slashed." He scrunched up his napkin and placed it on the table. "Another body'd turned up a week earlier. Another youth. Another slashed throat. Killings like that are not usual so that gets my unit—*me*—involved." He turned away from the table. "The first one had a gang tattoo. That gives the case even more significance."

"Go on," she urged him. "This is getting more and more interesting."

"There're a lot of gangs in Dili—not many criminal gangs but lots of organised groups of young Timorese. Timor-Leste is a country of young people. The median age of the entire population isn't quite twenty years. So some youth join martial arts groups, you know, sporting groups—they've become very popular. Some are known as ritual arts groups—more into spiritual and mystical stuff. Then there are groups of former resistance fighters, veterans, who've recruited younger members to bolster their numbers. All up tens of thousands of Timorese now belong to groups like these. And on the fringes there are a few groups which engage in criminal activity and worse."

"Worse?"

"You know about the 2006 crisis?" he asked and she nodded that she did.

"I read about that in the briefing papers the Embassy gave me when I first arrived," she said. "Police and military fighting each other and a whole lot of young people joining in. But the briefing papers didn't provide much detail—the focus was on the US aid response afterward." Her brow creased. "It was almost like giving too much away might cause offence to whoever for what they did or didn't do."

Cordero nodded. "Political leaders of all parties have to be very sensitive in Timor," he said. "It's no surprise your embassy people are as well. The situation exploded in 2006. That's why the UN had to send in a force to restore order. But the reasons the place exploded linger. You know, who can you trust? Who can't you trust?" He played with his spoon. "Two years after the 2006 crisis, an attempt was made on the life of the then President and Prime Minister. Three months later the men accused of trying to kill the two were tracked down and brought to Dili. But the security forces that tracked them down held a party for the accused and only served them arrest warrants the next day. In what other country would that happen?"

"I said this was a strange place," Carter reminded him. She leaned back. "You were in the police back in 2006. What was your involvement?"

Cordero laughed. "I kept my head down. Like all the sensible ones." His expression reverted to serious. "I was only a junior officer. And I'd only recently returned after years in Australia which meant I was considered an outsider. No one worried too much about me or what I was doing. The trouble in 2006 was largely fuelled by regional conflicts brought to Dili by people moving from villages destroyed by the Indonesians. You see, many gangs're made up of young people from the same area. The gang keeps alive local customs and beliefs. That's the thing about Dili—much of it's a patchwork of rural communities with all their prejudices intact. When things blow up between gangs, or in ways that involve gangs, it can spread like wildfire."

"You said the first victim had a gang tattoo. Not this latest?"

"No," Cordero said. "He had a fancy scorpion tattooed to his chest. Maybe a gang thing, maybe not. But no, no obvious gang tag. They're usually made by scarring the skin in an amatuerish way. This was a professional job."

"Are you thinking there could be a gang dispute about to blow up into something more serious?"

"That's my fear," he said. "But at this stage it's only one possibility."

Carter stared at the table and was silent for a moment. "I've done a lot of work with gangs back home." She looked up at him and raised her eyebrows. "They're big on the reservations, especially the Navajo reservation."

She waved an arm loosely.

"Generally starts with small acts of vandalism, develops into beatings of particular kids in middle school, and, left unchecked, stabbings, drug trafficking, sexual assaults and killings. I've worked it with tribal police and state cops. Can't tell you how many young Navajos in baggy pants and bandanas I've had to interrogate the past few years. Basically they're all troubled kids. Real troubled but simple as that. They all justify themselves in the same way. Say they're looking for respect. They're really missing a purpose in the family, the community, the work force."

"It's worse here," said Cordero. "Timor-Leste is a new nation, a new state. Not everybody identifies with it. Not yet at least. For a start the local identities I mentioned remain strong, stronger than any sense of national identity in many cases. Then there are those who refuse to accept that the new state we have is the new state people suffered and died for under the Indonesians. They see it as a state run for the benefit of the elite, not the common people and certainly not the young. So many gangs reject the state and all it stands for. They run their own welfare systems in the neighbourhoods they control, their own security systems. They refuse to accept the legitimacy of the state, its laws, its officials. That makes them dangerous in the hands of ambitious people."

"It's not that different," she said, glancing away. "Gang loyalties back home cut right across family, clan and tribal loyalties. And gangs back there are just as often manipulated in the same way, by the same types."

He played absently with his spoon. "There's more," he said and hesitated.

"What?"

"We found a betel quid in both victims' mouths." He looked up at her as if to check.

"I know what a betel quid is," she said.

"They'd been placed there after the victims were killed," he said. "Looks like it's a message of some kind. But what—"

His cell rang. He reached into his pocket, answered the call. "Sorry," he mouthed silently to her and then said: "Cordero. Yes... Really? Well that is interesting. Where is she now? Okay...Yeah, will do...Yeah...On my way. Thanks *maun*." He replaced the cell and wiped his mouth again with a fresh napkin.

"What's up?" she asked.

He rose from the table and reached for his car key.

"A girl's turned up who could provide some answers to the puzzle I just explained," he said.

"Turned up dead?" she asked.

"No. Very much alive."

Chapter 7

"Where is she?" Cordero asked Officer Helio Nelson, when he arrived at the police headquarters building on *Rua Jacinto Candido* in Caicoli.

"Interview Room Two," Helio said. "As soon as I saw the tattoo I remembered you asking about one just like it and that's why I called." He grinned broadly. "She wasn't trying to hide it, I can tell you that."

Cordero headed to the room where the girl had been told to wait. When he opened the door she was chewing a fingernail, arms folded tight across her chest, while pacing the floor in front of a bare table with two empty chairs.

"Who are you?" she asked, turning suddenly. "When can I get out of here?"

Cordero guessed her age as late teens, no more. She was a pretty girl with soft, coffee-coloured skin and long hair that had been straightened and braided so that it fell half way down her back. She wore a red, yellow and green crocheted dress—Rastafarian colours—that was very low on her chest and very high on her thighs. A small scorpion tattoo was visible above the left breast. Her fingernails were painted red and a thin coral necklace hung around her neck. The alluring façade could not soften the anger on her face.

"Jerujalem Lemos," Cordero read from a slip of paper Helio had handed him. He looked up at her. "Is that right?"

She stared at him, caution now displacing the anger.

"Yeah," she said before repeating more slowly: "Who are you?"

"I'm Investigator Vincintino Cordero," he said. He pocketed the slip of paper, sat down in one of the chairs, and rested an elbow on the table. "Sit down and tell me what happened, Jerujalem."

"I've already told that other officer," she snarled. "And the one before him. Why again?"

"Because it's me who's asking you this time," Cordero said. With his free hand he moved the other chair from the table and gestured for her to sit. She turned away, biting again at a fingernail. He waited. She spun back around and slumped heavily into the chair, her hands on either side of the seat and her arms rigid.

"Alright," she said, her teeth clenched. "For the third time! It was close to midnight. Three men were following me. In Bidau." She was reciting the account like it was well rehearsed while she gazed at the ceiling and jiggled one leg folded over the other. "They surrounded me. I knew they were going to rape me." She stopped.

"Go on," he said.

"What more do I have to tell you?"

"All of it," he said.

She grunted.

"People were coming down the lane. Carrying a statue, you know, like they'd been praying or carrying it to a church or someone's house."

"What kind of statue?"

"I don't know! You think I care about statues? Three guys were about to rape me!" she said spitting out her words.

He waited, holding her stare.

"Alright. *Nain Feto,*" she said referencing the Virgin Mary in Tetun. "It was a statue of *Nain Feto* all in pretty blue and white with her hands joined in prayer, alright?" He ignored the mockery in her tone. "And they were singing a hymn. La la la. I broke away by slipping in among them. They were so busy with their la la's that they didn't take any notice. When they reached the main street I ran."

Cordero nodded. "And these men—they didn't follow you?"

She looked at him with contempt.

"They can't rape you if you're in the middle of a crowd singing hymns, you know!"

Cordero kept his voice level and restrained. "Can you describe the men?"

She shrugged. "They looked like men out to rape someone."

"Can you be a little more specific?"

She started to jiggle her leg again.

"Young. Rough looking."

"That's not much to go on," Cordero said.

She huffed. "One had long hair, one had short hair and one— I don't know what he had. All were wearing jeans. Okay?"

Cordero stared at her, poker faced.

"I was scared! I was worried about me not them!" she snapped.

Cordero nodded and let it go. Clearly if she knew more about the boys who she claimed were trying to rape her she wasn't of a mind to tell him.

"What were you doing in that area at that time of night?"

"What's that got to do with it?"

"What were you doing?" he persisted.

"I was coming home from a friend's house. That a crime?"

"How did you get here?" he asked, ignoring her question. "To this police station I mean."

She lifted her eyes toward the ceiling.

"Didn't they tell you that already?"

"No. You tell me."

She let out a theatrical sound of exasperation. "A *Kareta Estado* drove past," she said, meaning a government vehicle, common in Dili, and all marked clearly with *Kareta Estado* on the sides. "Couple of guys coming back from a meeting or something, I don't know. They saw me running and stopped to see what was wrong. I told them what had happened and asked to be taken to the police station for protection. They brought me here. I stayed because I was afraid. Afraid I'd run into those men again in the dark. In the street."

She looked across directly at him.

"But now its daylight and I want to go home."

"Did they bring you straight here or did they drive around looking for the men you say were out to rape you?" Cordero asked.

She waved the question away. "They drove around a few streets but didn't see anyone except the people with the statue. They were singing hymns like nothing had happened. I tell you these church people—"

"Why did you think these men were going to rape you?" he cut in.

She rose from her chair and resumed her pacing. "Shit! How many more questions before I can go? I haven't done anything. I'm the victim here," she said raising her voice and jabbing a finger into her chest.

"Calm down," he said. "I know you're the victim. That's why I'm trying to help you. Why did you think these men were going to rape you?"

She stopped pacing, stooped across the table and said in an even louder voice: "A girl knows! It shows! Alright?"

Cordero sat back in his chair. "Nice tattoo," he said, nodding at her chest. She straightened up and tried to pull what there was of her dress across the top of her breast. She said nothing. "Where did you get that done?"

She appeared confused. "What are you looking down my dress for?"

"Did you get that tattoo done at the *Surfista*? By Octavio Cristarao?"

A wary look came over her face.

"I could ask him, you know. He has a good memory for his clients. Especially pretty ones."

She scowled at him before answering. "Yeah, the *Surfista*. So what?"

"With your boyfriend?"

She started pacing the room once more, hands on hips, weighing her options, wondering how much he knew and about what.

"Jerujalem?"

"Yes, okay. With him. But he's not my boyfriend. I just hung out with him for a few days, that's all."

"Hung out with him enough for him to pay thirty dollars for that tattoo," said Cordero. "That's quite a lot of money for a casual acquaintance to pay."

She avoided his eyes. "I'm not a *puta*," she said, meaning whore.

"I never said you were," Cordero responded. "What was his name?"

"What?"

"You heard. What was this boy's name?"

"What's this got to do with me nearly getting raped?" she demanded to know.

"That's what I'm trying to find out," Cordero said. "The boy who paid for that tattoo is dead. He was murdered last Sunday night. And now you—who knew him well enough that he paid for a smaller version of *his* scorpion tattooed to be put on *your* chest—claim to have almost been raped by three men. Too much of a coincidence for me. Tell me his name."

She stood still, thought about biting her fingernail again but instead said, "Jenito. That's all he told me and all I ever called him."

"Where did he live?" Cordero asked.

"In Perumnas," she said. "I don't know where."

It was an area near Comoro, in Dili's west, where the Indonesians had built housing for their civil servants during the occupation but which had been taken over by squatters from the rural districts when Jakarta pulled its people out of East Timor. Perumnas was overcrowded, largely derelict, and home to several gangs.

"You never went to his house?"

"Why should I?" She was becoming more petulant now the questions had turned to Jenito.

"Well maybe the two of you wanted to…you know."

She slapped her hands against the sides of her legs. "It wasn't like that!"

"What did Jenito do for a living?" Cordero asked.

"I don't know. It! Wasn't! Like! That!" she shouted.

Cordero placed his hands on the table. "You don't seem too surprised or upset," he said.

Upset?" She threw him a quizzocal look. "About what?"

"About your boyfriend being murdered."

"I told you, he wasn't my boyfriend!" she said through gritted teeth.

"Murder doesn't bother you?" he asked.

She bent down to his eye level. "Getting raped bothers me more!"

"When was the last time you saw Jenito?" Cordero asked.

She straightened and ran a hand across the braids on the top of her head.

"A week ago maybe."

"Maybe?"

"Last Wednesday!"

"Where?"

"In Caicoli," she said. "I was walking home. He pulled up on his motorcycle and gave me a lift. What's any of this—"

"How did he seem?"

"Seem? What do you mean?"

"Well, was he happy, tired, worried about anything?"

"He was the same as always," she said cutting off his list of suggestions and folding her arms tight across her chest again.

"But if you hadn't known him long, how would you know what he was usually like?"

She let out a groan. "He was normal, fine. Okay?"

"What type of bike did he ride?"

"Shit! A blue one! A red one! I don't know. I didn't take any notice."

Cordero stood to leave.

"Do you have a cell?" he asked.

"I did have," she grunted. "But I lost my bag when I was running from those rapists."

"Lost it where?"

She waved her arms around. "In Bidau with that group of crazy people singing to a statue! How should I know? I told you I was scared."

He watched her for a moment then told her she could go. As she stomped out of the room Officer Helio Nelson entered, almost bumping into her. Cordero closed the door and resumed his seat.

"You believe her story?" Cordero asked.

Helio grinned. "She is kind of cute," he added.

"That's not what I asked," Cordero said.

Helio looked at him and raised his hands in a gesture of 'don't ask me'.

"How many pack rapes have you heard of occurring in Dili?" Cordero asked.

A vacant expression came over Helio's face.

"How many rapes of any kind have you dealt with as a police officer?"

Helio looked awkward and frowned. "Two. Three."

"And how long have you been with the police? Four, five years?"

Cordero gazed back at the door. "She's hiding something," he said and rose to leave. "Let me know if her cell turns up."

• • •

After Cordero had left, Carter returned to her apartment to compose a letter to FBI headquarters in Washington to counter whatever was heading that way from the Embassy. She opened her laptop, pulled up a page, and addressed the letter to:

The Executive Assistant Director,
Human Resources Branch,
FBI,
Washington, D.C.

Why waste time on underlings, she'd decided. She spent a long time detailing her record, what she had achieved during her time with INTERPOL in East Timor, and the importance of her FBI work out of the Arizona field office. Then she deleted all of that and figured she'd get straight to the point: she'd completed her assignment, was due to go home, and resented what Ambassador Taylor and INTERPOL's Director were trying to do to keep her in East Timor.

She read through what she'd written, decided it exuded too much anger toward Taylor and Jacobsen, and deleted it. She composed another letter, short and sweet, but decided it was altogether too sweet and too short. In between drafts she drank more coffee—too much coffee. After a futile two hours the page on her laptop only showed the intended recipient's title and business address. She was now jittery from caffeine.

She'd never felt quite like this before. What was it—indecision? And if that, what caused it? Could it be that she was divided about going or staying? She'd certainly made friends here—Estefana and Cordero—*real* friends unlike any she could try to name back in the States. Was she torn by the thought of leaving them?

Or was it something else? When he picked her up at the hospital Cordero had made a crack about her always being the cop. Was he right and was she guilty of the very same defect she saw in INTERPOL's Danique Jacobsen—only caring about the job? She thought about that. Maybe she'd let too many other things pass her by that only here, now, in this country cut off from her normal responsibilities and usual routines she was free to enjoy.

She tried to focus again on the letter but found her mind wandering and her hands shaking. It had just gone lunch, the sun was blazing and the day was like a furnace despite the breeze that had built up through the morning. She thought of the beach. She slammed the laptop shut, slipped into her swimsuit, grabbed a wrap and a towel and headed outside to hail a taxi.

The letter could wait.

• • •

Cordero drove the few blocks from police headquarters to his own more modest office building where the scientific investigation unit was based. On the way he decided to buy lunch but couldn't at first think of what he felt like to eat. He drove around a few blocks, eventually stopped, parked his vehicle and walked. His mind was preoccupied with thoughts of two murdered boys, the betel quids found in their mouths, a possible outbreak of gang warfare, and a girl in a Rastafarian mini-skirt with a scorpion tattooed to her breast. That last had him thinking of Carter as well. He decided he needed to eat to get his mind off things and settled for an Indonesian restaurant close to his building.

Twenty minutes later, food container in hand, Cordero walked into his office to find Lucas Rama Savoy, feet propped on the desk, reading a newspaper.

"Busy day, Lucas?" Cordero asked as he sat down at his desk to a take-out lunch of beef sate *maranggi*. An aroma from the dish of lean beef cooked in shredded palm sugar, tamarind pulp, chilli, lime juice, and soy sauce drifted from its container across the room to Lucas' desk.

"Looking forward to Sunday?" Lucas asked, sitting up in his chair. The unit had been told Cordero would be representing its members at the reburial of dead guerillas in Metinaro as their chief couldn't make it back from a meeting in Singapore until Sunday evening.

"You know what I think about pomp and ceremony," Cordero answered.

Lucas ignored the comment. "Says here they dug up three bodies at the bottom of Mundu Perdido out Viqueque way. Then there's a bunch from Lautem and Manufahi and the remains of"—he checked the paper and read aloud—"eight from Ermera and another eight from Manatuto."

"I received the memo too, Lucas," Cordero said and opened his lunch releasing more of the appetizing aroma.

"That's nearly thirty, *maun!*" said Lucas, making conversation as he folded the paper under his arm and followed his nose toward Cordero's desk. "I knew it was going to be big with all the police assigned out there but I didn't know it'd be that big." He edged closer. "You think reburying all those guys in the same place is a good idea?" he asked to disguise his real interest in the food. "You know, that far from home?"

It was an argument Cordero had heard many times before. Some people said the cemetery at Metinaro, known as the Garden of Heroes, was an important symbol of the new nation and its struggle to win independence: traditionalists said the dead should be buried in their origin villages or they'd never be at rest. Cordero had no desire to discuss it now. He ignored the question and logged in to his computer.

"Then there's this other article about a wave of home-made weapons," Lucas said, shifting closer to the container of food. "A kid in Comoro shot his foot off trying to make a rifle. You hear about that? Another in Vera Cruz blinded himself with a bomb he was making. And someone in Becora burnt their house down making Molotov cocktails. Can you believe this shit? What's going on, Tino?"

"Let me see," said Cordero grabbing the paper from him.

"Hey!" Lucas said. Cordero raised a hand to silence him.

Lucas made a show of sniffing the air. "Something smells good," he said. "Think I'll get lunch myself."

"'All in the last few days according to the Dili district police commander,'" Cordero read aloud but to himself. "What's that you say?" he asked looking back at Lucas.

"I said I'm off to get some lunch."

Lucas opened his wallet and started to check what cash he had. He pulled out a five dollar note and two one dollar notes. He put a hand in his trouser pocket and felt for coins. Cordero's cell whirred. It was Officer Helio Nelson.

"Sorry *maun*," Helio said. "Me again. A woman in Bidau just reported she found a shoulder bag. Says its green, red and yellow. You know, Rasta colours. Like that girl with the tattoo on her... you know?"

Cordero placed his elbows on the desk, gripped the cell and placed it tight against his ear. "She bring it in?" he asked.

"No. Said she can't. Mother's sick or something. But she said she has it. Seems to think there might've been a cell phone found too. You asked me to call, remember?"

"Okay, give me the address," said Cordero. He wrote it in a notepad while Lucas was counting the coins.

"Thanks *maun*." Cordero looked at his *maranggi*, then at Lucas. "Your lucky day," he said, handing his lunch to his colleague and leaving with the newspaper clenched in his fist.

Chapter 8

It was mid-afternoon when Cordero pulled up outside the house of the woman who phoned in about the bag. He started sweating the moment he stepped out of his air-conditioned vehicle, the humidity fed by a line of heavy black clouds building to the west. The first rains of the wet season wouldn't be far off now. He wiped a kerchief across his face and neck and sent the woman's chickens scuttling as he walked to the front of her small green cement block house. When she appeared at the door he introduced himself.

"I didn't find the bag, *Senyor*," the woman said without exchanging pleasantries. "My boy Antonio did." She was wiping her hands on her dress. "He was playing with it. Using it as a giant slingshot, of all things, loading it with rocks, swinging it and then letting go of one handle." She motioned for him to follow her around to the back of the house. "He's always up to mischief like that. Well, one rock hit the house. Bang! Nearly broke a window. That was enough for me, I tell you. I scolded him but when I saw the bag it looked unusual, expensive, and I called the police." She stopped. "Antonio!" she shouted.

A boy of about ten years of age came moping from the back of the yard. He was skinny, bare foot, his hair flecked with dust, and he wore hand-me-down shorts that were too big for him. "Get over here!" the woman yelled. "I put the bag up here, *Senyor*," she said reaching to the top of a water tank. "To stop him running off with it."

The woman handed the bag to Cordero. He opened it and checked inside. It was empty. "Where did you find this, Antonio?" he asked.

The boy stared at the ground, hands in pockets, circling the dirt with the big toe of his right foot, and said nothing. The woman clipped him over the ears.

"Ouch," he exclaimed quickly covering his ears with his hands. "That hurt!"

"You'll get a lot more than that if you don't tell the police officer what he wants to know," the woman said.

"Actually I'm a police *investigator*," Cordero corrected her. He squatted down to the boy's eye level. "It's okay, Antonio. I just need to ask you a few questions. You're not in trouble." The boy looked up at his mother as if to say 'See'. "Where did you find the bag, Antonio?" Cordero asked.

The boy looked back at Cordero and bit his bottom lip.

"Tell me Antonio," Cordero said. "Where did you find the bag?"

"I didn't," he said.

"You didn't what?"

"I didn't find it," Antonio said.

Cordero looked up at the boy's mother. "But I thought—"

"My friend Raul, found it," the boy cut in. "Out in the lane," he said and pointed vaguely. "On our way to school this morning. He said it was in the drain."

"Was there anything in the bag?" Cordero asked.

The boy looked up at his mother and said nothing. She made as if to strike him again.

"A balloon," Antonio said

"A balloon?" repeated Cordero.

"Yeah. It came in a little plastic thing and when we tore it open and blew in the end it became a balloon."

Antonio's mother cursed softly under her breath.

"Anything else?" asked Cordero.

Antonia looked at his mother again and thought her embarrassment about talk of a *prezervativu*—a condom—was actually more anger.

"Some money," he rushed out.

"You didn't tell me you found money!" the mother exclaimed.

Cordero raised a hand to silence her. "How much money, Antonio?" he asked.

"Fifty centavos," the boy muttered. The mother held out her hand. The boy retrieved a few coins from the pocket of his shorts, showed Cordero but he held on to them. "There was a dollar too but Raul took that," he said.

"Is that all that was in the bag?" Cordero asked. The boy shook his head. "What else, Antonio? What else was in the bag?"

"Go on," Antonio's mother pressed him.

"A cell. Raul took it."

"A cell?" Cordero repeated.

The boy nodded. "But it didn't work," he said.

"Where does Raul live?" he asked.

The boy pointed down the lane. "The house with the two coconut palms at the gate," the mother explained.

Cordero thanked them both, took the bag, and said Antonio could keep the fifty centavos as a finder's fee. Antonio smiled and ran off before his mother could take the money from him. Cordero walked down the lane to where Raul lived. It was the same type of simple cement block house set back in a small yard. The father was home and he called his son to come out of the house.

Raul appeared to be the same age as Antonio but his expression suggested he was bolder and more stubborn. At first he refused to admit to anything, let alone hand over the cell he had hidden in the yard but Cordero's tongue-in-cheek threat of handcuffs and a jail cell for the night soon brought him around. Cordero took the cell back to his office to be examined. It had to be recharged which meant retrieving the call log would take time. He'd let Jerujalem Lemos know her bag and cell had been recovered after he'd found what he wanted to know from it first.

• • •

Carter spread her towel out on the sand, slipped off her sandals and her wrap, and headed into the water. It was clear and cool and she ran out to where it was deep enough and dived under. She came up flicking the wet hair from her face, checked the bruise on her forehead lightly with her hands, opened her eyes, and looked back to the beach. A few young children played in the shallows and three couples—two young, one old—lounged on the sand. The day was hotter now even though clouds were crowding the sun. The water offered pleasant relief. She swam across the front of the beach for fifty yards, turned and swam back to where she'd started. She tread water for a moment and repeated the feat. It felt good to be exercising again and even her head, she convinced herself, was feeling better for it.

As she strode out of the water one of the young children smiled at her. Carter decided to practice her limited Tetun. She tried for the child's name.

"*Ita nia naran saida?*" she asked.

"Alcinda," the child replied.

"*Naran bonita,*" Carter said—a beautiful name. "*Hau nia naran* Sara."

"*Bondia mana,*" the child giggled. "Sara!" and she ran off to her parents calling the name again and again. Carter could see the child explain her excitement to her parents and point in her direction and the parents waved. She waved back as she headed up the sand.

Carter grabbed her towel, rubbed it gingerly through her hair conscious of the bruise on her forehead, and wrapped the towel around her body. An old man trudged over the sand toward her, his toes showing through his worn sneakers. He carried mandarins in his hand and trinkets of various kinds hanging off ties from a pole balanced across his shoulder. He doffed an old sweat-stained hat and bowed slightly. He smiled a toothless smile at Carter, the white stubble on his jaw and the skin as dark and hard as leather on his face lending him a theatrical appearance. He offered her a mandarin.

"*Lae, obgrigada,*" she said, thanking him but declining the offer.

He took a small, carved outrigger canoe from his assortment of trinkets and offered that, the smile fixed like a clown's paint to his face.

Again she declined.

He tried a statuette of a crucified Christ and offered to add some rosary beads for five dollars—a number he indicated with his fingers. He pointed the statuette toward the bruise on her forehead as though a power it contained could cure the wound.

"*Lae, obgrigada,*" she repeated.

The man doffed his hat, bowed, and lumbered on.

Carter checked her cell. It was a habit she knew she should try to shake off at least while she was on vacation but there was a missed call. It was from the Embassy—an aide to the Ambassador who Carter had met when she first arrived in East Timor. She felt she ought to call him back

"Carter here," she said when the call was answered. "You just called me."

"Oh, yes, Agent Carter," said the aide. "Thanks for calling back. How are you today?"

"I *was* fine. What's this about?"

"Ambassador Taylor would like a meeting with you as soon as possible."

"I saw him only last night," Carter said. Her tone was decidedly cold.

"Yes, well, I think that's what he wants to talk to you about," the aide said.

"I'm on vacation," said Carter.

"Yes, well, the Ambassador was thinking that perhaps you could come this afternoon or tomorrow morning. Which would you prefer?"

"Neither," replied Carter. "I told you I'm on leave."

"Yes, well, the Ambassador has a very busy schedule." There was silence on the call for a moment. "I need to know what time you would prefer. Would this afternoon or tomorrow be best for you?"

"Shit," said Carter cursing away from the cell. "Shit, shit, shit!"

"I didn't catch that, Agent Carter?" the aide said. "Hello? Are you there?"

"Tomorrow," said Carter. "Nine o'clock. I don't want to lose any more of my duly approved leave time than the Ambassador finds necessary to take from me," she added and ended the call.

• • •

"You had no right to examine my cell," Jerujalem Lemos complained. "I've done nothing wrong." She grabbed the bag from Cordero, took out the cell and placed it on the table.

"Your bag and cell are evidence in a crime," Cordero bluffed.

"What crime?" the girl hissed.

"Your attempted rape, remember?" he said.

She rummaged inside the bag. "There was money here," she said. "Over a dollar. It's gone."

He tut-tuttered. "What are things coming to in Dili?" he replied.

He'd gone to the room Jerujalem rented behind a shop selling cheap shoes in Bidau. He figured rightly that she'd be there, resting, after a sleepless night at the police station. The room was small, tidy, and sparsely furnished. A single bed was set along one wall, its sheets crumpled from where she had been laying on them, a small table and two chairs were against the other wall. Jerujalem sat on one of the chairs. Cordero stood.

Three items had been hung above the bed: an old photograph showing Jerujalem in a school uniform with what looked like three younger siblings, an embarrassed mother and a sour looking father; a string of three small black-and-white pictures of Jerujalem pulling faces at the camera in a photo booth, and; a crude drawing of a scorpion Cordero imagined Jenito had made to illustrate the tattoo he wanted reproduced on their bodies. A line of thin rope hung across the wall opposite the bed and items of clothing she'd washed hung from it to dry—G-string panties, a bra. Behind the clothes a window had been cut into the wall. It was closed and locked. Two cardboard boxes on the floor contained more clothes, makeup and cheap items of jewellery.

Jerujalem was wearing a grimy T-shirt and ragged denim shorts. Her feet were bare. She crossed her arms across her chest and pouted.

"You told me you'd only known Jenito for a few days. That it was all very casual. Yet the call log on your cell shows regular calls between you two going back several months. How do you explain that?" Cordero asked.

She turned away from him and reached for the underwear hanging on the rope. She pulled each piece down, roughly, and folded them together with exaggerated movements.

"I don't leave here until I get an answer," Cordero said. "An answer I can believe."

She looked back at him, anger in her eyes. He pulled out a chair and sat. "Alright, he was my boyfriend," she snapped, shoving the underwear to one side. "So what?"

"Why didn't you tell me this before?" he asked but she turned away. "What was his full name?"

She kept him waiting for an answer. Finally she said: "Jenito Fuentes."

"And where did Jenito Fuentes live and what did he do for work?" Cordero tilted his head to the side when she didn't answer. "If he was your boyfriend you must know where he lived and what he did for work."

"I told you he lived in Perumnas. That's all I know. I never went to that shit hole. It stinks. Everyone's crazy there."

"Everyone except Jenito?" Cordero said.

"Whatever," Jerujalem replied.

"And his job? What did Jenito do for work?"

She looked at the pile of underwear as though seeing it for the first time.

"What do you do for work, by the way? A room like this wouldn't come cheap. Where do you get the money to pay for it?" Cordero asked.

She paused again before she answered. "Jenito gave me money," she said and locked her eyes on him. "I told you I'm not a whore. He loved me!" Cordero thought he could see tears welling in her eyes. "He did jobs—" She stopped.

"Jobs? What kind of jobs? Who for?"

She turned her face away again.

"*Forsa,*" she said. It was the name of a notorious Dili gang.

"What sort of jobs?" Cordero asked.

"I don't know," she snapped. "Jobs. Picking things up. Delivering things. How would I know?"

"There was a call to you from Jenito's cell on Sunday night just before ten o'clock," Cordero said. "He left a message." He noticed a red tinge colour her face. "What was that about?"

She chewed a fingernail, clasped her hands, and started rubbing them between her thighs.

"Jenito was murdered. Maybe you were involved," Cordero said. "Or maybe you're next."

She looked at him, remorse, fear, terror in her eyes.

"Well?" he pressed.

"He told me he was in the lane in Balide. He was being followed."

"What lane?"

She brushed a hand across her face. "It doesn't have a name."

"Where is this lane then?"

"Everybody knows it. It runs down from a Chinese bakery. We go—we used to go—there once in a while for the tarts they bake." She stared at nothing in particular. "Jenito loved their tarts."

"Who was following him?"

She pressed her lips together, looked away, said nothing.

"Who Jerujalem?" She shrugged her shoulders. "The call went for ten seconds," said Cordero. "What else did he say?"

She rubbed her hands together, harder this time.

"Come on Jerujalem. You've told me this much. If Jenito loved you do the right thing by telling me what you know so I can find whoever killed him," said Cordero.

She looked at him, fear in her eyes. A tear ran down her cheek.

"They'll kill me!" she said. "They've already tried once!"

"Is that what the attempted rape story was all about? Someone knew Jenito had talked to you that night and wanted to know what he'd told you?"

She began to sob and nodded her head.

"Do you know these people?"

She shook her head.

"I can get you protection but you have to tell me what you know," Cordero informed her.

"I don't know who they were. And I don't know who was following Jenito. He said he'd hidden a package at a house across from the lamp in the lane. There's only one lamp." She wiped her eyes with the back of one hand and let out a grim chuckle. "We used to laugh about how fucked that was. The new Timor-Leste. One lamp!" She wiped her nose. "I don't know where in the house or what was in the package. I don't know why he told me." She looked directly at him, her face scrunched up and eyes red and moist. "What was I supposed to do?"

"Maybe he figured one of his friends would get in touch with you if anything happened to him," suggested Cordero. "Has anyone tried to?"

Again she shook her head. "I was at my friend's on Sunday and Monday nights like I said and in that police station without my cell last night and this morning, remember?" she said. "I don't know if anyone was looking for me or called me."

"There was a text message to your cell from Jenito's the day after he was killed. It asked for a meeting," Cordero said. "And a second when you'd replied suggesting a lane in Bidau near a big fig tree at nine on Tuesday evening."

She nodded. "I didn't know Jenito was dead. I was at my friend Fatima's house and I texted back that I wouldn't be home until Tuesday night. We used to meet under that tree." She caught her breath. "I thought it was Jenito not...."

"Not the people who killed him?"

She nodded, sobbing uncontrollably.

"And so three men met you and demanded to know what the message was that Jenito had left on your cell on Sunday night—just before he was killed. Is that right?"

She nodded.

"And did you tell them?"

She put her head in her hands. "I had to. They were going to kill me!"

• • •

Later, as he was leaving his office to go to the lane in Balide and look around the area where Jenito Fuentes had told his girlfriend he had hidden a package, Cordero noticed Pinto Baptisto heading toward the police building. The old man was wearing the same jacket and the same cap with the Superman logo. It was too late to avoid him.

"*Botarde tiu*," Cordero muttered.

The old man stopped, took a moment to recognize Cordero. "He spoke to me again, *senyor*," he said.

"*Tiu* we found the body in the water tank, remember?" Cordero reminded him.

"Yes but even you said that couldn't have been my ghost because my ghost spoke to me before the boy you found had been killed."

Cordero was about to say something reflecting his frustration with ghost stories but he didn't. "*Tiu* I am driving now to the lane where you live. Let me give you a ride and you can tell me on the way."

"I would have come sooner but my legs didn't want to work this morning," the old man said. "Walking is hard on them some days."

Cordero made a point of checking his watch. "I'm sure it is but I'm in a hurry so please, come. My vehicle is just over here."

• • •

The clouds had covered the setting sun and were dark over Dili when they pulled up outside the house of Pinto Baptisto. The old man had repeated the same story he had told Cordero: he was woken in his sleep by a ghost saying he wanted his body taken back to his ancestral village for burial. "You know, for a proper burial," the old man repeated. Cordero had listened with as much attention as he could muster. As the old man slowly climbed out of the vehicle, Cordero noticed a group of boys huddled under what must have been the sole lamp in the lane.

"*Tiu*," Cordero said, calling the old man back to the window on the passenger's side of the vehicle. The old man turned. "Do you sleep on your back?" The old man nodded. "And when the ghost speaks to you, do you turn your head to hear him better?" Again the old man nodded. "To the left or right?"

Pinto Baptisto frowned and rubbed his chin.

"Left," he said.

Cordero remembered looking into the old man's bedroom. If the old man slept on his back and turned his head to the left, he would have been facing toward the window and, over the nearby fence, the lamp. There was no ghost: someone had been talking under the lamp and the old man imagined he was hearing a ghost. But why would anyone under the lamp repeat the same thing night after night?

"Thank you, *tiu*," Cordero said. "I hope you get a good night's rest."

The old man shuffled stiffly into his house. Cordero watched the boys. There were four of them and he guessed their age at ten or twelve years. Each was holding a sheet of paper. The boys were far too short to be seen from the other side of the fence—from Pinto Baptisto's yard or bedroom.

Cordero walked toward them, hands in pockets. "*Botarde*," he said.

"*Bonoite*," one corrected him, as it was coming on night.

Just then the lamp came on. Cordero stared at it for a moment. He nodded and smiled.

"Do you boys come here—under this lamp—often?" he asked.

The boys looked at each other. "*Sin*," one agreed, which meant yes, they did.

"What do you do here?" Cordero asked.

"Why you want to know?" one of the boys asked. His cockiness suggested he was the leader of the group. "Who are you anyway?"

"I'm here to check that the lamp's working okay," Cordero said. He didn't want to scare the boys into silence by revealing he was with the police. "Is it bright enough for whatever you do here?"

"We're rehearsing a play for school," said a boy on the left of the group. He held up his piece of paper for Cordero to see. "We come here because the light is good. Fernando has one light in his house but his parents sit under it. Abilo doesn't have any lights that work. That's why we come here. The lamp is good."

"That's interesting," Cordero said. "What school do you boys go to?"

"*Escola Catolica De Sao José Operario*," they sang in unison— the Catholic School of Saint Joseph the Worker.

"And what's the play about?"

"You said you were here for the lamp," their leader said, challenging Cordero a second time. "Why are you asking about our school and the play?"

"Well it's obvious the lamp is working well," said Cordero pointing. "I'm just curious. It happens when you get old like me."

"It's about God saving us," said an excited boy with a high-pitched voice. "I'm Jesus and I say: 'Wretched man that I am! Who will set me free from the body of this death?'"

"That's not Jesus!" said the group's leader. "That's San Paulo who says that."

"And I'm Moses parting the sea so the people can escape," said another boy in a shrill voice.

A shirtless boy jumped in front of Cordero. "Then I say: 'I am to be gathered unto my people: bury me with my fathers in the cave—" He stopped and checked his piece of paper.

"We must get this right!" the leader admonished the others. He turned to Cordero. "We're doing the play for a concert at school. Everyone will be there."

"How often do you come here at night?" Cordero asked.

"Most nights," the leader said.

"But only for the last two weeks," the boy with the high-pitched voice added.

"Were you here last Saturday night?" The boys faced each other. "Someone reported that the lamp wasn't working then," said Cordero who really wanted to know if this was the source of Pinto Baptisto's ghost.

"It *was* working then. We were here. And Sunday and Tuesday," said the boy with the high-pitched voice. "Need to rehearse."

"The lamp was working fine," said the leader of the group.

"Well I don't know who could have—" Cordero rubbed his chin.

"But we didn't rehearse on Sunday, Raul," the shirtless boy corrected the leader. "Remember?"

"There was a truck over there with a coffin on it," the leader named Raul explained to Cordero and pointed. "On Sunday. We were watching. Some people helped an old man come out of that house and he looked at the coffin. We thought he was going to climb in and die. It was scary! So we didn't rehearse that night. That's why we came back on Tuesday. We just watched them looking at the coffin on Sunday."

The shirtless boy interjected in a whisper. "But we didn't tell our parents that we didn't rehearse on Sunday. That would have made them angry."

They all laughed, Cordero along with them.

"After they'd walked the old man inside, a man on a motorcycle came," said the boy with the high-pitched voice. "Vroom, vroom," he said and made like he was controlling a bike with his hands.

"Vroom, vroom, eh?" said Cordero. "Sounds like a dog barking?"

"Yeah," said one of the boys.

"What did this man want?" asked Cordero.

"Nothing," said Raul. "He just climbed up on the truck and put something on the roof of that house." The boy stretched out a finger. Cordero's eyes followed the finger. The boy was pointing at the right edge of the roof of the house. "We were going to try and get it after the truck left but there was no way to get up there and—"

"Then other motorcycles came," another boy cut in, "and we all ran back home."

"Other motorcycles?" asked Cordero.

"Yeah," said the boy who'd cut in.

"Did you see them? How many?"

"Three," said one boy.

"No there was four," insisted another. "But we were all running home in the other direction by then. We didn't take much notice."

Cordero nodded. "The package still up there?" he asked.

The boys all shrugged.

"Well thank you, boys, you've been—"

"Then the men on the motorcycles came back," said the shirtless one. "And they weren't friendly like you."

"You said you all ran home. When did they come back?"

"Tuesday night," Raul, the leader of the boys, said. "That's when they came back."

"Tuesday night?"

"Of course it was Tuesday night," Raul said. "Monday we have soccer practice."

"Same motorcycles?"

"Looked the same. Sounded the same," the shirtless one said.

"Who were these other men?" Cordero asked. The boys raised and lowered their shoulders. "Why were you here on Tuesday?"

"I told you we didn't practice on Sunday and we need to practice!" stressed Raul, as though it was obvious. "But we keep getting interrupted. Like now!"

"I'm sorry," said Cordero. "Yes, you did tell me that. I'll leave you in a moment. But why did you say these men weren't friendly? Did they talk to you?"

"One said he'd seen us on Sunday night under the lamp. He asked us if we had seen the first man stop," said the shirtless boy. "We didn't answer at first and he grabbed Abilo by the collar and shook him."

"Yeah and Abilo wet his pants!" laughed the boy with the high-pitched voice.

"I didn't wet my pants!" the boy called Abilo yelled.

"Yes you did," the other repeated.

"That's terrible," said Cordero. "The man being rough with you, I mean. What a terrible person. And you boys are very brave. What did this man look like?"

Abilo shrugged. "He kept his helmet on."

"What did you tell him?" Cordero asked.

The shirtless boy wiped his nose on the back of his arm. He looked at the leader of the group. Cordero turned to face Raul.

"You're not in any trouble," Cordero said. "It's a good story. Like I said, I'm curious, that's all."

"I told him that the first man had put a package in the coffin and ridden away," said Raul. "But only because he was mean to us."

"What did the man do then?" Cordero pressed them.

"He had Abilo by the collar," the shirtless boy said. "He asked about the truck with the coffin in it. You know, where was it from, what it looked like?"

"And?"

"And Abilo told him that it had pictures of coffins and '*Tomas Pereira, Bidau*' painted on the side because he was scared," the boy said. "And he did wet his pants!"

Cordero thanked the boys and left them arguing about whether or not Abilo had embarrassed himself on Tuesday night. He walked to the house opposite.

A woman answered his knock and he heard the chatter of many more people inside. He introduced himself as a police investigator and asked delicately about the coffin. The woman's husband had been dying, she told him, but wanted to see his coffin before it was too late. She said a "nice boy" had brought it from the coffin maker's the previous Sunday night. Her husband had asked for small changes to the adornment on the lid. The boy had taken the coffin away and brought it back Wednesday morning. Her husband had died later that day. The mourning rituals were underway around the coffin in the house and they would bury her husband in the old Santa Ana cemetery in Bidau, in Dili's eastern district the following Monday.

Cordero asked if he could check her roof. "One of the boys over there said he threw a ball and it's stuck up there. I wouldn't want him trying to get it and disturb your grieving," he told her.

With her permission he drove his vehicle to the front of the house, climbed onto the bonnet, and reached along the guttering. Before long he'd found it. He stepped down, climbed back behind the wheel, switched on the interior light and examined the package. He guessed the weight of the methamphetamine it contained at about two pounds and, depending on where it was sold, its street value at many thousands of dollars.

Chapter 9

Cordero was running down the *avenida* but his shoe laces weren't tied and he was tripping over them. Up ahead he could see his parents smiling. Carter mouthed his name and Howard Brooks held out a package of methamphetamines. A police car pulled up in front of him, siren wailing.

He woke with a start. The cell on his bedside table was buzzing.

"Josinto's gone missing," were the first three words Carter uttered.

Cordero glanced at the time. It was seven thirty.

"Say again," he said rolling onto his side and rubbing sleep from his eyes.

"Josinto. He's gone missing. Estefana just rang me. She's beside herself with worry." She was rushing the words out and Cordero was doing his best to keep up through the fog in his head.

"He went off on a job yesterday morning and didn't come back. His boss rang Estefana around six last night. Needed his truck back. She knew nothing. Hadn't heard from him. She tried his cell. No answer. She went to his room last night and waited. No show. Cell still not answering. He hadn't come home this morning."

"She call the hospital?"

"First thing," said Carter. "Nothing."

"Well maybe...he was taken out for drinks. You know, by friends. Before the wedding."

"That's not what Timorese do, Cordero. You told me that yourself. And it's certainly not what Josinto would do. I doubt he even drinks. And what about the truck?"

"Well let's not get ahead of ourselves."

"Get ahead—"

"Look, it's not yet eight o'clock. Let's call Estefana again mid-morning and see if he's turned up. What are you doing this morning?"

There was a pause for a moment on the other end of the call followed by an audible sigh. She said that 'prick'—by which he figured she meant 'Ambassador Hudson Taylor'—had 'summonsed'—by which she might have meant 'invited'—her to a meeting at the Embassy at nine o'clock. "How do you like that? I think he's cooked up an extension of my time here and wants to present it as a done deal." The anger in her voice rose and then waned. "What are you up to?"

"Umm—" he began but she cut him short.

"Right. I'll call Estefana when I'm finished at the Embassy. If Josinto hasn't turned up we should catch up with her and report it to the police."

And with that she ended the call. He placed the cell on the bedside table and rolled onto his back, thinking through the meaning of Josinto's disappearance and the killers who'd been told that on Sunday night a package of methamphetamine worth thousands of dollars had been placed in a coffin which Josinto had driven away in his truck.

• • •

Cordero pulled up outside the US Embassy where Carter was waiting on the opposite side of the road, hands on hips, gazing over the sea. She opened the passenger's door, threw onto the seat a yellow envelope which carried an Embassy emblem, climbed in and slumped down unceremoniously on the envelope. She tried a wan smile.

"Hi," she said.

"How did it go?" Cordero asked.

"I don't want to talk about it," she said but immediately began to do just that. "He'd stitched the whole thing up. Him and that asshole Slaton in Flagstaff. And Jacobsen, of course. Gave me the papers to sign for another three months starting as soon as my vacation ends week after next." She was erupting with anger. "I said 'Fuck you' or words to that effect. He said, and get this, 'Calm down now—I'm sure you'll see this is in everyone's best interests in time'. Calm down my ass! Everyone's best interests come down to his best interests." She thumped her hand on the dashboard. "This isn't over yet!" She calmed herself. "Sorry," she said and rubbed the dashboard where she'd hit it. "I shouldn't be taking it out on you or your vehicle."

"Well—"

She cut him off. "He said he didn't need the papers signed for another few days since I'm on leave. Put them in this envelope." She slid it from under her and waved it about. "And dismissed me. Dismissed me, Cordero! Like he was the lord and master and I was his domestic servant."

"You're upset—"

"Damn right I'm upset!"

He thought it best not to comment further. "Anyhow let's forget it." She turned to face the sea, raising a hand to shelter her eyes from the glare. The clouds from the night before had gone without rain but another line appeared to be building on the horizon. The heat was climbing. "Josinto's still AWOL. Estefana rang me. She's worried sick, Tino. We're meeting her at Josinto's place in Bidau. Know it?"

"I think so," he said. "But there's something I need to tell you first."

"What?" She looked across at him.

"Remember the boy whose body we found on Monday? Turns out he was in a gang and carrying a package of methamphetamine when a bunch of guys caught up with him. He hid the drugs before they killed him but left a message on his girlfriend's cell to say roughly where he'd hidden the stuff."

"That the girl who'd turned up when we were having breakfast?" she asked.

"Yeah, the same."

"I'm guessing you've got the drugs then?" Carter said.

"Uh-huh," Cordero said. "Securely and secretly stored at police headquarters. I don't want whoever is after the stuff knowing we found it. You know how gossip can circulate among police officers."

"What's this got to do with anything?" Carter asked.

He overtook a microlet that was slowing to pick up a group of women heading to the market and slid back into the traffic behind a line of motorcycles.

"The killers—well, I assume they were the killers—scared the girl into telling them what the message was. They came back to where her boyfriend told her he hid the drugs and roughed up a few young boys who use the place for rehearsing a school play. Right outside the window of an old guy who claimed to be hearing a ghost."

"Let me take another guess: they're the voice of the ghost you told me you were chasing," she said.

"Correct. Anyway, the boys didn't like getting roughed up so they told the killers that the first guy had dropped a package in a coffin driven away in a truck that'd been parked outside a house opposite. A truck with a *Tomas Pereira, Bidau* decal on the side." He cast an eye across at her. "If the killers think the drugs were in the coffin—" and he left the rest unsaid.

She whistled softly.

"It could be completely unrelated to whatever's happened with Josinto," he said.

"Could be." She pursed her lips. "But sounds like an explanation for the break-in at the coffin maker's workshop and you join the dots from there."

• • •

Cordero turned right into *Estrada de Bidau* just before the bridge over the canal that separated Dili's administrative district of Cristo Rei from central Vera Cruz. The sky was reflected in the pools of stagnant water. He took the first right hand turn over the canal and wound through the backstreets until he reached Josinto's rented room. They stepped out of the vehicle and Carter rushed ahead to the door marked '3'. She knocked and Estefana opened it immediately. They touched hands. "*Mana*, he's not answering his cell," Estefana said. "I don't know what's happened to him or what to do."

The two went inside. Carter tried to reassure Estefana that there was a simple explanation for Josinto's disappearance and that he would turn up eventually. Estefana wasn't buying it. She paced back and forth rubbing her hands together nervously and looking around the room as if for a sign—any sign—of where Josinto had gone.

It was a small room, functionally furnished. There was a single bed, a small chest of drawers, clothes on a hanger, a small table with a single gas burner for cooking noodles and making coffee, and two plastic chairs. A picture of a smiling Estefana was on the chest of drawers next to the bed and a crucifix hung from the wall. Cordero lurked on the doorstep. "*Maun!* Sorry, come in," Estefana said when she finally noticed him.

Anything missing from the room?" Carter asked to get Estefana's attention.

"Missing?"

"Yeah, you know, clothes, bags, laptop, whatever," Carter said.

"Nothing, *mana*," Estefana said, although she appeared uncertain.

"Underwear—"

"I haven't checked, *mana*. We are not yet married."

"Tino," Carter said and Cordero inspected the chest of drawers.

"Looks like nothing's gone," he said after a few moments. He checked the clothes hanging on a stand on the other side of the bed and cardboard boxes stacked against the wall. "Can't see that anything's been grabbed in a hurry."

"When the coffin maker rang you, he had no idea where Josinto was?"

"No *mana*."

"Did the coffin maker say where he would be today?" Carter asked.

Estefana took a moment to answer. "Yes *mana*. He complained that he would have to do all the deliveries Josinto was meant to do. He said he'd be back about five o'clock." She looked at them both. "He sounded very angry."

"Have you reported Josinto missing to the police?" Carter asked.

"Just before you came, *mana*. They said I should take a photograph of him to the station."

Carter looked across at Cordero whose expression showed little sympathy. "Without proof of an accident or foul play I doubt they'll do much for a day or two," he said. He caught her annoyance at the lack of urgency. "But, yes, a photograph would be good. And one of the truck if you have it."

Estefana nodded. Carter turned back to her. "Have you been to police headquarters to sign the papers on your transfer?" Estefana shook her head. "Well I think you should do that as soon as you've dropped off the photo of Josinto."

"And the truck," Cordero added.

"And the truck," echoed Carter. "For one thing, completing the paperwork will ensure that you have legitimate police powers and we may need you to have them if the regular police are slow to get involved. And it's better than waiting and worrying."

Estefana protested that she had to stay in case Josinto came back but Carter insisted.

"I'll stay with Cordero for now in case something turns up. If not, I'll meet you back here just before five and the two of us will go talk to the coffin maker. Okay?"

Estefana, doubtful, scanned the room again.

"Okay?" Carter repeated and bent down to have direct eye contact with her friend. Estefana nodded. Carter picked up the motorcycle helmet, handed it to Estefana, and shuffled her out of Josinto's room. When she'd ridden off, Carter turned to Cordero. "So the cops'll do nothing? Is that what you're saying?"

"Do you know how many people go missing each week in Dili?" he said, raising a hand in frustration. "And remember most officers will be out of Dili doing crowd control in Metinaro on Sunday. That means there'll only be a skeleton staff on duty before, during, and after the weekend. Shifts and time off in lieu, remember?" He calmed himself. "I have to go to Metinaro on Sunday as well."

"It's not Sunday yet," said Carter. "How about you rattle some cages, call in some favours, do whatever it is you can do to raise some interest?"

"And what might that be? People are moving in and out of Dili all the time," he tried to explain. "They don't fill out travel plans, don't always tell anyone. People regularly move for ritual purposes. They keep their movements discrete, in other words. All we have is a missing person. There could be any number of simple explanations. That's how the police will view it anyhow."

"We have a person whose sudden disappearance may be connected to the drugs your murdered gang member was carrying," she said.

"*May be connected*," he emphasized.

"Well if the police aren't going to do anything it's up to us. Let's start with the murdered gang member and the drugs."

"What's with this 'us'?" Cordero asked, caught off guard.

"Well you don't expect me to stay here and do nothing, do you?" she said. She held the door open for the two of them. "Where are we heading?"

It was pointless to argue. "I want to talk to a friend of mine at the university. An anthropologist. About the betel quids we found on the two dead boys," Cordero said. "I'm happy to have you along," he added, "but remember you're no longer with INTERPOL. You're a tourist now."

"A tourist with a sudden interest in anthropology," Carter said, pushing him out of the room.

Chapter 10

They drove to the center of town where the national university, *Universidade Nacional Timor-Lorosae* or UNTL, was located. It had opened in 2000 on the site of a smaller Indonesian-era university that was razed to the ground by Indonesian military units and their militia allies in the lead up to the referendum on independence in 1999. Almost every school in the country was destroyed prior to independence as payback to Timorese students who had been at the forefront of demonstrations against the Indonesian occupation. In recent years UNTL had been renovated, expanded and was now a large operation and the country's only public university. The main building was an elegant white two-storey structure stretching along *Rua Jacinto Candido*. The entrance led to classrooms and offices around a courtyard where dozens of students mingled in small, excited groups or sat alone preoccupied with their cell phones and notebooks.

Professor Eurico Guterres was late for the meeting with Cordero. His lecture on the origins of the family of Trans-New Guinea languages spoken in the eastern regions of East Timor had raised questions from one female and three male students and he didn't want to dismiss them with glib answers. Carter and Cordero were waiting as he rounded the corridor that led to his office, a sheaf of notes under his arm. He seemed to be about Cordero's age but thinner, his face unshaven, his hair uncombed. He wore jeans and a crumpled T-shirt that read: '*Ema mate hanorin ita kona ba moris*'.

Carter began translating this as '"Dead people"'—but Cordero finished it for her—'"teach us about life'. Appropriate for an anthropologist I guess," he added.

Cordero introduced Carter to Eurico who greeted her in perfect English and Cordero explained that the two of them had become friends while both were part of the small cohort of Timorese at university in Australia. The corridor was filling with noisy students jostling and arguing as they moved between classes and Eurico motioned them into the relative sanctuary of his room. It was a simple office and quiet once Eurico closed the door.

A bookcase along one wall was half occupied by books on anthropology in English, Portuguese and Bahasa Indonesian. The other half was covered in student assignments, some of which were typed, most hand-written. There was a desk with an ancient bulbous computer surrounded by a clutter of papers, notebooks, and index cards. Piles of monographs spilled onto the floor, and a dusty plastic skull sat atop a filing cabinet.

Eurico cleared more student assignments off two chairs, invited them to sit, and settled himself at his desk. "So Tino?" he said.

"We have two dead bodies," Cordero began, getting straight to the point. "Youths. Their throats slit. Both members of different gangs. Each had a betel quid placed under his tongue post-mortem." Eurico was twirling a pen on his desk. "I think the killer or killers are sending a message by placing the betel. But about what? And to whom? Can you throw any light on that?"

Eurico nodded and sat motionless for a moment. "You want to know what the betel quid might signify."

"Exactly," said Cordero.

"A lot of things, I'm afraid," said Eurico. He stood, turned and stared out his office window. Clouds by now were heavy again and the sunlight in the courtyard was dimming fast. "As you know betel or *bua-malus* as it's called in Tetun"—he turned and addressed Carter—"*bua* for the seed of the areca palm and *malus* for the leaves of the betel pepper vine with which it's mixed"—he went back to the view beyond his window and continued what was sounding like a well-rehearsed lecture—"is a stimulant that produces a mild euphoric sensation when chewed. It might be chewed by people working their garden plots or when they're walking long distances to markets. It offers mild relief from the burden, you see. But ritually it's associated with uniting the living and the dead in order to summons the protection of ancestral spirits." He turned and faced Carter. "I'm sure you've noticed the red spittle marks on the sidewalks of Dili."

"Hard not to," she said.

"Chewing betel produces red saliva, as though the vegetative ingredients are transformed into blood. That's why some people liken the consumption of betel to the Catholic Eucharist—you know, consuming the body and blood of Jesus for spiritual and physical wellbeing."

Carter nodded. Eurico turned to check if Cordero was following him.

"Go on," said Cordero.

"If a person chews betel and spits black rather than red spittle, it's a sign that the ancestors disapprove, that they're maybe going to cause trouble for the person who spat or was spat on. Let's say drugs were involved in the killings—"

"They were," Cordero stopped him. "At least in the most recent killing."

Eurico resumed his seat. "Then the killer could be saying that the ancestors disapprove of drugs—the reason the boys were killed." He twirled the pen on his desk again. "But it wasn't spat on them; it was placed under their tongues without being chewed. And there was no black spittle."

"Back in the States," Carter said, "where I work among Native Americans, many believe in witches. Skinwalkers, the Navajo call them. They shoot beads made of bone, human bone if they can get it, into their intended victims. The idea is the bone causes a deadly illness known as corpse sickness. You think placing the quids in the victims' mouths could be a kind of hex on dealing in drugs?"

"Not in the way you're thinking," Eurico answered her. He took up the pen and pointed with it to a small map on the wall. "There are variations in custom and practice, even in the spice mix in betel quids, all over Timor," he said. "But the general idea associated with betel is the same. Betel is associated with good things—health, prosperity, security. It's not a thing of black magic or hoodoo. Even black spittle is essentially a warning, not something with power of itself."

"The killer may be trying to turn the victim's bad behaviour into something positive by placing the betel," suggested Cordero.

Carter turned sideways to face him. "You mean killing them in order to redeem them?" she asked.

"That's an interesting interpretation," said Eurico looking directly at Carter. "And, yes, a case could be made for saying that the killer is trying to save their souls. You see Timorese are not as hung up on the idea that death is the end as Westerners generally are. A rather busy life goes on in the spirit world only in a different form." He smiled. "But what you suggest would be a long bow to draw. More likely the killer is trying to discourage others from following the example of the ones he killed and in that way hoping for good outcomes. It's a more convoluted reasoning but it fits with what we know about betel and its uses." He glanced at Cordero. "No doubt accounts of the betel quids are getting around."

"Probably. You know how news travels in Dili."

Eurico nodded.

"It's the drug angle we should be focused on then?" asked Carter. Cordero's eyebrows rose again at the use of the pronoun 'we'.

"Or whatever the killer disapproves of," insisted Eurico. He reached across and took a folder off his bookshelf. "I have a monograph here that explains what I've just told you in sixty-eight pages." He offered it to Cordero. "But it's in Portuguese," he added.

"No thanks," said Cordero declining the offer.

Eurico smiled again. "Portuguese never was his strong point," he said to Carter.

"I don't like the way academics over-complicate things," Cordero replied. He rubbed his nose. "Anything else?"

"As I said, it could be any one of a number of behaviours the killer disapproves of. You said both victims were likely involved in gangs? Well, it could be a double-cross that's disapproved of. Someone cheating someone else. Disloyalty. That's assuming it is a warning the betel is meant to convey. Betel that's ritually-blessed from a person's sacred house is often carried by that person wherever they go to invoke the protection of their ancestral spirits for themselves and their offspring. If they were moving from one part of the country to another, for instance, they might take betel from their sacred house. If they were about to engage in something quite complex like marriage they might take betel as a way of calling on the spirits for assistance to make a success of it. But these quids didn't belong to the victims. They bore no particular relationship to either victim, I'm assuming. And you're assuming they were placed by the killer. Why not a passer-by appalled by the sight of the dead bodies? Do you know what's in the betel quids? Where they came from?"

"I don't know if the quids bore any relationship to the victims," said Cordero. "And I don't know where they came from either. Perhaps it's time the medical examiner took a close look at them."

They left Eurico fielding more questions and comments from students who had been waiting patiently outside his office door.

"Where does that get you?" Carter asked as they headed for the university exit.

"Not very far," Cordero replied. A loud rumble of thunder echoed across the top of the building. Carter flinched and looked up: everybody else was accustomed to the seasonal change. "But I'll get Brooks on to those quids."

"Your friend did have a point that you are only assuming the killer planted the betel quids," she said.

"Two murders a week apart. In different parts of town," he said. "How likely is it that a passer-by would happen upon both, each time be carrying a betel quid, and each time decide to insert it in the victim's mouth to make a vague point to a person unknown?"

Thunder boomed once more.

"That the only alternative source of the quids you can come up with?" she asked.

"You have a better one? No, it's the killer planting them alright."

They stopped abruptly at the door of the building. Drenching rain had started and students, dripping wet, were running inside for shelter.

Suddenly the rain stopped. Swirls of fine mist rose almost instantaneously from the warm ground.

"That was quick," said Carter.

"Usually is until well into the rainy season," Cordero said.

They made for his vehicle, Carter jumping a torrent of water rushing down the stormwater drain beside the road. She checked her watch. "Not yet four o'clock," she said. "Too early to meet Estefana." She looked across at Cordero. "Any suggestions?"

"Yeah," he said taking out his cell. "Pepe".

"You mean that gang expert of yours?"

Alberto 'Pepe' Marcelino headed a small section within the regular Timorese police that kept files on gang activity. Cordero and Carter had consulted him a month earlier on a case they worked that appeared at first to involve gang or militia activity.

"That's the one. I'd like to pick his brains. I'll see if he's in. If he is, we'll go see him then I'll drop you back at Josinto's and get onto Brooks."

While he made the call, Carter settled into the passenger's seat and checked her own cell. There were no texts from Estefana which meant there was no news on Josinto's wherabouts. Cordero climbed behind the steering wheel, his cell pressed to his ear. Carter couldn't hear what the person on the other end was saying.

"Bedois?" she heard Cordero ask. It was an area in Dili.

"Right. Thanks," he said and pocketed his cell. "Pepe's picking up his daughter from afternoon classes at school. It's on the way to Estefana. This won't take long."

He turned the key on the ignition and edged into traffic splashing rainwater off the road onto a group of students running passed. "Pepe's a cheapskate. This is a good Catholic school but it's cheap because volunteers from Australia do most of the teaching for nothing." He grinned and shook his head. "But cheapskate or not, nobody knows more than he does about gangs in Timor."

Chapter 11

After the heavy downpour the storm water canals were washing trash through the city and out to sea, the owners of convenience stores were reassembling their outdoor displays, and dogs were rummaging for any scraps of food discarded by people hurrying inside during the rain. Daily life was returning to normal and the humidity was building again.

Pepe was sprawled on a bench in a small cloister running along one side of the school's compact courtyard. True to his reputation among Timorese police as a big man with an even bigger appetite his attention centered on doughnuts he was devouring from a paper bag resting on his expansive stomach. Crumbs were scattered over his police uniform. He brushed them away when Cordero introduced Carter.

"FBI, eh?" Pepe said in his limited English, smiling. "I hear they're good. Want a doughnut? Remind you of home. There's a place near here makes them. They go down well with the kids and don't cost much." He peered into the nearly empty bag. "Unless you buy too many, you know?"

Carter thanked him but declined the offer and said she'd take a look around the courtyard.

"FBI," Pepe said in Tetun when she had gone. He sniggered. "I also hear they can be real stupid, *maun*. Like the dinosaurs—too much armour not enough brains." He turned to Cordero. "I heard about that boy you found Monday," he said. "That why you here?"

"Yeah," said Cordero, taking what was left of the bench next to Pepe. "Seems he was in *Forsa*. The one we found a week earlier—"

106

"*4:4*, I know," Pepe completed the statement. "They've both gone into the files."

"Any idea what's going on with the gangs?" Cordero asked.

"Well I don't know anything about either murder, if that's what you mean," said Pepe. He shoved the last of the doughnuts into his mouth, scrunched up the paper bag, and munched away heartily. "I do know there's a bit of activity out there," he said out of the side of his mouth. "We've had a lot of reports of guys, young guys, making their own guns and bombs and shit. But most end up using the stuff on themselves—by accident."

"I've been reading about that. You think it could be connected to the murders?" Cordero asked.

Pepe brushed a hand across his lips. "Could blow up again. Who knows? But seems here and there, you know? Not like a general weapons buildup."

"Are these two gangs—*Forsa* and *4:4*—still regionally homogenous?"

Pepe folded his arms across his chest. "*4:4* is largely guys from Ermera," he said. Ermera was a district west of Dili. "*Forsa* was originally from the east but I hear they'll take anyone these days. Anyone crazy enough to join."

"I want to talk to the people in both," Cordero said. "Who should I see?"

Pepe shifted his great bulk toward Cordero, the whites of his eyes suddenly pronounced. He swallowed hard. "You lost your mind, *maun*?"

"Think I lost it a long time ago," Cordero said.

"You scientific police guys got no experience with gangs, *maun*. No one's going to tell you anything. And those two gangs are the worst. More likely kill you than talk to you."

"I want to try," Cordero insisted.

"Crazy *maun*," Pepe repeated. "*Forsa* is small, but tough, you know? Real tough. Most of its members live—or better still lurk—in slums around Becora. But the guy who runs it—the guy you need to talk to if you're crazy enough—is Chiquito Santana. He lives in the Muslim quarter. Thinks it's safer there since 9/11." Pepe let out a cynical laugh. "Reckons the security forces are watching the area because it's Muslim, you know? Reckons they'll scare off his rivals."

Pepe shook his head as his daughter Agueda, who Cordero knew to be seven years old, tore out of a classroom, saw her dad and came stampeding across the courtyard.

"4:4 is based in Perumnas. They're even tougher, meaner, than *Forsa*. But smarter. Into all sorts of shit, *maun*. Some of it real bad. Some believe their real leader is high up in the Ministry of Transport. Others say the Ministry of Social Solidarity. Whichever it is, seems he's a powerful guy."

Pepe stood, opened his arms wide and let his daughter jump into them.

"Hey *doben*," he said. "You know Tino, don't you?'

"*Botarde tiu*," the little girl sang.

"*Botarde* Agueda," Cordero replied and ruffled the girl's hair.

Pepe's arms engulfed Agueda for a moment then he turned back to Cordero. "But day-to-day operations are run by a guy called José Magno."

Cordero nodded. "I've heard of him."

"I'm not surprised," said Pepe, brushing hair from his daughter's face. "He's been in trouble plenty of times but always slides away."

"Is it worth going through the UEP to him?" Cordero asked. The UEP, *Unidade Especial da Polisia*, was a special police unit based near Perumnas and set up to control gang violence and terrorism after the troubles of 2006.

"You kidding me?" said Pepe in a high pitched voice. "There you go—you don't know enough about gangs, *maun*. How long you been with the police, Tino? You should know by now that a lot of our guys are in the gangs. And you should know that other police are ordered to protect certain gangs or at least keep well out of their way. Orders come from on high, *maun*. It's political. The UEP would more likely arrest you then take you to Magno."

"Thought you'd say that," said Cordero. "Then I'll have to make a direct approach."

"You know he works in one of the ministries? I wouldn't be talking to him there—too many ears and eyes, you know? Gang business is a nighttime pursuit of his but that makes it even more dangerous for you. Things can happen in the dark when no one's around to see them."

Cordero was expressionless.

"I know what you're like when you set your mind to things, *maun*," Pepe said. He slapped Cordero on the back. "I'll have the priest here say a Mass for you."

• • •

Carter leaned against a pillar on the opposite side of the courtyard from Cordero and Pepe. The clouds were clearing and an intense afternoon sun had transformed the mist into thick, sticky air. She was happy for the shade but the humidity was making her sweat more than ever and she waved a hand against her face in a feeble effort to cool down.

Groups of young girls had converged on the courtyard to skip and giggle while older girls huddled over cell phones or sheltered in the shade like Carter. Each of the girls wore a neat school uniform of light blue with darker shorts or a skirt depending on their age. Watching them Carter was taken back to her own schooling in Missouri: happy times learning, playing, making friends—until her half-sister Bec was abducted in a supermarket car park and her father shot dead trying to prevent it. Nothing was the same after that.

"Good afternoon Missus," a soft voice slowly, carefully enunciated.

Carter was shaken from her thoughts to find two young girls, goggle-eyed and staring at the new foreigner in their midst. The one doing the talking was the brasher of the two because she held Carter's eye. The other was standing behind her friend not knowing whether to speak or to hide and half-hoping she'd not be seen until she'd decided.

"Well good afternoon to you too," Carter replied.

"How are you today?" the girl asked.

"I am well. And you?" asked Carter, figuring this might be the practical extension of an English class.

"I am well also. My name is Anetta. What is your name?"

"My name is Carter. Sara Carter. What is your friend's name?"

"Her name is Teresa. Are you the new teacher?"

But before Carter could answer a voice cried "*Mana!*" from across the courtyard. It was Eloisa—the girl who'd been struck across the face by the drunk on the beach—and she came running over so fast she almost tripped on her shoelaces.

"It's you *mana!*"

"Eloisa!" said Carter crouching to receive a hug. "The doctor let you out too?"

"Yes *mana*. Yesterday. But he said I had to stay at home. I've just come back to school today." Eloisa could hardly contain her excitement. "Come *mana* and I'll show you my classroom and my friends."

Before Carter could say anything Eloisa had her by the hand, the other two girls in train, and was dragging her across the courtyard, enjoying the attention the scene was creating. They entered a classroom that was a jumble of heavy wooden desks and plastic chairs bunched up before an old blackboard covered in chalk dust. There were no panes in the window spaces high up on the walls and tiny swifts flew in and out. Handwritten words describing animals in English—'small cat', 'big dog', 'tall giraffe'— were written on sheets of paper and pasted onto the rear wall. Six children escaping the heat of the afternoon in the relative cool of the classroom looked up from their exercise books when Carter entered with Eloisa.

"This is my friend *Mana* Carter," Eloisa announced, one hand waving toward the guest. "She has come here to school especially to see me."

"Well—" began Carter but Eloisa would broach no dissension.

"*Just* to see me," Eloisa added for effect. "Are you coming to my birthday party, *mana*?" she asked turning to face Carter "You must come, *mana*. You saved my mother's life."

"I didn't—"

"Promise me *mana*," Eloisa insisted.

"When is your birthday?"

"Twenty-two days. I can count down in English! Twenty-two, twenty-one—"

"I can't promise anything, Eloisa," Carter said.

"My mother knows how to contact you," Eloisa said as though that sealed the deal. "She asked the doctor at the hospital. She wants to thank you."

Through the open classroom door Carter noticed Cordero parting company with Pepe and looking for her in the school grounds.

"We'll see, Eloisa. That's my friend over there. I must go. He's looking for me," Carter said.

"Is that your husband, *mana*?" Eloisa asked.

"No," replied Carter.

"Your boyfriend?"

"Just a friend, okay? It's been very nice to see you and your friends and you have a lovely classroom," Carter said to change the subject.

"It is our English language classroom, *mana*," said Eloisa her tone deflating now as Carter headed out the door. "See you on my birthday," she added hopefully.

Carter ran a hand through her hair as she walked toward Cordero. "What were you doing?" he asked.

"Confronting another obstacle to my plans to go back home," she said. "Get what you want?" she asked to avoid further questions.

"Kind of," said Cordero. "But I may regret it."

Chapter 12

Cordero drove Carter to Josinto's room. As they walked to the door they could see Estefana through the window. Josinto's motorcycle was parked by the front door but there was no sign of him. Carter knocked and Estefana hurried to the door, her face dropping when she realised it wasn't her fiancé.

"*Botarde, mana,*" Estefana said, her tone deflated. She turned and went back inside.

Carter ignored the greeting.

"Any news?" she asked, stepping through the door.

"No, *mana,*" answered Estefana. She walked over to Josinto's bed and sat, hands listless by her sides, eyes wandering the room.

Carter motioned Cordero to leave them alone and he made his way back out to his vehicle. He sat behind the wheel, called Brooks and asked him to examine the betel quids retrieved from the two dead boys and let him know what he could about them. He ended the call and drove off.

Carter sat down next to Estefana. "You took the photographs?" she asked.

"Yes, *mana.*"

"What did the police say?"

"They said to let them know if Josinto turns up or if there was any new information about what happened to him."

"That suggests they're not in a hurry to do anything themselves," said Carter. "Did you do the paperwork on your transfer?"

"Yes, *mana.*"

"Good," replied Carter. "Then you can use your badge if you need to." She checked her watch. "It's nearly five o'clock.

Let's head to the coffin maker's workshop and find out what we can."

Estefana made no effort to move.

"Estefana!" said Carter. "Don't get all maudlin on me now."

"Maudlin, *mana*?" Estefana said.

"Yes. It means so full of self-pity you just sit here and mope. I can't do this by myself. You're a police officer. You have skills. I need you to put them to use now. Use them to find Josinto!" She picked up the motorcycle helmet and thrust it into Estefana's hands. "Where's the spare helmet?"

"Near the door," Estefana said, pointing with her helmet.

"Then come on, let's go." Estefana rose and made for the door. Carter put a hand on her shoulder. "We're going to find him, Estefana, I promise," she said. She slapped Estefana playfully on the bottom, picked up the spare helmet, and followed her friend outside.

• • •

Timor's Muslim population numbered less than ten thousand, most of whom were concentrated in a crowded neighbourhood between *Avenida Nicolau Lobato* and the seafront on the eastern bank of the Comoro River. The majority of Muslims in Timor were descendants of Malays and Arabs who had arrived in colonial times but there were a few local converts. If there had been a buildup of hostility towards Muslims during Indonesian times—Indonesia being the world's most populous Muslim country—it quickly receded with independence. Timor-Leste's first prime minister was a Muslim and soon after independence the government paid for two minarets to be erected on the green-domed *An-Nur* Mosque to show that, despite its Catholic majority, Timor-Leste was a country where people of any religion could live in peace. If the security forces saw a need to keep an eye on the Muslim quarter, as Pepe said the gang leader Chiquito Santana believed, Cordero saw no sign of it.

The compound Chiquito had taken over was in a rutted dirt lane off a road that fronted the mosque. Alone among the shoulder-to-shoulder cement block houses it was an old, free-standing, concrete structure behind a new security fence topped with razor wire. A heavy steel gate guarded by two young men in baseball caps opened to a gravel courtyard where six motorcycles were parked. Cordero figured his visit would raise less suspicion if he walked to the gate and so he left his vehicle on the corner. Young girls in open-faced hijabs passed him in the lane and an old man in a grimey kaftan exchanged greetings. When he reached the locked gate one of the young guards confronted him and asked what he wanted.

"My name's Cordero," he said. "I want to speak to Chiquito Santana." The youth waved him away. "I see you're a Real Madrid fan," Cordero said, pointing to the soccer team's logo on the young man's cap. "Great team. Better than Barcelona." He smiled but the youth said nothing. "I'm a police investigator. I'm not here to trouble Chiquito. I just want to talk," Cordero added.

The young man looked to his companion for guidance. Cordero handed his badge through the grille of the gate. "Show Chiquito this," he said. "But I want it back. Okay? Tell him I'm not here about him or anything to do with *Forsa*. I just want to talk."

The youth took the badge, looked again at his companion who shrugged, and turned back to Cordero.

"Wait," he said, and walked off into the house.

Cordero noticed a security camera angled toward the gate. He dug his hands into his pockets, started to whistle, and smiled at the passers-by. The youth behind the gate kept a close eye on him. Three minutes passed, then four, then five. The youth in the Real Madrid cap reappeared. He ran over to the gate, handed Cordero back his badge and took keys from his pocket.

"He'll give you ten minutes," the youth said, opening the gate. "See that guy at the door?" He pointed over his shoulder. "Go with him."

Cordero thanked him and slipped through the gate which was locked behind him. He walked to where an older man in jeans and an open short-sleeved checkered shirt was blocking the doorway.

"This way," the man grunted and led Cordero down a corridor

to the back of the house.

They entered a room that was sparsely furnished, windows barred and drapes drawn making the light dim inside. Chiquito Santana was sitting on a vinyl couch with a young Chinese girl in a red sequined skirt that rode high up her thighs. He looked to be in his thirties, possibly younger, possibly older—the shaved head and heavy coating of tattoos made it hard to be sure. He was wearing fashionably-ripped jeans, an orange singlet, and flip-flops. He stared at Cordero while the girl snuggled up by his side.

"What you want?" Chiquito asked.

"I'm Investigator Vincin—"

"I know that shit. What you want?" Chiquito repeated. The girl giggled.

"Last Sunday a boy was found murdered in Balide," Cordero began. "His body was found on Monday. His name was Jenito Fuentes." Chiquito's face remained expressionless. "Know him?"

"Why should I?"

"Because I'm told he worked for you," Cordero said.

"Who told you that bullshit?" Chiquito asked. He uncoupled himself from the girl, took a cigarette out of his pants pocket, and lit it with a plastic lighter.

Cordero could hear laughter coming from another room-- more gang members, more security for Chiquito.

"Seems he was a courier. Seems he was carrying drugs when he was intercepted and had his throat slit," Cordero said through the smoke Chiquito had intentionally blown toward his face.

"Why you telling me this?"

Cordero waved the smoke away. He noticed a desk in the corner, the man who'd brought him into the room standing behind it and watching his every move. He turned back to Chiquito to allay any suspicion that he might really be looking for something he wasn't going to mention. "A week earlier we found another one. Member of 4:4. His throat was slashed too."

"You come here to give me the news?" Chiquito said. "I can see it on the television." Again the girl giggled.

"I came here thinking there might be a turf war about to start.

If you can tell me anything about that, I might be able to help you," said Cordero.

"Help me how?"

"Provide protection, negotiate a truce—"

Chiquito stood, dropped his cigarette on the floor and the girl quickly picked it up and extinguished it in an ashtray on the armrest of the couch. The gang leader stood close to Cordero. "I look like I need protection to you, *maun*?" he asked. "Fuck your truce. We take care of business ourselves."

"That's what worries me," said Cordero.

"Don't worry me," Chiquito said and he gestured to the man behind the desk to show the visitor out.

Cordero stood his ground and the man hesitated. "There's nothing you're willing to tell me about Jenito Fuentes, what he was doing, why he was killed?"

Chiquito turned his back on Cordero and walked to the desk. The girl looked up at Cordero, went to giggle, but caught the look in his eye and thought better of it.

"A betel quid had been placed in both of the dead boys' mouths," Cordero said. "What can you tell me about that?"

Chiquito acted as though the news was no surprise. Clearly word had spread out from police headquarters as Cordero had expected. *Lian anin*, they called it—Tetun for 'voice on the wind', meaning rumour.

"What it mean to you?" Chiquito asked, turning his head to the side but avoiding eye contact with Cordero.

"I don't know," Cordero said. "That's what I'm trying to find out."

Chiquito seemed to toss things over in his mind. "The police have no idea?"

Cordero shrugged. Chiquito spun around toward him and glared. Then he turned back to the man behind the desk and lifted his chin in a more insistent manner. Cordero could see he was being ushered out. Just at that moment, from loudspeakers atop the mosque, came the call for prayer on sunset. Chiquito raised a hand to stop the man advancing further and uttered: "Shush".

When the call ended he lowered his head. "You believe what they say about the betel?" he asked Cordero.

Cordero turned, a little puzzled by the question. "What's that?" he asked.

Chiquito ignored the question.

"Muslims believe the new day starts at sunset. You know that? For them it's tomorrow now but for us it's today. How can that be? Like the living and the dead all mixed up," said Chiquito. "Maybe joined together by the betel." He looked up directly into Cordero's eyes. "Bad things coming, *maun*," he said. "My advice is be ready."

Chiquito turned away and searched his pockets for another cigarette.

Chapter 13

Senyor Pereira had been a cabinet maker when, sometime after 1975, the Indonesians forced him to make coffins due to the deathtoll from the famine brought on by their invasion. He'd stayed on in the job after independence, realizing a coffin maker in East Timor would never be out of work even if not all of his clients could pay the money that should have made it a highly lucrative job. He was now in his late sixties, a short, stocky man with a head of thick grey hair and bowed legs. A cigar stub dangled permanently from his mouth although no one could ever remember having seen it lit. His lips curled into a smile around the stub when he saw Estefana walk through the workshop door, a familiar figure these past few weeks and one he had already come to like very much.

"*Botarde, mana,*" he said. He looked at Carter, curious.

"*Botarde, senyor,*" Estefana said. "This is *Mana* Carter. She is a police woman from America. I told you about her, remember? She doesn't speak Tetun but she's helping me look for Josinto."

The coffin maker took the cigar from his lips and bowed slightly to Carter.

"That boy," *Senyor* Pereira said to Estefana. He gestured with his cigar stub to a back window. "There's the break-in to deal with. Everything's a mess. Now Josinto's disappeared. I've had to do all his work since he went missing. Finishing coffins and delivering them. And without my truck! I don't know where it is! I had to borrow one from a friend. It normally carries fish and it stank! Another job to clean it before I could carry anything. On top of everything else! People expect respect around the dead not the stink of fish."

His workshop was the size of a conventional Western double garage and was stacked with coffins of different sizes and in different stages of assembly. At the front, showing onto the street, lay three brightly varnished coffins, one in white with a gold trim, one in cinnamon with silver handles and a cross, one in a red finish with black trimmings. At the very rear of the workshop Carter saw the shape of three coffin frames covered by a tarpaulin.

"*Senyor*—" Estefana began but he hadn't yet finished.

"And I have to finish those coffins before the weekend for the burials on Sunday," he said, meaning the coffins for the re-interment of the *Falintil* guerrillas at Metinaro. He scratched his head with the hand that held the cigar stub. "They don't want Indonesians making them, understand? Thirteen coffins plus sixteen caskets for remains I've had to make! I had to rent another space in a disused shed in Cristo Rei and bring in extra help. That's why I left Josinto to manage things here by himself. I have to finish the varnish on six of the coffins." He waved a hand around the workshop. "And it's Thursday now! I'll be working all night tonight!" He replaced the cigar in his teeth and chomped down on it. "The dead don't wait, you know," he said. "And neither does the government when it commissions coffins like those!"

Senyor Pereira had grown flushed. He looked at Carter. A regretful expression came over him. "I've forgotten my manners," he said in Tetun. "Forgive me, *mana*. Hello and welcome to Timor. I hope the sight of the coffins doesn't bother you."

Estefana translated and Carter asked her to thank *Senyor* Pereira and reassure him she felt quite comfortable in the workshop.

"Do you have any idea where Josinto is or what's happened to him?" Estefana asked.

"No and no," he said, taking a rag and wiping his forehead. He could see the worry on Estefana's face and placed a hand crusted with dried varnish on her shoulder. "I don't know what's happened to him, *mana*. He was finishing a coffin for a customer in Balide. I know he went there Sunday because whoever was dying wanted to see it first. I wasn't taking much notice. I was busy with the government order. At the other place."

He threw out his hands in a gesture of despair.

"I think the man who'd ordered the coffin wanted changes. Just small things, you know? To the trim. Josinto may have taken the coffin home to finish the work and return the coffin on Tuesday or Wednesday. I don't know. Like I said, I wasn't here. I know he took the truck home but every so often he'd do that anyway. I haven't heard from him since." He looked apologetically at Estefana. "I don't know where he is or what's happened to him."

Again Estefana translated for Carter's benefit. "Ask him if he can give us the address of the house Josinto took the coffin to on Sunday," Carter said.

Senyor Pereira picked up a small hand plane from the floor where it had been thrown during the break-in and placed it on a bench. "There were two or three coffins he was working on for people in Balide," he said. "I was too busy to keep an eye on him. Besides, he's a good worker, reliable, you know? Not like that lot I've had to hire at the other place, I can tell you. Josinto doesn't need me telling him what to do all the time. He just does what's needed. I don't know which one he took on Sunday."

He chomped down harder on his cigar.

"The break-in," he said. "They went through the coffins and all the drawers."

He walked over to a large wooden packing case and rummaged through a chaotic scattering of papers it contained.

"My records. Haven't had a chance to sort them. I just collected them up and threw them all in here. The name, address—would be in this pile somewhere with other orders Josinto was working on."

They stood peering down at the wooden case that held the papers. "Ask *Senyor* Pereira again, if he could find the paper with the address," Carter told Estefana.

"I told you I didn't take any notice of it," the coffin maker told Estefana when she'd asked him. "I'd have to check the orders to know which it was and where Josinto took it."

"Could I check the orders?" Estefana asked.

Senyor Pereira shook his head. "You wouldn't know what you were looking for. There are lots of orders there from Balide, going back months but probably undated. Josinto is not the best record keeper." He laughed grimly at the mess in the shed. "I hope nothing has happened to him. When you work with the dead—" He looked at Estefana without completing the thought.

"Can you look for me, *senyor*?" Estefana pleaded.

"Yes. Alright. Of course," he said with a sigh. "Soon as I can. I'm sorry Estefana but I must finish varnishing the *Falintil* coffins first. I only came here for more varnish. Maybe I'll take a break to let the coffins dry. Then I'll come back and look. I promise."

"Then you will call me when you have something?" pleaded Estefana. "I don't care what time it is."

"Yes, yes. I will. I promise."

Estefana and Carter made to leave.

"And you call me if you hear anything," *Senyor* Pereira shouted after them. "I don't care what time of the day or night it is either! No sleep for me tonight!"

• • •

Carter had rung Cordero and suggested they get together and compare notes. Since they all had to eat, dinner seemed an appropriate occasion. They were upstairs in an Indian restaurant off the *Avenida de Portugal*.

"Have you been in contact with his family back in Suai?" Cordero asked Estefana as their food began to arrive.

Estefana nodded. "They don't have a phone but I rang a neighbour who does and they haven't seen Josinto or heard anything from him for the past week."

"Have you tried his friends here in Dili?" Cordero continued.

"The ones I know I've called. No one knows anything," Estefana said.

Cordero waited for the others to serve themselves. Neither was in a hurry and he took his chance to scoop beef vindaloo and saffron rice onto his own plate. Carter broke off a piece of garlic naan and nibbled at it but Estefana merely stared at her empty plate.

"You must eat, Estefana," Carter urged her. "You need your strength."

Estefana dithered for a moment and took a small serving of chicken masala onto her plate. She only played with it with her fork.

"And there's no word from the police?" Carter asked throwing Cordero an accusing look. Estefana shook her head.

"I don't know much about Josinto," Cordero said to Estefana. "Tell me about him."

"Tell you what?" asked Estefana.

"Well, what's his background? How did you two meet? What attracted you to him?"

Estefana placed her fork on the table. Her eyes grew moist and she dabbed them with a paper serviette. She straightened herself in her chair and sniffled. "We met in high school. When we were sixteen. He's twenty-two now, like me," she said and stopped.

"Go on," Cordero said.

"Just take your time, Estefana," said Carter glowering at Cordero.

Estefana wiped her nose.

"Josinto was living in the school dormitory because he'd run away from home. His parents are very traditional and he'd been expected to work in their garden plots and not go to school." She looked up defiantly. "But he wanted an education so he ran away!" They waited. Her defensiveness eased a little and she stared at the table. "I noticed how lonely he was at school."

Silence. She seemed caught in the memory.

"How did he pay for the dormitory?" asked Cordero.

"He worked at night for the baker."

"Okay. What then?" Cordero asked, his tone less demanding to avoid another sour look from Carter.

"I invited him to come home and meet my mother and my sisters and brothers." Another pause. "After the second or third visit, it was like he was part of the family. At first we'd all play together but he and I became boyfriend and girlfriend not long after." Her expression seemed pleading. "He was very thoughtful and kind and was always very honest with me, *mana*, about everything." She wiped her eyes.

"You stayed together after school?" asked Carter. "Tell us about that."

"When we finished school we stayed together even though I left for a while to train as a police officer. He remained in Suai, helping his family. The only job he could get was working on a building project but he did that and sent money to his mother and father. That's how he was accepted back. His father saw Josinto was making money because he'd gone to school, and instead of wasting it like many young men his age he was supporting his family."

She was unconsciously working the serviette through her fingers now and it started to shred into tiny pieces. Carter offered her another one.

"How did he get the job in Dili?" Cordero asked.

"Because of the work he was doing on the project in Suai, Josinto became interested in carpentry. He thought he'd make more money as a carpenter and be better able to help his family." Estefana looked at Cordero. "When he decides to do something, he works hard to achieve it. Like working for the baker at night and going to school during the day." She paused for a moment before continuing. "A manager where he was working knew *Senyor* Pereira and arranged for him to take Josinto on. He started here six months ago."

"Well, sounds like you two have been through a lot already. And that's too good a story to end badly, Estefana," Carter told her. "When this is all over and you're married I'm sure you'll look back on everything that's happening now and laugh. Now eat before it all goes cold."

"Yes, *mana*," Estefana said. She added a scoop of rice to the chicken on her plate and began to work her way slowly through it. Carter loaded her own plate as well and started on it.

"Did *Senyor* Pereira tell you anything useful about where Josinto might be or what he was up to?" Cordero asked.

"Not really," Carter said deciding not to mention they'd asked for the address in Balide where Josinto had taken the coffin on Sunday. She didn't want him to try to prevent her and Estefana going there to trace Josinto's movements. "He hadn't seen him for a few days. Busy finishing a big government order. Said he could usually trust Josinto to work on his own."

Cordero forked more curry into his mouth. After he'd finished it he looked back at Estefana.

"The last few times you saw him, Estefana, did Josinto say anything to indicate he was worried or concerned about anything?"

Estefana shook her head. "Nothing bothers Josinto." She hesitated a moment. "He was surprised my transfer came through. Said he thought it'd take at least a year. So now we're about to look for a house to move into after we're married and he mentioned how high rents were in Dili. He's hoping *Senyor* Pereira will pay him more. But none of that seemed to worry him."

They finished the rest of their meal exchanging occasional encouraging remarks. Carter offered to go back home with Estefana and stay with her but she said she'd rather be alone to think. Estefana said that on the way to where she lived, she'd pass a church. "Thank you both," Estefana said. "I may sit inside the church for a while. I can walk home from here."

"You sure?" asked Cordero.

"Yes, *maun*, I'm sure. Thank you again."

"I'll call you tomorrow, first thing," Carter said.

When Estefana had left the restaurant, Carter turned to Cordero. "I'm worried she's becoming fatalistic," she said.

"Because she wants to go to church?"

"No, because she's Timorese," Carter said.

"I'm Timorese," Cordero reminded her.

"Yes but you were brought up in the West," she said. "And you're a lot older than she is."

He appeared slightly offended by the comment. "I wouldn't say a lot older," he said.

"You know what I mean," she said. "Anyhow, what do you think?"

Cordero placed both hands on the table, and then raised one. "Could be he tired of waiting for the wage rise, thought about how much being married was going to cost him, and—"

"And what, ran?" she said and lent forward across the table. "Is that what you'd do if a person got too close to you and complicated your plans?"

"All I'm saying—"

"Josinto wouldn't do that."

"You heard her say he wasn't expecting her transfer to come through for another year," Cordero said.

"He wouldn't cut and run," Carter insisted.

"What makes you so sure?" he asked. "She said he ran away once before."

"When he was a kid. To get an education," she said. "Not when he was an adult, with a job and a wedding coming up."

"He was worried about money—"

"She didn't say he was worried. She said he'd raised the issue in connection with rents. I know Estefana and she wouldn't have stayed with a guy for six years if he was the kind to get the jitters all of a sudden and leave town."

"Woman's intuition?"

"Don't start me, Cordero! Men always claim that when all the signs go against their own intuition."

He raised both hands off the table. "Okay, okay."

She sat back in her chair. "We should be doing more," she said.

"Like what?" he asked.

"I don't know but the first twenty-four hours are critical."

"That's in a kidnapping," Cordero said. "All we have is a possible missing person."

"Possible?" She frowned and tapped her fingers on the table. "You find out anything useful from that gangster you went to see?"

"He's not a gangster he's a gang leader," he corrected her.

"Whatever," she said. "Answer the question."

"No," Cordero said. "He answered my questions with questions of his own. He only spoke to me to find out what I knew. Which is nothing."

"What now?" she asked.

He checked his watch. "Perumnas. I've another gangster as you call them to visit."

"At this time of night?"

"*Gangsters* don't work nine to five," he said to tease her.

She lent forward again. "Want back up? I could use a bit of excitement."

He smiled. "No. If I go alone I'm less of a threat and they may talk to me," he said, though the real reason was he feared for her safety. "But thanks."

"Then drop me home. I have things to do," she said vaguely. "I'll call you tomorrow. Just to make sure you haven't gone missing as well."

• • •

When Cordero had dropped her off and left, Carter sat down at the table in her apartment. Lying atop it was the envelop Ambassador Taylor had given her with the papers to extend her time with INTERPOL for another three months. She looked at it, stood, and paced the room. She came back to the table, checked the time, picked up the envelop, and called a taxi.

She was driven to Danique Jacobsen's condominium on the other side of the Comoro River. Jacobsen answered the door with a book she'd been reading in her hand.

"Why Agent Carter," she said. "How nice to see you. Come on in."

Carter said nothing and was shown into the small lounge/dining room. She spun around and held up the envelop to Jacobsen.

"You and Taylor don't seem to get it," she said in a calm but firm voice. "I'm not going to sign these papers. I'm not staying on. I'm going home."

"Calm down, Sara," Jacobsen said, placing her book on a side table.

"I am calm," Carter replied.

"Let's talk about this," Jacobsen suggested. "Please sit. Would you like a drink of some kind?"

Carter remained standing.

"I don't need a drink," she said. "What I need is for you to stop threatening to have Estefana dos Carvalho sent back to Suai. If that's the best you can do as the person in charge of INTERPOL here I must say it's pathetic."

Jacobsen took a seat herself. She folded her hands on her lap.

"I didn't threaten her transfer," she said. "I was merely pointing out that there are repercussions for her if you go back to the United States."

"Repercussions you'll make sure eventuate," said Carter.

Jacobsen ignored the taunt.

"Sara, you know how desperate we are here for staff. Timor-Leste is a very new country. Its institutions—government, police, justice system—are in their infancy and not fully understood or accepted by people. This is a small country. It is trying to make itself a stable functioning democracy. But it's impoverished, as you know. It's easily prey to outside interference of the worst possible kind."

"Nice speech but you're avoiding the issue," Carter said.

Jacobsen raised a hand. "No, I'm not," she counted. "I need you here."

"And the people I work with on the Native American reservations back home also need me. They're also impoverished and prey to all sorts of abuses."

"I know that and I know you do excellent work. But you are replaceable back there. Your country has resources aplenty to put into policing. Timor-Leste doesn't. That's the difference. That's why I want you to stay. If you were only half as good as you are you'd still be the most valuable member of my team."

"Don't patronize me!" said Carter.

"I'm not," Jacobsen said. "I'm being truthful."

Carter glared at the INTERPOL director.

"Have you been replaced back home while you're here?" Jacobsen asked.

Carter said nothing, knowing she had been.

"That's what I mean," Jacobsen said. "But if you go now, who's going to replace you here? I'm only asking for three more months."

"Then what? Another three after that?" asked Carter.

"No," said Jacobsen. "I promise you. Three months will give me time to find someone else."

"You've already had three months," Carter said.

"It's not easy finding staff willing to come here. I've tried. It took me almost five months to get you. I need more time to find your replacement."

Carter looked at the envelop in her hand.

"You know I can contest whatever that jerk of an Ambassador sent to Washington?" she said.

Jacobsen nodded. "I know. You told us that over dinner at the Embassy. But I hope you won't."

"Watch me," said Carter and stormed back outside.

Chapter 14

Cordero drove into the Bairo Pite neighbourhood, a six block enclave in Perumnas where hundreds of people lived in burned out houses, abandoned stores, and crude shacks made from discarded building materials and tarpaulins hoisted up against walls for stability. The area smelled of raw sewage and garbage, rubbish blocked the drains, and grubby alleyways ran off pot-holed roads into even filthier dirt tracks.

The place where Pepe had said 4:4 was based was a small former warehouse complex with what appeared to be a manager's residence inside the grounds. The entrance was dark—the only light coming from an unattended dumpster fire and the headlights of parked motorcycles. A group of youths hanging out around the motorcycles kept their eyes on strangers as guard dogs might. Half way along the rutted road toward the complex Cordero passed the shell of a yellow taxi cab propped up on its axles, engine, tires and wheels long gone. On its side was scrawled *Firacu beik ba imi nia rai*—'Go home to your own country stupid easterners'. Pepe had said that 4:4 remained a gang of youths almost entirely from Ermera, a district on the western reaches of the country. On the wall behind the wreck was painted a huge red 4:4 made to look like the numbers were dripping blood over graffiti which read *Ita oho ita nia funu-maluk*—'We kill our enemies'. Unlike Chiquito Santana, José didn't need security cameras or razor-wire. Cordero guessed the entire area around this part of Perumnas was his defense perimeter and everyone living there probably doubled as a lookout or a guard.

Cordero eased to a stop in front of the complex. Three youths stepped down from the porch of the residence, came through the gateway and surrounded his vehicle. One, smoking a cigarette, wore a T-shirt with the image of Che Guevarra on the front. The other two wore tattered soccer jerseys for different teams. The youth with the cigarette approached Cordero's window.

"What you want here, *maun*?" he demanded, blowing smoke through the window.

"My name's Vincintino Cordero," Cordero said, his hands firmly on the steering wheel in plain sight. He coughed a complaint against the smoke.

"So what?"

"I'm a police investigator," Cordero answered.

"That's your problem, *maun*. What you want?"

The other two youths circled the vehicle peering inside and rejoined their companion. One of them took a cigarette out of his shorts and lit it.

"I want to see José Magno," Cordero said.

"He doesn't want to see you," the first youth said. "Piss off."

"You haven't asked him," said Cordero.

"I'm saving time. Piss off."

"Tell him I have information that might interest him," said Cordero.

"You another police guy looking for money? We got enough of them already," the youth said.

"I don't want money," said Cordero.

"You don't want money?" he looked up and laughed to his companions. "Then you crazy, *maun*."

"The information I have is about Chiquito Santana and *Forsa*," Cordero said. "I wouldn't want to be the guy preventing José Magno hearing what I have to say."

The youth stood erect, looked at his two companions, and threw his cigarette onto the ground. He leaned back over Cordero's vehicle.

"You got guts, *maun*. Or else you crazy like I said." With his eyes fixed on Cordero, he called "Julião," to one of the youths standing to the side. "Go see what José wants to do with this guy." The boy Julião ran off. "You sit there, *maun*. Don't move."

When Julião returned, Cordero was led into a room off a shabby corridor inside the former manager's residence. He was surprised by a welcome rush of cool, dry air when he entered the room but could see no sign of an air conditioner. There was a desk, side cabinet and two leather easy chairs. The floor was covered in new parquetry and religious icons hung on the walls. A youth stood silent and motionless in one corner, arms folded. Cordero could see the handle of a small calibre pistol under his shirt which was not tucked into his jeans. José Magno sat behind the desk, a tea cup and thermos to his right, sheets of paper in front of him which he turned face down as Cordero entered.

Cordero had never seen José Magno and he was not the type of gang leader he was expecting to find. He was young, thin, bespectacled and dressed in trousers and a neat long-sleeved business shirt buttoned to the neck. His hands looked soft and manicured and his dark hair was neatly combed. To Cordero he looked like a bank clerk out to impress his manager or an accountant who'd come to check the books. He smiled when Cordero was shown into the room, though it was a cold, mistrustful smile.

"It's late for a police officer to be paying a social visit," José said.

"Actually I'm a police *investigator*," Cordero replied. "Two young men are dead and another may be in serious danger. I don't have the luxury of time if I'm to find him."

José offered Cordero one of the leather chairs. He sat. "Is that what you came to tell me?" José asked.

Cordero ignored the question. "The first young man we found two weeks ago. In Bemori. He had a cicatrix of 4:4 tattooed to his neck. I assume he was a member of your gang."

José smiled at the suggestion. "I don't have a gang," he said. "I help organise a social group for young men. Nothing more."

"Why does a member of a social group need a handgun?" Cordero asked tilting his head toward the youth in the corner.

José gestured for the boy to leave the room.

"Fernando watches too many pirated American movies," José said.

"If you say so," said Cordero. He folded his legs. "The dead boy had been murdered. Throat cut. We think he was ambushed, carrying drugs."

"You see any drugs here?" said José spreading his arms to indicate the room. "Since I have no knowledge of this unfortunate boy, why are you telling me this?" he asked.

"Whoever killed him placed a betel quid in his mouth after death," Cordero added.

José held Cordero's gaze for a moment before pouring tea from the thermos. He didn't offer any to Cordero. He took a sip and replaced the cup gently in its saucer on the desk. "An interesting story but I don't see what it has to do with me," he said.

"Last Monday we found the body of another boy," said Cordero. "In Balide. Member of Chiquito Santana's *Forsa* gang. His throat was also slashed and a betel quid was found in his mouth."

José adjusted his spectacles. "Sounds like a plague of strange murders," he said. "A serial killer perhaps. That should prove quite a challenge for a police"—he hesitated—"*investigator*."

"Lot of young men are stocking up on home-made weapons these days," Cordero said. "There may be a gang war about to break out."

Again José smiled. "As I said, we are a youth group, not a gang. None of this concerns me." He picked up his teacup. "And none of this explains why you are here," he said and sipped from the cup. "You told my friends outside you had information that might interest me. I'm curious to hear it."

Cordero unfolded his legs and shifted in his seat. That line had been a bluff and now it was being called. "I went and visited Chiquito today," he said. José waited. "He believes there's a crisis looming."

There was a moment's silence.

"That's it?" asked José.

"He thinks it involves the dead as well as the living. That's what he makes of the betel quids."

José held Cordero's stare before putting his cup back down. He placed the fingers of both hands together, his elbows on the desk. "When is there not a crisis in Timor?" he asked. "Chiquito is afraid of his own shadow. He's very superstitious. Do you know his mother claimed to be a *buan-manas*?" he said, meaning a witch who uses black magic.

"I didn't know that," said Cordero. "So his fears about what the betel could mean don't bother you?"

"Why should they?" said José. "He's a stupid man."

"And his stupidity doesn't bother you—what it could make him do?" Cordero asked.

"I'm an educated man, *senyor*." José Magno leaned back in his chair. "If the only information you brought me is that Chiquito Santana is shitting himself over a betel quid, please leave now. I have more important work to do than to dwell on his fantasies."

José turned over the pages in front of him and bent his head as if to study them closely. The interview was over. Cordero rose, thanked him for his time, and was escorted out of the complex.

He drove a couple of blocks out of Perumnas, pulled over to the side of the road and turned off his engine. Something was nagging him, something José Magno had said, something about guns and American movies. Where had he heard that before? In his office? Talking to Pepe Marcellino when he was picking his daughter up from school? No, none of those. He clicked his fingers. It was Sergeant Mateo Belo, when they were walking down the lane in Balide to examine the body in Cisco Mola's water tank.

Was it merely a coincidence that a gang leader like José Magno and a police sergeant like Mateo Belo both specified *pirated American movies* when accounting for the interest in handguns among young Timorese?

• • •

Carter returned to her apartment, lucky to have caught one of the last taxis operating in Dili so late at night. She tossed the envelop back onto the table, slumped into a chair, and opened her laptop. *Sanctimonious bitch*, she said to herself not for the first time in reference to Jacobsen. She pulled up the page she had started to write to FBI headquarters back in Washington.

Then she sat back to put herself in a calmer frame of mind to draft the letter.

She thought about the dry country of Arizona and New Mexico, its warm days, cool nights, and shimmering horizon at noon. She recalled the piñon pine and juniper, eagles and coyotes and the long-eared jackrabbits they both hunted. Those kinds of thoughts always settled her.

She turned her mind to her colleagues in the Flagstaff agency: Rozzetti, Rainey, and Tanner…and Sanchez, of course—who must have had the baby by now but nobody had bothered to message Carter to tell her.

In fact, nobody from her office in Flagstaff had bothered to message her about anything or even ask how she was doing. It was as though she was no longer considered part of the team.

Suddenly that riled her for reasons she couldn't quite fathom. She'd never really thought of any of the people she worked with as friends, but even so…

Her thoughts turned to Estefana and Josinto. She didn't know Josinto well, but what she'd seen of him she liked. He'd always been courteous and friendly and he doted on Estefana. As for Estefana—well, they'd become close, very close. And Carter often found herself experiencing things in Estefana's company that she'd brushed aside back in the States in the interests of her policing career--things like shopping for wedding presents--and she smiled at the thought.

She looked around her apartment, the boxes she'd packed, the book that held the note Cordero had written after he'd brought her home from hospital. She picked the note out, read it and put it back in the book. Fragments of thought flashed through her mind without forming clear images or coherent ideas. It was like there was a kaleidoscope whirling in her head.

Carter collected herself and pulled the laptop closer to type the letter:

The Executive Assistant Director,
Human Resources Branch,

FBI,
Washington, D.C.

She added *'Dear sir'*, paused a moment, and eased the laptop to one side.

She thought about the Native Americans among whom so much of her work back in the States was concentrated. The older ones who hadn't succumbed to depression or self-pity were proud, and in their own way dignified despite shabby housing, half-completed schooling, and entrenched health problems. They were suspicious of outsiders, and so, for the most part reserved among strangers like her, but who could blame them? They deserved much more than the lot they'd been handed--but she couldn't change that.

What she could do—in fact did—was seek justice for wrongs that became them including those they inflicted on each other. It might have been what was cynically referred to as "white man's justice", but then the crimes were increasingly "white man's crimes", even when committed by Navajos or Apaches or Zunis. Murders, rapes, child abuse, drug offences—these were unheard of in traditional tribal societies but common now on the reservations. She wondered if her replacement was as committed to solving these crimes as she was and as culturally sensitive in doing it as she tried to be.

Carter stopped her mind wandering into what were becoming conceited notions. Despite its faults, the FBI employed good people and, with few exceptions, those with whom she worked were dedicated professionals.Jacobsen, of course, was right: she *had* been replaced. Timorese were just as deserving of justice as anyone but the resources available to deliver it to them were hardly comparable to those in the US.

If she extended her time in Timor, and worked active cases, she could make a difference that otherwise likely would not be made; and there was more she could do. Estefana was a good police officer who could become a much better one. She looked up to Carter, sponge-like in the way she absorbed advice about policing. By mentoring Estefana a little longer Carter could help in a small way to address the paucity of policing talent in Timor.

"Timor," she said aloud to herself. It was lush, it was friendly, it had energy—all the things the reservations didn't have. But Timor wasn't home. She glanced across at the yellow envelop Hudson Taylor had given her, picked it up, and shoved it away across the table—but it wasn't about *home*.

She hated people telling her what to do, thinking they knew best, or making decisions that served them but at her expense. By extension that's how she lost her half-sister and her father to selfish men and that loss left her with a deep aversion to being pushed around—by anyone. She repositioned the laptop so it was facing her again and wriggled her fingers over the keyboard just as her cell buzzed.

It was Estefana.

"*Senyor* Pereira called me, *mana*," Estefana said, excitement in her voice as she rushed out the message.

"Slow down, Estefana," Carter said. "What did he say?"

"He found the order Josinto was working on. Where he took the coffin on Sunday and back again yesterday. It was ordered by an old man called *Senyor* Boavides. From Balide, *mana*."

"You have the address?"

"There is no address, *mana*, but there was a note with directions and *Senyor* Pereira read them to me. We could go now."

Carter checked her watch. It was close enough to midnight. She swore under her breath.

"What did you say, *mana*?"

"I said it's too late to do anything now—"

"But *mana*—" Estefana broke in.

"It will be midnight soon, Estefana. An old person won't be awake now."

"I think *Senyor* Boavides may be dead, *mana*. The coffin was for him."

"Even less reason to bother whoever he lived with at this time of night," said Carter. "We'll go first thing in the morning. Can you pick me up at eight o'clock. Better still seven. I'll be ready for you. Now go to bed."

"But *mana*—"

"Trust me, Estefana. There's nothing we can do tonight."

There was silence on the other end of the call.

"Estefana?"

"Yes, *mana*. I'm here. I will do what you say."

"One more thing," said Carter.

"Yes *mana*?

"Wear your police uniform."

"But I'm officially on vacation, *mana*," Estefana protested.

"You're officially assigned to the Timorese police in Dili after you signed the paperwork on your transfer today," insisted Carter. "Wear the uniform, okay?"

"If you say so, *mana*."

"I do. Now try to get some sleep," said Carter. "We've a lot to do tomorrow. I'll be waiting for you at seven o'clock."

Carter ended the call. She became quickly annoyed again that the police seemed blasé about Josinto's disappearance. Even Cordero seemed far too casual about it for her liking. It would be left largely to her and Estefana, she decided, to find Josinto and ensure that his wedding to Estefana went ahead as planned. Knowing where Josinto had gone in Balide was a start.

She looked at her screen, yawned, closed her laptop and decided to get some sleep herself.

Chapter 15

Cordero rose after a restless sleep. His visits to Chiquito Santana and José Magno raised more questions than answers and he'd tossed and turned thinking them over most of the night. Santana feared an upheaval of some kind but what could possibly bother him, tucked away as he was in the safety of a fortified headquarters? Magno was far more composed than Santana, even far too composed for a gang leader who'd just had one of his own killed and possibly lost a major shipment of drugs. What could explain that? Cordero walked over to his bedroom window and peered out. The sun was rising stark and intense in a cloudless sky and the day was already uncomfortably hot and clammy. It was not yet six-thirty.

He dressed in his sweat pants, singlet and sneakers, and shoved work clothes and good shoes into a bag. He forced down two glasses of water—coffee would have to wait. As he headed to his vehicle he recalled Howard Brooks saying he'd never known anyone in Timor brave enough to open up on gang activity. Cordero thought he did and he was off to find out if he was right.

Only a few people were using the gym this early in the morning but Fidelis was among them, as always, working a heavy bag, when he caught sight of Cordero coming across to the ring. Fidelis' arms glistened with sweat and his hair hung damp across his forehead. Cordero placed his gym bag on the ground, took out long white bandages and began to wrap his right fist. An overweight man kept attacking one of the bags next to Fidelis, throwing wild punches that made his stomach wobble each time. A boy of twelve or thirteen was working free weights, his arms not much thicker than the bar holding the load he was struggling to lift. The boy puffed and contorted his face as he slowly raised the weights above his head.

Fidelis's face broke into a broad grin. "What you doing, *maun*? This ain't Monday. Not your day to be here," he said as Cordero finished wrapping his right fist and started on the left.

"Couldn't sleep," Cordero replied. "How you feeling?"

"Feeling good, *maun*. You?"

"Me too," Cordero lied. "You up for four rounds?"

"Sure *maun*," Fidelis said tossing off his mitts and picking up the worn eight ounce boxing gloves the gym provided. Cordero finished taping his hands, slipped on his own gloves and stepped through the ropes. This was the last thing he felt like doing in the heat and humidity. All the same, it was the best chance he could think of to follow through with what he had in mind. With a little fumbling in the gloves he wore, Cordero set the round timer on the boxing app on his cell. Fidelis stepped through the ropes and swiveled his head from side to side to loosen up his neck muscles. The two inserted their mouthguards. They touched gloves. The bell sounded.

Cordero was conscious of the heavy hit he'd taken to his left eye in their last sparring session. He didn't want to make things worse. He kept his glove up against his left temple and he kept as far away from Fidelis as he could, on his toes dancing and circling. When Fidelis came forward, Cordero wheeled back. When Fidelis wound up to throw combination punches, Cordero slipped to the left or the right and if neither of these was an option he clinched and smothered Fidelis' arms to keep him in check.

Every few seconds, when he dared, Cordero studied Fidelis' eyes. The anger and meanness that was there when the boy first came to the gym full of piss and wind were gone. In their place was a steely determination to become good, very good at the brutal ballet that was boxing. His footwork showed it: rather than bounce around like a puppeteer's doll wasting energy, he now slid, heels off the canvas but only just so his feet remained firmly anchored to the mat and his center of gravity secured. Even looking at him through raised gloves and ever mindful of his ability to strike fast and hard, Fidelis was beautiful to watch in the ring.

By the end of the third round Cordero was exhausted from his constant movement around the ring. In the corner for the one minute break between rounds, he wanted to call it quits. He didn't have to keep going to serve his purpose today. But the fat man and the skinny kid had come to the side of the ring and were watching the contest, open-mouthed, like it was a title fight. *You can't lose face now*, Cordero told himself, and in a show of bravado he stood up and kicked his stool out through the ropes well before the bell sounded. When it did, he sprang forward into the center of the ring.

This time Cordero took the fight to Fidelis. He jabbed and moved then jabbed and was gone again. He danced around his opponent to the left, the right, constantly shifting his line of attack and taunting with sharp blows to the head. Suddenly he came at Fidelis with his arms low and appearing to lead with his jaw as though all energy and sense had been drained out of him. Fidelis fell for the ruse. He launched a jab which Cordero brushed away with a quick downward deflection of his left glove and, as Fidelis worked to regain his balance, Cordero slammed a right hook square into his jaw. The fat man swore and the kid let out an audible 'Aah' from ringside. Fidelis' eyes seemed to spin backwards in their sockets. He moved back, shook his head violently and shaped up again just as the timer sounded to end the round.

The fat man clapped and the kid glanced sideways at him and did the same. Cordero raised a glove to acknowledge their applause, walked over to Fidelis' corner, threw his hands across the top rope and leaned his body over for support. "You did well, *maun*," he said gasping. "Real well. You're coming along real good."

Fidelis looked at him, spat his mouth guard onto the ground outside the ring and grinned. "You too, *maun*," he spluttered. He sucked in a lung full of air through his nostrils. "Didn't think you had it in you to move like that and punch that hard."

"I surprised myself," said Cordero laughing and he tapped Fidelis on the back. They both shook off their gloves. Cordero stepped out of the ring, wiped his mouth, and turned back to Fidelis. "I've a favour to ask of you Fidelis," he said.

"Sure, *maun*. Anything," said Fidelis, ducking under the ropes himself. "I owe you, *maun*."

Cordero waited until the fat man and the young boy had moved away and resumed their workouts.

"No you don't owe me anything and if you say 'no' to what I'm asking I won't hold it against you, okay?" Fidelis waited. "I'm investigating the murder of two young men. One was a member of the *Forsa* gang, the other from 4:4. It's kind of urgent because a friend of mine has gone missing and may have been caught up in whatever's going on."

Fidelis's breathing eased but he stood eye-to-eye with Cordero, a blank expression on his face, and said nothing.

"I know drugs are involved. Crystal meth. Could be raids by one gang on another or a turf war. Either way it's bad and could get worse." Cordero unwound the tape from his hands. Fidelis remained silent. "I went to talk to Chiquito Santana and José Magno but they wouldn't tell me anything. Both victims had a betel quid placed in their mouths after their throats were cut. No one knows why, least of all those two. Could be a warning from another gang altogether."

Cordero bunched the tape in his hands and hoped for the best. "You still know gang members pretty well, right?" Fidelis nodded ever so slightly. "I need to know what's going on."

"I turned my back on the gang shit, *maun*," Fidelis said. "I was *gila-gila* them days but not now," he added using the Bahasa Indonesian slang for 'crazy'.

"I know and I admire you for it. But did you turn your back on all the other gang members you hung out with? Aren't you on speaking terms with some of them? Couldn't you make enquiries?"

Fidelis turned away. "No one wants to talk about killings or drugs. That gang stuff, *maun*. You fuck with that stuff, you better leave town. Even then they come after you, tear off your balls and cut off your head. I've seen it, *maun*. They don't mess around. Know what I'm saying?"

"I know. I didn't expect you to get involved," said Cordero. "I know I wouldn't," he said and chuckled.

"You been to Santana and Magno with this shit you already involved, *maun*," said Fidelis. "I'd watch my back."

Cordero nodded. "Good advice," he said. "Okay. No problem. I just thought I'd ask, that's all. No hard feelings."

Cordero slapped him on the shoulder. "See you next week," he said, picking up his bag and starting for the showers. "And remember that trick that dropped your jab and left your chin exposed," he said over his shoulder. "That's the second time I've caught you with a feint. Don't fall for it again."

Fidelis gazed up at the sky, and spat a little blood. "Hey *maun*," he called. Cordero stopped and turned. Fidelis approached and locked eyes with him. "Give me your cell number. Said I owe you. I mean it."

• • •

Estefana pulled up at Carter's apartment fifteen minutes before seven o'clock. Carter figured she would and was finishing her coffee on the landing outside. She was wearing jeans and a white T-shirt: Estefana, as instructed, was wearing her police uniform. They exchanged a wave by way of greeting. Carter placed her coffee cup near the door, threw a bag around her neck and over her shoulder, and skipped down the steps. When Estefana lifted the visor on her helmet, Carter noticed the red eyes from a night of tears and worry. She took the spare helmet, slipped it on her head, and mounted the back of the bike. She threw her arms around Estefana, more tightly than necessary, and they rode off into the bustle of morning traffic.

Outside a small cement block house in the laneway in Balide where *Senyor* Pereira said Josinto had delivered the coffin, Estefana parked the motorcycle and cut the engine.

"This is the house, I think, *mana*," she said and Carter dismounted.

She noticed the lamp post on the opposite side of the lane. "I think you're right, Estefana. I think this is where Cordero found the drugs."

As they approached the front door of the house, they heard a soft wailing from inside. Estefana knocked gently on the door. When no one answered, she knocked again, more forcefully. There was a rustling from inside and a stout woman of late middle age and dressed in black opened the door. The wailing from inside grew louder.

"*Deskulpa, senyora*," Estefana apologized for the interruption. She introduced herself and Carter and explained they were involved in a case of a missing person and needed to ask a few questions.

The woman slipped through to the porch and closed the door behind her. She introduced herself as *Senyora* Boavides. Her husband, Carlo, she explained, had died from a diabetic condition and he lay inside while the days of mourning required by tradition continued. Members of her family and his were in attendance day and night to recite the good deeds of Carlo in order for his spirit to make its journey to the other world.

"Did a man bring the coffin in a truck on Wednesday?" Estefana asked.

"Of course," *Senyora* Boavides said. "How else would we bury Carlo?" The woman clenched her hands together. "Carlo was satisfied the nice boy who showed it to him the Sunday before would make the coffin right. The boy did. And Carlo died very happy."

"How did the man who delivered the coffin appear to you?"

"Appear to me? What do you mean?" the woman asked.

"I mean did he seem worried, agitated, unusual in any way?"

"I didn't take much notice of him," the woman said, turning back to Estefana. "But if he were any of those things maybe I would have."

"Do you know where he went after he delivered the coffin?"

"No. We carried the coffin into the house. My sons and their cousins helped. We thanked the man who brought it and he left."

"Was that the only coffin he had on his truck?"

"Yes."

A younger woman, also dressed in black, opened the door to the house and popped her head out.

"*Ama*," she said addressing her mother. "Did you buy more coffee? I can't find it." She looked at the two visitors, the foreigner and the police officer. "What's happening?" she asked.

Estefana introduced herself and Carter and again explained their visit.

The woman stepped out of the house and closed the door behind her. She came and stood beside her mother. "There was another man there, on a motorcycle, watching the coffin get unloaded," she said. "I noticed him because he kept watching and I thought he showed no respect."

"Over there?" Estefana asked, pointing to the other side of the lane.

"Yes. Under the lamp."

"What did the man look like?" Estefana asked.

"He wore a helmet. He looked like anyone riding a motorcycle," the woman said.

"What did he do?"

"Just sat there," the woman said. "Watching. As the man with the truck left, he took out his cell and made a call. But I couldn't hear what he said. Then he went in the same direction. That way," she said and waved her hand in a northerly direction toward the center of Dili.

"And you can't describe this man?"

"No. Like I said he wore a helmet."

"Was he young, old? Did you notice that much?"

"Young I think but I can't be sure," the woman said.

"Can you describe his motorcycle?"

"I don't know anything about motorcycles." The woman put her arm around her mother. "We've answered enough of your questions. We must get back to my father."

"Just one more question," Carter interrupted and spoke to Estefana. "Ask her where her father is to be buried and when."

"Santa Ana cemetery," the woman said. "Monday afternoon. We must complete the *lutu* first," she added, meaning the period of mourning.

Carter and Estefana walked back to their motorcycle. "I pass that cemetery on my way to Josinto's, *mana*. It's in Bidau. Near the seafront," Estefana said.

Carter ignored the comment, weighing up options. She slid the helmet over her head and asked: "Which way would Josinto have gone back to the workshop from here?"

Estefana thought for a moment. "I think I know, *mana*. Why?"

"Let's retrace the route. If he had no more coffins to deliver it's likely he went back to Bidau. Who knows? Someone might have noticed the truck. Besides it's all we have to go on."

• • •

After he'd showered and dressed, Cordero checked his watch and walked to his vehicle. He decided to detour to police headquarters and the office of Alberto 'Pepe' Marcelino to go over what files Pepe held on Chiquito Santana, José Magno, and their respective gangs. He wasn't expecting to find much but there might be something there that would explain Santana's fears or Magno's calm indifference.

At police headquarters he found Pepe reclining in his chair, his feet on the desk, reading a newspaper.

"*Dia, maun*," Cordero said. "I'm back."

Pepe sat up straight and closed the newspaper. "Tino, *maun*. You see those gang guys?"

"Yesterday, yeah."

Pepe whistled. "And you're still alive? You're crazy, *maun*."

"So I'm told," said Cordero. "Listen, Pepe. I want to look at whatever you have on Chiquito Santana and José Magno and their gangs."

"What I have ain't much, Tino," Pepe confessed. "Told you what I know already."

"Doesn't matter. You might have overlooked small details that are useful. Can I see the files?"

"Sure *maun*. Felipe!" Pepe shouted and a junior officer in a uniform that was too big for his small frame came running. "Show Investigator Cordero our files on Chiquito Santana, José Magno, *Forsa* and the 4:4."

Felipe hurried off. "Nice kid. Works hard," said Pepe, raising his feet back onto the desk. "You need a computer, there's one over there," he said and gestured toward the far wall. "Anything else Tino?"

"Not right now, Pepe. Thanks."

"Nothing *maun*." And with that Pepe went back to reading his newspaper.

Chapter 16

Friday morning traffic was always especially heavy. Estefana stopped at the T-intersection of *Rua de Mascarenhas* and *Avenido Bispo de Mederios* and waited for a break in the tangle of cars, trucks, microlets, and motorcycles. Carter noticed a kiosk on the corner, tapped Estefana on the shoulder and asked her to pull over. At the kerb she dismounted the motorcycle, took off her helmet, and suggested Estefana ask the man in the kiosk if he had seen a truck with a decal of coffins on its side drive by on Wednesday. "It's a long shot, I know, but occasionally long shots pay off," she explained.

The man laughed when Estefana put the question to him. "You know how many trucks come by here each day?" he asked.

Estefana's shoulders were slumped when she returned. "He didn't see anything, *mana*." She dangling her helmet by her side. "It's now the third day Josinto's been gone. It's no good."

"Don't let those thoughts in, Estefana," admonished Carter. "Now think. Is there anywhere Josinto goes, you know, for coffee, gas, bite to eat when he's working this part of town?"

Estefana thought. A truck passed belching black smoke and they both had to cough away the fumes and brush dust and soot from their clothes. Estefana refocused on the question.

"There is a gas station in Lecidere I know he goes to," Estefana said. "He knows a boy who works there but I rang him yesterday and asked if he knew where Josinto was and he said no."

"Perhaps you asked the wrong question," Carter said. "It's on the way to Bidau, right?"

"Yes, *mana*."

"Right," said Carter replacing her helmet. "Let's see if Josinto made it that far."

• • •

As Pepe had said, the files on Chiquito Santana and José Magno were thin but Cordero was surprised by just how thin. Chiquito's file was two sheets of typed A4 paper. One held a brief profile: 34 years old, born in Baucau, finished primary school only, described as a member of a youth association, an official in a martial arts group, then leader of the gang *Forsa*. The second page listed charges and convictions. He'd been arrested twice in his mid-twenties for assault and once for robbery. Eight years ago he was cautioned for his role—undefined—in the riots of 2006. That was it. The usefulness of the file was close to zero.

José Magno's file consisted of just one sheet of paper. He was twenty-eight, born in the western district of Ermera. That made Chiquito and José potential adversaries on regional lines: one from the western district and one from the eastern. Cordero recalled the graffiti, warning off Easterners in Perumnas, but he also knew a lot of that was simply for show and that gangs occasionally worked together despite the threats they liked to make to each other. Besides, Pepe had told him that Santana's outfit was no longer made up exclusively of people from his region.

José Magno had a degree from the National University of Timor Leste in business administration and had worked for five years in the Ministry of Finance. It was during that time, Cordero suspected, that his talents came to the attention of an ambitious superior in that or another ministry and he was made an offer to moonlight with 4:4. That was it as far as the file went. No further information, no list of charges or convictions. José was either cleverer than Chiquito or he had friends who could make his past disappear from view.

The separate files on both gangs took the form of various reports in ring-bound folders—originally stamped with a blue UN logo and the initials 'UNMIT' representing the United Nations force that assumed policing responsibilities for a time after the break down of law and order in 2006. Several entries concerned the few brothels *Forsa* ran and its gambling activities at various cock fighting venues. There were photocopies of mugshots of various young men who had met violent ends including the suspected gang member recently found murdered in Balide. There were also entries about suspected drug trafficking but nothing concrete. The file told Cordero nothing he didn't already know.

The folder on *4:4* began in the same way: entries on the gang's main sources of income including the extortion of businesses in Perumnas and Comoro and the rents the gang charged stall holders for space and position in various Dili markets—none of which it actually had any rightful claim over. There were fewer mugshots of dead gang members and only one—the boy found in Bemori with the cicatrix of *4:4* tattooed to his neck—from the last six months. There were no reports about drug activity, not even entries for rumours or suspicions. That struck Cordero as odd.

He sat back and absent mindedly opened and closed the prongs of the binder while staring at the ceiling. He got a finger jammed in a prong and it pinched him—a sharp, stinging pinch. He swore, lifted the folder and thumped it back on the desk in anger. It was then he noticed he'd shaken slivers of the sides of perforated pages from between various files in the folder onto the base of its row of prongs. He examined the slivers closely. They were from several pages that had clearly been torn from the binder.

That was more than odd. It was suspicious.

He closed the folders, handed them with thanks to the junior officer Felipe, and walked back to where Pepe was slouched at his desk.

"Find what you want, *maun*?" came a question from behind the open pages of a newspaper blocking Pepe's face from view.

"Yeah, Chiquito comes from Baucau and José Magno from Ermera," answered Cordero.

"What does that mean?" Pepe asked.

"It means you don't have much in your files," said Cordero.

"Told you, *maun*," said Pepe.

"Anyone else been looking at those files lately?" Cordero asked.

"Lately? Sure," said Pepe lowering his newspaper. "Why?"

"Who's been looking?"

"Mateo Belo. Know him?"

"I know Mateo. What's he been checking?"

"I don't know," Pepe said. "Comes in regular. Always asking for files on gangs, especially 4:4. As if anything much changes."

"When was the last time you checked those files—the ones on Magno and 4:4?"

Pepe was sitting upright now. "A month, maybe more ago. Felipe enters anything new. What's this about Tino?"

"And has Belo been in since then?"

"Sure," said Pepe. "Comes in every now and then like I said."

"Thanks Pepe," Cordero said, heading for the door.

"Hey Tino? What's this about?" Pepe called after him but Cordero was already gone.

• • •

Estefana pulled up at the gas station in Lecidere where Josinto had once taken her to meet his friend and parked the motorcycle on the side of the pay booth away from the pumps. The smell of diesel hung in the air. Carter saw stickers on large metal containers warning they contained flammable liquid and she wondered about customers who puffed on their cigarettes as they filled their tanks.

The booth was attended by Flavio—the youth Josinto knew. He looked about Josinto's age, lean, and unshaven. His hair was long and tied in a ponytail and he wore shorts, a greasy 'Rambo' T-shirt and sneakers.

"Sure, he was here on Wednesday," said Flavio after Carter had framed the question for Estefana to ask. "You're the lucky girl, right?" he asked Estefana. "We met once. And I spoke to you yesterday on the cell."

"I should be the lucky girl but he's missing," she said.

"What? Backed out? I don't believe it," Flavio said and shook his head.

Estefana turned away. "We think it might be worse than that," she said.

"What kidnapped? Like in the movies? Shit!" said Flavio. He quickly apologized to Carter for the language even though he was speaking in Tetun. He turned abruptly and stared out at the pumps. "Wow."

"How did Josinto seem to you?" Estefana asked.

"When he came in here? Same as always. Fine."

"And when he left?'

"Same."

Carter had sensed a memory flickering in Flavio's mind as he looked across at the gas pumps. She told Estefana to ask Flavio why he'd stared at them.

"Oh it was nothing," Flavio said. "Just these guys, you know." He scratched his head.

"What guys?" Estefana pressed him.

They were interrupted by a customer who came in and handed over a ten dollar note to pay for gas. The bell on Flavio's antique cash register rang as he slid open the drawer, sorted the change, and handed it back to the customer who then left.

"What did you ask?" Flavio said. "Oh. Yeah. Four guys rode in behind Josinto's truck and stopped over there." He pointed to a gas pump. "Two motorcycles. Two pillion riders. Josinto came in and paid for his gas. We talked for a minute or two." He paused.

"And?" said Estefana.

"Look it's probably nothing. But they weren't getting gas, you know? I was wondering what they were doing. One of the guys pulls out his cell. Starts talking. I yell out that the sign says 'Turn off your cell phone at the pump' and he tells me to go fuck myself." Again he apologized to Carter for his language. "I came around the desk, to go and confront the guy for disrespecting me."

Another customer came in wanting to pay. She was a middle aged woman in a hurry because she 'Ah-humed' loudly to get Flavio's attention. Flavio turned to her, took her money, rung it up and she left without thanking him.

"Go on," said Estefana.

"Josinto puts his hand out to stop me, you know? Says ignore them. Says he'd noticed them all the way from Balide and they were probably just up to mischief. Anyway the guy puts his cell away, so I let it go."

"Did these guys say anything to Josinto?" Estefana asked.

"Say anything? No," Flavio said. "Nothing."

"What happened then?"

"Well Josinto walked back to his truck and drove off. And that was it." Flavio scratched his chest through his grubby T-shirt. "You really think he was kidnapped?"

"We're not sure what happened to him," said Estefana. "That's what we're trying to find out. Did he say anything to the guys on the motorcycles?"

"No."

"What did they do when he left?"

"They went too."

"Right after Josinto?"

"Yeah."

"Which way?"

Flavio considered that.

"Same way. Down there," he said and pointed down the road to the east.

"Can you describe these guys?" Estefana asked.

"They were just guys on motorcycles," replied Flavio. "I get hundreds in here each day. They all look the same. I don't take any notice."

They thanked Flavio and turned to head out of the booth.

"Except..." Flavio said and stopped.

Estefana turned back. "Except what?"

"Except the guy with the cell? I think he had a kind of red tattoo on his neck. He was wearing a helmet so I can't be sure. But he adjusted it before he rode off. That's when I saw it because I was watching him."

"Can you describe it?" Estefana asked.

"Not really. Like a line or a rope maybe. I only caught a glimpse."

They walked back to the motorcycle.

"Well now we know he made it this far," said Carter. "And that sounds like he was being followed. Could be those two pillion passengers managed to get into the truck and take Josinto to wherever they're holding him."

"But where's that, *mana*?" asked Estefana, her voice breaking.

"That's what we need to know."

"And that's what we're going to find out, okay?" Carter put her helmet on and threw a leg over the rear of the motorcycle.

"Where are we going now, *mana*?" Estefana asked over her shoulder as she kicked the stand back up.

"Where you filed the report that he was missing. If we upgrade that to 'abducted' the police might be more inclined to take it seriously."

• • •

They encountered Cordero coming down the steps to the entrance doors of the police headquarters.

"Where have you two been?" he asked. "And where are you going?"

"We traced Josinto's movements from the time he dropped off the coffin on Wednesday where you found the meth in Balide until he stopped for gas in Lecidere," Carter began.

"How did you know where he dropped the coffin?" asked Cordero.

"Don't worry about that now. Could be Josinto was being followed by a bunch of guys on motorcycles. Someone on a motorcycle certainly seems to have been keeping an eye on him when he dropped off the coffin. And four guys on motorcycles were following him when he stopped for gas."

Cordero nodded. "None of that proves he was abducted."

"But it does suggest he wasn't running away," Carter shot back.

Cordero raised a conciliatory hand. "Okay," he said. "But what are you doing here?"

"Estefana is going to upgrade the report on Josinto from 'missing' to 'abducted,'" said Carter. "Then we'll see if the police are more inclined to look for the truck at least."

"They'll still ask for evidence," Cordero said. "And there's the problem of officers being sent to Metinaro on Sunday which means many have been given today and tomorrow off."

"Whose side are you on?" asked Carter.

"I'm just saying—"

"Go on, Estefana," Carter said interrupting him. "Make the report."

When Estefana had entered the building Carter turned to face Cordero.

"Stop being so negative," she said. "We've got to keep her hopes alive. That means finding things for her to do so she doesn't feel helpless and start moping again."

"Look I know she's a close friend of yours and I know you want to help. But what you're talking about is therapy. You know as well as I do how police think and how they think is even less straight-forward in Timor. Don't let your personal feelings take over from your professional training."

"Therapy!" she said, straining to hold herself in check. "Since when did you become a psychoanalyst?"

"I'm not," he said. "I'm a police investigator. And investigate is what I'm going to do. You yourself said that the way to find Josinto is to get to the bottom of those murders and the drugs. Well let's dig deep." He paused to gauge her reaction. She was red-faced but silent. It struck him that he was the one now using terms that included her. "You coming?" he said.

"Where?"

"To see Dr Howard Brooks and learn what we can about those betel quids."

• • •

Cordero had suggested that Estefana leave the motorcycle at police headquarters and they go together to the hospital where the morgue was located. They waited in the hospital canteen until Brooks, who had taken the betel quids apart and carefully examined their contents, finished writing up his findings.

Because the quids had been placed in the mouths of the

murdered gang members after death they had not been damaged or contaminated by saliva. Both contained the nut of an areca palm, obviously, wrapped in a betel leaf, just as obviously, and an unsurprising paste of slaked lime.

Brooks had concentrated on a tiny spice mix he uncovered next to the paste. After countless interruptions from an impatient Cordero, he determined that the mix was the same in both: catechu—an extract of the acacia tree—cardamom and *malus*.

"But this *malus* is not from the leaf. From the catkin," Brooks said, meaning the flower cluster on the vine. "Stronger peppery effect, I suspect."

He approached the sink to wash his hands.

"I'm not an expert on betel quids, dear boy," he told Cordero. "That's as much as I can tell you. Hope it's useful."

Brooks was wiping his hands now on a towel by the sink, his back to Cordero.

"It's something, Howard," Cordero said. "Thank you."

"A lead, as you folk like to say?" Brooks said, not bothering to turn around.

"Maybe, yes."

"And where do you expect this lead to take you?" Brooks asked, turning now, curious.

"At the moment, Howard, to where people who *are* experts on betel quids hang out," said Cordero. "At the market."

Chapter 17

By the time they'd reached the main Dili market, out toward the Santa Cruz cemetery, it was late afternoon and a heavy low-hanging shelf cloud was creeping across the sky from the west. Merchants and vendors expected a drenching and many were packing up for the day. Brooks had reassembled the quids as best he could and placed each in a small clear plastic bag. Cordero gave one to Estefana and suggested she and Carter head down one line of stalls while he took the other bag and went down another line.

The further into the market they went the simpler and shabbier the stalls became. Steel-fronted enclosures stacked with bags of rice, cartons of beer, bottled water, and assorted packaged goods gave way to make-shift structures piled high with cuts of meat and assorted vegetables and sparse garden offerings laid out on the ground. Behind shelters made of poles and planks and rusting tin roofs, other merchants tendered racks of identical second-hand clothing.

Daylight was fading. Whole families—adults and children—squeezed onto motorcycles to head home before the rain.

After the tenth stall holder said she knew nothing about the betel quid, Estefana slumped down on the littered concrete steps leading up to an undercover area that had been selling meat, live chickens and fish. A rank odour wafted off the offerings. She clasped her hands over her knees and bent her head down. Carter could see the toll Josinto's disappearance was taking and joined her on the steps.

The two sat for a moment without exchanging words. Estefana sniffled. Carter placed an arm around her friend's shoulder.

"You're tired, Estefana. Worried sick. And you have every right to be."

Estefana began to sob uncontrollably. Carter rubbed her back lightly. People leaving the market cast furtive glances at the unusual sight of a Timorese police woman being comforted by a foreigner in such a way. If anything, it should have been the other way around.

• • •

Cordero had had no better luck getting answers to his questions. Heading back up a side alley through the market he felt the first heavy spits of rain, ducked under a canvass canopy and decided to call it a day. It had seemed a good idea in the absence of any other but now it seemed silly to think that it would produce results. A very old woman popped her head up from under a plank counter on which a few rancid vegetables lay for sale. Her face was withered, her grey hair a straggle and her body little more than bones held together by leathery skin. Cordero smiled at her. She smiled back, her toothless gums red from chewing betel.

"*Botarde tia,*" Cordero said, using the informal title 'aunty'.

"*Tarde alin,*" she replied, addressing him as a young sibling. "You don't look happy," she added. "Do you want an onion?"

Cordero laughed. "No thank you *tia.*" He looked at the rain coming down in wet sheets now and put one hand out to test the drops. The other hand extended back, under cover. It held the plastic bag with the betel quid.

"What you carry, *alin?*" the old woman asked.

He turned and held the bag up to the woman. "I was hoping someone could tell me what part of Timor this quid came from but no one seems to know."

"No one knows anything these days," the woman said taking the plastic bag without it being offered to her. "They go to school and it takes their knowledge from their heads," she said. "That's why nobody knows things anymore." She examined the bag. "Why do you carry the betel in a bag like this?" she asked.

"I'm a police investigator, *tia.* That quid is evidence."

158 • CHRIS McGILLION

"Oh, evidence," she repeated but he thought she might not know what that meant.

She turned the quid over in its bag, this way and that. He couldn't decide whether she was curious, simpleminded, or thinking of taking it to chew.

"The spice mix is catechu, cardamom and *malus*," he said, for want of anything else to say. "*Malus* from the flower of the vine, not the leaf." He didn't expect a reply. The downpour intensified, and the sound of the rain pounding on the canopy was deafening.

"Viqueque," the old woman said.

The canopy started to sag from the water pooling on top. The woman scooped her few remaining vegetables into a sack and Cordero took a piece of wood lying under her rickety counter and pushed the canopy up from beneath to expel water pooling there. It created a small cascade onto the alleyway and he jumped back to avoid the splash.

"What was that *tia*?" Cordero said. "I couldn't hear you with the rain."

"I said Viqueque. They like the peppery *malus* in Viqueque," the old woman said, her voice stronger. She was referring to a district in the southeast of the country. "They say it brings powerful blessings from the ancestors." She chuckled. "But I think they just like the taste."

"So the *malus* is distinctive of betel from Viqueque?" he asked. "Is that what you're saying?"

"In the west they prefer clove because they are near the *bapa*," she said referring to Indonesians. "Around here it's mostly tobacco they add these days because they think Dili is special, you know? But Viqueque is more traditional. They like that pepper. I know. I was married to one of them. But that was a long time ago, *alin*. Long before you came out from between your mother's legs, I think."

"And you say it brings blessings from the ancestors?" he asked.

"Not me, *alin*. That what they say. Blessings didn't do my husband no good. He died and is dead long time now."

Cordero took the bag from her. "Thank you, *tia*," he said. "You have been a great help. Maybe I will buy that onion from you after all."

She reached into her bag and pulled out a small, brown onion. He took it and handed her a fifty centavo coin—she'd asked for only five—and headed off to find Carter and Estefana.

• • •

After they'd driven back to where Estefana had left her motorcycle it was too late to do any more that night. Estefana said she'd like to go back to Josinto's just in case he'd come back or there was any sign that he'd been there. Carter told Estefana to call her if there was any news and said if there was none, they should talk early the next morning. She turned to Cordero and suggested they grab take-out food, go back to her apartment and go over everything they knew and, just as importantly, everything they didn't know.

It was drizzling still when they arrived at Carter's with servings of beef rendang, baked fish with tamarind, and Indonesian fried rice. Cordero shook the rainwater off his jacket while Carter set out plates, forks and paper serviettes. They sat and ate in silence until most of the food was gone.

"Wow, that was good," Carter said wiping her mouth and sitting back in her chair. "I missed lunch today."

"Yeah," agreed Cordero cleaning up what was left in the containers. "I'd forgotten how hungry I was too."

"You? Never," quipped Carter, scrunching her serviette onto the table. "I'm pissed off about the police not doing more to find Josinto," she said.

He waved a hand. "I've told you, they're short on officers because they're needed on Sunday for the big ceremony out of town at the Heroes Cemetery. Even I have to go."

"So you keep saying."

"Lot of officers off duty until then," he cut in. "Rosters, like I said. And, as I keep reminding you, we don't have any hard evidence to prove Josinto's been abducted."

"You're a senior police officer. Surely you could—"

"I'm a police *investigator*," he interrupted. "I don't have any influence over the regular police."

She folded her arms tightly across her chest and was silent a moment. "Tell me what the betel quids have you thinking now."

Cordero forked the last skerrick of rice into his mouth, devoured it, and placed both hands beside his now-empty plate. "The guy who heads the gang *Forsa* is from Baucau. His opposite number in *4:4* is from Ermera. Neither of them have connections to Viqueque, where the old woman said the style of betel in the dead boys' mouths is from. That suggests those two gangs are targets of another outfit, not perpetrators."

He wiped his lips and his hands with a serviette, brow creased, thinking.

"There could be a new gang from Viqueque muscling in on the operations of the others," he continued. "A vicious lot that doesn't play by the normal gang rules. That may be why Chiquito Santana and José Magno wanted to know what I knew. Maybe they're trying to find out who these guys are too."

"That doesn't explain why the betel was left in the dead boys' mouths," Carter said. "It's not as though anyone apart from the police would have taken the betel quids from the dead gang members and thought to analyse them to work out where they came from. It took Brooks to find out what was in them and you to trace that to Viqueque."

Cordero shifted uneasily in his chair. "Yeah, I know."

"Want to know what I think?" Carter put to him.

"Try me."

"Josinto's abduction is what we should be focusing on," Carter began, leaning in across the table. "The guys who killed the boy you found on Sunday bought the story you told me about the kids telling them a package had been put in the coffin in Josinto's truck. Right? So they ransack Pereiras' workshop on Tuesday night or early Wednesday morning but don't find it. Maybe the drugs are inside the coffin, say in the lining, where they didn't think to look. So they decide—or were told—to go back. By the time they return on Wednesday to have another go, Josinto is heading out with the coffin on his truck. They follow him and he heads back to Balide. They think that's a stroke of luck—he's identified the right coffin for them and all they have to do is search it more thoroughly. But then they realise they can't search it because it's now got a dead guy lying in it and too many people are there to seal him in and mourn his passing. What do they do? They grab Josinto."

She eased back in her chair.

"Why grab Josinto?" he asked.

"First of all because they're not sure if Josinto discovered the drugs, hid them, and is carrying on as normal so as not to raise suspicion. Second, if he didn't take the drugs and they can't get to the coffin before it's put in the ground, they have to know when and where it's going to be buried and who better to ask than Josinto."

"But they could find that out without abducting him," Cordero argued.

"You're forgetting my first point."

"Okay," he said. "Go on."

She came back over the table. "Okay, they grab Josinto but he makes out he doesn't know what they're talking about. Now they're not sure what to believe. Maybe he's telling the truth and the drugs are still in the coffin. Maybe he's lying and has kept them to sell himself. They can't be sure. So they decide to keep him until Monday when the old guy is buried and they can dig up the coffin and check."

She lent back. "I know that all sounds silly, but it would explain the break-in, the guys following Josinto—"

"The guys you think were following Josinto."

She ignored the interruption "—and his disappearance. Believe me I've seen criminals behave in a much more cock-eyed fashion than that."

"But what about the betel quids?"

"What about them? Maybe the guys we're looking for are from Viqueque," she granted. "Maybe there's a strange custom they're practicing for their own benefit when they kill. You know, to protect them from revengeful spirits or some shit. But I'm sure there're lots of people in Dili from Viqueque who chew betel. The betel quids aren't going to lead us to the bad guys."

She tapped the table repeatedly with her finger. "We were thinking the murderers would lead us to Josinto. Maybe it's the other way around and Josinto will lead us to them."

"I'm not entirely convinced. I can't help thinking the betel is a key to this. But I must say that's a fertile imagination you have," he said.

"It's known as hypothesizing from the facts," she said and grinned. "But I prefer to call it playing a hunch."

Chapter 18

The buzzing of his cell startled Cordero. He turned his face to the digital clock on the side cabinet in his bedroom. It showed 5:25. *Shit,* he thought as he rummaged for the phone, *what's happened now?*

"Cordero," he said. "Who's this?"

"It's me, *maun,*" the caller said. "Fidelis."

"Fidelis?"

"You said you needed information, *maun.* I've been talking to guys all night."

Cordero squeezed the bridge of his nose in an effort to become more fully awake. He sat up. "Where are you calling from, Fidelis?"

"Don't worry about that now, *maun.* Just listen. I gotta be quick. People don't like the questions I been asking."

Cordero threw his legs over the side of his bed. "Go on, Fidelis. I'm listening," he said.

"No one knows who's doing the killing. That's got them all shit scared. Not the killing but not knowing who's doing it, you know? That's why some of them guys are making their own guns and shit. For protection if things blow up."

"So there's no gang war looming?"

"No, *maun.* Nothing like that."

Cordero heard the growl of a motorcycle passing by wherever Fidelis was calling from. The boy said something inaudible, as though speaking with his head turned. "What was that, Fidelis? I didn't catch what you said," Cordero told him.

"I said drugs are the prize," Fidelis repeated. "Some of the gangs started bringing them in from Indonesia to sell to tourists and shit."

"I thought that might be the case," said Cordero.

"There's a guy who hangs out with tourists. He also knows guys in the gangs. Kind of a bridge between them, you know? He's the key."

Cordero stood up at his window trying to grasp what Fidelis was saying. "I'm not following you, Fidelis. Explain—"

"*Maun!* Lot of young guys in the gangs got money now, you know what I'm saying? Spend it on motorcycles and shit like tattoos. There's this guy who works the bars. Does tattoos. Guys come in, start drinking, get drunk and he gives them cut rates for information. Like when a shipment's coming in, where, and who's going to pick it up. You know? He passes this information on to a contact and the guys who pick up the drugs are ambushed. It was just the last couple of times they were killed."

"Do you know this tattooist's name?" Cordero asked to confirm his own suspicion.

"Octavio something, *maun*," said Fidelis. "That's all I know."

Fidelis started talking with his mouth away from the cell and Cordero found it hard to hear again. Then the voice came back loud and clear—"wondering why I'm asking all these questions and I think I'm being followed."

"Where are you Fidelis?" Cordero asked.

"Don't worry about that, *maun*. I won't be here long."

"Thanks Fidelis. You've done great. If you hear anything else—"

"Not hearing nothing more, *maun*. I'm leaving for a while. Like I told you, these guys don't fuck around if they think you betrayed them."

"Thanks Fidelis," Cordero said. "Take care and keep in touch."

"Nothing *maun*. Said I owe you. You been good to me," Fidelis said and ended the call.

• • •

Given the hour Cordero lay down again after the call from Fidelis tossing and turning as he imagined the danger he'd placed the boy in. Finally he'd gotten out of bed and paced the room, waiting for the café where he usually bought coffee to open, waiting for a suitable time when he could call Carter. It had now gone seven o'clock and he'd waited long enough. He was surprised to find that she was also up.

"I was talking to Estefana," she explained.

"How is she?"

"Distraught," Carter yawned. "Said she'd finally fallen asleep about two this morning—from exhaustion I'd say. I'm on my way to see her."

"Need a lift?"

"No. Thanks. I'll take a taxi. I think this is women's business. What are you up to?"

"The boy I coach at the boxing gym? He rang me earlier. Had information about drug trafficking that could be the break we need. I'm heading out to talk to a tattooist a second time. Long story. You don't want to come?"

"I'm busy this morning," she said. "I don't know what kind of state I'll find Estefana in. How about I call you later?"

"Okay. Call me later," Cordero said and with that he ended the call, drove to the café for a stronger coffee than normal, and made for the address in central Dili where the tattooist, Octavio Cristarao, said he lived.

• • •

Estefana was at the small table hunched over a sheaf of papers when Carter arrived, paid for the taxi, and walked in. The bed was made and Estefana was dressed neatly in her police uniform but when she looked up her eyes were red and moist from crying.

"How do you feel?" Carter asked, knowing full well what the answer was likely to be.

Estefana put the papers to one side and wiped her eyes. "I slept okay, *mana*," she said. "Thank you." She took a deep breath. "I was going through the arrangements for our wedding." Her eyes shut tightly. "It was supposed to be next week."

"It *will* be next week," Carter insisted. "And it's not like you to give up, Estefana. You're better than this." Carter and Estefana had been through some tight situations in the time they'd worked together for INTERPOL—Estefana encouraged by Carter to take part in every investigation she was involved with. In the course of their time together Carter had seen just how strong a young woman—and determined a young police officer—Estefana was becoming. "Don't fall apart on me now, you hear?"

"But *mana*—" Estefana started to protest.

"Look, we're making progress," Carter exaggerated. "We know that Josinto was going about his business as normal up until he went missing. We can be pretty sure he was being followed from Balide. That tells us a lot. And Cordero has a new lead. He received information earlier this morning about a guy connected to drug trafficking and he's off to interrogate him now."

Estefana turned back to the papers on the table. "It's no good, *mana*. It's too late now," she said.

It had rained heavily again over night but was easing now and the heat of the day made the air sticky. The sound of children playing in the street flowed into the room, their laughter a contrast to the melancholy inside. Carter put her hands on Estefana's shoulders and they locked eyes.

"That's enough of that kind of talk, Estefana," she said. "What have I been telling you ever since we started working together? You're a police officer, not a timekeeper. You search, you question, you examine and you don't give up. You never give up!"

"But *mana*—"

"My father used to always say 'You're stronger than you think you are but thinking you're not stops you from finding just how strong you can be,'" Carter said. "I've seen how strong you can be. I've seen it when we were set upon by that mob of villagers down near Suai and I've seen it when you saved a boy from being killed by men with machetes. I want to see it now, you hear?"

Estefana wiped her eyes again. "Yes, *mana*."

"There's nothing to be gained by giving up," Carter added. "Nothing."

"Can I come with you and *maun* again today?" Estefana asked. "Cordero doesn't need your police badge," Carter said. "He has his own. And I have things to do before I catch up with him. Besides I've a job only you can do. We need to know where Josinto's truck is. There's a good chance he's there with it. No sightings that we know of have been reported to the police but that doesn't mean nobody saw anything. You're in your police uniform. I want you to question police officers in various parts of the city. Starting where we know Josinto was last seen—in Lecidere. Work out from there east and west. If you hear anything useful, call me. Okay?"

Estefana bit her bottom lip.

"Okay?" Carter repeated.

"Yes, *mana*."

"Right. You go now. It's going to take you all day. I can catch a taxi back to where I'm going. If I don't hear from you, I'll call you later to check how you're getting on."

Estefana picked up her motorcycle helmet and sheepishly made for the door.

"Estefana," Carter called after her. "Never give up!"

• • •

It was a room in Caicoli above a store selling Chinese and Indonesian-made mattresses. The store was just opening for the day when Cordero took the stairs at the side to Octavio's room and knocked; no answer. Cordero pinched his shirt away from his sweaty body and grew impatient. He knocked again, more forcefully this time and called out "*Polisia*." The door opened a crack. Octavio was standing on the other side wearing only a pair of boxer shorts, scratching his chest and blinking.

"You again, *maun*," Octavio said.

"Thanks for inviting me in," said Cordero. He pushed the door open and brushed the tattooist aside.

There was a rustling in the corner and a woman—a foreigner—hurriedly threw on a skirt and top, grabbed her handbag and shoes and rushed out the door without saying a word.

"What is it this time?" Octavio asked, rubbing sleep from his face.

"This time I want the truth," Cordero said.

"About what, *maun*?"

"Who you gave information to about drug shipments," Cordero said.

"You crazy, *maun*," Octavio said. He slumped on a chair at the small table in the center of the room and lit a stubbed-out rolled cigarette. "I don't know what you're talking about," he said sucking in smoke.

"Members of various gangs are in the habit of coming to the bars you work when they have money. Maybe they want tattoos. Maybe they want to try their luck with foreign women. Maybe they just want to listen to music and drink. But they come. And they know you and you know them." Cordero kept his eyes on Octavio and leaned across the table. "And when they've had a few drinks, they start boasting about money. You know very well that's likely to mean a drug shipment. Maybe they tell you outright. And you pass it on."

"I've told you everything I know, *maun*," protested Octavio. "Didn't I tell you about that guy with the scorpion tattoo and his girlfriend?"

"Yes, but probably because he was dead, and you thought the girlfriend would be as well by the time you told me," said Cordero.

Octavio rested the cigarette in an ashtray overflowing with butts, clasped his hands together and stared at them. Cordero could hear his foot tapping.

"I have a witness who'll testify you passed on information about drug shipments," Cordero said, stretching the truth about the precise detail Fidelis could provide. "That makes you an accessory to two murders and probably an abduction that could end in murder. You can say goodbye to your artistic career, unless you want to specialize in prison tattoos for thirty years."

Octavio seemed a little less sure of himself but said, "Prove it, *maun*."

Cordero knew that for the moment at least, and certainly with Fidelis on his way out of town, he couldn't. He noticed the tattooist's expensive needles and ink he kept in a box sitting on a bench near a gas-fired kitchen burner. He walked over, took out a needle and dropped it on the ground.

"Hey *maun!*" said Octavio. "Those things're expensive."

"Sorry," said Cordero, as he looked down and scrunched the needle under his shoe. He took another out of the box as though to drop it as well.

"Okay, yeah, I pass on information," Octavio said. He reached over, grabbed the box and put it on the table. "But that's all I do. And I don't know what they do with it."

"Who's 'they'?" asked Cordero pulling up another chair and seating himself across the table from Octavio.

Octavio turned the box around on the table top, playing for time. Cordero put his hand on the box to stop his dithering. "Who's 'they'?" he asked again.

"Guys out in Comoro. I don't know," said Octavio. He reached for the stub of his cigarette, puffed on it but it had gone out. "I just have a number to call when I have information. Different people answer."

"How do they know it's you calling and not the police?"

Octavio picked up a plastic light and struck what was left of his cigarette. "I give them a code, *maun.*"

"A code? What code?" Cordero asked.

The tattooist blew out smoke and coughed but said nothing. Cordero picked up the box of needles.

"*Samea mean,*" the tattooist said. It meant 'red snake' in Tetun. He took the box back from Cordero.

"Why *samea mean*?" Cordero asked.

"It's a code, *maun,*" Octavio said. He puffed again, coughed again. He extinguished the butt. "How do I know? It's just what they use."

"How'd you get the number?" asked Cordero.

"Like I said, guys out in Comoro." Octavio waved a hand at nothing in particular. "They came into the bar a while back and we started talking. I didn't ask their names and they didn't tell me."

Cordero took a notebook and pen from his pants pocket. Octavio gave him the number and he wrote it down.

"How are you paid for the information you pass on?" Cordero said pocketing his notebook.

"When guys come to the bars, they hand me the money if the information I give them is correct." Octavio looked at Cordero and could tell he wasn't satisfied. "Again, different guys, *maun*! I don't know their names."

"But you must know more than that they're from Comoro. How do you know they're not police? How do you recognize them?"

Octavio started tapping his bare foot on the floor and rubbed the sides of his thighs.

"The only good thing you can do for yourself now is tell me," Cordero advised him.

Octavio stared at him. He wiped a hand over his face. "They say they're from Tristao, *maun*."

"Tristao?" Cordero considered that. "Is that a place or a name?"

"A name, *maun*," said Octavio. "What do you think?"

"Who is this Tristao?"

"I don't know. Guy who sent them maybe."

"You don't know him? Never met him?"

Octavio shook his head.

"You weren't ever curious?" Cordero pressed him.

"No. Why should I be? I just pass on information, that's all."

Cordero sat back in his chair. "What do you know about the gang members who were killed recently?"

"Nothing, *maun*. Honest."

"But you told these people in Comoro that they were carrying drugs?"

"I never knew who was carrying the drugs. I was told they'd be coming in, when and where. That's all. And that's what I told them. Nothing more."

"How often have you passed on information about drug shipments?"

Octavio looked down at the table and brushed a hand over it. "Five, maybe six times in the past few months."

"And how do the drugs come in?"

"Driven across the border from West Timor. Brought in by boat. Any way they can get them in. That's all I know, *maun*."

"You know anything about a guy abducted in his truck on Wednesday?"

The tattooist shook his head.

Cordero stood. He was uncertain whether the tattooist knew more than he was admitting but he'd told him enough to go on with for the moment. What he was sure of was that if he let Octavio go he'd get word back to Comoro.

"Get your pants, you're coming with me," he said.

"Where?" Octavio asked.

"Police station where else?"

"But I'm cooperating, *maun*! You can't prove I had anything to do with murders."

"I'm taking you in for having sex with an under-aged girl," Cordero said.

"Bullshit, *maun*. That *malae*," he said referring to the foreign tourist who had rushed out the door, "was at least thirty."

"Prove it," Cordero said, lifting him by the arm.

• • •

"Under-age sex with an unidentified foreign tourist," the balding, heavyset desk officer repeated. "That's a stretch even for you isn't it, Tino?"

He'd brought Octavio Cristarao to the police station in Caicoli and was now trying to have him taken to a cell.

"Look," said Cordero, out of earshot of the tattooist. "I just want him locked up for the time being or he could alert the wrong people to what I'm up to. If you can think of a better charge for the moment then use it."

Octavio was staring out the doors at the people coming and going from the building. "No, that'll do," said the desk officer as though he was a willing party to a conspiracy. "Actually, it's quite a clever idea, Tino. It'd take us a day to find this tourist—if we can find her at all," he said and winked. "Then of course we'd have to check her age and all. Let me see now, passport checks and visa." He looked up sharply. "But you'll owe me, Tino." The desk officer straightened. "Benigno!" he called.

A junior officer appeared from a back room holding a sheet of paper.

"Take *Senyor* Octavio Cristarao to a holding cell and make him comfortable," the desk officer ordered.

The junior officer looked from the tattooist to the desk officer and back at the paper in his hand.

"What have you got there?" the older man demanded.

"A motorcycle accident I'm meant to file. A fatality. Just in. Happened this morning. They need clearance to take the body to the morgue."

"If the person's dead they can wait five minutes, give me that," said the desk officer. "Fidelis Tau. Seventeen years old. No helmet," he read and let out a sigh. "When will they learn?" he asked no one in particular.

"Let me see that," snapped Cordero.

The report noted the victim had come off his motorcycle just outside Dili on the road that led to Dare and the mountains of central Timor beyond. No one had witnessed the accident but a passing microlet driver had called police and reported he'd seen a body on the side of the road. A police officer had been sent to check and had radioed in the report.

Cordero checked the details a second time. The body was spotted at six o'clock—thirty minutes after Fidelis called, honouring a debt he felt he owed Cordero.

Chapter 19

Cordero had asked for the name and cell number of the officer who handled the body found on the road to Dare. He called him now. Officer Eduardo Rios answered while he was dealing with a truck breakdown blocking traffic near the stadium in the center of Dili. In between shouting orders to frustrated motorists and motorcyclists, the officer tried to answer Cordero's questions.

"Did you find anything he'd hit that would explain what happened?" Cordero asked.

"Nothing in particular," Eduardo answered. "Why?"

"Did you look?" Cordero persisted.

"Wait, *maun*," Eduardo said.

Cordero overheard bits and pieces of an angry exchange between Rios and a truck driver that ended in "or I'll arrest you now" and a moment later the police officer was back on the call.

"What did you ask?" he said.

"Did you investigate the area around the body?" Cordero asked.

"What for, *maun*? He came off his motorcycle. Probably hit his head on the road or a tree or another vehicle. I don't know. Why would I look any further? It happens all the time."

"Did you speak to the driver of the microlet?"

"Who?"

"The driver of the microlet who rang the police, that's who."

"No."

"Did you get his name and number?"

"I asked the dispatcher who took the call but she said he hadn't left either. He was running late into Dili. Didn't stop. Didn't

173

know anything other than he'd seen what looked like a body and a damaged motorcycle on the side of the road," Eduardo said.

"When you got there, did you ask around if anybody had seen anything?"

"Ask who, *maun*? There was no one around."

Cordero was annoyed by what he regarded as Officer Eduardo Rios's lazy policing but he let it go.

"The body's been collected?" he asked, trying to disguise the emotion in his voice.

"Yeah. Taken to the morgue a little time ago. That's why I left and was ordered to sort out this mess down here," Eduardo said. "Shit *maun*. You should see it."

Before Cordero let the officer get back to the traffic problem he asked where the damaged motorcycle had been taken and where exactly the body had been found. Then he headed first to a towing yard in Comoro where the motorcycle had been impounded.

He found nothing instructive. The brakes of Fidelis' motorcycle seemed to be working fine, the tread on the tyres was good and they were fully inflated. He examined the fairings and frame and could see no tell-tale damage on any part that provided a clue as to why Fidelis had crashed and been killed. He asked to see the helmet only to be told that none had come with the motorcycle. He called Officer Eduardo Rios again who confirmed no helmet had been found at the scene of what he continued to call the 'accident'.

Cordero left the towing yard and drove to where Eduardo had told him he'd found the body. Traffic had built up on the road by now but Cordero parked his vehicle and weaved in and out of the trucks and motorcycles as he examined the road. Its surface here was intact—no ruts or potholes—although the visibility ahead for anyone riding up the road was poor. A sharp left-hand bend curled up a steep rise not thirty yards on. Traffic coming down the road would appear without warning. Fidelis would have—should have—been close to the hillside leaning into the side of the ridge given the left-hand driving rule in East Timor. But oncoming traffic often monopolised the entire road on narrow strips of bitumen such as this and could easily have collided with him.

Cordero refused to believe it. Fidelis's body and his motorcycle had been found on the wrong side of the road where it dropped off into a gully. It was unlikely he'd hit anything that far over—Cordero could see nothing to suggest that on nearby trees or what was left of an old guardrail. Might he have been hit by a truck moving fast in the opposite direction and spun across the road? Might he have slipped, hit his head on the road itself, and slid to where his body was lying?

Again, Cordero refused to believe either possibility. There were no signs of blood on the road and no skid marks. If a weapon had been used to kill Fidelis—as Cordero suspected—that would explain why. And if it had been tossed into the deep and heavily wooded gully on the right side of the road rather than taken away by the killer it was never likely to be found.

For now, and despite his best efforts to get to the truth of what caused the fatality, Cordero simply had no evidence to contradict the presumption of accidental death.

He'd parked down from the bend on a short, straight stretch of roadway. As he headed back down toward his vehicle he noticed a small girl, perhaps no more than eight or nine years of age, sitting behind three plastic litre bottles of gasoline set atop a wooden crate by the side of the road. If she had been there earlier, he hadn't seen her while he was studying the road surface and dodging vehicles but he noticed now that from where she was sitting the girl had a clear view of the bend where Fidelis had met his fate. He slowed his pace, smiled and walked over to the girl.

"*Bondia*," he said and the girl answered so softly he couldn't make out what it was she said.

He squatted. "You're selling gasoline," he said. "How much is a litre?"

The girl held up a finger.

"One dollar, huh?" Cordero searched his pockets and found a bunch of coins that totalled $1.10. He handed the coins to the girl who pocketed them without checking and pushed a bottle of gasoline toward him.

"You must see a lot of cars and trucks and motorcycles on this road," Cordero suggested and the girl nodded. "Did you see a police officer come this morning—up there on that bend?" The girl nodded a second time. "I'm a police investigator," Cordero said. "Do you know what that is?" The girl shook her head. "Well, a police officer takes care of accidents and an investigator like me tries to find out why they happened. You understand?" The girl nodded. "You think you'd like to help me?" The girl gazed up the road, turned back to Cordero and nodded a fourth time. "Okay. So tell me, did you see what happened up there before the police officer arrived?"

The girl went to answer but wheeled her head quickly and then rose to her feet. A woman was approaching up a track from the gully below.

"Nandi," the woman said. "What are you doing?"

Cordero stood. He knew the woman was inquiring about him and not the girl who presumably was her daughter.

"*Bondia, mana,*" he said. "My name is Vincintino Cordero. I am a police investigator. I'm looking into the motorcycle accident that occurred this morning and was wondering if this little girl had seen anything that might help me understand what happened." The girl had clasped her arms around the woman's legs but continued to eye Cordero. The woman remained silent. "Or perhaps you saw something when you set out the gasoline bottles," Cordero continued. "What time do you usually do that?"

The woman stroked the girl's head. "When the sun comes up, *senyor,*" she said. "I don't know what time that is."

Just before six, Cordero thought to himself. He looked up the road toward the bend. "We think the accident occurred around then too," he said. He looked back at the woman. "Did you see anything?"

The woman stared at him a moment. "You asked what time I *usually* set out the gasoline," she said. "This morning my boy is sick. I didn't set the bottles out until later and told Fernanda to keep an eye on them while I went back to check on her brother."

"There is nothing you can tell me about the accident?" he asked and the woman shook her head.

Cordero looked down at the girl and smiled.

"And you didn't see anything either?" he asked her.

The girl shook her head.

"Well, thank you for your time, Fernanda," Cordero said. "And thank you too, *mana*," he added.

As he turned to leave, the little girl called after him. He looked back and she was holding out the bottle of gasoline he'd paid for.

It was all he had to show for the morning's efforts to find out what had happened to Fidelis.

Chapter 20

Brooks opened his front door in a robe that was untied at the front. It was after eleven o'clock but he was still in pajamas. "You again, dear boy," he said. "Come in. I was just having a cup of tea. Would you like to join me?"

"No thanks, Howard. I have a favour to ask," said Cordero.

"Another one," said Brooks, walking him into the kitchen. "I thought you might."

"I want you to do an autopsy on a body found this morning," Cordero said.

"Dear boy, you do know it's Saturday?" Brooks said. "And if I was on duty, which I'm not, I do have other people calling on my services."

"This boy was a friend," Cordero explained.

"Oh," was all Brooks said. He picked up his tea cup.

"And now he's dead."

"Dead how?" Brooks asked, finishing the tea.

"They're calling it a motorcycle accident. On the road to Dare. I think it was murder."

"What reason have you to suggest that?"

"Thirty minutes before he was killed he called me with information that might help solve the murder of those two gang members and the disappearance of Estefana's fiancé," Cordero said. "He was scared. He knew he'd raised suspicions among dangerous people. He was leaving town for his own good."

"Maybe he was in too much of a hurry," Brooks suggested. "Did you think of that?"

"I sparred with Fidelis. At the boxing gym. On a regular basis including yesterday. I've never known a seventeen year-old with reflexes as fast as his were. And he was powerful too. I don't believe he hit a pothole or failed to take a turn. I think he was murdered."

Brooks nodded and put his tea cup down. "Then I'd best get dressed," he said and turned off into the bedroom.

• • •

Estefana had grown more and more disheartened with every blank she'd drawn from the police officers she'd spoken to. In total that came to twelve. On the day of Josinto's disappearance, two had been escorting a man charged with vehicular theft from a village 50 miles along the coast west of Dili to the capital to be held for trial, four had spent the day in court waiting to give evidence in a variety of cases, three had been assigned to desk duties, and three had no recollection of the truck Josinto had been driving.

In short, none of them could tell her anything.

She'd been at it for nearly three hours and had covered the administrative subdistricts of Lecidere, Bidau, and Bairro Grillos and was heading into Formosa near the center of the city. She was starting to convince herself that the whole exercise was pointless and felt like going home. But she remembered what Carter had said—"Never give up"—and forced herself to press on.

At the intersection of *Rua da Formosa* and *Avenida Xavier do Amaral* she spotted a police officer cautioning a man sitting behind the wheel of a heavy construction truck. The truck driver had reversed from a building site without another worker directing him as he backed into the traffic on the busy thoroughfare. That had almost caused a collision. An argument had ensued. Now trucks, microlets, taxis and motorcycles were banked up trying to get around him. Many were blowing their horns, a few yelling profanities. The police officer ignored the complaints and was cautioning the truck driver.

Estefana parked her motorcycle, took off her helmet, walked across and waited for the officer to finish with the man. When he was done the officer walked out into the center of the road, held up a hand to the traffic, and directed the truck out and off on its way.

"*Botarde maun*," Estefana said, as the police officer walked back onto the sidewalk and the traffic began to flow freely again.

"*Tarde, mana,*" the officer replied.

"My name is Estefana dos Carvalho," she said, trying as best she could to add a smile. "Can I ask you a question?"

"You just did," the officer said grinning. "I see you are a police officer. I haven't seen you around."

"I'm from Suai. I've been working here in Dili for three months with INTERPOL but I'm now with the regular police. Well, I am when I start in a week or so. I'm on leave at the moment. I'm supposed to be getting married next week."

"Supposed to be?" the man repeated. "Aren't you sure?"

"That's why I'm here," she said. "We—that is, two police colleagues and I—believe my fiancé has been abducted."

"Abducted!" the police officer said.

"He might have gotten innocently mixed up in a gang dispute four days ago. No one has seen or heard from him since." The police officer was looking at her intently now. "He works for the coffin maker in Bidau. He was driving a truck with signs for the coffin business on the side. We think a gang hijacked him and the truck. Maybe in Lecidere or Bidau."

"Why hijack a coffin maker's truck?" the officer asked.

"We think they thought there were drugs hidden in the truck," Estefana explained. "I've been asking police officers around town if they remember seeing a truck with pictures of coffins on the sides around midday on Wednesday."

The police officer scratched his chin. "I was not on duty Wednesday," he said and Estefana's hopes sank further. "All the rosters are messed up because of the ceremony in Metinaro on Sunday." Estefana made to put her helmet back on and thank the officer. "But now that you mention it, I think I did see that truck," he added.

• • •

Cordero had driven Brooks to the morgue and they were both standing inside now, under the harsh glare of the fluorescent lights, Brooks with a clipboard in hand. He ran a finger down the facing page and read aloud:

"'Motorcycle accident victim. Deceased. Location: main road Dare. Reported: 6.30am. Located: 7.10 am, Saturday November 22, 2014. Male. Fidelis Ado Tau. Born April 4, 1997.Last Known Address: Perumnas—'"

"That's where he used to live," Cordero interrupted. "He'd moved to Lecidere."

"'Entered: 8.00am, Saturday November 22. Case No 15/2014, Chamber 8'. That's good, dear boy," Brooks said replacing the clipboard. "He won't yet be too cold to work on."

Brooks walked over to Chamber 8 but before opening it turned to Cordero who was standing by the examining table. "We're short staffed today," he said. "Always are on Saturdays. I'll need your help to get him on the table."

Cordero nodded and approached Chamber 8. Brooks opened the door and slid out a black body bag on a metal tray. He checked the tag that had been tied on the zipper pull. It read 'Case No 15/2014, Fidelis Ado Tau'.

"This," was all Brooks said.

He and Cordero lifted the body and carried it over to the metal examining table. Cordero was surprised at how light it felt given the power Fidelis had been able to put into his punches. Rigor mortis had only just begun to set in. Brooks held up a finger in a gesture of 'Wait', went over to the side bench, slipped on his gloves, and brought a pair back for Cordero. He unzipped the bag. The body was clothed and unwashed. Cordero froze when he saw the cold, lifeless, bloody face of Fidelis.

"Tino," Brooks said but it brought no response. "Tino!" he repeated. "Help me get the clothes off his body for the examination. Be careful: any little thing could give us clues to his death. If you see anything that might be instructive, stop, don't touch it, just tell me."

Cordero did as he was told. The body bag was dropped to the floor beneath the examining table. The clothes were laid out on a bench to the side of the room. Brooks examined the body quickly for gunpowder residue, oil, and unusual deposits, but found nothing. He then looked for knife wounds and felt for bone abnormalities.

"Okay, Tino," he said, wiping his forearm across his face. "I'm going to wash the body now and examine the injuries. This will take a while and I don't need you here. In fact, you'll only be in my way. Go out and get me lunch. Come back in, let's say, an hour or two. You can bring me a sandwich and another cup of English tea. Milk, two sugars." With that Brooks donned an apron, ran hot water in the sink, and found a bowl and sponge. "Bye now," he added to send Cordero on his way.

• • •

"You saw the truck?" Estefana asked the officer. "Where? When?"

"I was picking up my daughter from school just after lunch. She attends that new Pentecostal school in Caicoli. You know it? We're Catholic but my wife and I aren't—well, you know, we haven't actually been married in a church so we don't have a marriage certificate and you need one of those to put your kids in a Catholic school. We'll get around to it one day—"

"Are you sure it was the truck I'm talking about?" Estefana interrupted him. "With signs for the coffin maker on the side?"

"Oh yes," the officer said. "I'm sure of that. It had pictures of coffins, a name I didn't catch and 'Bidau' written on it."

"Can you tell me exactly what you saw?"

"Well, this truck comes roaring down the road making a hell of a noise. If I'd been on duty I would have booked the driver, you know? Locked him up, in fact. All those kids. It was very dangerous."

"Where was this exactly, *maun*?" Estefana asked.

"I told you. Outside that new Pentecostal school on *Rua Caicoli*."

"Did you see who was in the cabin?"

"Yeah. I wanted to see the idiot who was driving. But actually there was a bunch of young idiots in the cabin. Three of them. I couldn't hear anything because the windows were up and they shot passed. But they seemed to be laughing and jostling each other around, you know. Not caring about how fast they were going or who they might run down."

"Where were they heading?"

The police officer rubbed his chin and stared at his feet.

"Well they were driving toward *Estrada de Balide*," the officer said. "But whether they went left or right at that T-intersection I couldn't tell you. I was too busy collecting my little girl by then."

• • •

Cordero had seen dead bodies before—too many in fact. And his own brother, a seminarian, had been killed by Indonesian troops in 1991 when they gunned down a crowd of Timorese gathered at the grave of a young man shot protesting the occupation in 1991. His brother at least was older than Cordero. Fidelis was young and had his whole life ahead of him, but it was not that which was haunting Cordero. He had become very fond of the boy and enjoyed the avuncular relationship that had developed between them. For someone who'd never thought about having children of his own, the way the role of father-figure had developed through the coaching had surprised him.

But again it was more even than that. Cordero blamed himself for Fidelis' death. It was he who asked Fidelis to go back into a world the boy had worked hard to escape and, he had to admit, there was a part of him that had hoped Fidelis would feel obliged because of the time Cordero had put in with him. *A boy's welfare subordinated to the job*, Cordero thought to himself. He'd got his priorities all wrong and whether it was an accident or a murder, it was on his shoulders.

He walked back into Brooks' examining room as the Englishman was cleaning himself up. Cordero carried a take-out cup of tea in one hand and a cheese sandwich in the other. When Brooks wiped his hands and reached out for both, Cordero noticed what he was carrying without remembering having bought it.

"Tea's a little cold," Brooks said.

"Sorry," Cordero muttered. "I've been wandering. What can you tell me?"

"Well it's clear what killed him," Brooks said placing the tea and the sandwich aside. "Massive contusion on the right side of his head. It fractured his skull and caused an intracerebral haemorrhage. I'd say it would have killed him instantly."

"Do you know what caused it?"

"You said you'd visited the crash scene," Brooks said. "Did you see any sign that he hit a tree, a concrete barrier, or rocky or concreted strip of road?"

"No."

"Was he wearing a helmet?"

"No helmet was found at the scene."

"Well any of those things I mentioned could have done it, especially if he wasn't wearing a helmet."

"Or someone could have hit him with a blunt instrument," suggested Cordero.

"That too," said Brooks nodding. "But I can't find any definitive evidence of a struggle." He lent his backside against the sink and lifted a hand toward the body. "Oh there is bruising on his ribs, solar plexus and around the jaw. But you told me you sparred with him only yesterday. You could have done that."

"Like I said he was strong, fast, could hit you with every punch in the book. I don't believe he lost control of the motorcycle."

"But you don't *know* he didn't," Brooks pointed out.

"There was no blood on any hard surface near the body," Cordero insisted.

"It rained earlier this morning," Brooks said. "That could have washed it off. Or he hit a vehicle passing in the other direction—a side mirror, a pipe or something of that nature hanging out of the back of a truck—and the driver just kept going. Did you check his motorcycle?"

"Of course."

"And?"

"Scrapes along the side," Cordero said. "Hard to tell whether they were old or fresh."

"Hard to tell or you didn't want to tell?"

"Whose side are you on, Howard?" Cordero said angrier than he had wanted.

"The side of science and logic, dear boy," replied Brooks. "Look, I know you want it to be murder. That would take responsibility off this young man for being careless."

Cordero glared at Brooks.

"All I'm saying is that there is no conclusive evidence of foul play. Unless you find some, this will have to be written up as what it appears—an unfortunate motorcycle accident."

Chapter 21

Carter had rung Cordero that afternoon and he told her he was following a lead out in Comoro. To Carter the word 'lead' had the same effect as the word 'bone' to a hungry dog and she insisted on going with him. He was unusually grumpy as he pulled up to collect her from a busy corner in central Dili. He was grumpier because he was grumpy around her. If INTERPOL's Danique Jacobsen and Ambassador Hudson Taylor couldn't arrange for Carter to extend her stay in East Timor she'd be heading home in a little over a week. He didn't want her remembering him as moody or worse a grouch, but he couldn't help himself and that made him even grumpier still.

"Hi," he managed as she climbed into the passenger's seat. "How are you?" he added after a pause.

She stared at him. "A lot better than you, I think," she replied. "What's up?"

He shifted uncomfortably in his seat. "Remember the boy who gave me the black eye in the boxing gym?"

She nodded.

"His name was Fidelis."

"Was?"

"I've just come from Brooks. He just autopsied the boy. Found this morning beside the road to Dare. About half an hour after he rang me with what he'd found out." Cordero rubbed his face. Carter said nothing. "Looked like a motorcycle accident but I think he was murdered. Brooks claims there's nothing definite to support that."

He accelerated away from the kerb and into the traffic.

"Brooks should know what he's talking about," Carter offered, looking straight ahead.

"But he didn't know Fidelis. I did," he insisted. "If you could have seen him move around that ring—" and he let the statement hang.

"I don't have to tell you what that road is like," said Carter slipping on sun glasses. They'd driven it on a case a few weeks earlier. "And a motorcycle is not a boxing ring."

Cordero grunted.

"Was he wearing a helmet?"

"No one found a helmet," Cordero admitted.

"Well—" Carter left the statement unfinished.

"He'd spent the whole night talking to different gang members to get information I asked him for," Cordero said. "When he rang me, he knew he was in danger. He wasn't panicking or anything. Fidelis wasn't like that. But he told me he was leaving town just in case. And they didn't *find* a helmet. Fidelis always wore one. I'd say whoever killed him took the helmet to make it look like Fidelis hit his head in an accident."

"You're only assuming that," Carter said.

"Like I said, he always wore a helmet," he said in a more emphatic tone. "He didn't want to risk any damage to his face or his head that could make him vulnerable in the ring."

She gazed sideways at him. "Are you mourning the kid's death, angry with Brooks, or feeling guilty that you may have been responsible?" she asked.

She noticed his knuckles whiten as he gripped the steering wheel.

She turned and faced forward. "You're the one who's big on hard evidence," she said. "And you're the one who told me not to let personal feelings get in the way of professional training."

He looked away from her, out the driver's window.

"Point taken," he said and paused. "Where've you been?"

"A little business I had to attend to."

He looked across. She gave no more away.

"How's Estefana?" he asked.

Carter took off her sunglasses and pinched the top of her nose. "Not good. As you'd expect," she said, and replaced the glasses. "I suggested she go out and talk to police officers all over town today. See if any of them saw Josinto's truck. No offence but I don't trust the reporting system in your police force. Besides, it'll keep her busy so she doesn't start feeling sorry for herself."

"You can be hard, you know," he said.

"You're telling me I can be hard when you keep telling her there's nothing the police can do until next week!" she said. "Because they're short-staffed and not even then without more evidence."

"Okay, sorry. I shouldn't be taking my problems out on you."

"No you shouldn't. And you shouldn't let your 'problems', as you call them, distract you from what we're here to do. That's to find the killer or killers of two boys before they make Josinto number three."

"I think Fideli's death is connected."

"Then let's prove it," she said.

Neither spoke for a moment.

"What's this lead you spoke about?" she asked.

"Fidelis told me a guy who works the bars would pass on information about drug shipments to a phone number in Comoro. I'd questioned this guy before, in connection with the tattoo on the second boy who was killed. I suspected he might know more than he was letting on. When I confronted him with what Fidelis had told me and threatened him with being charged with accessory to murder, he opened up. Said when he heard about a drug shipment he'd call a particular number. Said he'd identify himself by using a code—*samea mean*. It means red snake. The—"

"Wait a minute. The guy who worked the gas station in Lecidere where Estefana and I went on Josinto's trail said he thought he saw a tattoo on the neck of one of the motorcyclists following Josinto's truck. From his description it could have been a red snake."

Cordero nodded. "Okay that figures then," he said. "Anyhow the guy who seems to run this racket is called Tristao. That's who we're going to find and question."

He looked across again but she was staring out the windscreen. "I called Pepe. He'd never heard of a Tristao. He made a few calls. Nothing. He said that was a good sign—if any police were connected to Tristao or his group there would have been word of it among some officers at least. I traced the number the tattooist was told to call to a landline in a convenience store in Comoro. We'll start there."

He sighed.

"Tomorrow I'm off to Metinaro. Couldn't come at a worse time. You can add that to everything else that's annoying me. If we don't get a breakthrough today in Comoro—" and he waved his hand in a gesture of exasperation.

They drove along the *Avenida de Portugal*, the sea on their right sparkling in the afternoon sun. A few old women and young children sold fish off bamboo frames along the stone wall separating the road from the beach. It was late in the day for fresh fish and most hawkers had turned to BBQing what they had and turning it into what Timorese called 'Fish on a stick'—their version of fast food. The aroma of the BBQ was appetizing where it wasn't lost in the gusts of diesel fumes.

Cordero turned left and zig-zagged up to and across the intersection with *Avenida Nicolau Lobato*. He threaded through Comoro's narrow streets to a corner on which sat a small ramshackle convenience store with two doorways flanked by security shutters. Along the front was a display of shovels, hoes, rakes and yard brushes together with bags of rice and stacks of bottled water. Two youths slouched against the rice bags arguing with two more who stood in front of them. One of the youths who was standing wore a loose-fitting singlet and was gesturing wildly with a cigarette. On the side of his neck was a tattoo; long, thin, and red.

Cordero parked up from the store and he and Carter walked back to where the youths were arguing. The boy with the cigarette and what clearly now was a red snake tattooed to his neck was angry and swearing loudly. "*Nia kidun kuak,*" he barked, calling someone an asshole. One of the youths resting on the rice bags rose to challenge him, was pushed back harshly, slipped over the rice bags and landed on the ground. The boy slouching against the bags told him to calm down but was dismissed with "*Het inan ba tiha!*" which loosely meant "Get fucked" in English. The boy standing to the right laughed.

"*Botarde*," Cordero said, and all four youths turned and glared at him. Carter stood to Cordero's left, against the front of the store. "I'm looking for Tristao. Maybe you boys can tell me where I can find him," Cordero put to them.

The boys looked at each other.

"What you want him for, *maun*?" the youth slouched against the rice bags asked but the one with the cigarette thrust his arm out to shut him down.

"Who are you?" he demanded of Cordero.

Cordero chose to answer the boy on the rice bags. "I hear he's a wise man. I want to ask him if I've got a future with this *malae* woman," he said, tilting his head in Carter's direction.

The boy with the cigarette gave her a looking over, his nose turned up. Cordero hadn't translated, so Carter had no idea what the conversation was about only that evidently she was at the center of it.

"We don't know no Tristao, *maun*, so piss off or else," the boy said and took another drag on his cigarette.

"That's a nice tattoo on your neck," said Cordero ignoring the threat. "A red snake isn't it? *Samea mean*. I hear Tristao is connected to a group called *Samea Mean*. You must know where I can find him."

"My tattoos got nothing to do with you," the boy said. "And I don't know what you're talking about, see?"

"Oh, I think you do," said Cordero.

The boy squared up to Cordero. "I told you to piss off," he hissed and flicked his cigarette butt into Cordero's chest. "Not going to tell you again!"

Cordero casually wiped the ash off his shirt.

"How about you?" he asked the youth on the rice bags. "Or you?" he said looking at the boy on the ground. "Either of you know where I can find Tristao?"

The two said nothing.

"What about you?" Cordero said to the fourth boy, looking over the shoulder of the one who'd threatened him.

The boy nearest Cordero pulled a knife from his back pocket and held it just below Cordero's chin. "I told you to piss off, *maun!*" he said. Cordero didn't flinch. "Do it now!"

It happened so fast it was easy to miss.

Carter grabbed one of the display shovels. A whoosh of air was followed by a loud 'clang' as the flat of the shovel slammed against the head of the knife-wielder. He collapsed to the ground as though his legs had suddenly given way. Two of his fellow gang members edged back quickly into the doorway of the store. The boy on the ground scurried backwards on his hands and feet. He held up a hand to Carter thinking she might be insane. She looked at Cordero. "My father used to say shovels have many more uses than people give them credit for," she said and replaced the shovel neatly in the row of garden implements.

Cordero checked the boy on the ground. He was groggy but there were no broken bones or open wounds. "He'll live," he said. He took the knife from the boy's limp hand, and took a step towards the three youths in the doorway.

"I'll tell you where you can find Tristao," blurted the one of the ground, staring at the knife. "But put that down and keep her way," he added.

"I'll send this to Brooks," he confided to Carter, pocketing the knife. "What's your name?" he asked the boy.

"Rogerio," the boy said.

"Well Rogerio, my name's Tino. What can you tell me?"

Rogerio regained his feet, dusted himself off and gestured to Cordero and Carter to follow him around the corner while his two companions attended to the boy Carter had knocked senseless with the shovel.

"It's not far," Rogerio said.

"You were having an argument when we approached," said Cordero. "What was that about?"

"Zico is always angry," was all Rogerio said.

He led them off the sealed road to an unsealed laneway. Fifty yards along they came to a compound where two youths, both with a red snake tattoo, paced the entrance puffing on cigarettes. Rogerio spoke to them before escorting Cordero and Carter through the open gate. Other youths in the courtyard peered suspiciously at the two visitors. Rogerio spoke to an older youth, at the entrance to the main building before turning back to Cordero.

"He's running late," said Rogerio. "But we can go in. The *pose* hasn't finished," he added, referring to an investiture of some kind.

Rogerio led them around the back of the main building to a roughly constructed undercover area out back.

The roof was rusted corrugated iron, the floor packed earth. No walls enclosed the area under the roofing which was smaller than a tennis court. Five young women sat on plastic chairs, two nursing small children, on one side of a crooked aisle. Across from them were eight male youths in two rows, standing with their hands clasped in front of them, their feet slightly apart, like soldiers ordered to stand at ease. Presumably the women were partners of the youths and had been invited to attend the ceremony. Each of the males wore a light blue karate training suit with a red stripe down the sides of the pants, a red belt around their waists and a red ribbon diagonally across their backs. Cordero guessed their ages to range from sixteen years to early twenties. All were barefoot. They were facing a small platform, two steps high. On the platform a figure in the same light blue colours but wearing a cloak rather than a training suit crouched, his back to those assembled. When he rose and turned, they could see the man was wearing what looked like the chasuble a priest would wear, a snake embroidered in bright red on the front, and a white stole that bore images of stars and new moons.

This was no Catholic priest, but rather Tristao aping priestly garb as he prepared to induct the boys into a group, gang, association—or whatever it was *Samea Mean* was meant to be.

It was hot under the iron roof and one of the children began to cry. The mother tried to hush the child but without success and she stood and shuffled through the chairs to the open yard where the sound would be less distracting. Cordero and Carter stepped aside to let her pass. As they did, they noticed the boy Carter had hit with the shovel was being helped into the main building by two other youths. He looked angry and, when he set eyes on Carter, began cursing and struggling but the others held him and ushered him away.

Cordero and Carter turned their attention back to the ceremony. *"Imi mak soldadu sira iha luta foun,"* Tristao was intoning, the thick lenses of his glasses glistening in the sunlight that streamed through holes in the roofing. *"Laran-moos nafatin no sai prontu ba."* Cordero whispered to Carter that the new recruits were now to be known as soldiers and were urged to stay pure of heart for the struggle ahead.

Tristao clapped once and from the side of the platform a youth held up a strong box to him. Tristao gestured to the boys in the rows and they formed a line leading up to the platform. From the box he extracted betel quids and placed one in the mouth of each of the boys. When the last boy had received his betel, they each headed back and joined their women folk with broad smiles on their faces. The *pose* was over.

"We must give him time to change," Rogerio said, as Tristao left the area. "Sit here," he motioned to them.

"So this is how you become a member of *Samea Mean*," Cordero said.

Rogerio nodded. "The women will now sow the red snake on the back of the suits. Many like to get it tattooed as well. You only wear the bar while you are a *novisu*."

"A novice?" said Cordero. "Like in a religious order, you mean?"

Rogerio nodded again.

"This whole thing was like a Mass," whispered Cordero.

"Tristao says *Maromak* was here long before the Church," Rogerio said, using the Tetun for God. "But people have forgotten that and are Catholic now. He says he has to lead them through what they are familiar with to the truth and that's why the *pose* is like this. That's why he gives the betel like priests give communion."

"Do you think I could have one of those betel quids?" Cordero asked.

"What for, *maun*? You're not joining," said Rogerio. "Tristao keeps the betel. Only he hands it out. The boys who guard the quids won't give them out unless Tristao says to. Not to anyone."

The area quickly cleared. "Come," said Rogerio jumping to his feet. He led them to the back of the main building and ushered them inside. They followed him down a corridor where all the doors were closed to a room where Rogerio knocked, entered alone, and shut the door behind him. After a few moments he opened the door and invited them in.

Chapter 22

The light in the room was dim and Cordero and Carter had to adjust their eyes after the glare outside. There was a small wooden table, two straight backed chairs, a pitcher of water with one glass set next to a tiny call bell, and a notepad and pen resting in the middle of the table. The priestly garb hung from a peg on a side wall. Tristao was crouched on the floor in the corner furthest from the window, the shades of which were closed. He could have been forty years old—it was hard to tell because he kept his head bent toward the floor. His shoulders were now draped in a *tais*—the traditional Timorese woven cloth which might have demonstrated respect for those around him, connection to the ancestors, or a simple taste in attire. Around his neck were strings of beads made from seeds and a large *belak* or medallion used as a chest ornament and occasionally signifying the wearer's importance as a ritual leader. The skin on his face was pale and his hands small and delicate as though never used for manual work.

"The boy told me you came here to find out if you should marry the *malae* woman," Tristao said in a raspy voice. "I know that's not true."

"My name is Vincintino Cordero. I'm a police investigator," Cordero said. "My companion is an American, *Mana* Carter." He hesitated. "She is an FBI Agent who works here in Timor-Leste with INTERPOL. She doesn't speak Tetun. I will translate for her."

"Then you can translate that INTERPOL is useless," the man said. "It can't protect our people. Just like the Timorese police. Useless."

"Protect them from what?" asked Cordero.

"Evil," the man replied.

"Who will I tell her is saying this?"

"My name is Tristao," he said. "It is no secret. I hear even you used it."

"Just Tristao?" asked Cordero. "No second name?"

"It's what a man does in life that's important," said Tristao, "not what he's called."

"Not many people seem to know of you," Cordero said.

"The people who need to know me, know me," the man said.

"And who are they?" asked Cordero.

Tristao shifted so that he was facing Cordero and Carter. But through the thick glasses his eyes seemed strangely vacant. "Why are you are here?" he said.

"We've found two boys dead—one was a member of the *Forsa* gang, one a member of 4:4. We suspect both were couriering drugs."

Cordero stopped, gave a brief summary of what he'd just said to Carter while he watched Tristao carefully. The man sat still and showed no reaction. Cordero turned to Carter. She too was focused on Tristao. He remained silent and unmoving.

"Ask him about Josinto and the truck, and the guy who looked like he had a snake tattooed to his neck who seemed to be following him," said Carter.

Cordero did as she asked. Again, no response from Tristao. Cordero rubbed the back of his neck. They waited.

"There is a story told where I come from," Tristao began without prompting. "About a beautiful girl called Biloi. She was not only beautiful she was good. She took care of her parents for she was their only child and she weaved beautiful *tais* that she would take to the village market. People would come to buy them and while they were there they'd buy things from the other villagers. Everyone benefitted."

He stopped to make sure they were following his story.

"She wove her *tais* by the river," he continued, "and while she worked, she'd sing. Biloi had a lovely voice and her singing would serenade a *fohorai boot*," he said, referring to a big python snake.

"The *fohorai* would curl itself on a branch in a tree above Biloi and listen to her song."

He reached for the pitcher of water. He filled the glass but took just a sip.

"Many men in the village wanted to marry Biloi but she turned them down. She told them she must take care of her parents and make *tais* to ensure people come to the village market and spend money. The men grew jealous and they began to meet to drink palm wine."

He took another sip of water.

"One day they got so drunk they decided to have their way with Biloi. They finished the palm wine and staggered to the river to find her. She was sitting there, weaving and singing. They each forced themselves onto her in turn and when they'd finished they killed her so no one could identify them."

He placed the drinking glass back on the table.

"The *fohorai* could do nothing because it was in the tree. But it had seen what the men had done. That night it visited each in turn and squeezed the life out of them. When the evil they had brought to the village was gone, it was safe for Biloi to come back to life. Again she attended to her parents, again she weaved, and again she sang by the river."

He closed the *tais* more firmly around his body.

"Timor is like that girl. It has been fouled by evil men. When the evil is removed, Timor will flourish once more."

He looked directly at Cordero.

"My people are not evil," he said. "They do not kill. They are not violent. They do not abduct people. I tell them they must remain pure. The struggle they are preparing for is a spiritual struggle."

"Is that why you give them the betel?" Cordero asked.

"It connects them with those who have gone but will return," Tristao said. "And with each other," he added.

Tristao fumbled for the bell and rang it. Rogerio and another youth entered the room. Cordero studied their expression and told Carter there'd be no point seeking more information. Tristao had bent his head back toward the floor.

"Did he say anything that could help?" Carter asked as they walked along the corridor. There'd been no time for translation of the story.

"I'll tell you on the way back," Cordero said.

Shouting came from behind one of the closed doors and Carter stopped. Rogerio and the other youth escorting them seemed edgy and tried to hustle them along. Carter held back, listening.

"That voice," she said to Cordero. "That sounds like the guy on the beach—the one who hit the girl and clocked me with the bottle. I'm going in." The youth with Rogerio threw his arms out to stop her reaching for the door knob.

Cordero tried to force his way into the room but three more youths came running down the corridor and surrounded him. He held up his hands to signal he'd got the message but continued to listen until ushered away.

"The guy in there is using a lot of Portuguese," he said. "My Portuguese isn't good but I think it might be Brazilian Portuguese. There are differences in pronunciation. But I've no idea what he's yelling."

On their way back from Comoro, Cordero related the story about the girl Bilol and the snake which had revenged her murder and brought her back to life. "I think it's a folk tale about redemption. I'll call Eurico and ask him if he's heard—"

His cell rang. It was Estefana. She'd been trying to call Carter for the past hour but Carter's cell was switched off. He looked across to Carter. She checked.

"True enough," she said. "Must have happened when I decked that kid with the shovel. What does she want?"

Cordero listened to Estefana rush out her words. He nodded and ended the call. "She says she has news."

• • •

They caught up with Estefana at the room she rented. She was excited and rushed out the account of her meeting with the police officer who said he'd seen Josinto's truck with three youths in the driver's cabin and about how he said the truck was heading west toward *Estrada de Balide*.

"He said the three in the truck looked like they were having fun," Estefana said. She stopped and her expression changed from excitement to concern. "*Mana*, if Josinto was in the truck, and they were laughing, it would mean he was one of them—that he was part of whatever it was they were doing."

"Or it could have been two gang members arguing and wrestling with Josinto and the police officer just thought they were laughing," said Carter. "Either way it tells us he's alive."

No one spoke for a moment. Carter turned to Cordero. "I don't care how many police are left in Dili, one of them has to keep an eye on the compound where that Tristao character lives."

"I didn't see anywhere they could be hiding a truck," Cordero said.

"The betel quids, the kid with the knife, the snake tattoos, there's more to that guy and his group than quaint village folk tales," Carter said.

"Okay, you're right," Cordero conceded. "At the very least we have enough circumstantial evidence to get surveillance on the place. I'll put in a request. And I'll get an alert out for police in the area to keep an eye out for the truck and to ask around," he added to sound more convincing.

"What about television, radio appeals?" asked Carter.

"In the areas we're talking about people don't have television and the only thing they listen to is music," said Cordero. "We need police officers. But we're not going to get any of them tonight or tomorrow because of the numbers being sent to Metinaro."

"Then you and I'll spend tomorrow looking around that area," Carter said to Estefana. "Cordero's has to go to the burial ceremony."

"*Mana*, what about tonight?"

"We don't know where to look and it's too dark now to just ride around."

"Tomorrow may be too late, *mana*," Estefana said. "He could be dead!"

Carter lent over the table and touched Estefana lightly on the shoulder. "Enough of that talk," Carter insisted. "You've already established that our suspicions about what happened to Josinto are correct, Estefana. You've done good work. And if, as Cordero and I think, they'll hold Josinto until they can get to that coffin on Monday, they're not going to harm him."

Estefana focused on Carter's eyes and drew confidence from what she saw in them. "Then I'll go to Mass first thing tomorrow, *mana*. Before we go out looking. I'll pray for Josinto and that we find him safe," Estefana said.

Carter had been raised Catholic but hadn't attended Mass for years. She eased back, took a second to think, and played with a strand of her hair.

"Then I'll come with you," she said.

"To Mass, *mana*?" asked Estefana.

"Yes, to Mass. Why not?" asked Carter, who didn't relish the idea or the time it would take out of their search day but wanted to support Estefana in any way her friend felt necessary. "Last I heard everyone was welcome."

Chapter 23

Cordero was feeling hot and constricted in the formal police uniform he was required to wear as the representative of the Scientific Police for Criminal Investigation unit at the re-burial ceremony in the Heroes Cemetery in Metinaro. Lucas Rama Savoy and Manuel Fonseca were technically his juniors which is why the honour—or burden—had fallen to him. He had to park 300 yards from the arched entrance to the cemetery because of the crush of people who'd come to watch the spectacle. He passed the army barracks built alongside the cemetery as he walked to the entrance, noticed troops in dress uniforms, and headed up through the terraced gardens.

He showed his police ID at a security check-point and was directed down a path toward rows and rows of the identical graves of guerilla fighters and, at the end, the platform from where the Mass would be celebrated and official speeches given. Off to the side he noticed members of the permanent honour guard outside the building meant to house the remains of the nation's two 'founding fathers'. The body of Xavier do Amaral, Timor-Leste's first President upon the unilateral declaration of independence from Portugal on November 28, 1975, lay there; the sarcophagus for Nicolau Lobato, first Prime Minister who led the armed resistance against Indonesia after it invaded ten days later, was empty. Lobato was killed by Indonesian troops in 1978 and the whereabouts of his body had never been disclosed by Jakarta.

The cemetery had been laid out on a stretch of land below a range of hills sloping out to the sea. When it was inaugurated in 2009—the 10th anniversary of the referendum that led to the end of Indonesian occupation—it was an arid area of spindly eucalypt trees. Now, with a full-time force of gardeners and funding from successive governments, it was a lush and green garden with brightly coloured urns of flowering salvia, mallows, and peace lilies set among broadleaf evergreens. Today the perimeter of the cemetery was festooned with Timorese flags.

Cordero took his seat among lesser dignitaries at the back of the platform where he was only partially protected from the sun. In the row in front of him sat members of parliament and officials from the political parties. In front of them were army generals who, by law, had the responsibility for approving those who would be buried in the cemetery. They sat behind the current President and Prime Minister who were flanked by the Minister of Defence and the Bishop of Dili. Following a brief welcome from the President and various speeches, the Bishop, aided by six priests, would conduct a Mass ahead of the actual burials.

Cordero knew how much government officials and bishops liked to hear their own voices in front of a captive audience. This was going to take three, maybe four hours. He was growing restless already.

After a delay of twenty minutes while the crowd settled, the President rose and welcomed everyone to the ceremony. He was brief and everybody clapped when he sat back down. Cordero realised he hadn't caught a word of what was said. "Impressive, isn't it?" whispered a decorated police service commander seated next to him. The Prime Minister rose to the microphone. "Makes you proud to be Timorese," the commander added.

Cordero didn't know whether the man was talking about the cemetery or the ceremony but he didn't care. He merely nodded. The Prime Minister droned on. Cordero felt hotter, even more bored, and was anxious to get back to Dili to help in the search for Josinto.

• • •

Estefana suggested an early Mass at the church of *Santo António de Motael* on *Avenida de Portugal* across from the seafront.

It was a beautiful Catholic church, Estefana had explained, and of immense historical importance as the oldest church in East Timor, dating from 1800 originally. The remodeled 1950s version of the church had preserved the beauty of the original, boasting an elegant white bell tower and portico. But it was the congregation rather than the building which grabbed Carter's attention.

Inside the church, where she and Estefana crushed in between families of Timorese fanning themselves from the heat with hymn sheets, were two hundred or more people dressed in their Sunday best. Outside stood another hundred men, women and children following the Mass on loudspeakers. There was energy in the pews as everyone participated in the service with enthusiasm. The last time Carter attended a Mass she was one of only a few young people sitting bored in a scattering of elderly parishioners mumbling responses. She wondered what had changed to make American Catholic worship services so lifeless compared to this Timorese one.

Before the service concluded the priest stood at the altar rails and invited any foreigners whose time in East Timor was coming to an end to step forward for a blessing. Estefana urged Carter, due soon to leave, to go up and she reluctantly joined the twenty people gathered in front of the priest. The priest thanked those who had worked in the country—in a voluntary capacity, for an NGO, or for state agencies—and wished the tourists among them well. He then blessed them and the congregation clapped as they returned to the pews. The priest then asked any foreigners who had just arrived to come forward. Another ten people did. These the priest welcomed to the country, blessed them also, and, again, the congregation clapped. The last hymn was begun, people filed out into the already blistering sun, and the grounds of the church were soon crowded with people lingering in clumps to exchange news. No one seemed in any hurry to leave.

A few people exchanged pleasantries with Carter—a foreigner—and Estefana—a newcomer to the church—but the two knew no-one and had no reason to hang around. They went back to Estefana's room in Lecidere to change out of their formal clothes and into more functional attire—the police uniform for Estefana, jeans and a light blouse for Carter. Estefana made coffee, laid a map of Dili out on the table, and they planned where to go on Josinto's motorcycle in search of his truck.

• • •

Cordero surveyed the crowd of perhaps ten thousand people. Immediately below the platform where he sat was a military guard of thirty troops in camouflaged uniforms and black berets. Beyond them was a collection of invited dignitaries. Cordero noticed US Ambassador Hudson Taylor towering over officials from Asia and Australia. Taylor seemed to have brought his own photographer—a crew-cut young American in a business suit taking photos from angles that featured the Ambassador in every shot. Further back were lesser Timorese political party officials and donors, a number of senior bureaucrats, business men and women, representatives from several dozen NGOs, and a large local media contingent.

Out among the graves old women were wailing. Off to the side, beside the new coffins and caskets containing what was left of the guerrillas, stood a contingent of troops wearing white gloves for handling the remains. Each of the remains was covered in a Timorese flag. Cordero noticed another line of troops standing to attention with weapons by their side. This would be the firing party for a 21-gun salute. People lined the walls that fenced in the cemetery. Some were old and wore traditional clothes but many were young and dressed in skirts or jeans or shorts. Among them mingled the legion of police officers brought in from Dili to ensure the day went without incident.

The bishop had begun the Mass with Cordero barely noticing. He quickly blessed himself and refocused his attention. An hour later the faithful were invited to take the wafer they believed had been transformed into the body of Christ. As a choir sang people spilled out of the rows of graves and lined up before the many priests distributing communion. Cordero noticed his anthropologist friend, Eurico Guterres, in a queue and remembered he had a question for him. He also needed to stretch his legs. He jumped off the back of the podium and threaded his way through the crowd, keeping an eye on Eurico. When he saw him return to his spot and kneel in prayer, Cordero waited until Eurico blessed himself and stood and only then went over to join him.

"I didn't think I'd see you here, Eurico," Cordero said.

"You kidding? This is how myths take shape, *maun*. Textbook anthropology," Eurico replied. "On one level what you see is a re-ordering of the landscape. They gather the bodies of the fallen that were disrupting the harvests and haunting the locals, and rebury them here so they can rest in peace. On another level it's the state claiming to correct the horrors of the past for a bright future." He turned back toward the front. "Textbook."

The old people around them scolded Cordero and Eurico for talking while they were trying to pray. Cordero took his friend by the arm and walked him off to the side.

"I was going to call you," Cordero said.

"More questions?" Eurico joked.

"Yeah."

Cordero recounted the story Tristao had told about the girl Biloi and the snake who had avenged her rape and murder so that she could live again. Eurico bent his head and listened carefully to what Cordero was saying. "That mean anything to you?" Cordero asked.

"I haven't heard that particular version but it's a variation on a theme. There are a number of traditional stories about a girl called Biloi who was very desirable but unattainable. In all of the stories she's killed, avenged by one means or another, and brought back to life. It's like the story of Noah and the flood—things have turned to shit in the world, there needs to be a reset, and then things are put right again. Most cultures tell a version of that tale."

Eurico waved a hand out toward the graves.

"This process of gathering and reburying the dead guerilla fighters has re-ignited interest in such stories. I'm sure you've heard stories about dead guerillas rising from the dead to bring forth a new Timor. One version has it that the day will come when the body of Nicolau Lobato is finally brought here to lead the resurrected army."

Cordero had thrust his hands in his pockets and was thinking this information through. It wasn't helping.

"Who told you this story, anyway?" Eurico asked.

"Guy out in Comoro called Tristao. Strange character. Dresses like a priest and initiates boys and young men into some kind of cult called *Samea Mean*."

Eurico nodded. "They take on the role of the avenging snake," he said. "See themselves as heroes cleansing the country of its vices so the new age can dawn." He nodded again. "Typical millenarian thinking," he said.

"You think this cleansing could involve murder?" Cordero asked.

"If those killed are seen as part of the evil that must be destroyed, yes."

"And drugs?" Cordero asked.

"Again, drugs could be viewed as part of the evil that's corrupting Timorese." Eurico faced forward again. "This about your betel quids again?" he asked.

"Maybe it's all tied up," said Cordero.

"Sounds like it," agreed Eurico.

"Thanks," Cordero said. He turned to walk back to the podium for the central part of the ceremony when the dead guerillas would be interred.

"The thanks are all mine, *maun*. Now I have another version of that old Viqueque tale to catalogue."

Cordero stopped. "Viqueque?"

"Yeah Viqueque," Eurico said. "Biloi is a Viqueque name and stories about how she was avenged are from Viqueque, whatever the details may be."

• • •

They took *Rua 25 de Abril* to *Traversa Tafu'i* and cut back into *Avenida de Portugal* where it changed from one-way to two and they could follow the seafront west to the Timor Plaza shopping complex and across *Avenida Nicolau Lobato* into Comoro--at least that was the plan until Carter realised she'd left her cell in Estefana's room when they were changing their clothes.

"We'd better go back and get it in case we get separated," Carter, riding pillion, shouted over Estefana's shoulder. "Sorry."

Estefana made a U-turn and headed back to Lecidere. As they came up to *Portu Dili*, the country's tiny international seaport, people were spilling onto the road in a frantic rush. Traffic was choked in both directions and horns were blaring. Women and children were pushing aside the heavy iron gates of the port entrance and screaming to get outside; men were swearing, shouting, yelling instructions and trying to keep hold of their possessions.

Estefana pulled up, raised the visor on her helmet, and asked an old man hurrying past what was going on.

"*Asasinatu*," he said and ran on.

"He says it's an assassination, *mana!*" Estefana told Carter. They dismounted, slipped off their helmets and shoved their way through the crowd to the gates. Estefana, the smaller of the two, managed to squeeze through first but was almost hit by a motorcycle accelerating around the derelict Indonesian-era administration building that dominated the center of the port area. The rider careened around a group of children, barely missed two old women, and took off into the city.

Carter bustled her way through the crowd and joined Estefana. "Look *mana!*" Estefana pointed to a body lying near a support for a container crane further down the pier. They were running toward the body when a boy staggered from behind a rusted container up ahead and stooped over whoever it was lying on the concrete. As they approached they noticed blood from a gash on the head of the injured person and heard him cry in pain. It was another youth of a similar age to the one standing over him. Carter grabbed the first boy's arm and locked it behind his back. She noticed a scarring that looked like *4:4* tattooed to his shoulder under a ripped T-shirt. Estefana attended to the boy on the ground.

"It's a bad cut, *mana*," Estefana said, placing a kerchief over the gash and strapping it tight with her own belt. "We'll have to get him to hospital."

The boy Carter held was struggling. "Can you call for help while I keep a firm hold on this one?" she asked. Estefana reached for her cell.

By now most of the crowd had cleared the port area and were huddled in bunches watching what was happening from the park across the road. Food items, household goods and clothing littered the area where they'd been dropped in the panic but otherwise the pier was empty. A motorcycle stood parallel to the main ferry to Atauro Island. Another lay on its side on the other side of the pier alongside a smaller ferry from Indonesian West Timor.

As Estefana made the call for police backup and an ambulance, a motorcycle started revving from behind a line of containers. It roared out heading straight toward them. Carter noticed a pillion passenger wielding a machete over his head and pushed the boy she was holding aside for his own safety. Estefana had seen the threat, grabbed a pole carrying baskets of vegetables someone had abandoned and swung it at the rider. He ducked but his pillion rider couldn't see the pole coming toward him. It hit his helmet and he tumbled with a thud onto the concrete. Carter managed to put a foot to his neck, pinning him to the ground, took the machete, and tossed it to one side. The rider made a sharp, skidding U-turn, came back, and kicked Carter clear of his companion. The pillon rider quickly clambered to his feet and reached for his machete but Estefana managed to kick it clear. He remounted the motorcycle and the two raced off. Just as they cleared the gate a second motorcycle emerged from behind the containers. It tore past Carter and Estefana out the gate of the port and was gone.

"Are you alright, *mana*?" Estefana asked as Carter stood and brushed down her clothes.

"Yeah, I'm fine," Carter said. "You?"

"I'm good too, *mana*," said Estefana. "What was all that?"

"Well it doesn't look like an assassination to me," said Carter reclaiming her hold on the boy with the 4:4 tattoo. "Perhaps our friend here can tell us what this was about when we get him to a police station."

They waited thirty minutes for the ambulance and another ten before two police officers arrived and took the boy into custody.

"Sorry it took this long, *mana*," one of the officers said to Estefana. "There aren't many of us on duty and they've spread us all over Dili."

• • •

As he headed back through the crowd Cordero noticed the gang tattoos on some of the younger members of the audience. He even recognized faces from Chiquito Santana's *Forsa* compound and from José Magno's *4:4* headquarters. There were members of other gangs and a few youths sporting red snakes tattooed to their necks or shoulders. Suddenly the crowd rushed forward and Cordero was propelled along with it. An honour guard was marching the coffins and caskets toward the platform where the dignitaries sat, the heavy military boots clip-clopping in step on the concrete tiles of the laneway. A *karau dikur*—a traditional instrument made from buffalo horns—sounded and the Defense Minister was shuffling notes as he rose to speak.

Cordero shouldered his way through the throng catching the occasional phrase from the Defense Minister as he went: "—spirit of the dead...heroes of the Fatherland...gave us freedom...." As he drew near the small contingent of *Samea Mean* members, Cordero spotted Rogerio, the boy who'd led him to Tristao, hoisted on his toes to see over the heads of the people in front of him.

"*Maun*," Cordero said to get Rogerio's attention.

"*Tarde*," Rogerio replied, lowering himself when he recognized Cordero but quickly raising himself up again to watch the proceedings.

"I've seen a lot of gang members here today, Rogerio," Cordero said. "I'm surprised they all seem to be getting along."

"Bigger things happening today than gang shit, *maun*," Rogerio said, shifting his head from side to side to get a better view. "Could be today."

"What could be today?" Cordero asked.

"Coming back, *maun*," Rogerio said cryptically. "Soon. Rising up and coming back. That's what Tristao says. He was there when some of these guerillas were buried first time years ago. He knows, *maun*. Maybe today."

"Speaking of Tristao," Cordero began, "I can't see him."

"Quim bringing him, *maun*," Rogerio replied. "He be somewhere."

"Who's Quim?" Cordero asked.

"What? Oh, he helps Tristao. Drives him around because Tristao don't see too good. Quim tells everyone what Tristao is thinking so he don't have to do it all the time," said Rogerio.

The Defense Minister pressed on with his speech, interrupted by high-pitched screeches from audio feedback: "—develop our country…provide for widows and orphans….the new Timor-Leste."

"You seen Quim yet?"

"Huh?" asked Rogerio.

"I said have you seen Quim here," Cordero repeated.

"No."

"You haven't seen Tristao either?"

"Not yet," Rogerio said growing impatient. "But he'll be here, *maun*. You see."

"What's Quim's full name?" Cordero asked. Rogerio was ignoring him now and was soon swallowed by the crowd as he pushed forward with it.

Timid applause broke out as the Defense Minister finished. Cordero thought it wise to get back to his seat quickly. He skirted around the crowd and climbed back onto the rear of the platform. The service commander seated next to him gave Cordero a disapproving look.

"Touch of food poisoning," Cordero offered by way of explanation. The service commander huffed and his medals rattled as he adjusted himself in his seat.

Quim—a popular Brazilian name but not a common one for Timorese, Cordero was thinking. *Could that be the man we heard yelling on the other side of the door when we left Tristao's office?*

Chapter 24

"You say you couldn't identify the others?" Cordero asked. He'd returned from Metinaro late on Sunday night and they'd woken him with a call early the next morning. He was tired and a little cranky as a result.

They'd met at Estefana's room and were heading to the police station to question the boy Carter had detained at the port. His friend had been taken to the hospital.

"The others wore helmets, long-sleeved shirts and bandanas around their necks," Estefana answered. "One seemed more heavy set than the others but that's all I could see."

"That it?" he asked.

"I don't think they wanted to be identified," said Carter, not trying to disguise her sarcasm.

"Did you look around Comoro for the truck?"

"Yeah and lots of other places," Carter said. "When they finally let us out of the police station. But we didn't find anything."

They inched along through the stop-start Monday morning traffic that only made Cordero crankier.

"You haven't told us about the ceremony. How was it?" Carter asked.

"Long and boring," Cordero answered. He wiped his face and tried to brighten up. "I saw Eurico there. I told him the story Tristao told us. He said it's linked to the idea that Timor's been corrupted by outside influences since independence and things need to start over."

He looked across at Carter. She made no comment.

"Eurico also said the story originates in Viqueque," Cordero added. "Tristao said it was a story from where he came from."

"Have you checked with whoever was keeping an eye on his compound?" she asked.

"I called before we caught up. Apart from the fact that a number of his boys left the compound yesterday—I saw them in Metinaro—nothing to report."

At the police station they were told that the boy from the port—Sefriano de Cruz—had been released. "What were we going to hold him on?" the desk officer complained when he saw their frustration. "There was no evidence he'd committed a crime. Everything pointed to him being a victim."

Cordero slapped his hand on the desk and turned to head out of the station. "He's gone to the general hospital, by the way," the desk officer added. "The other boy with the gash on his head? That's his brother."

They drove to the Guido Valaderes National Hospital on the eastern side of Dili and found Sefriano de Cruz in the general ward standing alongside his brother's bed. The brother seemed either sedated or asleep. Sefriano was a thin boy of fifteen or sixteen. The cast-off jeans, the torn, grubby T-shirt, and the worn flip-flops suggested Sefriano was very much part of the Dili underclass and probably a member of a gang for that reason.

They could see from under the bandages wrapped tightly around the top of his head, that the brother was a little older, perhaps eighteen or nineteen. The edge of a 4:4 tattoo on his neck protruded from the sheet draped across him.

Cordero introduced himself and his companions, and picked up the patient's record on a clipboard at the end of the bed. Sefriano was ignoring him. Cordero summarised what was on the clipboard for Carter and Estefana:

"'Salvio de Cruz. Lacerated forehead requiring ten stitches and suspected moderate concussion. Bed rest. Hydrate every two hours.'"

He replaced the clipboard, stared at the patient a moment, and turned to Sefriano.

"What was this about?" he asked.

Sefriano kept his eyes on his brother and said nothing.

Cordero placed a hand on Sefriano's arm, swung him around and asked again.

"What was this about, Sefriano?"

His brother stirred and Sefriano pivoted back to the bed.

"I don't know," Sefriano said. "I don't know nothing."

"A group of guys attacked you and your brother and you're telling me you don't know what it was about?"

"Yeah," he said.

"They nearly killed him, Sefriano," Cordero said, but again the boy ignored him.

The older boy seemed to be listening to the exchange. He coughed, put a hand to his head then gestured for the younger boy's attention.

The two brothers started muttering together. The only word Cordero could hear clearly was "*Polisia*". Salvio urged his brother to move closer and whispered in his ear. They argued for a moment but Salvio seemed the more insistent of the two.

"What are you two talking about?" asked Cordero. Sefriano wiped dribble off his brother's chin.

"I ain't admitting to nothing," Sefriano said.

"I'm not asking you to admit to anything," Cordero assured the boy. "You've been released without charge. We're not after you, we're after the people who attacked you and your brother. And we can't get them unless you tell me what this was about."

Sefriano rubbed his hands on the sides of his pants: they came away even grubbier than before. He stared at Cordero, looked back down at his brother, and lent back against the wall at the head of the bed.

"They say drugs are unloaded at the port," he began, distancing the account from himself and his brother. "Drugs that come in on that fast ferry from West Timor."

"What kind of drugs?" Cordero asked.

"Pills and stuff, *maun*! How should I know?"

"Okay, go on," said Cordero not wanting to scare the boy into silence.

"They say guys get the drugs from the ferry and take them into town. Used to be there was only one guy went to get the drugs but now there's more so no one knows who's carrying the drugs when they leave." He stared at Cordero. "More dangerous now," he explained.

The boy in the bed started coughing. Sefriano pushed himself off the wall and calmed his brother by stroking his hair. The coughing stopped and Salvio gestured to his brother to continue.

"They say others want the drugs now. Don't have the right connections to get them themselves, you know? Or maybe not to get them fast. Maybe that's what happened yesterday."

"You mean a shipment came in, the couriers were attacked, and someone took off with the drugs?"

Sefriano looked at Cordero directly. "Maybe something like that, *maun.*"

"What happens to these drugs?" Cordero asked.

"Maybe sold to tourists in the bars. Maybe sold to *zinzan*," he said using the derogatory expression for Chinese working long hours on the projects. "But that shit money." Sefriano paused. "Bigger shipments can be sent to other countries for more money."

"Why would the drugs be brought here only to be sent out again?" Cordero asked.

Sefriano shrugged.

"I think I can answer that," Carter said. Estefana had been translating the conversation. "From what I've read at INTERPOL, shipments from Indonesia are carefully scrutinized in places like Australia, Malaysia, Thailand. It's mainly to do with people being smuggled out of Iran and Afghanistan by criminals operating out of Indonesia. People smugglers don't operate out of East Timor. And the country's seen as low risk. There are no hard drugs produced here and no systemic police corruption. A shipment from here wouldn't attract as much attention as one from Indonesia."

Sefriano showed no interest in what Carter was saying and didn't ask for a translation. He bent back over the bed to check on his brother.

"Where were the customs officers?" Cordero asked.

"What?" Sefriano asked.

"I asked where the customs officers were on Sunday."

"They say the shipments come on weekends only," the boy answered. "No one wants to work on weekends. Want to be home with their families. So they don't look too hard, you know? Besides, yesterday people were at those big burials. Especially the bosses. Others lazy because there's no one to check what they do."

"Do you know who these 'others' who want the drugs are?" asked Cordero.

"No," the boy said. He lent back against the wall. "Three months ago a brothel we—I mean other guys—ran in Balide was fire bombed. The ones meant to guard the place ran to a shed out back to get a parcel. They didn't care about the fire or the girls, you know what I'm saying? Girls are easy to find—from China, Thailand, anywhere. Drugs are hard to find. Someone was watching and that must have given them the idea. We—I mean a gang—lost a rider two weeks ago. Lost his stuff too, you know? He was killed. I hear the same thing happened to another guy a week ago."

"Have you heard anything about someone who was abducted after that second boy was attacked and killed?" asked Estefana.

"No," replied Sefriano. "But it don't surprise. These guys will do anything to get their hands on the drugs."

Cordero was starting to see how things connected. "What I can't understand is if a shipment was coming in yesterday, why wasn't it better protected by the guys taking delivery?" he asked.

"Like I told you, *maun*, lot of guys went to Metinaro. The cop said he'd make sure no one left in Dili would be around the port to bother us." He checked again on his brother. Salvio was reaching for water and Sefriano helped him.

"What did you just say?" Cordero asked, jerking back the boy's shoulder.

"I said we were told they'd be no police there to bother us," he said.

"Who told you this?"

"How should I know, *maun*? Some cop. Only saw him once talking to José inside the gate at the warehouse. I remember because I trod on the fucking gum he spat out and spent a lot of time scraping it off my shoe."

• • •

"An officer who can guarantee to a gang leader there won't be police around the port when a drug shipment comes in? Sounds like a senior officer to me," said Carter as they left the hospital and walked to Cordero's vehicle.

"Maybe," agreed Cordero. "Or maybe an officer given the job of deploying a skeleton staff across the city. Who'd raise questions about why there were police in one location but not another? Everyone knew there weren't enough to go around." He stopped at the driver's door and tossed his keys from one hand to the other.

"Even so, it could be a problem," Carter said.

"It's not our priority," he said.

"What the hell, Cordero!" she complained.

"Who's investigation is this anyway?" he asked, annoyed by her second guessing him. "You don't have policing authority, remember?"

He unlocked the vehicle and climbed in behind the driver's seat. She climbed in beside him.

"It's *Samea Mean* we're looking at," he said, composing himself. "I'd say our friend Tristao dredged up this old legend about the fallen guerillas rising from the dead to renew the country, spread it among impressionable young guys in gangs who don't feel they've benefitted from independence, and told them the city needs to be purified of drugs before anything can happen. Then he makes the connection to the burials in Metinaro on Sunday to give the idea urgency and get most gang members out of Dili. The few boys he trusts stay in the city to intercept Sunday's shipment and retrieve the other drugs he thinks are about to be buried in a coffin on Monday. After that, Tristao disappears with the lot as things start getting too hot to stick around."

"What do we do now, *maun*?" asked Estefana, taking the back seat. "What about Josinto?"

"First we go to my office and arrange backup for tonight. After that we'll keep watch at the Santa Ana cemetery. We wait until they come back and dig up the coffin. Then we follow them and get Josinto. We'll have them for abduction and detention. That's eight years jail time in Timor—just for starters. We can link them to the drugs I found in Balide. And we can link them to the murder of Jenito Fuentes. His girlfriend will probably be able to identify them as the guys who tried to kill her. With a bargain to reduce a possible thirty years or more in prison, I'm sure one or two will give up Tristao. Then we go after him."

Cordero turned the ignition. Clouds were thickening and darkening over the sea to the north and wind was gusting. He ducked down for a better look at the sky through the windscreen.

"More rain on its way," he said. "A quick stop at my office, then it's off to what's shaping up to be a drizzly graveyard."

"How appropriate," Carter muttered.

Chapter 25

"You're saying a coffin maker is the key to this?" asked Cordero's superior, Chief Investigator Francisco Jada. "That seems implausible."

Jada had flown back to Dili the night before. He'd been sitting behind his desk, in the offices of the Scientific Police for Criminal Investigations, going through the memos that had piled up in his absence. He was a big man with a greying burr cut and a dark and heavy moustache. His uniform was spotless, the braiding bright and impressive in contrast to the subdued light in the room as another storm prepared to hit the city. Cordero stood in front of Jada's desk, Carter and Estefana slightly to one side.

"He's the coffin maker's apprentice and he's the key," answered Cordero. "A witness saw his truck being followed by suspected gang members and another saw three men in the cabin of the truck a little later after we think he was abducted."

"You *think*?" repeated Jada.

"We suspect the people who took him are the people responsible for killing the boys from different gangs recently," Cordero continued, ignoring the sarcasm. "They've been led to believe the missing drugs they're after—the drugs I turned up last week—were placed in a coffin the apprentice was working on. When they dig it up and don't find the drugs tonight we could have a third murder on our hands."

"Is this some kind of prank on your part, Tino?" Jada asked.

"No sir."

Cordero's superior grunted. "We're a specialist investigative unit," he said. "We investigate crimes. We don't kick down doors. Why aren't the regular police doing this?"

"All of the police officers assigned to the burials at the Heroes Cemetery in Metinaro yesterday have been given today off," Cordero explained. "Most of the officers on duty tonight are junior."

A thunderclap rolled across the sky.

"Alright but why aren't you asking them for backup?" Jada asked.

"This is going to take people with considerable experience and maturity," Cordero explained. "That's why I'm asking for Lucas and Manuel."

Jada picked up a pen and tapped his desk. "This one," he nodded toward Estefana. "She looks young and inexperienced to me."

"Estefana has a vested interest in the case," Cordero said. "The coffin maker's apprentice is her fiancé."

Jada looked at him sharply. "You're joking," he said. "And you want a young, inexperienced female officer with an emotional connection in the case as part of your team? Haven't you learnt—"

More thunder masked the start of Cordero's answer but he continued "—on two previous cases. It's in my reports. She's a very capable officer and I can rely on her completely." Cordero turned to Estefana. "Besides, she won't be armed."

"And the American woman?" Jada grumbled, eyeing Carter but continuing to talk in Tetun. "I don't want her involved. Understand? If she gets hurt we'll be in a lot of shit with our government, her government. And if she injures anyone else we'll be in just as much shit." He rose from the desk, thrust his hands in his pockets and paced the room. "She's definitely out!"

Estefana was translating for Carter who, when she heard this remark, opened her shoulder bag and produced her INTERPOL identification card.

"Show him this," she said to Cordero. "Tell him we're dealing with imported drugs and that's a legitimate reason for INTERPOL to be involved." Cordero took the card and passed it to his superior. "Tell him I'm just an observer," she added. The man looked at the card and sniffed acknowledgement. He handed the card back to Carter and began pacing again. Thunder cracked over Dili a third time, a bright flash of lightning lit the room, and the first heavy raindrops began pounding the window. Jada peered out as the downpour began.

"All right," he said and turned to Cordero. "You can have Savoy and Fonseca, but only if they volunteer."

"They'll need authorization," Cordero pointed out. "To carry arms and use them if necessary."

"I know that," the superior barked. "I'll give them authorization but only if they volunteer, you hear?" He turned back to the window. "Yours isn't the only ass that needs covering here, Tino."

As they walked down the corridor to Cordero's office he leaned across to Carter. "That was a close call," he said. "Always is with him. He's calculating the political consequences of every decision he makes." They reached Cordero's office. "Good thing you kept that old ID card," he added and opened the door for Carter and Estefana to enter. "Both of you trust me in here," he whispered as he let them pass.

Lucas was sitting with his feet on his desk reading a newspaper and he didn't turn toward the door when it opened because he figured no one of interest would be coming in. Then he noticed Manuel's surprise and almost knocked his computer terminal off the desk in his haste to stand and greet Carter. Lucas had met Carter before—briefly—and was smitten by her. Manuel shifted his eyes from Carter to Estefana and he broke into a grin.

"You know FBI Agent Carter," said Cordero. He walked to his desk, leaned against it, folded his arms, and faced them. "And this is Estefana dos Carvalho from the regular police. She's on vacation but has agreed to help us." Cordero gestured to his colleagues in turn. "Lucas and Manuel," he said by way of introduction.

"It's a—" Manuel began to mumble.

"Pleasure," Lucas interjected in his limited English. "It's a pleasure to see, I mean *have*, both of you visit. Could I get either of you a coffee, tea?"

"No time for that," said Cordero. "We have an operation tonight that we want you both to be part of."

"A cool drink, perhaps?" said Lucas, taking no notice of Cordero.

Carter smiled and moved next to Cordero. Estefana remained by the door.

"Lucas!" Cordero said. "I need you to pay attention. You too, Manuel," he said, noticing Manuel's eyes had settled on Estefana.

"We have reason to believe the people responsible for the two murders I've been investigating are holding a hostage until they retrieve drugs they stole and believe were stashed in a coffin to be buried in Santa Ana cemetery this afternoon. Tonight we suspect they'll dig the coffin up. When they don't find the drugs, they'll head back to wherever they're holding this hostage and take out their disappointment on him. Before they do that we're going to jump them, release the hostage, and convince those who abducted him to lead us to the mastermind behind these murders and stolen drug shipments."

"I'm not on duty tonight, *maun*," said Lucas.

"Me neither," said Manuel.

They were both still focused on the women in the room.

"I have, umm, a law lecture," Manuel added. "You know, at university."

Cordero ignored them and went on. "We think a guy in Comoro by the name of Tristao is behind this. He pretends to be a spiritual leader who initiates people into his cult by giving them betel quids with a special spice mix he makes. I believe these were the quids found in the mouths of our two murder victims. This Tristao tells his followers that if they clean up the drugs in Dili, the dead *Falintil* will rise again and win the country for them. If we convince the grave diggers to talk, we've got him."

"Interesting case," said Lucas. "But I'm not on duty, like I said."

"I know that," said Cordero. "But the boss says he'll authorize you to take part if you both volunteer."

"Well sorry, Tino," Manuel said turning to face him. "You know I'd help you out but this is an important lecture and I don't want to miss it."

"You missed the last two," said Cordero.

"That's why I don't want to miss tonight," answered Manuel.

"Yeah and I'm about to start an eight day shift, *maun*," Lucas chimed in. "There's things I need to do first."

"The way I figure it," Cordero continued, ignoring their objections, "we'll follow these guys from the cemetery to the hideout. Neither of the women here will be armed. Lucas, you'll have to partner *Mana* Carter and Manuel, you'll partner *Mana* Estefana."

Instantly Cordero saw the faces of his two colleagues brighten.

"Well of course they'll need protection if they're not armed," said Lucas, smiling at Carter. "Why didn't you say that in the first place, Tino?"

"I'd be only too happy to help out this young lady," Manuel said, standing up and moving alongside Estefana. "The lecture is only theory about the law whereas this will be a very practical expression of the law in action. And if you are a new police officer *mana*—"

"Okay that's settled," Cordero cut in and headed behind his desk. "I'll tell Jada you've volunteered." The rain was now bucketing down and it was hard to hear across the expanse of the office. "Gather round," Cordero shouted, "and we'll go through what I've got in mind."

Cordero took a map of Dili from a drawer, spread it on his desk, and tapped one spot. "Here is the Santa Ana cemetery," he said above the torrent of rain, "and we think they're holding the hostage over here in Comoro or Balide." All were bent over the map now. "Carter, Estefana and I will keep an eye on the cemetery. We don't expect them before nightfall when they can dig up the coffin unseen," Cordero continued. "But we need to be in position beforehand so as not to arouse suspicion. Carter and Estafana will keep watch together because two women hanging about will not seem unusual and I'll keep watch from the other side of the cemetery. I want you two to park here," he said and pointed to a place on the map two blocks from the cemetery entrance, "and keep out of sight."

"You sure the burial will go ahead with all this rain?" asked Lucas.

"The rain'll be over soon," said Cordero. "The burial starts around five o'clock. Water may pool in the grave but I'm sure they can deal with that. The family've already held on to the body for days. They'll want to bury it."

He leaned over the map. "I'll follow the grave robbers in my vehicle, Estefana and Carter on a motorcycle, and you two in your vehicle. That way, if it looks like they suspect a tail, the lead can peel off and there'll be another who can stay with them. When we get to wherever they're heading we're going to have to move fast. Lucas and Carter pair up, Estefana and Manuel pair up. I'll be okay on my own. That gives us three points of attack." He stood again. "These guys will be furious and they'll get to work on their hostage as soon as they get the chance. We'll have to decide how we'll approach and do it quickly. Remember, these guys have tortured, kidnapped and killed twice. They don't fool around."

He folded the map. "I'll organise three police radios. You two," he said gesturing to Lucas and Manuel, "sign out a pistol each. We don't know if these guys are armed but they certainly have knives and machetes. It won't be dark until after seven o'clock but be ready from half five. Okay? Any questions?"

Lucas and Manuel shook their heads, all business now... almost.

"When this is over," Lucas said and grinned toward Carter, "and we have released that hostage, we'll all have to celebrate together."

"*Bele deit!*" offered Carter in her limited Tetun. It meant 'Of course' and she said it with a practiced smile.

Chapter 26

The Santa Ana cemetery had been dedicated during Portuguese colonial times. Now it was congested, almost derelict and due to be closed. Only those few Timorese with space left in family plots were allowed to be buried there. *Senyor* Sebastien Boavides was one such: his grandfather had purchased a large family gravesite over one hundred years earlier and the Boavides had been laid to rest there ever since. Sebastien would be the last.

On the rusty gates opening on to the cemetery was a sign that read '*Sidade ne'ebe ema mate ona*'—'City of the dead'. Beyond the gates lay rows of graves with professions of affection and faith eroding on headstones weary from marking the resting place of loved ones for years. Weeds grew out of the sunken graves and vines snaked along what long ago were neatly pebbled paths. Time and the salt air had taken its toll on monuments that stood cracked and worn while others were on a lean and many had collapsed completely. Against its original intention the cemetery had become a stark reminder of the impermanence of all things and little more now than a shrine to the macabre.

The rain had long ceased falling and the storm had drifted off. Eerie veils of mist now hung through the headstones and above the few tiled vaults in the fading light. Carter and Estefana had positioned themselves in a small kiosk diagonally opposite the cemetery gates. The owner, a woman in her sixties, made space for them in a small back room crowded with supplies to be sold. Against a dusty window she attached a rag to act as a curtain so they couldn't be seen from outside. Carter balanced uncomfortably on a tiny stool, Estefana sat on an unopened box of Chinese canned tuna.

When they first arrived, the Boavides burial was in progress. Twelve adults and fifteen children in their best clothes huddled around the grave while a priest in solemn vestments recited prayers and three young men from the entourage began shovelling damp soil onto the sunken coffin. Eventually the crowd dispersed, the widow of *Senyor* Boavides sobbing as she was helped along on the arms of two younger women.

Now only two very old women dressed in black and unrelated to the Boavides family were in the cemetery. They finished a rosary over a grave at the rear and blessed themselves. Each in turn placed a hand lightly on the headstone, turned and shuffled out the gate arm in arm.

"Perhaps they were visiting the husband of one of them," Estefana commented. "Maybe it was his birthday or their wedding anniversary."

"Could be," Carter said, taking little interest.

A motorcycle pulled up at the kiosk and the rider offered a cheery *"Botarde"* to the owner. The voice was a woman's. She continued to chat as she dismounted. Carter snuck a peek and could see she was middle-aged and neatly dressed in a business skirt and blouse. She cut the engine and bought gasoline in a plastic bottle. She unscrewed the cap on her tank, poured in the fuel, returned the bottle, thanked the kiosk owner, and rode off.

"I don't know what I'd do if I lost Josinto," Estefana was saying. "What would I do without him?"

"You're not going to lose him," Carter said, tiring of Estefana's negativity.

"Have you ever been in love and lost that person, *mana*?"

"One way or another most people of a certain age have, Estefana," Carter answered. "That's life."

"I don't think I could bear it, *mana*. I don't know I could start again."

Through the curtain they could hear the giggling of two very young children as they approached the kiosk counter. The older one, a boy, asked for a package of cigarettes saying they were for his father. Carter and Estefana caught the sound of coins as the boy dropped them on the counter, and scooped them into a pile. The kiosk owner handed the boy the cigarettes and separated fifty centavos from the pile of coins in change. The younger child, a girl, reminded the boy that their father had said they could spend ten centavos on themselves. They quibbled over what to get: the boy said a soda, the girl a chocolate bar. They compromised on a bag of boiled candy, thanked the kiosk owner, and raced back down the muddy road to their home.

"I wish I was strong like you, *mana*," Estefana said. "You can come back from a loss like that but I don't know that I can."

A woman carrying a newborn in a sling strolled up to the kiosk and asked for baby formula in a weary voice. Behind her a man pushed through, excused himself, paid for a plastic lighter, and left leaving a trail of cigarette smoke in his wake.

"We're going to find Josinto, Estefana," Carter said to avoid having to rake over her own past. "And then you and he are going to get married, just like you planned. So let's just concentrate on what we're here to do."

• • •

Cordero had parked in a concealed part of the yard of a large, two-storey house built along the boundary line at the side of the cemetery. The house was deserted and locked but stairs on the side led up to an overgrown rooftop garden where he could keep watch over the whole cemetery without being seen. A lamp near the cemetery gate came on, throwing a pale yellow beam across the first few rows of graves. Off in the distance a baby began to wail and a rooster crowed even though it was on nightfall.

He knew he could be wrong about this whole thing. His superior, Francisco Jada, was right to be skeptical. The idea that a gang would come back to dig up a coffin in search of drugs was far-fetched. Indeed, it seemed more and more far-fetched as the minutes ticked by. Perhaps they'd stolen Josinto's truck for other reasons such as a robbery or a hit on a rival gang. But why would anyone use a truck adorned with images of coffins and bound to draw attention for either purpose? Perhaps they hadn't stolen

Josinto's truck or abducted him at all. What had the police officer Estefana had spoken to said? Three men in the cabin of the truck he saw seemed to be laughing.

Then there was Tristao. The only connection Tristao had to any of this was that he told a story about a legendary girl called Biloi from Viqueque which is where an old woman selling onions claimed the spice mixture in the betel quids had originated. What had Cordero insisted all along about solid evidence?

He brushed a hand across his face, cleared his mind of doubt as best he could, and turned his attention back to the graves below.

• • •

Lucas and Manuel sat in an unmarked police car on the corner up from the Santa Ana cemetery where Cordero had instructed them to park. There were houses either side of them and a group of children sat on the gutter in the half-light flicking marbles onto the sidewalk, racing after them, sitting back down and doing it all again.

Lucas and Manuel were eating the take-out satay chicken and rice Manuel had picked up from an Indonesian restaurant on the way. Manuel stopped chewing, his plastic fork poised above his container.

"They say you never want to be shot on an empty stomach," he told Lucas. "You bleed out more slowly if your stomach is full."

"Is that right? I thought it was because they put you on a liquid diet for days in the hospital," Lucas countered.

"Whatever," Manuel said, taking another mouthful.

Two girls strolled passed their car in miniskirts. Manuel's eyes followed them.

"That Estefana's cute," he said, when the girls had turned a corner.

"So?" asked Lucas.

"Well, I'm an experienced investigator," said Manuel. "I could show her a thing or two she might find useful. You know, in her career as a police officer."

"You wish," replied Lucas.

Manuel laughed. They finished their meals and placed the containers in a plastic bag on the floor of the vehicle behind their seats. Lucas wiped his mouth and hands with a kerchief. Manuel used the back of his hand and wiped it on his trousers.

"What makes you think you're a chance with the American?" he asked Lucas.

"Who says I think I am?" Lucas said.

"Come on, *maun*," taunted Manuel. "I saw how you looked at her in the office. She does have a nice figure." He smiled at the thought. "And what was that about us all celebrating when we catch the bad guys?"

Lucas eased back in his seat behind the wheel. "Let me explain something, *maun*," he said. "These American women—they're all looking for something different, something exotic, you know what I'm saying? I've seen it in movies. Why else you think she's here, in Timor-Leste? And me—well you can't get more exotic than that, see? I'm about her age and her type—fit, handsome. And she's looking for novelty and adventure. Like all American women. Simple as that."

Manuel laughed at the explanation. "You might have to argue the case with Tino, *maun*," he said.

"Tino? Come on, *maun*," said Lucas. "He's not interested in such things. Have you ever known him to take an interest in women? He likes his freedom too much to care about the hard work they require."

"What hard work?" asked Manuel.

"You know, *maun*. All the stuff you gotta say to them, all the fuss you gotta make. None of that's for Tino."

They were silent a moment.

"You ready for this shit tonight?" Manuel asked.

"What shit—with those two women?" Lucas said.

"No *maun*, the gang shit and the guns and stuff," said Manuel.

"Ready as I'll ever be," said Lucas. He looked across to Manuel. "Besides, *maun*, you want to impress Estefana, don't you? What better way to impress a girl than by being a hero tonight?"

They were laughing when the police radio came to life. It was Cordero. Three youths had entered the cemetery with shovels and a lamp and they'd started to dig up the grave of the late *Senyor* Sebastien Boavides.

Chapter 27

The youths had left their motorcycles twenty yards from the cemetery entrance—far enough to suggest they were visiting a house nearby but close enough to make a quick exit if the need arose. From there they'd strode into the cemetery, two carrying shovels and one a kerosene lamp and a crowbar. From his rooftop vantage point Cordero watched them search the rows of graves for the one of Sebastien Boavides. They soon found the family plot with the fresh flowers and got to work.

They collected the wreaths in a heap and started to dig. The soil was soft and after ten minutes they'd uncovered the coffin. Two were standing in the grave, showing no reticence about the dead typical of Timorese. The youth with the lamp handed the crowbar to one of the others whose head popped up from the hole. Cordero imagined they would jimmy off the lid of the coffin, take out the body, rip open the lining, and ferret around for the drugs—and come up empty. Sure enough a shrouded body was lifted out and dumped onto the side of the grave. A minute passed, then two, then three. The body was flung back roughly into the coffin and the two youths hoisted themselves out of the pit. Both were caked in mud. They quickly refilled the grave, haphazardly replaced the wreaths, and extinguished the lamp. They ran out of the cemetery, mounted their motorcycles, and took off kicking up slush behind them.

Cordero was already on his radio to Carter. He told her and Estefana to follow the three because two women close behind on a motorcycle would raise the least suspicion. He would come next, followed by Lucas and Manuel. They should radio if anything went wrong.

The youths rode off at speed but Estefana, Cordero and Lucas had lined up at a distance behind them by the time they were on *Avenida 20 de Maio* and heading west. There wasn't much traffic at this time of night and it was easy to make out the three motorcycle tail lights in the distance. *A smarter lot would have split up,* Cordero was thinking, *but they're probably young, obviously in a hurry, and have no reason to suspect they're being followed.*

Everything was going according to plan until the motorcyclists approached the intersection with the arterial *Rua de Catedral.* A truck carrying a load of live chickens had collided with a microlet, toppled on its side, and spilled wooden cages of terrified chickens across the road. People who'd been sitting and chatting outside houses nearby went to the aid of the truck driver or were trying to collect chickens and secure them in what was left of the cages. Feathers drifted like snow across the scene. Traffic was banking up in all directions. Only motorcycles had any chance of getting through the blockage.

The three motorcyclists kicked chickens and cages out of their way and made short work of the obstacle. Estefana managed to do the same but Cordero, and Lucas behind him, were brought to a stop. Cordero radioed Lucas to back up before more vehicles hemmed him in. He and Manuel should take *Travessa de Vila Verde* and make their way beyond the cathedral into Comoro. Cordero was in position to try a shorter route through alleyways and would try to catch up with Estefana further along *Rua de Catedral.*

It didn't work. Lucas negotiated his way along back streets and emerged on the edge of Comoro but could see no sign of the motorcyclists he'd followed from Santa Ana or of Estefana. Cordero hadn't gotten far at all: he'd been blocked in the first alley by an abandoned yellow taxi, its wheels removed, and a scraggy old man organising himself to sleep across the rear seat. He radioed to get Carter's position but was told Estefana had no idea what road they were on.

"Damn it!" he said.

"They're not big on road signs around here, Cordero, and Estefana has been in Dili less time than me," replied Carter. "Start thinking."

"Are there any landmarks you can see?" he asked.

As he waited for an answer he reversed out of the alley and back onto *Avenida 20 de Maio*. He'd just have to force his way through.

The radio crackled and Carter came on again. "We just passed a large compound behind a high wall with a few of soldiers milling around and we're now near a poor excuse for a sports field or something," said Carter.

"Okay," said Cordero. "I think I know where you are." He picked up Lucas on the radio. "I think they're on the south side of the defense force headquarters, near that field where Australian peacekeepers used to play football," he said. "There are abandoned industrial buildings on the west of that, warehouses, garages—the kind of place you could easily hide a truck. Know where I mean?"

"Sure," said Lucas. "I'm on it."

Cordero shouted to the people chasing chickens to clear a space for a police emergency. It took half a minute but a man and a woman shifted cages out of his way and he was able to mount the sidewalk and drive through the wreckage. People cursed and raised their fists in protest but he ignored them, drove onto the other side of the road around the truck on its side, forced a motorcyclist off his bike, and shot down the thoroughfare and around the corner.

It was then he noticed a police officer on a motorcycle chasing him. He was probably one of the junior officers on duty tonight and he had the siren blaring and the lights flashing—the last thing Cordero needed if he was to sneak up on the gang holding Josinto. He could stop, show his badge and explain himself but that would take more time than he had. Police officers, especially junior ones, were slow to dismount, slower to walk to the driver of a vehicle, and slowest of all to comprehend what they were being told and accept it.

Instead Cordero executed a park brake turn—something he'd perfected as a bored teenager fooling around with old cars in

Northern Australia. He spun the wheel, pulled on the park brake, and threw the car wildly around through 180 degrees almost on the spot. Tyres smoking, he accelerated toward the officer who'd been chasing him. It took the officer a hundred yards to comprehend what had happened and turn safely. By then Cordero was nowhere to be seen. A few more alleys—not blocked by abandoned taxis—and he was in the general area he'd told Lucas to head for.

He drove past several intersections checking this way and that. He couldn't see either Lucas or Estefana.

"Shit!" he cursed and hit the steering wheel with the palm of his hand.

Seconds later he caught Lucas's car emerging from a side street and pulling to a stop on the side of the road. Estefana and Carter were right behind him. Estefana dismounted, removed her helmet, and snuck in a crouch up the darkened street they had just exited. Cordero pulled up next to Carter.

"They went into a kind of mechanic's workshop or garage or something just up that street," she said, taking off her helmet. Cordero waved to Lucas and Manuel to join them.

Estefana hurried back, puffing. "I can't see any security cameras," she said. "And the main doors are just tin sheets, *maun*. I think they will give way if we can hit them hard enough."

Chapter 28

They snuck up as far as they dared to get a good look at the workshop and its immediate surroundings. Either side were repair shops of various kinds protected by heavy steel grating that the weeds growing through the bearing bars indicated hadn't been opened for years. The workshop they were focused had also seen better days. Once it had been painted white but neglect had seen the paint wear and, in the unforgiving tropical climate, the rawness of the cement block walls was showing through instead. A window was boarded up, the glass missing, and a sign advertising the business over the roof had faded to a smudge and was covered in razor wire. The main double doors, as Estefana had said, were little more than sheets of rusted tin nailed to timber frames. A separate single door near the window may have led to a small office. It was securely bolted up.

They could make out the roof of a large warehouse at the back flush against the rear walls of the row of buildings in front. That meant no rear access and no meddling neighbours that the gang would have to worry about. It also meant no entry or exit except through the front. The whole area seemed to Cordero to date from the days when the UN administered the country and needed garages and workshops for its trucks and machinery. Abandoned now, it was the perfect place to hide a stolen truck and its driver.

"I'll crash straight through those double doors," said Cordero. "That'll get their attention." He turned to the others. "Carter, you follow Lucas in on my left. Estefana you follow Manuel on my right. Let's go!"

Cordero ran back to his vehicle, climbed in, and swung into the street. When he could see the others had taken up their positions he pushed the accelerator to the floor, roared up the street, turned sharply, and hit the brakes just as the vehicle impacted the double doors. There was a defeaning bang followed by the crack of sheared wooden frames and the clang of metal sheets shattering into the center of the garage. Cordero jerked to a stop inside the workshop just behind Josinto's truck, knocking over two motorcycles as he did. Dust clouded his view in the dingy interior. One gang member had been struck by a sheet of tin and fallen backwards onto the floor. He staggered to his feet and ran toward the gap Cordero had made in the entrance. Cordero swung his driver's door into his path and the youth collided with a thud and collapsed unconscious on the ground.

Lucas rushed through on Cordero's left and forced a youth stunned by the mayhem onto his knees. He scanned the darkened interior of the garage with his pistol extended. Carter was close behind. Manuel and Estefana made their way gingerly over the wreckage of the double doors but she abruptly stopped, grabbed Manuel and pulled him back. At the rear of the garage, by the flickering light of a kerosene lamp, was Josinto, tied, blindfolded, tape over his mouth, and propped up by someone pressing a knife to his throat.

"Don't come any closer!" the figure yelled. "I'll fucking kill him if you do!"

As his eyes adjusted to the poor light, Lucas could make out Josinto and the gang member clutching the knife to his throat. He stopped advancing but kept his weapon trained on the youth holding Josinto. Cordero had jumped out of his vehicle, kicked a timber strut out of his way, and come to the front of Josinto's truck. He studied the figure with the knife. Though the light was faint and the dust still settling, Cordero made out a huge red lump on the side of the youth's head. He recalled that Carter had caused it with a shovel when they'd gone looking for Tristao.

"Hello Zico. I see you got yourself a new knife," Cordero said.

"Fuck you!" the boy shouted. The eye near the lump was twitching as though trying to focus. "I've got another knife, yeah, and I'll use it if you don't all back off."

"That wouldn't be smart, Zico," Cordero said.

"I don't give a shit about smart. I'll kill him!"

"Then my friends here would have to shoot you," Cordero said. "Why don't you let him go and give me the knife?"

The blindfold had slipped down over Josinto's face as he'd struggled to free himself. The whites of his eyes were enlarged with fear and he was sucking air through his nose above the tape covering his mouth. His neck remained exposed to the blade. Estefana moved closer toward him, stopped, and extended a hand in a pitiful gesture of support.

"Put the knife down, Zico," Cordero urged him. "Nobody has to get hurt."

Cordero inched closer.

"Stay where you are!" Zico shouted and his grip tightened around the knife.

The boy under Lucas's foot wriggled and he tried to sit up. Lucas kneed him in the head without taking his aim off Zico. Manuel also had his pistol pointing squarely at Zico but every time the boy struggled with Josinto a support column in the building would block a clear shot. Manuel slid to the side hoping for a better angle.

"Stop!" Zico shouted turning in Manuel's direction. "I know what you're trying to do. I'll kill him, I tell you. If you come any closer I'll kill him!"

Carter had edged through the shadows along a wall of the workshop until she was almost within reach of Josinto. She was on the side of Zico's injured eye. He sensed the movement but couldn't quite make her out.

"You!" he shouted. "Get back! You hear! Get back!"

Carter stopped...waited.

"Come on, Zico," Cordero said. "It's over. Give it up before you get hurt."

"Fuck off! All of you!" Zico shouted. As he did he moved slightly so that he was facing Carter directly and the kerosene lamp threw a slither of light on her face. Zico recognised her immediately. "You, you bitch!" he yelled and lunged at her instinctively.

As he thrust down with the knife, Carter grabbed Zico's wrist with her left hand and came up hard under his elbow with her right. The grip on the knife loosened. She swivelled slightly and elbowed Zico solidly in the face once, twice, until he dropped the knife and fell to the ground.

Cordero rolled Zico over, grabbed both his arms behind his back, and cuffed him. He took out a kerchief and collected the knife.

"Good work," he said, pocketing the knife.

Estefana rushed to Josinto, removed the tape over his mouth, and untied his hands.

Manuel and Lucas holstered their weapons and cuffed the other two who lay on the ground.

"There's another," Cordero said to no one in particular.

"What?" asked Lucas.

"Only one of these guys is covered in mud. Where's the other one who dug up the coffin?" Cordero asked.

"He's right," Manuel called from the other side of the workshop. "Three guys on motorcycles plus one on the door. That's four. We've only got three. There's another here somewhere."

Lucas redrew his pistol and slid into the abandoned office. A stack of chairs was piled in the corner, empty food containers covered a desk, and a rusting filing cabinet lined one wall. But there was no fourth gang member.

"Nothing here," he called.

Cordero carefully checked a stack of dust-covered cardboard boxes piled high against the rear wall…nothing. Manuel checked the cabin of Josinto's truck. Again, there was nothing.

"There!" shouted Carter.

A boy was crawling from under Josinto's truck. He rose to his feet and scrambled over the wreckage of the doors to get outside. Manuel was nearest and went after him.

It was dark outside. To his right Manuel made out no movement. On the other side he heard the youth's flip-flops and saw a shadowy figure heading up the muddy road. The boy slipped in the slosh caused by the rain and Manuel gained on him. Forty yards on he caught the silhouette of the youth in the headlights of a truck moving up fast behind them both.

The youth was looking over his left shoulder at Manuel not the right shoulder and the truck. Just as Manuel drew near the boy made a sudden dash out and across the road. The truck made no attempt to stop or veer. The boy froze. Manuel dived at him to thrust him clear. The side of the truck hit them both but the fugitive hardest of all. The two tumbled onto the side of the road, the youth screaming in pain.

"Manuel!" Lucas cried as he ran up the road.

"Over here!" answered Manuel.

"You all right, *maun*? I thought that truck wiped you out for sure," said Lucas. "Thought I'd be scraping you off the road. You fool!"

"Shit my leg hurts," Manuel complained, rubbing his right shin and ankle. "Check him," he said gesturing to the youth at his side.

Lucas examined the boy. He was screaming and trying to rub his legs but that only made the pain worse. Lucas clearly made out the shape of a broken bone in the boy's right leg. The left leg also seemed badly damaged. He thought it best not to touch either and leaned back over to Manuel.

"Military trucks," Lucas said. "I've warned you before they're trained not to stop for anything." He placed his arms under Manuel's shoulders. "Can you get up?"

"Yeah, I think so," said Manuel. "How's he?"

"His legs don't look good but I'd say you saved his life," Lucas said.

"All in a day's—oh shit, that hurts!" said Manuel as he pushed himself up.

Back in the workshop Cordero secured Zico and his companions in the back seat of his vehicle. He checked Josinto.

"You need to go to hospital?" Cordero asked, examining his neck while Josinto rubbed the circulation back into his wrists where he'd been tied.

"I'll take care of him," said Estefana. "He says he can ride with me back to his room."

"You sure?" Cordero asked Josinto.

"Yes, *maun*," he said. "I'm okay."

Cordero nodded and gestured to Carter to climb into the passenger's seat of his vehicle. Apart from a smashed headlight and some scratches and dents, his old SUV had survived the ramming of the double doors with little damage. He reversed over the remains of the doors and onto the road. He drove up to where Lucas and Manuel were hovering over the injured youth. Carter got out first and went straight to Manuel when she realised he was injured. She checked his leg and decided he'd survive. She tried the boy whimpering on the ground. His injuries were clearly more serious.

"He needs a doctor," she said to Cordero.

"What about me?" Manuel protested.

"You too," said Carter. "But you can wait."

Cordero exited the SUV but left the engine running. He patted Manuel on the back and helped him over to the vehicle's bonnet for support. He took a quick look at the injured youth and stood to face Lucas.

"Josinto's a little shaken but otherwise unharmed," he said. "He says he'll go home with Estefana who'll take good care of him. We'll stay here while you get your car. Take Manuel and this boy to hospital. I'm going to take these three to the holding cells at police headquarters. I want to question them tonight. Meet me there after you drop these two off, okay?"

He climbed back in behind the wheel.

"What about the vehicles in the workshop?" Lucas asked.

"What about them?" Cordero replied leaning out the driver's window. "I've got the keys to the truck. If anyone takes the motorcycles, that's too bad." He looked across to Carter. "You coming?" She jumped in next to him. "Good thing you joined us tonight," was all he said before driving off.

Chapter 29

It was almost midnight by the time Cordero arrived at police' headquarters and settled the three gang members into holding cells. They would be held there for 72 hours before appearing before a judge. Under the weight of evidence against them, the judge would surely see the need for a trial and send them to prison until one could be arranged. Since his capture Zico had kept cursing Carter and threatening his two companions to keep their mouths shut. Cordero and Carter had paid him no mind.

Inside the building Cordero suggested Carter take a nap on a sofa in the office he'd commandeered. She resisted at first but eventually agreed: with Josinto safe, the immediate crisis was over and the rest was up to Cordero. He made himself a bad coffee and was sipping it and grimacing when Lucas came back from the hospital.

"How's Manuel?" he asked as Lucas, noticing the look of distaste at the coffee on Cordero's face, declined the offer of a cup.

"He'll live," Lucas said.

"And the boy?"

"Finally shut up when they gave him a shot to ease the pain," Lucas said. "He'll live too." He spied the sleeping form of Carter in the corner. "Did you see how she took that guy down, Tino?"

"Yeah, impressive huh?"

"Impressive? Shit *maun*, she's dangerous. Imagine what she'd do to you if you treated her the wrong way!" he whispered.

"Let's not worry about that now," said Cordero. "You ready to question these guys? I want to leave Zico 'til last. He's the hardest of the three and the other two just might give us something to work with when we question him."

They made their way to the interrogation room, Cordero leaving what was left of the coffee on his desk. The first gang member they questioned gave his name as Carlos Bacalao. He was the boy Lucas had kneed in the head in the workshop. Carlos claimed to be nineteen years old. He was skinny, his eyes were furtive and small beads of sweat covered his forehead and upper lip. Cordero guessed his real age at sixteen. The boy wore tattered jeans and a blue T-shirt with the remains of an elephant logo on the front. His clothes were dirty but not with mud. He said he'd been told to stay with Josinto while the others went out, but claimed he didn't know why or where they'd gone.

"Where are you from Carlos?" Lucas asked.

"From?" the boy replied.

"From?" Lucas repeated. The boy made no response. "I'm sure you were born someplace. Where was that?" Lucas asked.

The boy looked sideways at nothing in particular. "Ermera," he said.

"I don't see any red snake tattoos on your neck or arms," said Cordero. "How long you been with *Samea Mean*?"

"*Samea Mean*?" repeated Carlos.

"Yeah. The group run by Tristao?"

The boy shook his head and said nothing.

Cordero sensed the boy's fear. "You don't have to be afraid of Zico," he said. "He's locked in a cell and he'll be going to prison for a long time."

The boy stared directly at Cordero but his eyes glazed over and he dropped his head.

"How long, Carlos?" Lucas repeated. "How long have you been a member of *Samea Mean*?"

Carlos remained slumped and silent.

"What do you know about the two gang members who were murdered recently—one from *4:4* and one from *Forsa*?" asked Cordero.

Silence.

"What can you tell me about the drugs?"

More silence.

"Okay, how about the abduction of that guy you were guarding? Tell me whose idea that was," said Cordero.

They waited. Lucas slapped his hand on the table and the boy jumped in fright. "We've got you for abduction, deprivation of liberty, and resisting arrest," Lucas said. "That's about ten years. If we connect you to the murders and drugs you can add another twenty. You might want to cooperate."

The boy shivered but said nothing. Cordero put his hand on Lucas's arm to calm him.

"What are you afraid of, Carlos?" he asked.

The boy looked directly at Cordero again, his face buckled, and he began to cry. But he shook his head and said nothing.

Cordero turned to Lucas and shrugged. "Call the officer to take him back to his cell," he said. "Maybe time will make him more willing to cooperate."

The next boy was the one Cordero had hit with the driver's door of his vehicle. He was older than Carlos, though not much. He had a nasty red welt on his forehead from the car door and his nose seemed to have been pushed out of shape. His hair was greasy, his arms covered in dirt and grime. Dried mud caked his bare legs. A red snake tattoo jutted out of the neck of his faded T-shirt and he sat with his arms folded tightly. A grimy identity card in his pocket gave his name as Silvio Moniz and his birthplace as Hatilua in Ermera.

"Why were you digging up a grave tonight, Silvio?" Cordero asked.

The boy tapped his foot, said nothing.

"I'm sure you know that grave robbing is a serious offence," Cordero said. "Not to mention abduction and resisting arrest. What was this all about?"

Silvio looked away and continued tapping.

"Your friend Zico is pretty handy with a knife," Cordero said. "Did he kill Jenito Fuentes, you know, the 4:4 guy, the Sunday night before last in Balide?"

The foot stopped tapping. Silvio continued to stare at the wall.

"You didn't find the drugs in the coffin, Silvio," Lucas said. "So what were you going to do with the guy you abducted? Was Zico going to slit his throat too?"

"Drugs, coffins, throats—I don't know what you're talking about," Silvio said, still gazing at the wall.

"Okay, tell us what you know about Tristao," said Cordero. Silvio turned sharply and faced him but his lips tightened as though he was afraid something might spill out.

"Is he the one who ordered the killings in order to get the drugs?" Cordero asked. The foot tapping started again. "Is he?"

"Time to get smart and cooperate, Silvio," said Lucas, "or you could spend the rest of your life in prison. Nothing good happens in there, *maun*."

They waited. Silvio gave them nothing except more foot tapping and a frozen expression of defiance. This time Cordero called the police officer standing outside the interrogation room.

"Fuck you!" Silvio said as he was taken back to his cell.

Lucas let out a groan, rose and paced the room. "We're not getting very far, Tino," he said.

"Early days," Cordero replied.

The door re-opened. Zico pulled his arm sharply away from the police officer who led him into the room. He slumped down into the chair opposite Cordero and Lucas, thrust his legs out, crossed his feet and leaned back, sneering. Along with the lump on his forehead from where Carter had hit him with the shovel he was now developing bluish bruises from her elbows to his face.

"Let's start with your full name," said Lucas, resuming his seat.

"Fuck you," said Zico. "I don't have to tell you nothing."

"But we know your first name is Zico," said Lucas. "Why not tell us your second name? You embarrassed by it?"

The sneer turned to an angry, sullen silence.

"Every time I see you, you look more beaten up than the last time, Zico," Cordero said.

"That bitch!" the boy hissed.

"What's the bet," Cordero began, "that when we examine the knife you were wielding tonight, or perhaps the one I took off you in Comoro the other day, we'll find traces of the blood of Jenito Fuentes who you killed last week?"

"I didn't kill nobody," Zico replied.

"But you were going to kill Josinto Veddo tonight," Cordero said.

"Who's he?"

"The man you were holding at knife point in the garage," Cordero said.

Zico said nothing.

"I don't think you were going to kill him when we confronted you," Cordero continued. "That would have been silly because my friend here"—he gestured to Lucas—"would have shot you immediately and we'd be looking at your corpse now. Even you're smart enough to have known that. I think you were planning to kill him before we arrived because you didn't find any drugs in the coffin you dug up and you thought he was holding out on you. We just interrupted your plans. Is that right?"

Zico leaned across the table. "I'm not saying nothing and you can't make me," he snarled. "Fuck you?" He titled toward Lucas. "Him too."

"Well your friends are going to tell us what we want to know. It doesn't really matter if you don't," Lucas replied.

"That's shit. Those guys won't tell you anything," Zico hissed. He leaned back in his chair and grinned.

"Because you'll kill them if they do?" asked Cordero.

Zico wiped the grin from his face and turned away.

"Now this guy Tristao who runs *Samea Mean*," Cordero began. "Did he order the drug interceptions?"

"Told you before, I don't know any Tristao," Zico insisted.

"So you're prepared to take the blame for two murders, an abduction, several drug offences, disturbing a grave, threatening a police officer—"

"Fuck you!" Zico spat.

"Zico," Cordero mused. "That's a Brazilian name isn't it?"

"What if it is?"

"I'm wondering if you know a guy called Quim," Cordero said.
"No I don't but if I did, he'd rip your head off," said Zico.

• • •

Cordero fell asleep across his desk and woke with a start when he heard a cell phone buzzing. He blinked, looked around, noticed Carter asleep on the sofa and Lucas stirring from an easy chair where he too had dozed off. Lucas fumbled in his pocket, retrieved his cell and stumbled outside to take the call.

"Manuel! Hey *maun*, what time is it?" Lucas said.

"Nearly eight, *maun*," said Manuel. "I've been up for an hour."

Lucas rubbed his face and ran a hand through his hair. "Well you just woke me. I'm still at the office. So's Tino and the American. They're asleep. Long night. How are you?" he asked.

"Fractured ankle. They took x-rays and set it. Eventually. Said I was in a queue and had to wait my turn. That was hours, *maun*. They're letting me out as soon as I can make my own way home. You able to come and give me a ride? I can get a taxi otherwise."

"No, no, I'll come, *maun*," said Lucas. "Just need to wake up first. Been a long night, like I said."

"You get anything from those guys we caught?" Manuel asked.

"Nothing," said Lucas, yawning. "The one with the knife has convinced the others he'll kill them if they talk. It'll be hard to connect the guy Tino thinks is behind it all unless one of these guys or that guy in hospital with you talks."

"Well at least we got the killers Tino was after," said Manuel. "That's something."

A second time Lucas yawned. "Yeah," he said. "Maybe."

"Hey, *maun*, there's this pretty nurse in here," said Manuel, his voice dropping to a whisper.

"Do you ever give up, *maun*?" asked Lucas.

"No, listen. She's cute. Says she knows my cousin. Well anyhow I figured I'd talk with her real nice, you know, and then when my ankle's fixed I'll track her down through him and ask her out. Her name's Ina."

"I'm happy that your broken ankle could have a happy ending, Manuel," Lucas said. "Now let me find a coffee then I'll come get you."

"No wait, *maun*. Listen. So I was talking to her just now. I said 'You look tired. Long night?' You know, *maun*, so she thinks I'm the caring sort."

"If you weren't the caring sort, Manuel, you wouldn't have risked your life to save that boy from the truck," said Lucas.

"Forget that, *maun*, listen. So she says, 'Yeah, it was the boy you brought in with you. Had three breaks in his legs, one really bad. So we gave him morphine.'"

"Do I really need to hear all this, Manuel?" Lucas asked.

"Yeah, you do. Now listen. Then she says 'But he had another drug already in his system. Whatever it was we didn't know he'd taken it when we gave him the morphine. When you mix morphine with other drugs you get all sorts of reactions like hallucinations.' So I say, 'You mean he was talking to you?' And she says 'Well, yelling mostly. He was calling out all night. I had to keep an eye on him to make sure he didn't have a seizure. Plus do all my other rounds. That's why I'm tired.'"

Lucas was starting to think this might lead somewhere. "Go on," he said.

"I say 'What was he yelling?' and she says he kept calling out that he'd got the stuff from the list someone wrote. 'I got it, I got it!' Shit like that she said. So she asks 'What stuff, what list?' She couldn't think of anything else to say to calm him down. Then he tells her 'The spices for Tristao's betel. I got it. I got the list. It's in the pocket of my jeans.'"

Lucas was fully alert now and walked back inside the office to catch Cordero's attention. Carter was woken by the movement in the room. She yawned, stretched, and slide off the jacket Cordero had placed over her during the night. She stood up and almost collided with Lucas. He stepped back from her, still thinking about how she took down Zico, and headed for Cordero's desk.

Cordero sat upright. "I've got Tino here," Lucas said to Manuel, placing his cell in front of Cordero and switching it to speaker. "You say there's a note in that guy's jeans hand written by this Tristao listing the ingredients for the spices he mixes with his betel quids?" Lucas asked, looking directly at Cordero.

"No *maun*," said Manuel. "I was trying to impress her, you know? I told her I was a police investigator. That seemed to do it. She took the list from the guy's jeans and gave it to me. I'm holding it here right now."

Chapter 30

"We had to run a toxicology test to find out what we were dealing with," the doctor told Cordero. They were standing at the nurses' station just outside the ward where Manuel and the gang member with the injured legs had been sent. The doctor was Emilio Tranto, Cuban trained and highly competent. He was scanning a patient report on a clipboard he was holding. "It was methamphetamine," the doctor continued. "He hadn't smoked it or injected it. He'd crushed a tablet and swallowed it." He made a note on the clipboard and handed it to a nurse sitting at the desk. He pocketed his glasses and faced Cordero. "The release is slower that way and the effect lasts longer."

"He'd been told to dig up a coffin that had just been buried," Cordero said.

"Then he was probably shitting himself—you know, disturbing the spirit of the dead and all that—and took the drug to calm himself."

"When can I question him?" Cordero asked.

"Not for quite a while. The mixture of morphine and methamphetamine isn't too kind on the body. You can see him tomorrow—maybe," said the doctor. "You wouldn't get any sense out of him before then anyway."

Cordero joined Carter and Lucas in the ward where the two were helping Manuel to dress.

"You okay, *maun*?" Cordero asked.

Manuel flashed a gleeful grin. "The doctor says no work for two weeks and only light duties for another two after that," Manuel said. "And I met Ina."

"I'm happy for you," said Cordero. "Do you have the note from the boy's pocket?"

"Sure *maun*," Manuel said. He reached over to the small side table near his bed, but too quickly and almost tumbled. Carter had to steady him. "This is going to take a bit of getting used to," Manuel said. He retrieved the note on the second attempt and handed it to Cordero. Four words were scrawled on it.

"'Catechu, cardamom, catkin *malus*,'" Cordero read aloud. "The spice mix from Viqueque."

"He must have written the items down thinking this kid was too stupid to remember them," suggested Lucas. "By the look of him I'd say he was right."

"When we match the handwriting it will connect Tristao to the abduction of Josinto through this patient here, to the interception of the drug shipments, and to the deaths of the two boys from the other gangs through the betel," said Cordero. He pocketed the note. "But we can't wait. We need to pay Tristao a visit. He'll know things have gone wrong when the boys sent out to retrieve his drugs don't report back. When he does he'll cut his losses and run."

• • •

Cordero called police headquarters. The normal police roster would be operating again after the reburials in Metinaro and he could count on experienced officers as backup. He requested four to meet him at the convenience store in Comoro where he'd first encountered Zico. First though, there was Manuel to deal with. They drove him back to his house and Lucas helped him inside. Manuel hopped, hobbled and cursed the whole way. By the time Cordero, Carter and Lucas arrived at the convenience store, the officers had relieved their colleague who'd been keeping an eye on the area and were sitting in a police car smoking cigarettes. "Young guy conducting surveillance had nothing to report," one of the officers told Cordero. "But he was asleep when we got here."

No members of Tristao's group were hanging around the store so there was no need to station an officer there. Instead Cordero led the way to the side laneway off the bitumen road where Rogerio had taken him and Carter into Tristao's compound. Cordero pointed out the entrance and instructed two officers to look for a rear exit. If they found one, they were to stay there and stop anyone from leaving. With the other two officers in tow, he, Carter and Lucas walked into the compound through the front gate. There was no one on the gate or immediately inside between the laneway and the main building. The front door hung open and the building looked deserted.

Cordero told the remaining two police officers to wait in the forecourt and keep their eyes open. He moved to the left of the doorway, Carter behind him, while Lucas went to the right and drew his pistol.

"*Polisia!*" Cordero shouted and his voice echoed down the empty corridor. There was no movement. "*Polisia!*" he repeated. *Nothing.*

He put his arm out to hold Carter back. "Stay here," he said and nodded to Lucas. Cordero entered first, flush against the wall of the corridor. Lucas took the opposite side, his pistol extended. Cordero checked the first room on his left. Empty. Lucas checked the room on the right; also empty. Cordero slid slowly down the corridor to the closed door of the room where he and Carter had met Tristao. Lucas skipped in front of him and quickly checked the back of the house. He returned shaking his head.

There was a sound like something being knocked to the floor from the room opposite. Cordero and Lucas moved to either side of the doorway.

"*Polisia!*" Cordero shouted. *Silence.* He tried the door knob. It turned. He thrust the door aside and leaned back against the corridor wall. He looked at Lucas, held three fingers up in turn and rushed into the room, Lucas right behind him. The room was dark. It offered no movement and no sound until a cat meowed and darted out the door. Lucas checked the room. *Empty.* They moved back to Tristao's door.

"*Polisia!*" Cordero shouted for the fourth time. The call went unanswered. Again he tried the knob and again it gave. He elbowed the door open, barged in and pressed against an inside wall. Lucas came in behind him.

Lucas stayed to Cordero's left, moving cautiously, his pistol held in front of him. There was a crunch of glass underfoot. Lucas had trodden on a drinking glass. Cordero went to the window and ripped open the shades. He'd stirred the dust and it drifted into the beam of sunlight now penetrating the room. The beam shone on the lifeless face of Tristao lying on the floor beside the table.

They checked the body. The man's throat had been cut and his thick glasses lay stuck in a pool of dried blood. There was no sign of a struggle save for the drinking glass which had dropped to the floor: the pitcher of water, the notepad and pen, the tiny call bell were all on the table.

"Rigor is dissipating," Lucas said. "I'd say he's been dead for twelve hours at least."

Carter entered the room and made her own examination of the body. She stood and looked over the articles on the table. "The notepad," she nodded.Cordero took the shopping list for the betel spice mix from his pocket and compared the paper it was written on to the notepaper. It was the same.

"You think the others know he's dead and that's why they've cleared out?" Carter asked.

"Looks that way," said Cordero. "Probably scared the killer's lurking around."

"But I don't figure it," said Lucas scratching his head. "We've locked up the killer." They both looked at him. "Zico," he said.

"How could Zico have done it when he was at the cemetery last night?" Cordero asked.

"How do we know he was there?" Lucas countered. "He wasn't covered in mud like the other two."

"He was probably giving instructions to the two who were digging," said Cordero. "Someone was holding a lamp over the grave. And he's the type to give instructions rather than take them."

"We only have that boy Carlos's word for it that he was the one guarding Josinto," said Lucas. "What if Zico told him to say that? What if it was Zico who stayed back with Josinto while the others went to the cemetery? While they were gone he slips out and kills this guy. You've seen how fond he is of knives."

"Josinto might be able to tell us who was guarding him and if that person left the workshop at any stage," Carter offered. "Let's go ask. There's nothing more we can do here that those officers outside can't do."

Cordero told two of the officers to seal off the building and stay with the body until a forensic team arrived and someone came from the morgue. He told the other two officers to take into custody anyone from Tristao's group who happened to show up. He rang Dr Howard Brooks and told him to expect another body and that he needed it examined as soon as possible. Brooks had said 'Of course you do, dear boy' in a tone meant to demonstrate his exasperation. Cordero drove Lucas home to get a little rest and took Carter to grab coffee on the way to where Josinto lived.

• • •

Estefana looked drawn but sounded relieved and happy when she opened the door to them at Josinto's room. "He's just waking now, *mana*," she said to Carter. "He had a restless night," she said and averted her gaze, "until I lay down on the bed and held him." She looked up again. "But I kept my clothes on, *mana*. The whole time."

"I'm sure you did, Estefana," said Carter. "But you won't have to after you're married. Remember that and you'll have a happy marriage."

Estefana blushed.

"How are you feeling, Josinto?" Cordero asked.

"Good *maun*," said Josinto. "I want to thank you again—"

"Later, *maun*. What can you tell me about what happened?"

Josinto sat up in his bed and rubbed his eyes.

"Well, they stopped me in Lecidere," he said. "One rode up beside my truck and said something had fallen off the back. When I stopped to check, they grabbed me. They forced me back into the truck and drove me to that workshop or whatever it was. I tried to fight them off but there were two of them."

He looked at Estefana. She poured him a glass of water. "Thanks *doben*," he said, took a sip, swallowed, and grimaced as if it had caused him pain.

"Go on," said Cordero.

"When we got to the workshop they tied me up and blindfolded me. Then they started asking me about drugs." He stared, befuddled, at Cordero. "I didn't know what they were talking about. One guy hit me but I couldn't see who it was. 'Where'd you put the drugs?' he kept yelling. I told them I didn't know anything about drugs. They started talking among themselves and then asked me where the coffin was I'd taken to Balide on Sunday night. I told them I left it in my truck to finish it at home on Tuesday night and deliver it back on Wednesday. They asked if the coffin was lined. I said of course it was. They asked who the coffin was for and I told them *Senyor* Boavides who was being buried on Monday at Santa Ana cemetery." He took another sip of water and handed the glass back to Estefana. "They said if I was lying they'd kill me."

"Did anyone apart from those boys enter the workshop while they were holding you?" Cordero asked.

"Most the time only one would stay with me," Josinto said. "I don't know which one. He'd talk on his cell but I couldn't make out anything he was saying. The building was big and I was tied up in a back corner, blindfolded, and scared."

"And early last night did the boy who was guarding you leave at any time?"

Josinto thought for a moment.

"I couldn't say. Like I said, I was blindfolded and too tired by then to pay attention to what was going on. They made me sleep sitting up in the chair. I only stirred when I heard the motorcycles come back to the garage and they all started swearing at me. Next thing I know, you arrived."

• • •

Cordero and Carter, who'd both skipped breakfast, grabbed a quick bite to eat and headed for the morgue to talk to Brooks and hand him the knife Zico had threatened to use on Josinto. Josinto's account neither proved nor discounted Lucas's speculation that Zico was to blame for the killings, including that of Tristao. If that was true, a bit of luck on the forensic front and a bit more pressure on the other boys they had in custody might close the case. The only thing missing would be any drugs from earlier intercepts of couriers including the first murdered gang member, and those taken from the port on Sunday. But they'd get to that and maybe even to Cordero's suspicion that someone—Zico again?—had killed Fidelis Tau.

Brooks had only just begun examining the body of Tristao when they arrived. He was bent over the cadaver, the fingers of one hand in a red plastic glove delicately holding open the man's eyelid.

"Tino," he said looking up. "And the lovely Miss Carter," he added. "How utterly delightful."

"Hello Howard," Carter replied.

Cordero took the latest knife he'd taken from Zico and placed it in a plastic evidence bag on the bench against the wall. "Another knife for you to examine," he said.

Brooks glanced over the bench and gave the knife a quick inspection. "Anything for us?" Cordero asked.

"Policing may be a hasty business, dear boy, but pathology is a slow, painstaking practice," said Brooks and bent back over the body. "If you want to do it right."

"I stand corrected," Cordero said. "But is there anything at all you've found that could help?"

"Not much, I'm afraid," said Brooks. "I've only just started my examination." He stood again. "I can tell you he suffered from uvietis."

"Uvietis?" Cordero repeated.

"Inflammation of the uvea, dear boy," said Brooks. "In the eye or, in this case, eyes plural. It is not uncommon among children in this part of the world. Causes blurred vision, sensitivity to light, pain and eventually blindness if not treated. His is untreated and seems fairly advanced."

"What causes it?" Cordero asked.

"Oh any number of factors but most commonly a genetic condition," said Brooks. "Can be dealt with in most cases if addressed early enough but we do live in Timor."

"Interesting," said Cordero, "but it doesn't help us with his murder. Would you say it looks like the same killer who murdered those two gang members?"

"Well you can see the same markings on the forehead from a tight hold from behind. And the cut is similar, yes."

"Anything else?"

"Not yet, dear boy," said Brooks. "As I said, pathology—"

"Okay, thanks Howard."

"You must come to my humble abode for a drink, Miss Carter," said Brooks. "Before you leave Timor, I mean. That is, if you can spare the time, of course."

"I'll check my diary," she said.

She and Cordero turned to leave.

"Oh there is one other thing, Tino," said Brooks, wiping his gloves on his apron. "That knife you had dropped off here the other day—the one you seemed to think might have been used to kill those two gang members?"

"What about it?"

"Well it wasn't, dear boy. That's all."

"What do you mean? You didn't find any traces of blood on the knife?" asked Cordero.

"Didn't need to look. The blade was serrated. As, I can see, is the one you just brought in. When a serrated knife is used to cut a throat it leaves striated scratches on the wound. There were none on the other two victims. Haven't found any on this chap either," Brooks added, pointing to the body of Tristao.

"Are you sure?"

"Do you really have to ask me that, dear boy?"

Cordero thanked Brooks and he and Carter headed out of the hospital.

"I think it's time we had another talk with Zico," Cordero said as they climbed into his vehicle.

"What makes you think he'll tell you anything more?" asked Carter.

"This time I'll take a secret weapon," he said.

"And what's that?"

"The person he fears most." He glanced across at her and started the engine. "You!"

Chapter 31

On the way back to police headquarters he told her what he could about his own interrogation of Zico—the boy's anger, his hostility, and his tough guy theatrics. Carter listened but said nothing until they were mounting the steps into the building.

"We do this my way," she said.

He stopped. "Which is?"

"You sit back and translate," she said. "Nothing more. You don't move, you don't comment. No matter what he says or what happens. Got it?"

"You have no official capacity. Anything he tells—"

"You want me to do this or not?" she cut him off.

He rubbed the back of his neck. "Okay," he agreed.

She stopped as he opened the door to the police headquarters building for her, grabbed him by the arm and looked into his eyes.

"Got it?" she repeated.

"Yeah," he muttered. "Your way it is."

Zico was brought into the interrogation room. He shrugged away the police officer who led him by the arm and cursed after the man left. His hands were cuffed, his hair disheveled and his face now a patchwork of nasty wounds from being hit with the shovel and from Carter's blows as she knocked him senseless with her elbow. He turned and slumped into a chair across the table from Carter. Then he seemed to notice her for the first time.

"You!" he shouted and rose as though to spring across at her.

Carter remained seated but shot a finger toward Zico's face. He froze, eased slowly back down and spat on the floor beside his chair.

"Bitch!" he grumbled.

"Calm down, Zico," Carter said folding her arms. "I'm only here to talk."

"I've got nothing to say to you," he said.

Cordero was sitting back, translating the exchange. Zico seemed to become aware of him for the first time. All three of them sat motionless and quiet. Carter let Zico's apprehension build.

"*Ita hola malu ho nia ka?*" Zico asked Cordero to break the silence.

Cordero said nothing.

"Tell me what he said," Carter demanded and she inclined her head to Cordero without facing him.

Cordero coughed.

"Tell me," she insisted.

"He asked if I sleep with you," he said, moderating the verb.

Zico was smirking at her.

"Ask him what difference it would make if I did," Carter said.

Cordero translated for Zico's benefit and the boy's face hardened.

"*Ita puta,*" he spat and slammed the palms of his hands on the table.

"You don't have to translate that," Carter told Cordero. "I've lost count of the number of times I've been called a whore."

She grabbed Zico's hands. He tried to pull them back but her grip was too strong. She turned the hands over and examined his forearms. Her touch grew softer and for a moment Zico looked her in the eyes and seemed not to resist. When she let go of his hands he thrust them under the table. She looked closely at his face. He looked away as though embarrassed.

"You have a lot of bruises," she said. "Older ones, I mean, not the ones I caused. Why's that, Zico?" she asked.

He said nothing.

"Ask him to take his T-shirt off," Carter told Cordero. He did but Zico refused.

Cordero yelled at Zico to do as he was told but Carter held up a hand and stopped him.

"That's okay," she said. "The fact he won't tells me what I want to know." She gazed at him. "You get hit a lot, Zico," she said in a matter-of-fact tone.

"I fight a lot," he said through gritted teeth as he leaned over the table.

"Seems to me you lose a lot," Carter said.

He sniffed and turned side-on in his chair away from her piercing eyes.

"You act tough, Zico," Carter said. "But you know what I think? I think you're scared."

He spun back around to face her. "Take these cuffs off and I'll show you how scared I am, you bitch!"

"That wouldn't be smart on your part, Zico," she said.

He made a growling sound: her composure only seemed to irritate him all the more. "Fuck you!" he said and once more turned away.

"Resisting and threatening me aren't smart because, you see, I'm the only one here who can help you. I'm not a police officer. I don't care what you did. I don't care who you did whatever it was you did to. I just want to know why."

"I've got nothing to say," he said. He threw his head back and up at the ceiling.

"There was a time once I felt like you do now," she said. "Felt I could've torn the whole world apart with my bare hands. You're not the only one who got a shitty deal in life."

His face was flushed with anger but he made no sound.

"We know you didn't kill anybody, Zico," Carter said. "You see neither of the two knives we took from you was the knife we're looking for. Maybe you have another you only use for slitting throats but I doubt it. If you did, why would you exchange it between killing Tristao and coming back to kill Josinto?"

He flinched at the name 'Tristao' and the eye closest to where she'd hit him with the shovel began twitching as he made eye contact. Carter read that as surprise to learn that Tristao had been killed.

"That's right," she said. "Tristao's dead. Throat slit like the others. What was your role in all of this?"

He snorted.

"I can wait, Zico."

"Stop calling me Zico!" he shouted. "You don't know me, you're not my friend."

"That's true but I'd like to know a little about you," said Carter. She leaned across the table. "Tell me about your family and where you're from, Zico."

"Fuck you!"

"Okay," she said and eased back in her chair. "Let me tell you about my family. My mother walked out on me when I was five years old. My father married again but I never liked my stepmother. In fact, I hated her. She was cruel and bullied me. At times she beat me without my father knowing and told me she'd do it even worse if I told him what she'd done. When I was fourteen, my father was shot dead by two men abducting my half-sister. I never saw her again. I left home soon after and I've lived on my own ever since."

Zico was staring at nothing in particular on the table. A minute passed. Carter didn't interrupt it: she could see he'd listened closely to the translation of what she'd said and was thinking. Eventually he mumbled a question. She turned to Cordero but he shrugged his shoulders.

"What was that?" Carter asked. "I couldn't hear you."

"I said did your father love you?" Zico repeated.

She was struck by the question and ran a hand through her hair.

"You know," she began, "you're the first person who's ever asked me that. Usually I'm asked if I loved him." She paused a moment, dropped her head and looked up again. He was watching her now, curious it seemed. "Yes. Yes, he loved me every minute of every day," she said and nodded. "He loved my sister too. That's why he lost his life trying to save her from those men. Not a day goes by I don't miss him."

Zico brushed a shoulder against his nose and sat motionless, head forward over the table. He tested the manacles on his wrists, gazed around the windowless room in a building crawling with police, and fixed his eyes on this foreigner—a woman—who didn't flinch in the face of his outbursts. Clearly bluster and threats were no longer getting him very far at all.

Carter waited.

"Fuck you!" he said but there was less venom in his tone. He pushed back his chair and stood to leave the room. "Fuck all of you!"

• • •

"I told you I've interrogated a lot of boys like him," Carter said, brushing the hair from her face. "They put on a tough front because they're mostly damaged and hurting inside. If you can ignore the front and focus on what's behind it sometimes you can connect because no one else has bothered to try. I'd say Zico's been abused quite a bit. Beaten, bashed. I didn't see defensive wounds on his hands or arms and if those bruises and scratches came from fights I'd expect to. Let him think things over for a while. He may reach out. We all find different ways of calling for help."

Cordero had been staring at the ground but he straightened as though something had suddenly struck him.

"What did you say?" he asked.

They'd taken a break outside the police headquarters to consider their next steps. The day had turned cool, a gust of wind had blown up, and rain threatened again.

"I said they're usually hurting—"

"No not that. You said we all have different ways of calling for help."

"It's obvious isn't it?" she said, paying his interest little notice. "Sometimes people will—"

"So obvious that even Pinto Baptisto knew it," said Cordero, cutting her off.

"Who?" Carter asked, not sure what any of this was about.

"The old guy in Balide who said a ghost had spoken to him. Remember? He said we all have different ways of crying out for help."

"So?"

"It's not likely that Tristao killed those two gang members. He was almost blind, Brooks said, and he ended up a victim himself. Right?"

"Okay."

"And when he was killed there was no betel quid placed in his mouth."

"Go on," she said.

"Since the way Tristao and the two gang members were killed was the same, the absence of a betel quid in Tristao's mouth suggests it wasn't the killer who placed them in the mouths of the two murdered boys. It was somebody who was there when they were killed or at least knew soon enough that they'd been killed and where."

Cordero was pacing back and forth and clicking his fingers as he explained each point.

"If we'd been smart enough, early enough, we might have traced the betel quids back to Tristao's group. The guy didn't make a secret of using them, after all. Everybody in his group knew about them. The place he gave them out had no walls to hide the fact, remember?"

He stopped pacing and faced her.

"What if the betel wasn't there in the victims' mouths as a warning or a spiritual thing but was a cry for help—a clumsy, confused, childish way of trying to stop what was going on by drawing attention to the people behind it?"

He looked to Carter to see if she would draw the same conclusion he had.

"Zico?" she said.

"Remember that kid who took us to meet Tristao—Rogerio? When I asked him for one of the betel quids Tristao was handing out, he said the boys guarding the quids wouldn't give them out to anyone without Tristao's say-so. Who is the only other person they might have been scared enough to make an exception for?"

"That's a long stretch even for you, Tino," Carter said.

"But it's worth a try." He looked at her hopefully.

Slowly she nodded.

"Yes. It's worth a try."

• • •

Zico was brought back into the interrogation room. He leered at Carter but this time didn't wrench his arm from the officer leading him in. She and Cordero had taken up their positions in the room as before. Zico eased himself down in the chair opposite Carter and said nothing.

"Hi Zico," Carter began. "Sorry to bother you again so soon. I want to tell you a story."

He placed his hands on the table. She sensed she had his attention.

"When I was starting out as a policewoman, I was given the job of investigating a series of house robberies. What was strange about them was that in every house that was robbed a baseball card had been left somewhere in the living room. You know what a baseball card is?"

Zico shook his head.

"Well, it's a little card with the picture of a player from a particular baseball team on it and you collect them until you have the whole team. Anyway I was able to trace the baseball cards to a kid who lived in town. He had a reputation for trading them with other kids. He was only fourteen years old. When I pulled up at his house to question him, his mother was lying in bed unconscious from a drug overdose. I managed to get her to hospital and she survived. Thing is, she had forced the kid to rob houses to pay for her drugs. He wanted her to stop. The only way he could think of to do that without being beaten up by her was to get the police around to his house. Hence the baseball cards left in every house he robbed. They were his way of calling for help."

She sat back in her chair while Cordero finished translating the story.

"What do you think of that story?" she asked.

He shrugged but remained speechless.

"If you were that kid, might you have done the same?" she asked him.

Zico scratched the back of his chair. "I don't have no cards with pictures," he said.

"No. But you had betel quids," Carter said. "Or at least you knew where to get them."

He looked away from her.

"I think you put those betel quids in the mouths of the boys who were killed. I think you put them there hoping the police would trace them back to Tristao and be able to prevent more killings."

She let the thought hang.

"Police don't know nothing," he said. "Supposed to protect people but they don't do nothing."

It was a complaint but not directed at the point she'd made.

"And I think you did that because you were getting beaten up yourself, probably by the killer, and you were sick of all the violence," she said.

She noticed his shoulders slump a little. He wiped a hand across his face.

"Last time you wouldn't tell me anything about yourself, Zico," she said. "I still want to know. I told you about my family. Tell me about yours."

He gave her a severe look which quickly softened. He sniffed and turned away from her.

"Mother's dead," he said. "She died when I was twelve." He turned back toward her. "Left me. We got things in common, bitch."

So he took in my story, Carter was thinking to herself.

"How did she die?" she asked.

He didn't respond. "You've told me that much, why not tell me the rest?"

Zico chewed his bottom lip, weighing things up. She looked at him and tilted her head slightly to encourage him.

"It was eight years ago," he said. "When the gangs were fighting and killing people. They came to our house. My father wasn't there. They burned down our house and when she ran out with me in her arms someone hit her with a machete."

He sniffed like he might have been holding back tears. He placed his hands on the table and stared down at them. She placed her hands close to his just short of touching.

"She'd gone to Mozambique with her family when the Indonesians came," Zico continued. "Met my father there. He'd left the army. Been a paratrooper in Brazil." He raised his eyes, a hint of pride flashed momentarily across his face. "They're the toughest guys." He looked back down. "Got a security job with a mining company in Mozambique. I was born there. My mother wanted to come back after independence and so my father brought us here. I didn't want to come. I didn't want to leave my friends. And I only spoke Portuguese. Everyone here laughed at me and called me names."

His eyes were moist now.

"My father lost everything when they burned the house," Zico said. "My mother was dead and he had no money to get back to Brazil. He wasn't a bad man. He was sad. That's all." Zico rubbed a hand under his nose. "At first. But then he started to drink. Soon he started to blame me and beat me. Said it was for my own good. Make me strong." He turned away, ashamed.

"And he still beats you?"

He said nothing which she knew to be an admission.

Carter waited to see if there was more he wanted to say but Zico was struggling to hold back his tears.

"Is that how you came to join Tristao's group?"

He nodded. She had no need to push him to talk now.

"Six months ago my father met Tristao. He told my father this crazy story about stopping all the shit in Dili so the country could start again." He put his head in his hands.

"What shit?" Carter prodded him.

"Drugs and shit," he said.

"And your father saw an opportunity to make enough money to get back to Brazil?" Carter asked.

Zico wiped his nose on his forearm. "After my mother died he hated it here. So he told Tristao he could organise a group, you know, a gang, to take care of the drugs and he made me recruit boys I knew. He told me to beat them up if they didn't join and do as I say."

Zico slumped back in his chair. He lifted his shoulders and dropped them again. "Tristao would find out when the drugs were coming in and send me and some boys to steal them," he said. "Then I'd take the drugs and stash them and give Tristao pills or shit my father got at the market in their place. Tristao doesn't see things good. He couldn't tell the difference. He'd burn the pills in front of the group thinking they were drugs. 'We're cleaning up the streets, purifying Dili!' he'd tell them."

He huffed with contempt.

"But my father got greedy and wanted to get more valuable shipments. The kind the big gangs control. He'd go himself, but take me and a couple of boys. He'd kill the couriers so they couldn't report him to the guys who ran their gangs."

"Tell me about the betel quids," Carter said.

He went to fold his arms, found he couldn't with the manacles, and placed them back on the table.

"I couldn't stop him. Every time I'd try he'd just hit me. The only thing I could do was slip a quid into the boys' mouths so he couldn't see what I'd done. I thought the police might…" but he didn't finish the statement.

"When was the last time you saw Tristao?" Carter asked.

"Sunday afternoon," Zico said. "We were supposed to dig up a grave on Monday. The boys were scared. I wanted to know what to tell them."

He rubbed his eyes. "Tristao said he didn't know what I was talking about. Said he'd talk to Quim."

"Quim?"

"That's my father. Quim Alvarez."

"Did your father get on well with Tristao?"

"He thought he was crazy," he said. "He hated him. He hates everybody. I think he hates me. He just wants to go back to Brazil."

"Did you see your father there, when you were with Tristao on Sunday?"

"Yeah, he was there but we didn't speak."

"Where can I find him?"

Zico broke eye contact with her and said nothing.

"Better I find him than my friend here, Zico," Carter said, gesturing to Cordero. "As I told you before, I'm not a police officer. I don't carry a gun. My friend does and your father could be shot."

He looked from Carter to Cordero and back at her.

"Time to be smart, Zico," she said. "What would your mother want you to do?"

He rubbed his eyes and stared straight into Carter's.

She held his gaze and waited.

"Supposed to meet him at four o'clock today outside a restaurant opposite Timor Plaza," he said. "After I got the drugs from that coffin guy."

"Were you told to kill the coffin guy after you got the drugs?" she asked.

He broke eye contact. He nodded. "But I wasn't going to do it," he insisted. "I only held the knife to his throat to scare you off."

"I don't scare that easily," Carter said.

"I know that," he said. He wiped his nose on his forearm for a second time.

"When I called you a whore—" he began to say but stopped.

"That's okay, Zico," Carter said. "I've been called a lot worse than that."

• • •

"I thought he might open up a little but I didn't think you'd get that much out of him," Cordero said as they drove back to his office.

"First week on the reservation," she said, buckling her seatbelt, "I was questioning an old Navajo woman about a guy suspected of murder. I asked a bunch of questions about the guy's movements and she just sat there ignoring me. Then she says 'All you *bilagaana*—it's Navajo for 'white person'—are the same: you just take and never give'. I didn't know what she meant so I asked. She said 'You want information from me but you don't give anything in return so we don't trade as equals'. Taught me a lot. Taught me to put a little of me on the table so I'm not just a cop but someone who's been through shit just like them. That's why I mentioned my mother, father and step-sister in the first interview with Zico. Tried to come down to his level. I call it a Navajo transaction."

"Well it worked with Zico," he said.

"Works with most people," she said. "You should try it."

When they reached his room he took out his cell and woke Lucas. Then he made a call to request police officers meet them opposite Timor Plaza at three o'clock that afternoon.

Chapter 32

The restaurant was called *Funan Kontente*—Happy Flower—and was squeezed into a row of eight rundown storefronts directly across *Avenida Nicolau Lobato* from the new Timor Plaza shopping center. The entrance to the restaurant was a glass door off to the side of a large display window. Faded photographs of various menu items were stuck to the window and on a hoarding above the glass were Chinese characters and a lotus that had once been red but had faded to a dull pink.

The few lingering patrons had been told to finish their meals and hurry along and staff to go home and come back later for the dinner trade. Cordero and Carter concealed themselves behind bead curtains that separated the dining area from the kitchen. They retained a view through the row of tables to the front door and on to the sidewalk outside. To the right of the counter just before the doorway into the kitchen sat Lucas Rama Savoy, pretending to be absorbed in the contents of a week-old newspaper. Zico sat opposite, a bowl of soup going cold in front of him alongside a package made to look like the one Cordero had found in the guttering of the Boavides's house. At the table nearest the door were two young police officers, casually dressed and fondling like lovers. If any member of the general public came in after food, they would tell them the kitchen had closed due to a blown fuse.

With the restaurant cleared and everyone in position, they waited. A digital clock on the wall showed 3.50.

"I hope that boy was telling us the truth," Cordero whispered to Carter.

"What's your problem?" she replied.

"He's schemed and connived most of his life. You saw how he manipulated the other boys. I just hope he's not trying to manipulate us."

"Victims of domestic violence are taught to believe they're responsible for their abuse," she said. "Once they realise the opposite, they don't accept that shit again."

The minutes passed. The clock showed 3.57.

A motorcycle stopped outside the restaurant and a woman in a bright blue dress slid the visor up to greet another woman walking by holding a string bag full of vegetables. They exchanged chit-chat and the first woman dropped her visor again and rode off.

The two officers pretending to be lovers seemed to be enjoying their role. They had interlaced their fingers across the table, smiling and laughing. Cordero knew the female officer was single. He wondered about the male.

The time was now 4:01.

Zico seemed to notice the soup in front of him for the first time. He picked up a spoon, took a sip, and put the spoon down on the table.

They waited.

A yellow taxi pulled up at the kerb, reggae music blaring from loud speakers in the cabin. Two girls—foreign backpackers—approached the passenger's window. The driver turned the sound down. The girls bargained over a fare. They started to walk away, were called back, haggled a little more, looked at each other, then shuffled into the back and the taxi took off.

4:08.

"He's not coming," grumbled Lucas without lifting his head from the newspaper.

"Give it more time," said Cordero.

Two minutes later Quim pulled up on his motorcycle outside the restaurant. He was a big man, unshaven, hair slicked back. He wore tattered jeans and a grubby, sleeveless floral shirt. He planted a foot on the ground and looked around for his son. Zico went to the door, took hold of the handle and hesitated. Cordero primed himself to go after him, still believing the boy might try to run or be having second thoughts about giving up his father. But Zico seemed to study Quim a moment, stuck his head outside, told his father he was eating and to come inside. He returned to his seat before Quim could argue.

Cordero could just glimpse Quim yelling obscenities at his son but eventually slap a thigh in frustration and look up and down the thoroughfare, checking the area. A young woman strode by the restaurant talking on her cell. Off to the far side of the neighbouring store she passed two police officers dressed as road workers, covered in dust and grime, squatting over bottles of beer and following her with their eyes. On the other side of the restaurant, two stores down, another middle-aged officer in shorts and a singlet was cleaning a motorcycle on the sidewalk. Quim looked back at the front door of the restaurant. He slipped off his helmet, kicked out the side stand of his motorcycle, dismounted, and strode toward the door.

Before entering he cast an eye around the inside of the restaurant. He pulled the door open and strode toward Zico's table. From behind the bead curtain Carter recognised him immediately as the man on the beach who had slapped the little girl and hit her with a bottle.

"What the fuck is this?" Quim bellowed. "I told you to wait outside. Can't you get anything right?"

The boy looked at him. "Can you?" Zico asked.

"What's that supposed to mean?"

"Why did you kill Tristao?" the boy asked.

Quim checked to see if anyone in the restaurant had overheard the question.

"Who told you that?" he asked, leaning in across the table.

"Word gets around. Why'd you kill him?"

Quim straightened. "He was crazy. All that shit about cleaning up Dili so the dead would rise from the fucking grave. He was in the way."

"The way of what?"

"Me!" he snarled.

Again, he checked that no one was listening to their conversation.

"He was almost blind," said Zico.

"So what?"

The boy fumbled the package on the table.

"You were never going to take me with you, were you?" he said.

"What?"

"You've strapped a bag to the back of the bike," Zico said pointing in the direction of the motorcycle outside. "Where was I supposed to sit?"

"Shit *maun*! I'll send for you once I get settled. Okay?"

"You're full of shit," Zico said. "You were always full of shit!"

Quim slapped the boy across the face and reached for the package. As he did, he sensed a threat behind him. He spun quickly, grabbed Lucas by his shirt as he approached, and hurled him hard against the counter.

"Bastard!" Quim screamed at Zico.

He grabbed the package and ran for the door. The male of the couple by the entrance blocked him but Quim thrust the heel of his left hand into the man's face. The officer slumped to the ground, his nose broken and blood streaming down the front of his T-shirt. The awkward position in which he lay prevented his companion freeing herself from the table in time to stop Quim.

Outside, the two police officers disguised as road workers and the one who'd been cleaning the motorcycle made to encircle Quim. He drew a knife and swung wildly to keep them at bay. He was about to mount his motorcycle when he noticed the key had been taken from the ignition. He swung his knife again at the middle-aged officer forcing him to jump back. Quim cut the ties securing the bag to the tail fairing of the motorcycle and shoved the package he'd taken from Zico inside. He hoisted the bag over one shoulder, kicked the bike over in front of the policemen and darted across the road through heavy traffic toward Timor Plaza.

Motor vehicles screeched to a stop to avoid him, a heavy construction truck rear-ended a microlet crammed with school girls who tumbled over each other screaming, and motorcyclists swung this way and that in a wild confusion to avoid collisions. A chorus of horns beeped and blared in anger.

Cordero had stationed motorcycle officers at either end of the block on which the restaurant was situated in case Quim managed to get away by road. He radioed them now to seal the back entrance to the plaza. He ordered the two young police officers in the restaurant to keep an eye on Zico and weaved his way through the traffic chaos behind Carter, Lucas and the three other officers who were heading after Quim.

Quim stormed up the ramp to the front of the shopping center. The big, heavy automatic glass doors were slow to open as he approached and he kicked at the join in the middle of them. As the doors slowly slid apart Quim pushed his body through. A security guard approached from inside the building and Quim slashed the man across the face with the knife. The guard fell to the ground holding a hand to a cheek gushing blood.

Quim swivelled left then right as shoppers leapt out of his way in fright. He took the stairs toward the main retail level shoving people aside. A woman in a neat business suit was thrown and landed heavily on the stairs, a bottle of orange juice shattering and bread rolls spilling out of her bag and bobbling down the steps to the floor below. A young man stooping to catch the bread rolls blocked Quim's way and was elbowed into two young children who'd been trembling in fright at the bottom of the stairs next to their mother.

People were screaming. As Cordero entered the building, he signalled to one of the officers to attend to the security guard and another to the people struggling on the stairs. He, Carter, Lucas and the third officer rushed to the balustrade overlooking the ground floor. The trail of mayhem Quim had created left no doubt of the direction in which he'd gone.

• • •

At the bottom of the stairs was an open area around which were accessory stores, a pharmacy, a travel agency and a money exchange. Off to the left was a food court but the kitchens were closed and the area was deserted and chained off. To the right was a supermarket. They caught sight of Quim disappearing inside.

It wasn't a big supermarket, just eight aisles. Each of the aisles was stacked floor to ceiling with boxes, cartons and assorted goods making it impossible to see from one into the next over the shelves. Cordero figured several shoppers would be in the supermarket but how many was anyone's guess. He instructed the officer with him to block the entrance. He pointed Lucas to the cash register where an old man was joking with a young female cashier as he counted out coins to pay for cigarettes. Lucas held up his badge and told them to leave. Then he drew his pistol and waited.

Cordero told Carter to wait outside the supermarket as he started down an aisle stacked with cereals and biscuits. But Lucas noticed her slinking in. "Shit, *mana!*" he whispered and raised a hand to hold her back. She ignored him and crept toward the far aisle.

Cordero moved into an aisle of canned and packaged goods. A woman stormed out at the end near Lucas. She looked around for the cashier. Finding no one else to complain to, she turned to Lucas and said a man was knocking customers aside and stalking the aisles. He showed her his badge and told her to leave. She hurried out passed the officer at the entrance but eyed his dirty worker's clothes and clutched her bag to her chest as though he might steal it.

Lucas was still looking to see where Carter had gone when Cordero re-appeared, signaled him to call out to Quim, and slipped into an aisle for soaps, shampoos and toothpaste.

"Quim Alvares," Lucas shouted. "This is the police. You're surrounded. Throw out the knife and give yourself up."·

There was a loud clanking of cans spilling from a shelf and a yelp that was caught in the throat. The sounds came from the aisle nearest the last.

Lucas slipped forward and noticed Cordero doing the same on the other side of the store. Quim spotted them both and held a knife to the throat of a terrified woman, the other hand clasped firmly around her forehead.

"Back off or I kill her," he said. "Now!"

Lucas raised his pistol but Quim dragged the woman behind shelving. She tripped over the shopping she'd dropped to the floor when first grabbed and started to slip from his grip. He grabbed her hair and she squealed in pain.

"Give it up, Quim," Cordero said.

"Fuck you!" shouted Quim. He looked from Cordero to Lucas and his fingers opened and closed on the handle of the knife. "If you don't get back—"

He didn't get to finish. Carter appeared from the drinks aisle with a large bottle of liqueur and struck him solidly on the side of the head. The force of the impact smashed the bottle, spraying liqueur and blood all over Quim. He collapsed, a hunting knife dropping from his hand.

Cordero and Lucas came up and stood over him.

"The doctor at the Embassy told me that a full bottle packs far more punch than an empty one," Carter said, licking liqueur off her fingers. "He was right."

• • •

Quim Alvares was taken under guard to the hospital to be examined for concussion and have the gash to his head stitched. From there he was taken to a police cell with his forehead wrapped in bandages. Cordero sent the knife to Brooks for confirmation it was the blade that killed Tristao and the two young gang members. Among a few items of clothing in the bag Quim had taken off the back of his motorcycle they found two packages of methamphetamine pills worth tens of thousands of dollars plus the package he'd taken from Zico which had been filled with glucose tablets.

The case was almost concluded as far as Cordero's involvement was concerned…almost, but not quite.

He had Quim brought into the interrogation room.

After a barrage of curses and threats, the man settled down, angry and resentful but now quiet and seated at the table in the center of the room.

"A friend of mine was found dead on the road to Dare last Saturday morning," Cordero said. "His name was Fidelis Tau.

The police report said he'd fallen from his motorcycle and wasn't wearing a helmet." He looked Quim directly in the eyes. "But I think you killed him."

Quim turned away and said nothing.

"Fidelis had been asking around on my behalf for information on the two boys you killed and the drugs you took from them. I think you got word of that, tracked him down, killed him and dumped his body to make it look like a motorcycle accident. Is that what happened?"

"Why should I tell you anything?" Quim asked.

"One more victim is not going to make any difference to the prison time you'll serve. You'll never get back to Brazil now. What've you to lose?"

"Who told you I want to go back to Brazil?"

"Is that not true?" asked Cordero.

"Damn you," Quim said.

"So you won't tell me about that boy near Dare?"

"I won't tell you anything," Quim said.

Cordero studied him before rising to leave. He remembered Carter's story about the Navajo transaction.

"I had a brother killed by the Indonesians in 1991," Cordero said. "I miss him to this day. Your wife was killed. I gather you miss her. You have a son. He's alive and before too long he'll get out of prison. You're luckier than you deserve to be. I don't have any children. But your son's now all you've got. Think about that. Are you going to alienate him and the only chance you have to stay connected to life outside of a prison cell?"

"That boy betrayed me! I disown him!" Quim growled and slapped a cuffed hand on the table. He looked away. Cordero waited a moment, stood and headed for the door.

"You won't tell me anything?" he tried one last time before leaving the room.

"Go to hell," replied Quim.

Chapter 33

He picked Carter up from her duplex apartment in Motael mid-morning for the long drive to Suai. She put her overnight bag in the backseat next to his and climbed into the passenger's seat.

"Is that a wedding present on the back seat?" she asked.

"Yeah," he said.

"What is it?" she asked, fastening her seatbelt.

"A microwave," he said.

"A microwave?"

"You bought Estefana a breadmaker so I got a microwave," he said. "What's wrong with that?"

"Soon she'll be able to open her own white goods store," Carter said.

They drove through the Saturday morning traffic and turned right in the direction of the Santa Cruz cemetery and the road leading to Dare. Beyond there they'd drive to Maubisse and across the mountainous spine of Timor to the south coast and Suai. Estefana and Josinto had gone a day earlier. Before she left Dili Estefana had hugged Carter—something she had never done before—and held her tight until the American's embarrassment eased and she allowed herself to mould her body into the embrace as Timorese do.

"Is that a boxing trophy I saw in the back seat as well?" Carter asked.

He sniffed. "Yeah. I won it in a university championship years ago in Australia," he said. "I thought I'd put it on the road where Fidelis was killed. It's on the way. I've had a sign made with his name on it. It's a common thing to do on roadsides in Timor. People will respect it."

She slipped on her sunglasses and made no comment.

"He would have been better than me," Cordero said. "Faster, stronger. He boxed like a lion. I box like a fox—cunning but slow. He would have been better than me," he repeated.

They drove on in silence for a while.

"I booked two rooms in that guest house we stayed in the first time we went to Suai," he said. "Remember?"

"The Syrian manager who undressed me with his eyes? How could I forget?" she said.

The wedding was to be held the following day. It would be an all day and most of the night affair. They'd return the next morning.

They arrived at the spot where Fidelis's body had been found. Cordero parked off to the side, took the trophy, the sign he'd had made, and a hammer from the back of his vehicle and walked off on his own. She watched him. He chose a spot, hammered the sign in, and placed the trophy alongside it. Then he blessed himself, stood motionless for a minute, and came back.

"You still feeling guilty about that boy?" she asked.

"Sort of. He'd pulled himself out of the gutter and could've made something of himself."

She glanced across at him and touched his thigh. "I think he did make something of himself," she said.

"I just feel the loss, you know?"

She paused a moment.

"Back where I come from people like to talk about 'closure,'" she said. "Like you can shut a loss like that behind a locked door and just walk away. But the kind of loss you're talking about rips something out of you. You're never the same again. I know—it's happened to me."

Cordero looked across, a little surprised by the pain she'd acknowledged. But her time in Timor was about come to an end and he wasn't prepared to explain the complexity of the feelings he'd had toward the protégé he'd coached.

He started the vehicle and waited for a break in the traffic. Three vehicles went by followed by a man on a Timorese pony, and a swarm of motorcycles lined up behind him.

"Anything become of that bent police officer involved with the gang?" she asked to lighten the mood.

"Too little evidence to prove anything against him but I've arranged for him to be stationed in Viqueque for the next few months," Cordero said.

"I thought you told me you have no influence over the regular police?"

"I don't," he said. "One of my unit is being sent to Viqueque to investigate the embezzlement of road construction funds. Couple of companies seem to be involved. Complex case. Francisco—Francisco Jada, my boss, you met him—says he'll need a uniformed police officer to help with the investigation. He asked me a week ago to recommend someone. I recommended our suspect—Sergeant Mateo Belo. Said he'd be perfect for the job. That'll keep him out of Dili and out of gang affairs for quite a while."

An old truck laden with bags of cement belched its way up the hill and Cordero saw his chance to rejoin the road that would take them to Suai.

"You all packed for next week?" he asked. "Leaving Timor, I mean."

"Not quite," she said and stared out the passenger's window.

"How do you feel about going home? Back to eagles and coyotes and—what is it you love, the pinon pine?"

"*Piñon*," she corrected him. "It's *piñon* pine. You say it by kind of squashing the 'n' in the middle."

"Okay, so you must be getting excited," he said.

They overtook a motorcycle laden with bags of rice strapped to the sides and rear fender.

"You remember when I gave you my INTERPOL card to show to your superior?" she said. "You know, when he objected to my being part of the stake-out team at the cemetery?"

"Yeah so?"

"You didn't look at it did you?"

"Why should I?"

"Because if you had you would have seen that it's valid for another three months," she said. "Your superior certainly noticed that."

"What?" he said, turning sharply to face her. "How? Why?"

"Last Saturday? When you picked me up in the center of Dili? I'd rung Jacobsen and told her I'd sign up for another three months if she met me at the office, did the paperwork there and then, including adjusting my ID card."

"What changed your mind?" he asked.

She smiled.

"Well I told her I'd realised she was right and I could do a lot of good work in Timor." She laughed. "But really it was more personal than that."

He glanced at her. "My charm?"

"Hardly," she said. "Estefana changed my mind. Well, Josinto's abduction and what that was doing to her. As a friend, I wanted to help get him back and, if the worse came to the worst, to be there for her to deal with his loss. Your police weren't doing anything so, when I knew there were drugs involved of a kind that had to come from outside East Timor, I thought INTERPOL could claim a role and I'd have a valid reason to be part of the investigation."

She took off her sunglasses and cleaned the lenses.

"Besides," she said. "I've been invited to a little girl's birthday party."

"What little girl?"

"Eloisa. The girl Quim knocked unconscious on the beach." She replaced the sunglasses. "Haven't been to a party in a long while."

Cordero puffed out a breath. "So you're here for another three months?"

"Looks that way."

"Why didn't you tell me?"

"There were more important things to focus on, Tino."

He eased back in his seat and found it hard to suppress a smile.

"Tell me more about how this is going to work, you know, with your Ambassador and with Jacobsen," he said.

"Oh, I'll be okay," she said. "After all, they're the ones who want me."

They both laughed at that.

"You'll need another interpreter," he pointed out.

"That, or Estefana may be seconded back to INTERPOL—when she gets back from her honeymoon, of course."

"Of course," he repeated.

"The only thing that worries me is—" she began.

He looked across at her. "Is what?"

"Taylor—the Ambassador—is going to think he won. My staying will inflate his bloated ego even more," she said.

"Well if anyone can burst an inflated ego it's you," he said.

"You think so?" she asked.

"I know so," he said.

She was looking straight ahead but he could see the smile.

About the Author

Chris McGillion is a regular visitor to East Timor where he has been involved in media development initiatives and conducted research into the communication of agricultural science in remote mountain communities. He is a former journalist whose work has been published in Australia, the US and the United Kingdom and has taught politics, philosophy and communication skills at four universities in Australia. He has authored or co-authored a number of non-fiction books on subjects as diverse as US-Cuban relations, clerical sexual abuse, and religious sociology. He lives in the Blue Mountains west of Sydney, Australia.